KU-193-718

The
Everlasting Answer

"There is only one answer to every problem in the sphere of human relations and that answer is love."

By the same author

SOURCE OF THE RIVER

THE UNRELENTING DAY

JAN

"Stella Morton's novels reveal practised ability plus the talent of story-telling and the sincerity and restraint of good character-drawing." *The Sphere*

STELLA MORTON

The Everlasting Answer

THE ROMANCE BOOK CLUB
121 CHARING CROSS ROAD
LONDON W.C.2

To L. M.

Who fortuitously peddled drama as well as drugs

THIS EDITION BY ARRANGEMENT WITH HODDER AND STOUGHTON LTD.

The characters in this book are imaginary and bear no relation to any living person

Chapter I

"HE comes home on the thirteenth," she said. "I had the letter this morning."

She watched his eyelids lower over his eyes—he never gave anything away—and then she saw him take a pencil from the glass tray on his desk, and he prodded the point into the blotter and laid it down again.

She saw his hand as he moved it, the rather prominent knuckles, the waisted fingers and large nails, and she thought, 'It's terrifying to think that my life rests in those hands. It does, though.'

He was still looking at the blotter, his head slightly bent. She wondered if he were regretting the promise he had made. She could hardly blame him; but the thought disturbed the surface calm she had adopted, and she shifted her position in the chair, recrossing her long legs.

She half expected him to look up and smile and say, "Don't exert yourself to play a part. You don't believe in it and I see through it, so nothing's to be gained, is it?"

But he didn't look up and smile, neither did he speak. He sat quite still, staring at the blotter.

She glanced round the surgery. It was so painfully like a station waiting-room. Why? The dark-green walls, the antiquated horse-hair couch, the ugly, shabby steel filing-cabinet? Possibly it was not these so much as the grate and the mantelpiece. The grate was black and barred, with red tiles embellished with a blue rose surrounding it and, because it was summer-time, a piece of white pleated paper fanning up at the back. She wondered who had put it there. The house-keeper? The 'daily'? She pictured a woman kneeling on the hearth-rug folding the paper with precision, then placing it behind the bars and opening out the fan till it filled the grate. Did whoever put it there get a glow of satisfaction when they saw the frightful finished work? Or was it merely a piece of domestic routine, the corollary to the last fire of winter and the spring cleaning?

Did he, Philip, even 'see' it? Did he 'see' any of the hideous ugliness of the room—the repulsive reproduction of 'A September Morn' over the mock-marble mantelpiece; the bamboo table, the drab curtains; or did he 'see' only in terms of human anatomy? Curious to categorise everyone not by whether they were good-looking or attractive but by whether they showed signs of an over-active thyroid or kidney trouble. Or had he ever forgotten all that, swept the whole business of 'bodies' aside to be madly attracted to one body? Had he ever forgotten iris and cornea and pupil to be lashed with the desire or pity or love that shone from the mind behind the physical features? She tried to picture him making the actions of love, and couldn't do it. She tried to picture him as a little boy, and couldn't do that, either. There was never any other way to picture him but exactly as he was—sitting in the chair staring at the blotter. Yet there had been a time when he'd had his coat off and his sleeves rolled up and—— Oh, God, not that.

Why not that? It had caught up with her now. There was no escape, except that there was still time to run away, simply disappear. But she'd been over that argument so often, and she knew as well as she knew her own name that she wouldn't run away or disappear. Not, she half-smiled at herself with a clutch on humour, after all those plans! And she added, Funny to the last, that's what we are. Funny to the last.

Even now she could make this into a humorous situation if she wanted to. It only needed the fraction of a twist, the flick of an eyelid, to turn it into a music-hall joke. But the salt went out of the music-hall joke when you yourself happened to be at the receiving end. Fat women, false teeth, the *risqué* little story that wasn't *risqué* at all but only rather dull, took on a different guise if you happened to have lost your shape or had your teeth out or become the central figure in the *risqué* story.

She watched the thought stab home, and saw herself writhe under the impact, though reason still remained aloof, untouched. Almost untouched. Why had she fallen for it? Why did one? If anyone in the world knew the answer, there wouldn't be a question. And the sickening monotony of asking it! You vowed to yourself that you'd never do it again, and it seeped up from your subconscious, or whatever the thing was called, ten minutes after you'd sworn you'd seen the last of it, and round you spun on the old circle.

She caught a glimpse of Andrew then, walking across her memory as he'd walked across the sand, his hair blown into a sideways silly cock's-comb, his shoulders looking as though they'd been oiled in the sunlight.

He walked as far as the edge of the sea where the placid little waves lapped, and then he was gone and Guy stood in the drawing-room, one shoulder propped against the mantelpiece, reading from some typewritten papers in his hand, and as she came into the room he looked up and smiled slightly at her and said, "Want a drink? I'll get you one in a couple of minutes."

That was the Guy of a year ago, and even his figure was assured, not so much as touched with middle-age but assured for all that. She remembered that Andrew, speaking of someone or other he'd known, not even remotely connected with Guy, had said, "He's a self-made man and he's made himself very nicely."

She'd been irritated by the phrase, and yet it did fit Guy. And Guy had never, to her, at least, denied it. Even the first night she'd been to supper with him. . . . Why recall that? There was no need to recall it, but it was all there in her memory, part of the chain of events which led unerringly to this moment.

She was wiping the grease-paint from her face when Carrie came in and said, "Toby's party. I'd forgotten it. S'pose we'll have to show up. And my feet giving me what for. They would be."

She hadn't forgotten Toby's party. Neither had Carrie. With the run ending in a couple of weeks and Glynne Thorne back from the States with a new Manheim play in his pocket, the date was marked in your mind in headlines. But you had to pretend it wasn't, even while you knew perfectly well that everyone else was doing the same thing—and knew that you were doing it, too. What an infantile game it was, with no one deceived, least of all Glynne Thorne. Or yourself. Or wasn't that true? Perhaps the majority of them had grown so accustomed to the everlasting pretence that they no longer saw it as such. If you never told the truth, it was possible you'd reach a point where you were totally unable to recognise it. Just as if you continually acted a part—and who didn't?—you'd become quite out of touch with the person you were. But what was 'truth'? And what was 'yourself'?

"Does my parting show?" asked Carrie, and she peered into the mirror and then turned her face towards her, her head down, the comb dangling from her fingers.

"Not enough to notice."

"Sure? You're not just saying it? That girl made hell of it last week, only I couldn't afford Fernando, not at this end of a run." She went back to the mirror and pushed her hair up a little each side of the parting. "Is George going?" she asked. "If he is, that means Anna and I might as well go home and soak my feet for all the chance I'll get."

"Mightn't we all?" she answered, and she thought, 'Why didn't I learn to pound a typewriter and become a businessman's bright girl?' And hard on the heels of the question came the answer, 'Because you'd have been bored to tears, and because if you want to get anywhere it's less unpleasant to get there under the protection of a Glynne Thorne, who is at least decently thin and still keeps a faint memory of Winchester and Magdalen under his maroon pullover, rather than a business magnate who wears his Savile Row's as though they were armour and is only too anxious to forget Wimbledon Grammar and Night School.'

What did she want, then? At this precise moment—what did she want? And back came the answer to that, too. A bathroom with a clean bath in it. Hot water gushing from a tap, and bath towels, also clean, on heated rails. And a separate lavatory that wasn't perpetually stained with the tea-leaves someone else had just thrown down it. But when she'd had all that—and a dining-room with an oval rosewood table and a drawing-room with Liberty curtains—she'd loathed the lot. Told herself they were stifling her. And she hadn't been a fool over it, either. It was never the glamour of the stage seen from the second row of the stalls which had got her. She'd had a pretty lucid idea of what her mother had called 'the seamy side', but it was the 'seamy side' that interested her, for the simple reason that, so she'd thought, there was more 'life' in the 'seamy side' than there was in the Liberty drawing-room. She wanted—how immature it sounded now—to 'go out and meet life'. To make her impact on it. To smash into it, and beat on it with her hands and say, 'This is me. You've got to recognise me, you great, silent, inexplicable thing.' She wanted to argue with it, prove to it that she was right, but it hadn't occurred to her then that the permanent structure that was 'home' wasn't permanent. It hadn't occurred to her because she'd never given it a thought. It was as much a part of her make-up as her hair and the shape of her mouth, and as such 'her own', something which would last as long as she lasted. And the first two years had proved her right.

Now she was living. Lodgings in dingy houses; baths with a rime of grease, cheap stained dressing-tables with cream jars and lotions and lipsticks making little islands in the week-old film of powder, suspicious smells, the eternal 'sex' talk—they were all part of the pattern, the weapons of her 'impact'. There were the parties, or the journeys from one town to another on a wet Sunday, when heated arguments about everything under—or over—the sun lashed round the room or the compartment, giving everyone vast gratification and leaving all the questions wrapped up nice and cosy just as they were in the beginning.

And there was 'love', of course. Only you called it 'experience', which, perhaps, taking it by and large, was a more precise description for the inexpert caresses of too-long-haired youth which, while the promise of them raised you to heights of wild enthusiasm, left you more often than not flat as a pancake and feeling 'sold'.

But it was only now that she saw it in that light. Then it had been 'fun'—and slightly wicked fun, especially when, as you often did, you cast an eye towards your father's study and your mother's Women's Institute activities and thought deliciously, 'If they could see me now!' And every now and then you went back there, and drooped round the lanes in slacks and sweaters and remembered to enunciate your consonants and, if possible, drop famous names into any suitable conversation; while you told yourself how insufferably boring everything was. But it never struck you that one day the whole thing would be wiped away, leaving only a gaping hole where it had stood. For who, least of all herself, had suspected that the whole place had been nothing but a façade behind which was virtually nothing? At one minute her father and mother had been sailing through the clouds above the Jungfrau, the next, in the company of thirty-nine strangers, they were lying dead on its rocky slopes, and when the dry, slithery little lawyer had finished his addition and subtraction, he whispered the total to her. And the total was nothing. Not even minus. Just nothing.

A façade. A 'sham'. A three-hundred-pound butcher's bill. A hundred pounds' worth of bread. Five hundred for drinks. And no one bothering because Sir Maxwell and Lady Randolph had lived at Mannings Court for thirty years and Sir Maxwell's father for lord knows how many years before that. And it wasn't till the whole thing had fallen down that she'd come to see that she'd regarded it as being as indestructible as the Jungfrau on which its owner had died.

She barely had time to pack her remaining clothes into trunks and to wonder if her father were a knave or only a fool before the bank snapped up the house and she was on her way back to London. She'd never been able to stand her relations even when they were merely envious, and she certainly couldn't stand them now that their envy had somersaulted into a cloying pity. So she returned to the rooms in Oakley Street, where Carrie, who had just finished putting the grips into her hair for the night, looked up and said, "Mrs. Wood's been at the cigarettes again, would you believe it? One of these days I'll have her guts out with a pen-knife, see if I don't." Which, when you come to work it out, was about the only comment to make to anyone who'd lost home, parents, money and background in the space of time it took for an aeroplane to fall eighteen thousand feet.

Curious, or not so curious, the difference it had made; but then, however clever you might fox yourself you were, you rarely valued the obvious and the securely possessed till they'd become the unobtainable because finally lost. But it wasn't only that, it was the totally different light their loss threw on to a life which had been amusing, invigorating even. Why, because a house you hadn't been inside for a year and two people whom, you'd bragged often enough, you were 'quite out of touch with' were no more, should the rooms you shared with Carrie, Carrie herself, and your whole circle of friends, to say nothing of your 'career', become suddenly tedious and more than a little sordid, you didn't know. The point was, they had, and the second point was that, as the stage was your only known means of making a living, you'd better stick to it and hope that you'd made a mistake in your calculations and were a great actress after all. But a further two years of touring, followed by the present small part in London, hadn't done a lot to convince you, and as far as you could see, unless Glynne Thorne remembered your existence and was gasping to give you the maid or the nanny or the girl behind the haberdashery counter, or any or all of their equivalents in the new Manheim play, it looked like a spell round the agents till something turned up in repertory or on the road.

Sitting beside Carrie in the taxi on their way to Toby's, she thought again of the bathroom and a big bed in a spacious bedroom where, when you lay in them, the sheets weren't stained with the tea you'd spilt last night when you had your supper in bed, and you didn't even care how much the rent was because you weren't responsible for paying it.

But she didn't know that it was all going to be there waiting for her in Toby's crowded room.

It was. And she'd often thought since, how nearly she'd missed it, because in common with twenty other actresses she kept her eyes pretty well glued to Glynne Thorne, who was being studiously indifferent to everyone but Anna Delahenty whose dead straight black hair hung lankly each side of a face on which there wasn't even a smatter of make-up, and who in spite of it was beautiful past belief, and barely noticed the man, so obviously a stranger, who was hovering about with Meg Metcalfe and her gang on the other side of the room. If Raines, Meg's husband, hadn't caught her eye and beckoned her— but he had, and in that moment, even as she dodged her way past dinner-jackets and tails and ballet-length dresses and waves of Lançôme and Lelong, towards Meg's barmaid's laugh, she was changing the entire course of her life.

"Hello, there!" said Raines, and Meg shouted, "Darling! Any luck with Glynne or is he too busy eating Anna, boots and all? Isn't she the complete cad to walk in here straight out of her bath and make us all look like Jezebels?" And then, remembering she'd just come back from the States, she slipped into the American language and said, "Come here, Guy darling, will you? I'd have you meet a little friend of mine, Gina Randolph, who's in Rex's play at the Windsor. Gina, this is Guy Taylor, with whom we gotten acquainted on the *Queen* coming across."

His hand was firm, the skin, even in Toby's steam-heated turmoil, cool. Her future husband bowed slightly and said, "How d'you do."

She loved him. Love woke in her, and it was a totally different thing from 'experience'. She wanted to 'care' for him, look after him, only he looked after himself with the efficiency he did most things. And she liked him. She liked being with him. She liked his touch of arrogance and the deft way he used his hands. But she couldn't, at first at any rate, 'place' him. He was so obviously not an actor nor an artist. Neither was he one of the drooping mock-humble university men who hung around on the edge of the theatre. She didn't know what he did, and Meg, who might have known, had gone to Stratford and never answered letters, anyway.

He owned a Sunbeam-Talbot, a flat in Kensington and an income which included the better restaurants. There were one or two things about him which made her wonder until one night, after they'd finished supper, he said, not suddenly but as though the moment had been arranged for, "I want to tell you about my parents and my home. My father kept an ironmonger's shop in the back streets of Brighton. He mended bicycles to eke out a living. My mother died when I was fourteen, and my father last year. I went to a free school and got a scholarship to a Grammar School. I left when I was fifteen and helped my father in the shop, because by then he had the beginnings of arthritis."

She wanted to laugh and say, 'I don't care if your mother was a tadpole and your father a fish and you got your education reading comic strips,' she loved him so much. She said, "I've never quite worked out how much our parents matter, have you? I suppose it depends on whether you can open your mind wide enough to include another person's experience or not. My father was knighted for something or other in the First World War, and when he died we found he'd been diddling the tradesmen for years."

He smiled and said, "Meg told me. About the knighthood, I mean. She didn't mention the diddling."

"I'll bet she didn't," she answered shortly, and he said, "I've never told anyone that before. I wanted you to know." And she thought, 'If only he'd stop talking and love me.' But instinct had warned her from the first that this thing was different, and he hadn't even kissed her yet.

She said, "It's a pretty big jump from an ironmonger's shop in Brighton to a Sunbeam-Talbot and a Kensington flat. How did you make it?"

She saw an expression cross his face which subtly changed him, made him look harder. Older, then.

"I hated it," he said. "We lived in a room over the shop, and it was cold and cluttered up with piles of tin pails and boxes of nails. My father was a Catholic, and he bore it all for Christ's sake, amen. I couldn't bear it for anybody's sake, and I determined to get out. I'd always been keen on the way things worked, so I went to night school and took a course in engineering. I didn't find learning hard, I liked it. And everything I did I looked at as one step nearer escape. You've either got to hate or love to get out of things, haven't you?"

He seemed to expect an answer, so she said, "If you're going to live. You don't need to do either if you're content to go around in a coma, like most of us do."

"Possibly," he said, and continued, "I invented a new kind of screw when I was eighteen, and one of the masters at the technical school was interested. He introduced me to J. B. Harris, who lived in the country outside Brighton at that time, and he took the screw and me up."

She said, "I haven't a notion who J. B. Harris is, but he's evidently a man who knows a good screw when he sees one. Then what?"

He smiled slightly and answered, "He's an arms manufacturer," and added, "Not Madame Tussaud's, fire." He sat back in his chair as though the worst was over and said, "A year later I borrowed enough money on the patent to set up plant in an old garage on the

Great North Road beyond Hendon, and two years after got a small factory going. It did well, so I built a bigger one, and when that was looking after itself I put a manager in and branched out a bit."

She was excited, thrilled. Poor boy makes good was always a winner—it got you every time, and when the 'poor boy' was Guy, it made her want to laugh and shout.

"What happened to your Dad?" she asked. "Did he stay on at the shop?"

He stared down at the table-cloth. "I did everything I could," he said, "bar using force."

"But he stuck to the tin pails," she said lightly. "They do, don't they?"

A shade of an expression came into his eyes and, she thought, 'I've hurt him.' And immediately realised, 'That kind of remark would. I mustn't do it again.'

He didn't say anything more about himself, and they finished the meal talking of other things; but he stopped the car on the Embankment on the way back to Chelsea, and they sat watching the red glow from the power-station thrown down from low cloud and the lights on the far bank drawn like floating strips of gold-foil in the river.

She sat beside him, loving him and thinking how different it was from all the other things—the difference between a puddle and the sea; but she didn't so much as move her hand because she knew the moment must be his, not hers.

And out of the darkness and the red glow and the floating gold-foil strips that were vaguely Chinese, he said, "There's something else I meant to say at supper and I didn't. I'm thirty-eight. I've known women, of course, but not your sort."

He stopped and she said, "You ought to see Carrie whom I share a room with. What is 'my sort'?"

But he went on as though she hadn't interrupted. "There was no fuss with the others," he said. "I could be myself without question or questioning. I suppose I'm trying to say your kind always made me conscious of the ironmonger's shop. I was afraid of making a mistake, perhaps."

She wanted to say, 'In these days! And with an income and a

Sunbeam-Talbot and your looks!' But she said, "Couldn't you forget all that?"

"That's the point," she heard him say, and a car passed and a bus rattled by with people in it, remote, yet intimate, part of it all. "I want to, yet I can't. Not altogether. And why should I?" he asked. "I come from those people."

"We all come from 'those people'," she answered, and she wished more than ever that he'd stop talking and take her in his arms. "What about my 'diddling' parent?"

"He didn't live in a slum."

"No, he only lived on the butcher. Where is all this getting?"

"I want to marry you," he said.

"Because you love me or because my father was at Eton?"

"Because I love you."

She was weak with a mad laughing happiness.

"Got the ring in your pocket?" she asked, and she held out her hand.

He turned and looked at her, and the depth of the expression in his eyes went down into her heart like a sword thrust.

"No," he said. "Only a bit of fuse-wire."

"That'll do," she answered.

When she got in, Carrie, who'd been walking round the agents all day, was lolling in a chair with her feet up eating sardines on toast. She had taken her shoes and stockings off, and even her naked toes looked tired, still rather squashed together from the pressure of her high-heeled shoes.

The sardines smelt strongly, and Carrie's nylons, wet from their 'dip', were hanging from the mantelpiece, secured there by a green china cat with black spots.

Carrie licked one finger and said, "The theatre's bitched, if you ask me. I went into Sammy Golden's and he said, 'Why don't you take up baby-sitting, dear, and make a decent living?' How did you get on? Meet Guy all right?"

"Yes," she answered. "I'm going to marry him."

"As if I didn't know," said Carrie.

They were married in the Church of the Assumption, Great Hill Street, three months later. His insistence on a church wedding surprised her, but she willingly went to a rather gloomy presbytery on three or four occasions, where she was given some instruction on the permanence of marriage by a priest with an Irish brogue who wore a cassock with buttons all down the front.

She didn't listen overmuch because she kept thinking that if he'd shared a room with Carrie for five years and used a grease-rimed bath and trailed round the provinces living in even more depressing rooms than the one in Oakley Street, he wouldn't worry so much about marriage with Guy being permanent. As far as she was concerned, whatever he did to it he couldn't make it too permanent for her liking.

They flew to Paris on the afternoon plane after the wedding, and that night, for the first time, he made love to her. He led her all the way, was strong and tender and patient, and it was all just as she had known it would be.

They stayed in Paris for a week, and then went on to the south and, lying on the sand, giving herself up to indolence, she thought, 'I'm the living answer to the pet phrase of all the women's magazine writers—I'm blossoming like a rose.'

She was, too. She could even see the outward signs of it in the smooth newly-ironed look that was coming over her skin and her hair, and in the sense of well-being which was repairing the strain of the last two years.

And this, too, was Guy's doing. Turning over on her elbow, she looked at him as he lay beside her, his eyes closed, his face held to the sun. Now not only his mind but his body was known to her. His flesh itself was dear, intimate, and she thought how strange was that knowledge which came through the body. No other was to be compared. You could come close to another person in mind, talk to them for hours or years till you'd swear there wasn't another thought left to be revealed, and yet the mental knowledge ended where the other began.

Carrie wrote her a letter, which shouted the fact that she was either creaming her face or eating fish and chips, saying that at last she'd got one of the twin idiot sisters in Rudy Blair's *Day Must End* at the Sheridan, and that Olga Moore, who was now sharing the rooms in Oakley Street, never washed the teapot clean. She ended, "How's life with the self-made man?"

She bought the gaudiest card she could find and scrawled on the back, "It's fine. And this one doesn't worship his own creator."

Carrie mightn't appreciate it, but it gave her enormous satisfaction to write.

Guy couldn't be away from London for more than two weeks. They flew home and took up their lives in his Kensington flat, giving themselves time to look for a house at leisure. Change came over him, and she could see the drive and will-power that had sent the ironmonger's son plodding through the streets to night school on his way up to the super-tax class. Occasionally a hesitation over a word or a slight mispronunciation produced him even more clearly and woke a tenderness in her that she didn't know she possessed.

On one of their journeys to see a house, which by the agent's description was exactly what they were looking for but turned out to be a damp ruin of a place, she took him to see the only relative she had either respect or liking for—her Great-aunt Claire, who happened to live in the district.

She smiled a little, after she'd indicated the west-drive gates and he was running the car up through the park, at the expression on his face, and she saw his hand go to the knot of his tie and back to the wheel again. It was the only concession to nervousness he made, and she loved him for it. He so seldom disappointed her.

Her ladyship, Carter said, was in the garden, and they found her looking as she always looked, not over-well washed, with two inches of petticoat drooping below a cotton dress, and the brooch that held the front together unfastened. She introduced Guy, and she peered up at him and said, "How d'ye do", and turned to her with an "I'm glad you managed to get somebody at last. Old maids are so tedious; it affects their kidneys of course. Come and see my zinnias. They're particularly good this year." And as they trailed after her, she said over her shoulder to Guy, "What d'you do?

What's your work? They tell me you make pails or nails or something, and I do wish you'd see the heads are bigger. I'm everlasting hitting my thumb." And when they reached the zinnias, "There you are. Woolworth's. The best I've ever had. Your Uncle George always got them from the Society, but all he did was pay through the nose. A seed's a seed whichever way you look at it, and I've always said it's the dung that matters. Ever seen a finer show than that? Pig. Got it from Stapleton, the old rogue."

She gave them historic sherry before lunch, and some fat, tough mutton and a potato baked in its jacket at lunch, and she treated Guy neither as if she knew him well nor yet slightly.

Later she herself took him over the house, and she knew that he was impressed with the drawing-room and the portraits, and on the way home he said, "You ought to be in a place like that. You belong there."

"The day I want to live in a museum, I'll tell you," she said. "I'll take the flat, thanks. I see no point in twenty bedrooms when you can only occupy one a night, and the only entertaining Aunt Claire can afford is to let the general public in at three bob a time to gawp at Uncle George at the end of a line of very dead Conway-Coutts. She hasn't even got a radiator in the place, poor old girl."

He made no reply, and she said, "You're not a snob, are you?"

"Don't think so," he answered; but he added, "You can't get away from facts, can you? I can't stand not seeing the truth."

"What particular truth had you in mind?"

He didn't answer for a minute, and she saw his bent knee and the stretch of his leg ending in his sharply defined ankle bone and brown shoe planted squarely on the rubber matting, and she thought, 'He's just another human being. He's someone shut up inside himself, just as I am, and all this talk of "knowing" him means nothing at all.'

"Portraits," he answered, "and pails. You come from one, I come from the other."

"Someone's not told you the truth," she said lightly. "I come from what the Bible calls 'my father's loins', and unless I'm mistaken you did, too. A portrait never conceived anything. Nor, to my knowledge, did a pail. I shall begin to think you're envious in a minute."

But she determined not to take him to any of her relations again.

They were better on their own, two individuals each in their own right.

He rarely spoke to her of his work, and she didn't ask questions. It was still too novel, and too pleasant, to have money to spend without giving a thought to how it was made. "If," she said to Carrie on one of their infrequent meetings, "I'm going to be a man's cherished possession, I'll be a man's cherished possession. The little wife who is her husband's business inspiration never did appeal to me. That kind usually end up with a duodenal and false teeth while hubby takes a blonde feline covered in sequins out to dinner on his board meeting nights."

"You've changed your tune, haven't you?" asked Carrie, and she eased the last bit of lipstick out of the case with the end of a kirby-grip and put it in an old cream jar.

"I don't think so. Not really. I'm a woman, and I've never wanted to be anything else at heart."

"I've never heard you talk like one of those articles before," said Carrie.

She smiled and left it at that. She could hardly tell Carrie that love stripped down all your pretences and left you naked and unashamed, because Carrie would have thought she was talking about taking her roll-on off.

He flew to New York and she went with him. The thought of the Stratocruiser terrified her, and the diabolical poise and nonchalance of the air-hostess did little to inspire courage. Over the Atlantic, while her stomach suddenly lurched, she thought, 'A couple of inches of steel between us and a 30,000-foot drop into all those waves!' She put her hand on Guy's knee and pressed her shoulder against him, and he turned and smiled at her. "All right?" he asked. "All right," she echoed.

He mightn't be able to do much about it if the great brute had come crashing down the stars, but the very nearness of his body strengthened her and she thought, 'If he'd been an intellectual he might have proved to me that the Greeks had a word for it, but what a woman wants is someone who'll fend off mad dogs and push her behind him when the burglar says, "Put 'em up".' Thank God, he was one of those.

Sometimes he asked her to entertain men he was associated with in business. She discovered she could cook and enjoyed it, which surprised her. The men were all of similar type though of varying shapes. Their wives when they brought them with them usually had one diamond clip too many and were very very pleasant.

She wondered what they were really like beneath the façade of not quite the right clothes and the pleasant manner, but they were putting on their fur coats and picking up their little evening bags before she had time to discover. Her point of interest was centred in Guy himself, and with one dutiful eye on the diamond clips and the signet-rings she watched the swift brain at work keeping one move ahead of the, for the most part, older men, and she began to get a clearer picture of what the publicity people would call his 'spectacular rise'.

After one of those dinners and when their guests were gone, he was looking over some typed notes, while she, as she often did, sat on the rug at his feet, her head against the arm of the chair, smoking a cigarette.

"This kind of thing's very dull for you, isn't it?" he said, but he was giving most of his attention to the notes.

"I don't find it dull," she answered, and he continued reading and, almost absently, his free hand caressed her cheek. His touch roused her as it always did, and she relaxed to it and closed her eyes. Suddenly, with a slither of paper, he flung the notes across the room, bent down and kissed her.

"I'll get you out of this," he said, and she saw that his eyes were very bright. "I'll get you back where you belong."

He carried her into the bedroom and made love to her. It had never been quite like that before. But just before she slept, she wondered what had caused that swift, dominating mood in him. Her final thought was that to be made love to by any other man would be impossible. Not wrong—impossible.

After eighteen months they were still living in the flat because they had not found the house they wanted.

Neither had she conceived a child. She wanted his child with a desire which surprised her. But the child did not come.

One night, while she still lay in his arms, she said, "I went to a doctor yesterday." She felt the breath suspended in him, then he said, "What for? Are you ill?"

"No," she answered. "I wanted to find out why I can't have a baby. There seems to be no reason why I can't."

She thought she could almost hear his brain taking that in, turning it over till it formed an idea. He lay very still.

"You're hinting that it's my fault," he said, "aren't you?"

"I'm not 'hinting' anything. It may be, I suppose."

He hated that. Resentment, the supposed slur on his virility, the thought that there might be something wrong with him was, she knew, churning about in his mind.

And there was something else churning about in his mind, too, the almost suburban reticence he had about discussing such things.

"If you think I'm going to be mauled about by some damned medical——" he began, and she interrupted with, "You don't have to be. I want a baby. I can't seem to have one. And it appeared the only sane thing to do."

"You mean he examined you?"

"Of course."

She thought for a moment that he was going to make a fuss about that—how cryingly sensitive he was over some things—but at last he said, "And he said you could?"

"He said there was no apparent physical reason why I couldn't."

"Oh, damn the man!"

She thought of the efficient, precise little doctor and wanted to smile. Didn't he realise that one body was so like another body to them as to be unrecognisable? Or was he damning the poor little creature for not faulting her and imputing fault in him?

"Do you want a baby all that?" he said.

"All that," she answered, and she laid her hand against his neck. "Don't you?"

"I don't know that I do. If you want it, I do," he answered. Then he said, "There's nothing wrong with me. What could there be?"

She turned her head and kissed his shoulder.

"Don't fuss about it. I do want a child, but if we can't have one we can't."

He wasn't satisfied, though. She knew that.

Two days later he left for Germany, and when he came back he said, "Well, there's nothing wrong with me, either."

That he had gone to a doctor, after all, touched her, for she had sensed his deep repulsion, even perhaps his fear. But now he was pleased with himself again—a man, whole, able, if he wished, to father a child. And she found herself being pleased with his own pleasure.

She laughed and said, "It's really rather funny, isn't it, both of us scrabbling about trying to find out why we can't reproduce ourselves when people who don't want children have them just like that? P'raps we will now the medical profession has told us we may."

But six months later there was still no hope of a child.

They bought a house that spring. It was an hour's run from London, three miles outside Aberlane, a genuine but unpretentious Queen Anne, with three reception-rooms and a kitchen and scullery downstairs, four bedrooms and a dressing-room up, a couple of bathrooms and some rather attractive out-buildings.

He said to her, "Now look, this is yours. Do what you like with it. I'll go into figures and tell you just how much we can spend on furniture and decoration and all that, then you go ahead. I've got some big things on at the moment, and I'll have to give most of my time to them."

She was excited and told herself it was as good as going in for interior decorating without the risk that the customer wouldn't like the result or settle the account. He bought her a small car so that she could be independent of the trains, and she drove down there three or four days a week. A local decorator, a good craftsman, and his men, moved in, and two months later moved out, leaving her what she thought of as a prepared canvas on which she would paint the picture of their home.

During that two months she hadn't allowed him to go near the place, but when the last ladder and bucket had gone trundling back to Aberlane in Elias Withers' Ford van, she invited him to inspect this 'first stage'. His enthusiasm delighted her, although there was a quality in it which brought her near to tears. She had forgotten in her own excitement and pleasure that this was in a way his first 'home'—the succession of rooms he had inhabited leading up to the Kensington flat being merely milestones on the road to his becoming, in a small way, a 'landowner'. Once again she caught a glimpse of the ironmonger's son who had lived in a room cluttered up with tin pails and boxes of nails over the shop and had trudged off in his cheap shoes to grapple with signs and steel while others of his year stood around on street corners unable to grapple even with their dreary little desires which ended in furtive passes at the girls who tottered by on high heels. And she wondered what quality of blood or will or spirit it might be which could single out one from amongst so many. The Greeks, she'd thought, had a word for that, too—character *is* destiny. He had character and the destiny was coming along nicely. She loved him more than ever.

She'd taken Carrie down there once during that stage, too. Carrie had dressed for the country in tartan drain-pipes and an emerald turtle-necked sweater with, for luck, a diamanté clip on the shoulder.

She was too simple to disguise her disappointment and too kind to express it. She trailed round the empty rooms with her, smoking cigarettes, and at the end said, "Fancy two bathrooms!" But she cheered up over a drink and lunch at the hotel at Aberlane, and told her that Olga was trying for a job at Stratford next season and if that wasn't funny she didn't know what was. She said she went round the flat moaning 'Will these little hands ne'er be clean' till she could scream, and she'd dyed her hair black and let it grow long like Anna's, but instead of looking like Anna she only looked like that advert for death on the roads, and Sammy Golden had said if she went on being such a clot the only job he'd be able to get her was the body in a whodunit. She drove her back to London in time for the evening show, and noticed how, once they turned into the Fulham Road where the lights were shining on the wet streets, the slightly strained expression she'd been wearing all day left her.

"You wouldn't like my drain-pipes, would you?" Carrie said as she stood by the car. "They're too tight for me, really, and I don't like them for Town. Might come in for you down there, though."

She suggested she should keep them for when she came to stay with them.

By the end of another six weeks she had carpets laid in two rooms downstairs, one bedroom furnished and the kitchen fitted out. She knew to within an inch the effect she was aiming at, and was prepared to wait for the precise pieces of furniture which would complete her 'picture' for each room. She travelled miles in the little car to attend sales, and became quite expert at bidding. When she was ready, she 'invited' Guy to stay in the house for the first time.

He had planned to arrive at eight on the Friday evening. She had gone down there on the Thursday and stayed overnight, so that by the time he was due she had a wood fire lighted, more for effect than necessity, and a meal ready and everything in order. Waiting for him, she stood in the drawing-room trying to 'see' it with eyes other than her own.

Framed in the heavy brocade-draped windows, the last of the day was passing over the distant hills. Three shaded lights deepened the patina on wood which a craftsman had fashioned. A bowl of flowers from the garden was delicate as the spring itself against the apple-green wall.

She wondered what Guy would think of it. Would his mind go back to the room over the shop, to the ugliness and the pile of tin pails? Would there even be a barely felt undercurrent of nostalgia now that all that was so far behind?

She heard the car, and she went through to the panelled hall and opened the door.

"Hello there!" she said, and as he hurried up the steps, "Come and see what can be done with six-pennorth of screws."

They stayed on down there. He drove to London every day, and when necessary slept at the flat. Twice a week she went up to make sure that the daily woman was keeping the place habitable. He was, she knew, working very hard, and she thought he was going through a period of extra strain; but he never discussed it with her, and she saw no point in forcing him to talk if he preferred silence.

On two occasions, once in London and once while they were at Ladysmere, he had surprised her by going to church. He had made no fuss or comment, simply stating the bare fact that he was going and driving off in the car.

She could not see the way his mind was working, and she said, "Do you go because you want to or for business sake, amen?"

She watched his expression change, then a smile touched his lips. "I always went with my Dad when I was a boy. Didn't you ever go?"

"Of course. Father read the lessons. He must have had fun with 'Pay what thou owest and in everything give thanks'. He had quite a bit to give thanks for, but I've often wondered what the butcher, who was the gentleman who took the little bag round, thought of it. I don't think I ever got the hang of it quite. It always used to make me think of fish-bones. I've never known why."

He frowned. "It must be right," he said. "It isn't as if it's a new idea, it runs all through man's history in one form or another."

He didn't say more than that, and the subject was left.

He decided to give up the Kensington flat, and she began to plan the furnishing of the other rooms so that they could settle down to life at Ladysmere. A couple of weeks went by, and one night when he came down she sensed change in him.

After dinner he said, "Something to tell you."

"Yes?" she answered, but there wasn't the slightest apprehension in her mind.

"Yes," he repeated; then, "You remember J. B. Harris? I told you about him."

She was back in Mastrani's sitting opposite an unknown, exciting person who was telling her that his father had kept an ironmonger's shop. She was intrigued and she knew she was going to love him. At the next table a waiter in a white coat turned the frying-pan with a flick of his wrist and the lemon and rum blazed up in an electric-blue flame. The elderly woman sitting there watched his every movement with knowledgeable eyes. The waiter spooned the rum over the pancake, pursing his thick Jamaican lips a little. The smell of coffee, suddenly strong, consumed the smell of the lighted rum till there wasn't a trace of it. Guy looked down at his plate.

The memory was sharp and strong, more real for the moment than the Ladysmere drawing-room.

"The screw-man?" she said to Guy, but for another second or two she remained in the restaurant, loth to let those first exciting hours slip back into memory.

"Yes," Guy answered. His hands were clasped between his knees. "This week I've pulled off the thing I've been aiming at for months. We're all right now. I'm where I wanted to be."

"You mean J. B. Harris has 'taken you up' again?"

He smiled. "You could put it that way," he said. "Perhaps you could say we've taken each other up. I said I'd get you back where you belong."

"I belong here," she said, and she saw him fighting every inch of the way—the kid from the ironmonger's shop.

"There's a snag, though," he said. "It means I'll have to go to Korea for a spell. Not long—six weeks possibly."

"To *Korea*?"

"I know," he answered, "but I'm afraid it's necessary. Will you hate it very much?"

"I shall come, too."

"No," he said. "That wouldn't be possible."

"Of course it would be possible."

"No," he said again. "And, anyway, you couldn't get a permit."

"Then I'll come to the nearest point I can. Singapore or somewhere."

"I'd rather you stayed," he said. "I'd know you were here, and feel more secure in my mind. I'd hate you to be alone in Singapore."

"But there's fighting in Korea."

"I shan't be mixed up in that."

"You don't know you won't."

He put out his hand, and she came across and knelt on the rug before his chair.

"If I were a soldier, you wouldn't make a fuss," he said.

"Of course I should make a fuss. I'm not one of your noble women."

"Well, an explorer, then."

"All this talk! I should explore, too."

He smiled very slightly.

"Listen," he said. "I'm going for six weeks, and it's safe as houses. A lot safer than driving to London. And when I come back . . ." He put his hands on her shoulders. "I want to give you everything in the world," he said. "All this is for you."

"What in the name of nonsense would I do with everything in the world?" she said. "Do *you* know what you feed a hippopotamus on?"

He wiped the tears from her eyes.

He left a week later. The night before he went she thought, 'If I could love him more, I would. I can't, for I haven't any more love in me.'

The next day Bessie arrived with her battered trunk sewn into a grimy covering which made her think of an old elephant. She had kept in touch with her after her parents' death, and had suggested some time ago that she come to work for them at Ladysmere. It was good to see her 'solid oak' legs again and to have someone living in the place while Guy was away.

She missed him to the point of pain, but she decided to spend the time he was away in completing her work on the house, and often as she drove or walked she imagined his homecoming.

The six weeks passed, but he didn't return. Then when two months had passed Meg Metcalfe rang through to say that she and Raines were down at their house at Alban Bay, and why not come over for the week-end? Even Bessie had given a further little push by saying, "If you do I'll take the chance to slip home and see my Dad." What had Bessie's Dad, twisted into his bed with rheumatism, to do with it?

She went.

Driving down there, hatless, the car roof folded back, she thought, 'What did I say I'd go for? I don't want to go. I thought I'd got out of that idiotic habit of saying I'll go somewhere and regretting it the moment I have to get ready. It's so spineless. Even if I turned back now, I don't suppose one of them would notice I wasn't there. And what would it matter if they did? Not even Meg will remember who was present or absent in a week's time.'

The house was white and modern. There seemed to be a great deal of glass and there was a vague likeness to a ship about it. Windows and doors were opened wide; and there were no flower borders, but a lawn of smooth brilliant emerald and a low stone wall with the sea at high tide breaking a few yards from it.

There was broad blue-and-white striped garden furniture, and as she arrived, Barney, Meg's dresser, was taking the tea out to the garden.

There were many more people than she had expected. Meg, of course, with the usual three or four adoring youths round her, Raines and his monocle, some young girls, a couple of older men, Anna, her hair pinned up anyhow with a few 'old lady' hairpins, Glynne looking Oriental in a cretonne jacket over white shorts, and another man.

"Darling!" Meg said. "So you have! I was just saying to Dickie I bet you wouldn't. You're looking wonderful. You know everyone, don't you? Pretend you do, will you, darling? It's too hot to introduce people. Give her that chair, Raines. No, the big one. . . ."

Be honest, she told herself. Make yourself see straight. Don't hedge.

She was aware of him from the beginning. Raines said, "Since Meg's so dilatory, I'll try to be civil to my guests. Andrew! Come and let me introduce you to Gina—Andrew Wharton, Mrs. Taylor—Gina."

Right from the beginning. Why? In heaven's name why? She hadn't even thought that there might be such a creature as a man present. It hadn't occurred to her. Raines? Oh lord yes, Raines, but he wasn't a man. He was vintage Henry Irving with a monocle on a broad band, acting far better off than on stage. But the other one. He wasn't even good-looking, too heavily built with broad shoulders and a large mouth. He was quiet. But he had lovely hands. Right from the beginning. The attraction was so strong that there wasn't anything to fight. There wasn't any question of liking him, she didn't know him.

They were pulled together by a force as inevitable as gravity, some damned primitive thing that was as far outside convention and discipline and loyalty as an electric storm was outside a tea-cup.

There just wasn't anything to fight. And no one else had any entity or being; only he. The rest might have been figures painted on a backcloth, not even present as he and she were present. He alone, they alone had reality.

Was that eye-wash? Hot air? Excuse? No, it wasn't. It was the truth. If ever there was truth, it was that. She wasn't an adolescent or an inexperienced spinster. Passion and desire weren't things she had merely read about. She'd gone out into life, travelled, been on the stage, was married—and that thing at that velocity had never touched her before.

They had tea and the sun was still high and hot in the sky. Someone suggested bathing again, and the whole lot of them were over the other side of the little stone wall playing with an enormous striped water-ball on the wet sand, while the sea became calm and white as the house. They bathed, and he swam out far beyond the rest of them, with a slow leisurely stroke, quite at home in the water.

While he was still swimming, Raines sat beside her on the sand as she dried herself and said, "A most un-typical American, isn't he? Have you read his stuff?"

"I didn't know he had any 'stuff'," she answered, and Raines clicked his tongue. "He's over here to see his English publishers. They're bringing out his *Single Track* in a couple of weeks. It was all over the States when we were on Broadway. . . ."

He had reached shallow water and was wading towards them. When he came up to them, his eyes were more startlingly blue than ever.

They went back to the house, changed, had drinks, while the inevitable, silent thing went on. He didn't leave her side. They talked together as though they were isolated, quite alone. There was no time to think or to reason or to remember, and it was possible that if there had been it wouldn't have made any difference. She, both of them were mesmerised, living in a world which contained nothing and no one but the other. They had dinner, with champagne because it was Meg's birthday. Anna, without so much as a safety-pin on her night blue dress looked unrealistically beautiful, and everyone talked and laughed a lot, while the two young girls became younger and more girlish than ever. They sat out in the garden under the warm June stars, while inside the room the shaded lights picked up Glynne at the piano. The little lapping waves, far away now, were taken back into the darkness of low tide, and his voice came clearly out on the quiet air.

'There was a night when my burden was love,
My burden was love . . .'

Beside her Andrew said, "What's happening to us? I stopped falling for this sort of thing before I left college." He put his hand over hers. "I can't get a grip of anything at all. These people are all zombies. They've been dead a century. Only you are real. Gina, what's it all about? Tell me, for Pete's sake. I'm swimming out of my depth."

"I don't know," she whispered. "I don't know."

"If I say this has never happened to me before you'll think I'm joining in with the pretty lights and the little song, but I swear it's true. I've never felt so old, ageless then, in my life. Have you?"

"Never."

"My novelist's mind wants to analyse it, tear it to bits and stick a reason on it. I can't. Reason died when the sands piled up over the cities again. Oh hell, what's all the talk? Believe me that it's never happened to me before, will you, Gina? I swear to you."

The young girls went home. Car lights swung over the side of the house, making it dazzlingly white, and passed on, leaving everything shadowed and still again. Voices called 'good night'. Engines roared and died away.

And still there were only the two of them, he and she, in a world made up of the far beat of waves at the edge of the inexplicable sea under a skyful of worlds and planets whose light had died a million years ago.

He slept with her that night.

She thought, now, sitting in the surgery, that it was only as she was driving back to Ladysmere that she had come to herself again, and coming to herself had been the most agonising experience of her life. Between one mile and the next she had passed from one plane to another as surely as a lift slid from a sunlit top storey to a basement.

As the white house with its queer company of Meg, Raines, Anna and the rest faded into unreality, isolation hemmed her in. She watched herself as she might have watched another figure performing the actions she had performed. And she herself and her actions were as unreal as the rest.

The image of Andrew came and she tried to force it away, but he stood by the car as she was leaving, snatching a moment to say, "Are you all right? Do you hate me? You can't go like this. I'll call you. . . ."

She didn't hate him, because reason refused even the benison of hatred. How could she hate when the thing had been so totally shared between them? She wanted Guy and the security of their lives together with a need that was pain. If he had been there, she told herself that she would have gone to him and cried it all out. Disgusted with the maudlin self-pity of that, she tried rationalising the whole thing. Face it, she told herself. You are married, you love your husband, and while he is away you have slept with another man. You are not the first to have done such a thing, and you most certainly won't be the last. Those were the facts all right. That was the set-up, but the facts didn't make the slightest difference to the sense of isolation to the self which, below the surface, cried, 'Why did I? What happened to us? I didn't think of myself, let alone Guy or loyalty or love. I didn't think at all. And I haven't the excuse of loving him. You can't love anyone you've known less than twenty-four hours. And yet he, too, at first anyway, was as bewildered and mesmerised as I was. 'What's happening to us?' he'd whispered to her. 'For Pete's sake, tell me. I'm swimming out of my depth.' How should she know? Like any cheap little bit, she had lost control of herself and bartered love for Guy and loyalty to him for a few hours' sensation. Can you never count on yourself, she'd asked the unwinding ribbon of road? Is my will so weak that it goes down without a whimper? Was there something primitive and unusual about the whole thing, or was it that I behaved with the promiscuity I've always despised? And finally, it's no good wallowing in self-pity or trying to analyse the thing away. There'll come a time when the thought of it will cease to give me nausea. It's over.

But as she turned in at the gates of Ladysmere she would have given ten years of her life if it had never been.

Andrew didn't call her. He wrote.

"I am worried about you. Will you let me come and see you? It doesn't seem possible to leave this thing as we have done without explanation. I feel you may hate my even referring to it, but I must. I still swear to you that all I said was true. And I still insist that I have never experienced anything like it in my life. If I say I'm sorry, I shall be lying. The part of me that isn't anxious on your behalf glories in the memory. Do please cut this very real agony of anxiety short, and at least let me come and talk to you. I shall be staying at the above address. . . ."

She didn't know what action to take. The sincerity behind the letter touched her, but what good could come of her seeing him? The thought of discussion nauseated her. She wanted to forget the whole episode, put it behind her, never by thought or word refer to it again. That might not be fair to him but at least it was an attempt, at this late hour, to be fair to Guy. And he would soon forget. . . .

Half an hour later she saw his name on the front page of the paper.

'Andrew Wharton, the American novelist, was killed yesterday afternoon when his car collided with a lorry on the London-Worthing road at Washington. Mr. Wharton, aged 37, was the author of several books including the best-selling novel *Single Track*, the English edition of which is to be published by John Holland next week. Mr. Wharton was unmarried.'

Two months later she knew that she was to have his child.

Why go into that now? Because she was bound on the wheel of it, caught up in the pattern of the whole. And because, after a year,

Guy was coming home in four days' time. There was the agony of fear made certain; the impulsion to get rid of the child or even take her own life rather than face him. There was the rat-in-a-trap visit to Carrie and Carrie's surprised, "But there's that man over Batemans. He put Shirley right that time. You don't have to have it." She'd known that would be Carrie's answer, and yet she had gone up to London to hear it spoken. For a week she tossed on the pitching boat of indecision, then it was over. She couldn't do it. And Guy? The sentimental hope that, because they couldn't have children he'd forgive and forget as easily as though she'd overspent her dress allowance? And then in the middle of argument, the fantastic, agonising news that Guy had been taken prisoner in Korea, and down had come J. B. Harris, a little five-foot-four gnome with dark brown eyes, in a Daimler many sizes too large for him, to explain nightmare and procedure, and to leave her again telling her not to worry, that everything that could be done was being done and that the whole thing was a mistake on someone's part, and was she all right for money, if not please to let him know.

There were moments when the whole thing took on the elements of farce, so crazy had her life become, but beyond farce was fact—and the child developing in her body.

She looked at the list of doctors in the vicinity, picked one out with a pin and went to him. She told him the truth, and he sat as he sat now, staring down at the blotter on his desk, saying nothing. When he did look up he said, "I think you've done a very brave thing, you know, and I agree with you that to have got rid of the child would have been disastrous. I'll do what I can to help you."

He had and his friendship had been unlimited. She had, in fact, told herself that for the first time in her life, she had come to comprehend the meaning of the word. There were days when she knew that her mind, rocking on the brink of despair, would have pitched over into darkness without his hand there to steady her. Of his personal life, barring the fact that his wife was dead, she knew little, for he never spoke of himself.

Some four months before the baby was due to be born, she decided to close Ladysmere and find somewhere to live where she was unknown. It was true that, being new-comers to the district, they knew no one, but for Guy's sake she wanted to avoid scandal. She had heard from him once through the Red Cross, but there was no knowing when the fighting would end and he himself come home; nor in what condition. There was always, too, the faint, feeble hope that he would, by a miracle, understand and they would take up their lives again; but the near-certainty that he would do neither was stronger than the hope.

Besides the doctor, Bessie was her other crutch, though sometimes Bessie's 'Us pore girls' attitude was not easy to bear. But it was Bessie who found her the little flat over her cousin's tobacconist's shop in Melford, a market-town twenty-five miles away from Ladysmere. The tobacconist's shop was down near the station in a narrow little street of ugly stone houses, and had once been an old bow-fronted sweet shop. There was little chance of her being discovered by any of their friends there. The first night she slept in the place after she had closed Ladysmere, she knew that the isolation she had experienced on that drive home from the Metcalfes' house at Alban Bay was a mere shadow of a thing before the isolation she knew now. It was not only black as pitch but grimed with an appalling sordidness.

"I wanted a baby so much," she cried into the crook of her arm, "and if Guy had never gone away and it had been his, it would have been perfect. And the baby would have been wanted, longed for. I fell for the nonsense of champagne and stars and a little song, and the baby's got to be born in this hole-and-corner place while I fight off shame in case it'll hurt it. I know it's no one's fault but my own, but if only it could have been the other way. If only it could have been Guy's. . . ."

And if Andrew hadn't been killed in a car crash? The twists of fate were preposterous. Andrew Wharton the novelist was dead. He died unmarried, childless—but he didn't, a bit of him was still living in her, and no one in all the world knew it.

She wondered sometimes if his mother were alive.

Bessie's cousin was kind and she didn't ask questions. But, talking to her one night when loneliness had become intolerable, she said,

"If you're lucky, it'll be all over before your husband comes back, won't it? I don't see why he need know, not really."

She was astonished and she answered, "But of course he'll know. Even if he came home now, I couldn't let him think it was his. And if he doesn't come home for another year, he'll know without my telling him."

"Oh, you're going to keep it, then? I thought Bessie said you were just going to have it and put it in a Home. A lady I knew did that. She was the daughter at the place where I was housemaid, and she wasn't even married. She went away for a bit and had the baby, and it was sent straight off. I don't think she even saw it."

Back in her sitting-room over the shop she felt sick with nausea, and for the first time the unknown baby took on personality.

"Don't listen," she found herself saying to it. "Whatever happens I won't do that to you. I promise."

The doctor, Philip Blake, put her in touch with a nurse and doctor in the town, but he promised to come, if it were possible, when the baby was born.

Bessie's cousin, saddled by her patriotic parents with the name Dardanella—her father had taken part in the Suvla Bay landing in 1916—agreed to look after her while she was 'laid up'.

When the time came, Philip Blake, as he had promised her, delivered the baby, and it was he who brought him into the room to her.

'My son,' she thought. 'My son. . . . Guy. . . . Guy. . . .'

When, a month later, the doctor came again, she said, "Do you think I ought to put him in a Home?"

He thought before replying, and she sat there watching him, fascinated by the line of his brow and nose and the set of his lightly closed lips.

"Could you put him in a Home?" he asked her. "I don't fancy you could. Some women seem to be able to, but I can't see you doing it."

"He didn't ask to be born," she said.

A queerly helpless expression came over his face, making him look young. "No," he agreed.

He didn't say anything else, and she thought over the last month —the isolation of it, the crying solitariness. If the baby had been Guy's she could have shared him with not only Guy himself but everyone else they knew. There would have been laughter, celebration, fun. As it was, she had had to suffer only Bessie's faithful and funereal visits with her letters, or the solid Dardanella's limp condolences. Dear heaven, she thought, what a terrible price to pay for one mistake. She'd made it, but was there no end to the exacting of the full account? No, because the full account hadn't been presented yet. There was still Guy to come—if he ever came.

"Why did I have a baby by another man, when my husband and I wanted one so much?" she asked the doctor.

"I can't tell you," he answered. "I've known people go without a child for years, adopt one, and then have two or three of their own. It's one of those things."

"If you were Guy and we hadn't had children, would you accept him?"

"How can I answer that?" he asked.

"There's a chance he might, I suppose," she said.

"You know him. I don't. And you've got to remember that it will hurt."

"Perhaps it would be kinder to my husband to put the baby into a Home," she said. "It would, wouldn't it?"

He was silent a long time.

"Could you keep up the deception?" he asked at last.

"I don't know," she said. "I don't know. I wish I did. Sometimes I think I could, then at other times. . . . He didn't ask to be born," she said again. "And I love him. I do, you know. Sometimes I hoped that I'd hate him, but I don't. It would have been easier if I'd hated him, wouldn't it?"

"I don't think you're the kind not to love your own child."

"I don't know what kind I am."

"Do any of us?"

"Some people seem so—uncomplicated."

"Seem," he said.

"They wouldn't have done what I did."

"We each have our own temptations."

But it hasn't even been a temptation, she thought. Temptation was a thing you could fight. This thing was like a firework, blazing up into the night in a cascade of stars and falling to earth again.

"The other night I thought I'd try to find someone who'd take him," she said. "But every time I dropped off to sleep I woke thinking he'd gone."

"That's what I mean," he answered.

That night they arranged that, when Guy came home he would meet him and tell him, not in order to spare her, although the very thought of telling him appalled her, but because she had decided that until Guy knew she would not return to Ladysmere. If he refused to have her back, then not to appear there at all would make it at least simpler both for her and for him.

"It's only fair," the doctor said before he left, "to give him the chance to make a decision. Human beings are capable of heroic generosity at times."

"Are they?" she said.

She went down the stairs with him, and stood beside his car under the quiet spring stars. A year ago she and Guy had bought Ladysmere and she was furnishing it. . . .

"Heroic generosity," he repeated.

"It sounds like one of those things people say," she said.

"It is, but it's true, too. Good night."

"Why are you good to me?" she asked suddenly. "Or am I just a job of work?"

"I'd like to see it come right," he answered. "You haven't been *un*-generous," he added.

When he had gone she took the baby out of his cot and fed him. Even in the turmoil of solitude and indecision and fear, there was peace in looking down on his head against her arm, and in a half return to her old surface cynicism she thought, 'Child of my sin! But, dear lord, how I love him.'

Three months later, this morning in fact, she had received the news from Guy himself that he was flying home on the thirteenth.

She became aware of the surgery again. The fan of paper was still in its position behind the bars of the grate. The 'September Morn' woman still had her hair dangling about her fish-white shoulders. The doctor still stared at the blotter.

She looked at her watch. She had been in the room five minutes. In five minutes she had relived years of her life. Her parents, Carrie, the Metcalfes, Anna, Glynne, Guy, Andrew; houses, theatres, rooms, the sky, the terrifying depths of the Atlantic, a Stratocruiser, Ladysmere; scents, words, sounds, actions, colour, queer details of things like the old-lady pins in Anna's hair; the people in a passing bus on the Embankment, the man in the shop at Nice where she'd bought a post-card for Carrie—they had all been there, not dead and filed away, but living, coloured and fresh and crowding her memory just as they had done in life. And they took up no space, no time. Somewhere, somehow, she had even carried a Stratocruiser about with her, but it took up no more room than the diamond clip on Carrie's turtle-necked sweater.

"All right. I'll meet him," the doctor said.

Chapter II

THE crossing-gates closed, the signal cables below the platform shuddered and up the line the signal rose into place. Philip Blake felt for his cigarette-case, opened it and took a cigarette.

George Harrison, the ticket-collector, swung the handle of his clippers. "She's on the way, Doc. Any minute now."

Philip nodded, thinking what a curious fascination a mock-American accent held for so many people today. Soon our own identifying dialects would be totally lost, and you wouldn't be able to tell if a man came from Yorkshire, Sussex or Chicago.

"Trade good, Doc?" George asked him, with heavy humour. "Still fitting the customers out with wigs and corsets? Got to have something for our money. Don't pay to be well today."

The doctor smiled slightly. He had heard the whistle of the approaching train, and he wasn't awaiting its advent with enthusiasm. It wasn't the first time he had had to tell a man that his wife was the mother of another fellow's child, but he'd never disliked the doing of it more.

The train came in. The engine vibrated and was suddenly silent. Doors opened and slammed shut. A group of schoolgirls came down the platform, talking and laughing. One had the over-bright eyes of the highly sexed; one incipient goitre. A woman with a shopping-basket dragged a small child by the hand. Every now and then its feet went from under it and it lurched at an alarming angle, but the woman plodded on, her lips set. His glance left her and passed on. Coming towards him he saw a man whose clothes hung on him proclaiming the fact that he had lost weight. There were pouches of fatigue beneath his eyes. His mouth was a thin, hard line.

As he came up to George Harrison and surrendered his ticket, Philip stepped forward.

"Mr. Taylor?" he enquired. But he knew the answer.

"What is all this?" said Guy. "You say my wife's not ill. I've come to your surgery with you. What are you driving at?"

Philip Blake looked at him, and for a moment his passion for wresting the truth from things deserted him. Why had he taken this on?

He said, "I have to tell you that your wife has had a child."

"A what?"

He watched a flush take the place of incredulity on Guy's face. His muscles relaxed. A smile touched his mouth and his eyes were bright.

"Why on earth didn't you say so in the first place? All this mystery! I thought there was something wrong with her! It's the one thing we wanted. Is she at the house? I must go to her. . . ."

Philip Blake sat very still. He'd muffed it. Given the man to imagine the child was his. It had never occurred to him. . . . But, of course, Taylor had been a prisoner and in prison time lost its value.

"You're not hiding anything, are you?" he heard Guy say. "Trying to put me off?" A white patch came round his mouth. "She *isn't* dead, is she?"

He didn't answer.

"Well?" Guy said.

He looked directly back at him, and he watched truth come to him as though it were tangible, a substance. His nostrils dilated a trifle as he drew a breath. He closed his eyes and opened them, and a smile that was more of a grimace came about his lips.

"I see," Guy said. "Of course . . . I see." He lifted his head and looked over at him. "Of course, I've been in prison for a year, haven't I? While my wife's been having what they call 'a good time'. You're the father, I suppose?"

That supposition, strangely, hadn't occurred to Blake.

"I'd have told you if I had been," he answered. "I attended Mrs. Taylor when she was confined."

"How do I know that's true? Or were you only one of them? Who is the father, if you're not? Or doesn't she know?" He turned away and bent his head down on to his arm on the mantelpiece. "Christ, I can't bear it."

Philip poured brandy into a glass and brought it to him, but Guy didn't move.

"All these months. Thinking of her. Keeping my courage alive because of her. Believing in her. And she——"

"Brandy," Philip said. "Better drink it. I'll tell you all I know."

He told him all he knew. It wasn't, and he was aware of it, the exact truth, but it was Gina's interpretation of what had occurred, coloured possibly by her own mentality and imagination, and as near truth as might be; but watching Guy's face he knew there was to be no easy solution, and even when he had finished speaking he made no answer. He sat in the chair where Gina herself had sat four days ago, and his mouth was drawn down and his eyes held no pity.

At last he said, "I suppose you and my—you and she made up this story between you? You don't expect me to believe it, do you?"

"It's true," he answered.

"True!" Guy muttered. "Who was the man?" he shot at him.

"He was an American novelist over here to see his publishers. He was killed on his way to that appointment."

"She told you that?"

"Yes."

"An easy way to get rid of him. I wonder how many more there were? Did she pick him up?"

The torture on the poor devil's face was sufficient curb on temper, Philip told himself. Anger would serve none of them.

"As far as I know, she met him at a party given by friends of hers—Margaret Metcalfe and her husband."

"The stage crowd! So she ran back to them the moment I was out of the way."

Philip Blake picked up a pencil from his tray and put it down again. "I know this is a shock to you," he said. "It was bound to be, but try to keep a sense of proportion, if you can. You know as well as I do that your wife's not promiscuous. I tried to explain to you that this was one isolated instance and that there's no question of anyone else in her life. I don't expect you to believe that, but it doesn't serve any useful purpose to exaggerate the whole thing." He drew a breath and said, "Have you never fallen from grace, Taylor? Have you never made love to another man's wife?"

"What business of yours is it what I've done? It's got nothing to do with it. You know only what she chooses to tell you. And you believe it. Well, I'll tell you something now. When I first met her she was a third-rate actress in second-rate touring companies, and if she was lucky she got small parts in London. She was living in a hole of a room in Chelsea, and I picked her up out of all that and married her. And, like a bloody fool, I believed in her. If it ever came to my mind that she'd lived with a dozen men before me, I shut my eyes to it. I trusted her—God, I trusted her, and she acted as though she loved me. Acted! I'd even forgotten she could act, but it's clear as a bell now. She wanted the money. I had it. And the moment I'm out of the way she goes back to the old racket."

Pain of body, pain of mind, thought Philip, and how differently men met them. It was possible the chap had been a lion of courage in his prison cell or whatever they'd shut him up in, but this thing had beaten him. Well, what had he expected?

"Then you refuse even to see your wife?" he said.

"I do." The answer was rapped out without compromise.

"There's little more to be said then, is there? Mrs. Taylor asked me to let you know that the house, Ladysmere, is ready for you to go to, and there's a servant there who'll look after you."

But Guy didn't move.

"Why are you her spokesman?" he asked. "Hadn't she even the courage to come and tell me herself?"

"Oh yes, she could have told you herself. She chose this way in order to simplify matters. Had the child been born here and then you had refused to live with her——"

"Simplify matters! You know where she is?"

"I do. Yes."

"Is she here?"

"No."

"You're not going to tell me where she's hiding?"

"There's not much point, is there?"

"You needn't worry. I shan't run amok and kill her. She isn't worth it. You can tell her that, too. And you can say that I shall divorce her as soon as it's possible to do it."

"That would come better from a solicitor, wouldn't it? I'm a doctor."

Guy stood up. "God, what's the use?" He put his hand over his eyes. "I know you've done what you thought was the best you could do. I'm not a fool. She got round you to try to make me agree to have her child, just as she got round me for everything she wanted. Why did I ever trust her?"

"Because you've pretty sound judgment, I imagine."

"I don't want soft soap."

Philip Blake left his chair and came round to the other side of his desk. "I'm not in league with your wife in an attempt to fool you, Taylor," he said. "I'm only in this thing because she is my patient. I'm not defending her—I've no right to judge one way or the other—but there's one thing I am sure about, and that is that she's telling the truth. She could have had an abortion and you'd never have known a thing about it. She could have had the child sent away to an orphanage before you came home, or she could even have foisted the fatherhood on you. It wouldn't have been hard to fool you, you know, but she refused to fool you."

"Talk," said Guy wearily. "I'm so sick of it." He took his hand from his eyes. "I've been faithful to her," he said, "because I believed in her. Don't you see, nothing can make this thing right? It's she who's smashed our marriage, not me. I know it's the fashion to laugh unfaithfulness off and tell stories about how you found your wife with her lover; but I'm unfashionable. Neither of you see any reason why I don't say, 'Come back and bring the other fellow's baby, and go off and do it again any time you like.' That's what you hoped I'd say, isn't it?"

Philip Blake looked into his drawn face and fatigued eyes.

"No," he said, "that's not what I, at least, wanted you to say. I hoped—and I think she did—that you might have found it in your heart to forgive her."

Guy pushed himself away from the mantelpiece.

"I'll go. We're getting nowhere." He swung round to the doctor again. "I could never trust her any more. Don't you see that? She's broken my faith in her." He went to the door and turned the handle. "You did what you could," he said. "I realise that. Good-bye."

Guy stood on the pavement outside the house. There were cars parked in the square. Two buses were waiting one behind the other outside the bank. Women with baskets went into the shops on the far side. A policeman chatted to a farmer who stood by an estate car spattered with mud. An errand-boy trundled past with his bicycle basket piled precariously with wooden boxes, whistling as he went.

This was what he had pictured all the way home. This and Ladysmere. And Gina.

He fended off the thought of her with a barrier of the will, and asked himself instead whether he would take a taxi out to the house or catch the next train back to London. He was deadly tired, and the thought of another journey with nothing but an hotel bedroom at the end of it seemed more than he could endure. Yet, to go back to Ladysmere. . . .

He walked across the square and into the hotel garage. Five minutes later the taxi had left Belsted behind and was heading for Aberlane.

The car drove through the gates. He got out, paid the man and turned to the house. The front door stood open. There were flowers in the hall. For a moment of instability he wondered if he had imagined all the rest, that it was all part of the nightmare of the last year. Gina, he swore it, had arranged those flowers. She had a touch with them that no one else had. Everything was as he thought it would be. Gina was here. . . .

The door at the end of the hall opened and a stocky little woman came through. Large eyes looked up at him from a pale face. Her unshapely hands clasped one another.

"Mr. Taylor?"

"Yes."

The woman stared at him and then lowered her eyes.

"I'm Bessie. Everything's ready for you and the kettle's on. If you'll go into the drawing-room I'll bring your tea."

The drawing-room windows were open. There were flowers there, too—flowers that Gina had arranged. The room bore her touch about it as tangibly as though she had left ten minutes ago. Possibly she had. Where was she now?

Bessie came in with the tray. She moved a table nearer to the chair he had taken, spread a cloth, laid the china and food, tea-pot and water-jug on it.

"There's plenty more water if you should want it," she said. "Will you ring, sir?"

"Thank you."

He poured himself tea and drank it; ate some sandwiches; cut cake.

'My first meal in England,' he thought. 'The thing I'd dreamed of for nearly a year. Oh God, what a fool. What a fool.'

But he refused to allow himself to think. Not yet. He was too exhausted. He hardly cared.

He finished his tea and rang for the woman. He wondered who she was; where she had come from. How much did she know?

"I should like a bath in a quarter of an hour," he said. "I'm very tired and I shan't dress again. I believe I've got a dressing-gown somewhere in the house."

"It's in your dressing-room, sir. And your pyjamas are laid out ready for you. The bath water's beautiful and hot."

"You can get me a meal?"

"Oh yes, sir. It's all ready. Only needs cooking."

"I'd like it early. Seven o'clock. Then I shall go to bed." He looked at the woman's bending figure as she gathered the tea-things on to the tray.

"What did you say your name was?" he asked her.

"Bessie."

"How long have you been here?"

"I came just after you left, sir."

So she knew the whole story. She was probably laughing at him for being fooled. She and Gina had made jokes about it, certain that he would forgive her and take her and the child back.

Vaguely he remembered something else and he said, "Was it you who were with the Randolphs?"

"Yes. I was there for six years."

"I see."

So she knew more than the story. She had known Gina before he had. She could tell him what she was like before she went on the stage. He wanted to question her, to wrench from her the fact that she'd always been promiscuous. He'd have liked her to tell him that this wasn't the first time by a long shot.

"Is there anything else, sir?"

"Nothing else."

She turned round again when she reached the door. "Your bath-towels are on the rails," she said. "Shall I run the bath for you?"

"No, thank you," he said curtly.

He bathed, put on pyjamas and dressing-gown and went downstairs again. The woman had set drinks on one of the tables and he took some sherry. She had closed the windows and put a match to the fire.

He was afraid. He'd staved off thought even when he went into their bedroom, but now there was no escape.

He hated Gina. He'd like to have seen her disfigured. He wished she'd come to him herself so that he could have seen her grovelling at his feet, crying to be taken back. She was too clever for that. She'd twisted her rotten charm on to that poor fool of a doctor and got him to do her dirty work for her. He'd never thought, when she'd made the excuse to stay down here while she was furnishing the house, that she was entertaining her lovers in the place. And he'd bought her a car to make it easier! How they must have laughed over that—she and the Metcalfes and the lank-haired Anna with her undisguised perversions. Like attracted like. If he hadn't been besotted, he'd have realised what she was from the very fact that she was with Thorne and the Metcalfes at Toby Vane's party. But you could go farther than that. She'd told him herself that her father had rooked the tradesmen for years, and she hadn't even had the decency to feel shame. She'd laughed and called him her 'diddling parent'. It was probable that she admired his skill.

His brain stopped pouring out the stream of malice, and a picture of her came before him with startling clarity. It was the first week of their marriage and they were in the hotel bedroom at Cannes undressing, and he thought that he could never have enough of watching her; that all eternity would be too short. And while he watched her, he'd suddenly remembered his bedroom over the shop in Mark Street, Brighton. It had no curtains, and only a strip of old carpet by the bed, just large enough for his bare feet to tread on. The blankets were thin and grey, and his pillow was hard and smelled of many heads. He remembered being cold and drawing his knees up close to his body to try to get warm, and he remembered the misery which was the dynamo that had given him the energy to get out. Now he was not only 'out', but he'd made money. And he'd married Gina Randolph, whose father had been a knight and mother a viscount's granddaughter. Their names were in the history books—Maxwells, de Courcy, Lancaster, Conway-Coutts. Now he was lying in bed in a luxury hotel in France and Gina was brushing her hair, the slim lines of her back showing through her night-dress. And she loved him. It didn't matter to her that he hadn't come from the same class as she had. He'd told her all about himself, and it didn't matter to her. He'd learned how to behave and how to talk, and now he need never tell anyone that he'd ever been anything other than he was.

Gina drew the curtains back and turned out the lights, leaving the star-lit sky framed by the long windows. But instead of getting into bed she sat on the end of it, her knees raised, her hands clasped round them.

"Come to bed," he said. "You'll catch cold."

She laughed slightly and didn't move.

"I so nearly didn't go to Toby's party," she said. "If I hadn't I'd never be sitting on this bed peering at you. Lord, what luck! Do you think it was luck?"

"Not so bad," he'd answered.

"I always knew that if I loved I'd go right in, boots and all," she said. "It's no joke, is it? It seems—almost too big sometimes. Outsize. It's a curious business, isn't it?" she asked. "There's you and here's me, never seen each other till a few months ago, and now I can hardly bear it even when you go away from me to shave. I really do believe it's for ever and ever, amen," she said. "The one undying thing. . . ."

He thought, then, that he'd never forget her saying that and when he'd held her in his arms he'd had to fight back tears. "The one undying thing. . ."

And that, too, had been part of the 'act'—Gina Randolph playing the part of Gina Taylor in the new comedy at the Imperial, Cannes.

He walked into restaurants and saw other men looking at her, and something inside him had laughed—he was so sure of her. And all the time she'd been tricking him, giggling her head off if he'd made a slip in the pronunciation of a word.

He lay back in the chair, his head pressed against the back of it, his hands gripping the arms. 'The one undying thing. . . .' God! God! *God!* He'd loved her. Loved her. He'd have lived for her, died for her—anything. Anything. He'd believed every word she'd spoken, everything she'd done. He'd believed her when she said she loved him. He'd believed her to be true, loyal, good. He'd *loved* her. Gina. . . . Gina. . . . Gina. . . .

Gina knew the telephone would ring. She'd been keyed up to hearing it for the last quarter of an hour, and suddenly the impersonally personal croak that this particular instrument made came from it with the sound of a mechanical duck.

She picked up the receiver.

"Philip Blake here."

She sat down on the edge of the chair.

"Yes?" she said. "Please tell me."

He only hesitated a second, but it was a second too long.

"It's hit him pretty hard," he said. "We'd counted on that. He's in a low physical state, too. He hardly knew where he was. He says —but for heaven's sake remember he's not over the initial shock yet—that he won't see you. I told him Ladysmere was ready for him to go to, but whether he went out there or not, I can't say."

She sat very still. She felt she'd got to protect herself with her own shoulders. They were curved round over her body, and the mouthpiece of the telephone was pressed against her.

"Are you there? Gina?"

Even then she thought, 'He used my name.'

"Yes," she answered. "It's all right. We knew, didn't we? We didn't expect——"

"I told you the initial shock would probably knock him out. You must wait for a true reaction."

"Did he look ill?"

"Very thin. And showing signs of fatigue. That's only natural."

"I wonder—oh no, it doesn't matter."

"What were you going to say?"

"I wonder if I ought to have met him myself. All day I've wondered."

"You can't go back to that now. You chose this way because it seemed the best to you. It did to me, too. I'm still sure of it."

"Did he—did he say what he was going to do? Go to a solicitor? Please tell me. I can bear anything as long as I know."

"He did say that. He spoke of divorce. But I insist you remember that most of what he said was a shock reaction. I don't want to give you a false hope, God forbid, but I'm as certain as I can be that his attitude will be modified after a few days' rest."

"I'm afraid to think that."

"Maybe it's as well you are. It's better that way."

"There was no—no sign of his understanding."

"Not on the surface."

"You did tell him, didn't you, that—this is so difficult to say over a telephone—it was only that one thing? I was so afraid he'd think I was in the habit of it. He's so sensitive under that hard exterior."

"Yes, I made it as clear as I could, but he wasn't in the mood to see much hope anywhere."

"No."

She closed her eyes. Even in the darkness behind them there were bars and zig-zags of light. She longed for total darkness.

"Would you like me to come over?" she heard him say. "I could do. Later. I've surgery at six and a couple of visits. I could be there by nine. Or would you rather go to bed? What I don't want you to do is sit there alone exaggerating the whole thing. It's easy enough to do."

"There doesn't seem a lot to exaggerate, does there? You can't exaggerate a baby. It's just there. If it weren't there, none of this would be, would it?"

"Do you want me to come over?"

"I'd rather go to bed. I feel wretchedly tired."

"Take one of those soneril I left you. And eat some food. Got an egg or something light?"

"You sound like a doctor," she said.

"God forgive me. I'm coming out your way tomorrow about tea-time. I'll look in then."

"I'm trying to say 'thank you'," she said.

"Well, stop trying to say thank you. Sure you'll be all right?"

"Oh yes."

"Good-bye, then."

As she put the receiver down she thought he called her name again, but when she lifted it to her ear, the line was dead.

She sat as she was, with her arms folded high against her shoulders, her chin pressed down on her left hand. All that Philip Blake hadn't told her was there in her mind, clear as a bell. She had known what the answer would be, yet she'd still hoped for the miracle. If only she could see Guy, explain to him that she was just the same person she had always been. That one night hadn't *altered* her. She'd never stopped loving him—not even then. He was still there in her heart. But he—no one—would believe that and she couldn't blame either him or anyone else. If she herself had heard a similar story she'd have said, "She couldn't have loved her husband much, could she? No woman could go as far as that with another man if she did. It simply doesn't add up." It didn't add up. There'd just been that mad, primitive, overwhelming attraction and—she saw it with a knife-like clarity—the result of it would never be wiped out. She and Andrew Wharton, two strangers meeting for only a few hours, had between them created a child. And while the child remained, that night would remain. But Guy. . . .

She rested her elbow on the back of the chair and lowered her head into her arm. This morning, arranging the flowers over at Ladysmere, she'd found herself praying 'Oh God, let him understand. Let him understand. I can't bear the pain for him.' Even now, thinking of him there alone, she couldn't bear the pain for him. That awful year in Korea—and then to be met with the empty, silent house where they'd been so happy. She'd put so much care into it. So much love. Surely he'd still believe those things to be true, wouldn't he? Or was everything she had done stained now, made ugly and false? Ought she to have put the baby in a Home? Wouldn't it have been better for them all in the long run? Guy, then, would never have known, and Christopher, the baby, would never have known either. Or would he? Would the impression have remained somewhere in his little mind? No one could tell. No one.

She stood up and went over to the cot where he lay wide awake. He stared up at her with his brilliantly blue eyes, and she had the idiotic notion that he knew all about it. Gravely, with a slight frown, he considered her; then suddenly a wide all-encompassing smile came over his face. His eyes twinkled and screwed up at the corners. His toothless mouth opened in a silent guffaw.

When one of her tears fell on his hand, he licked it and made a grimace. Then he laughed again, and kicked his knees up and down and waved his arms about like a drum-major.

Guy went to London the following day. Before he left, he said to Bessie, "My plans are uncertain. I've a great many things to see to at the moment, and I can't tell you when I shall be down again." He looked into her oddly sad eyes. "Do you stay on here when the house is empty?"

"I can do."

"You aren't afraid?"

"I don't like it all that. Not at night."

He thought, 'I suppose she knows where Gina is, she must do. She'll probably report every movement I've made.' Again the notion came to him to question her, but he knew it was impossible.

"Can you find yourself somewhere to sleep if I don't get down for a bit?"

"I could go home," she answered. "It's not far."

"Better do that. When I've sorted things out, I'll telephone."

A stubborn expression settled over her face, but her black eyes remained sad. She drew a quick breath and said, "Isn't Miss Gina coming back, then, sir?"

He could have hit her heavy face, smashed into it with his clenched fist.

"Is that any business of yours?"

She looked down. "I shouldn't be staying if she isn't," she said. "My dad doesn't like me staying where there isn't a lady."

He laughed. "I can assure you and your dad that you are quite safe," he said. "More than safe." He took up his case. "If you want to leave—then leave," he said. "It's possible that I shall sell this place very shortly. You may tell my wife that when you see her."

He left her standing there, still looking heavy and stubborn and sad.

Driving to London he was certain that she knew that he came from the same class as she did. Otherwise she would never have asked him such a question, the insolent, dough-faced fool of a woman.

John Benjamin Harris sat back on his specially made high chair and said, "Of course, one would never have considered your going if one had contemplated such a thing. Both Sir James and I were appalled. You were not ill-treated?"

"The winter was pretty bad."

"Food?"

"Occasionally."

The change in him, thought John Benjamin, was frightening. He remembered the under-nourished sharp-faced lad whom Tennant had brought to him twenty years and more ago. The man had receded into the lad again—except for the expression in his eyes. The boy had had hope written there.

"You'll want a long rest," he said. "And good food. You'll soon pull up. Your wife will see to that, I'm sure."

"My wife unfortunately is away."

His tone jerked John Harris away from the chair-back. He peered at Guy's set face. "Oh dear," he said inadequately and added, "Not for long, I hope. I met her, you know. Went down to Ladysmere to see if there was anything I could do. She took the news with tremendous courage, I thought." He looked across at Guy again. He had not moved. There was absolutely no indication of his thought on his face. But that there was trouble was obvious. He couldn't believe that the girl had gone off with someone else while Taylor had been sweating it out in captivity in Korea. It didn't fit in with his impression of her. It didn't fit in with her clear eyes and her free walk. One of the Conway-Coutts lot, so he'd heard, and going down there he'd wondered how she came to marry Taylor. Rather off her beat, one would have thought. Yet, meeting her, seeing the charming home she'd made for him—sizing her up, he'd thought that the two of them were, in a manner of speaking, 'cut out of the same cloth'. Character, not background, of course. But perhaps 'background' had proved the insurmountable barrier. If it had, he was sorry. More than sorry. Taylor was a man after his own heart. He would have called him 'class-less' because by sheer initiative and personality he'd risen above the petty lines man had laid down for himself. Taylor, he'd have said, would have founded his own new and original dynasty. And the Conway-Coutts girl would have provided the necessary touch of breeding to his heirs. And if he knew Taylor, there'd be something worth inheriting when he died.

"I hope she won't be away long," he said to Guy. And he added, "I'd intended to ask her if she would invite Sir James and myself down to dinner at Ladysmere one night. Both of us have a great affection for that part of the country, and there are one or two things which I think we might discuss in a more leisurely way there."

But any hope he had of Guy's enlarging on the matter faded as he replied shortly, "I should be delighted." And then, consciously discarding the subject he said, "I think it would be as well if we tackled the whole position of the merger right away. I want to get up to the factory tomorrow to see Cartwright, and I'd like to have some kind of over-all picture to work on. When I left, the question of the Nigerian bridge was under discussion. I'd like the latest decisions on that and——"

"But, my dear boy," Harris broke in, "aren't you being rather precipitate? Surely you should get your health right before plunging into work? Everything has gone very satisfactorily and, if I may say so, apart from the inconvenience caused you, your reports from Korea were most gratifying. I assure you there is no need for you to rush into harness before you are recovered."

"I prefer to get down to it now," Guy answered coldly.

He took a room in an hotel, and spent the rest of the week in

London, regretting bitterly that he had given up his Kensington flat. He piled into work—and heaven knows there was enough leeway to make up, though the bite had gone out of the game and he had to fight off attacks of both physical weakness and mental inertia.

He also fought off thought, till, in spite of drugs, thought caught up with him before he slept. It oozed up from his unconscious mind, and swam before his eyes in repulsive pictures of a Gina he did not know who laughed and enticed a man whose face he could never see.

He had occasion to go down Shaftesbury Avenue and saw the boards announcing "Margaret Metcalfe and John O'Riordan in *This Way To Yesterday*, with Anna Delahenty and Peter Gourlay, under the direction of Glynne Thorne." Despising the masochism, he stopped and looked at the photographs. Neither lighting nor skill could, for him, disguise Meg's ageing vanity. Anna was beauty—and evil—incarnate, he told himself. Thorne, Winchester and Cambridge, superciliously clever. And they were her friends. They had applauded and sniggered when the American went to her room. Her unfaithfulness had been a joke, another bit of amusing gossip. He turned away, but thought was there now, forced there by their twice-life-size faces.

He couldn't go on like this any longer. He'd got to make up his mind what to do.

Flung down on his bed in the hotel, he knew only one thing. He must see Gina. He must see her to pour out on her the hurt and pain that was seething in his mind. He'd got to tell her what she had done to him, make her realise the desperate injury she'd given him. Weakness? No, it wasn't weakness. He didn't want her pity. What he wanted was an ease from this revolving wheel of the memory of their lives together. He'd striven to release himself from it, and he couldn't. He was sick with trying to fend off the constant turning of his mind to her. If he saw her again, watched realisation of all she had torn down show in her face, then at last he might be able to despise her. Wipe all she was and had been from his life.

He'd go down to Belsted. Get her address from the doctor who was her self-constituted protector.

He saw him then, behind his closed lids, standing in the surgery in his reach-me-down jacket, a small-town medical who went in for diplomacy and the patching up of broken marriages on his day off. "No," his quiet voice repeated out of memory, "that's not what I, at least, wanted you to say. I hoped—and I think she did—that you might have found it in your heart to forgive her." To forgive her. Did they really think that forgiveness was as simple as that? Even the Bible held that a man could put his wife away for adultery. "Forgive us our trespasses as we forgive . . ." That was all very well for the lesser things. God knows he wasn't unforgiving. But this thing was beyond forgiveness. Even Christ Himself. . . . He didn't want to think of Christ Himself. Why should he be kicked around and fooled and betrayed? He'd been loyal, faithful. Never once since the night he'd first seen her. . . . Not again. The wheel was beginning to revolve, and he couldn't stand it.

He swung his legs from the bed and reached for the telephone.

"I want my wife's address," he said to Philip Blake the next day. "I would prefer to ask you for it rather than the servant at the house," he added.

He watched the lids go down over the fellow's eyes. How he detested that trick of his of staring down at his blotter, considering every word before he spoke.

"You've a perfect right to have it," the man said at last.

"Exactly." He rapped the word down and left it.

The doctor picked up a pen and wrote on his prescription-pad. "You'll remember, won't you," he said as he drew a line across the sheet, "that she's suffered, too?"

"It was her own choice," he answered shortly.

"Few people choose to ruin their happiness," Blake said slowly.

"I had an idea that it was a question of my happiness, too, doctor."

He still looked down at the damned blotter.

"Her happiness is bound up with yours," he said.

"That," Guy answered, "I find difficult to believe." He held out his hand for the paper. "Thank you. Good night to you."

There were four people still in the waiting-room, but Philip Blake did not ring for the next patient.

Had there been a slight softening in the metallic hatred of Guy's mind? He thought there had. And if there were? Gina in her way had been through as much—more—than her husband, for Guy's suffering, however humiliating, was free from shame and remorse. Humiliation, bad as it was, could be overcome by confidence and success, but a living shame and a living remorse caused a scar which could only be touched by hands that had been pierced. If only Taylor knew that. . . .

Guy was driving to Melford on his way to see Gina. The car slid along the arterial road between the fields. He tried not to rehearse how he was going to behave, what he was going to say, but the wheel of his mind continued the rehearsal as though he himself were permitting it.

He approached the town, asked his way from a policeman, and turned down Station Road. Almost at the end of it, he came to the tobacconist's shop. He put on the brakes and switched the engine off.

A badly painted green door at the side of the shop window was open showing a steep flight of stairs covered with worn linoleum. On a postcard drawing-pinned to the wall was written, "No. 19A, Mrs. Taylor."

He went up the stairs.

Gina heard the car draw up.

Last night, Philip Blake had said to her, "I thought that you should be prepared. A shock of that kind is better avoided if possible."

"Didn't he say why he was coming?" she'd asked him. "If he really is going to divorce me . . .?"

"You've got to remember," Philip said, "that he regards me as an accessory both before and after the fact. He'd hardly make me his confidant."

"Why do you think he's coming?"

She noted his hesitation and wondered if he were keeping something from her.

"Please say it," she'd added.

"There isn't anything to say," he said. "You know I'd tell you if there were. He didn't act any differently, merely demanded your address. I may even be wrong in thinking he will come to see you."

"Yes, but you do think he will, don't you?"

"Yes. I do." He smiled slightly. "That's why I came over."

"I know," she said.

Now he was here. She had left the lower door open so that she could meet him in the flat away from the street and passers-by. She had taken Christopher into the bedroom.

The little shilling brass ship that was the knocker gave its inadequate rap. Just for a moment as she walked across to the door which opened straight into the room, she thought, 'Suppose he has come to kill me.'

She opened the door.

Guy saw her standing before him. In his imagination she had been unable to meet his eyes, but she was thinner, that was all. She looked at him, and the sadness, not the shame, in her expression struck down into his heart.

He said, "I thought it was better to come and see you."

She inclined her head a fraction in assent.

Absurdly he said, "May I come in?"

"Of course."

He stepped past her and she closed the door.

"Sit down, Guy," she said, but he shook his head. He couldn't say a word of all that he had rehearsed. He saw the tears come into her eyes and spill down her cheeks, but she didn't brush them away. Her shoulders drooped a little as though she were tired, but she still looked back at him. He fought to retain the humiliation and injury, but he couldn't. He made an involuntary movement with his hand; lifted it and let it fall to his side again.

He heard her say, "Guy, I——"

Nothing mattered. Nothing but that she was there, and he wanted her as he'd never wanted her before.

"Gina. . . ."

He took the couple of steps between them and she was in his arms, easing his hunger for her with herself. Nothing mattered but that.

An hour later he was sitting in the one easy chair and she, as she so often had done at Ladysmere, was sitting on the rug at his feet.

During the year she had known periods of exhaustion, but she thought now that she hadn't touched the edge of the hem of the robe of it. Even that had no significance. Guy was there.

She said, "How can I tell you? I must tell you, Guy. . . ."

She felt the recoil in him and he said, "No. I simply don't want to know. I never want to hear you speak of it again."

His tone made a barrier to something which had been eased, almost fluid, in her mind, and she thought, 'If only he'd let me tell him. Then it would be done.'

Or was that solely for her own relief? Hadn't he been through enough?

He said, "Gina. If we're going on with our lives together, it must be put right behind us. I want to forget that it ever happened."

Again a warning bell rang in her mind. What of Christopher? How could either of them forget while he was there? Surely the thing ought to be faced between them? But he, Guy, had his hand on her hair, and what he asked must be done, because he still loved her, wanted her to share his life again.

"I can't live without you," he said. "I hoped I could. I came here today hoping that I'd be able to hate you. I can't. Will you come back to Ladysmere, Gina?"

She wondered if you could die of relief and love.

"Oh yes, yes," she whispered.

"When?"

"Tonight. Now. Can't we?"

She felt his fingers grip her arm.

"Gina. You must understand this. I love you. I want to forget what's happened. I tell you, I never want to think of it again. But I can't have the child. It simply isn't possible. Perhaps, if I were a finer person than I am, I'd be able to. I don't know. I only know that I couldn't bear it. Every time I saw him. . . . No, I couldn't do it. It wouldn't be fair to him, either. I've been through so much. . . . You must see it's impossible. . . ."

Yes, she saw. That was the point—she *saw*. There was no answer to what he said, not from his point of view. It was all logic, common sense. Of course every time he saw Christopher he'd remember. Of course. She had been stupid. When he said, "Come back to Ladysmere," she'd immediately included her baby. She couldn't think of life without him. He was there. And she loved him. Loved him. She'd thought for a moment that it was all over, the account squared. She'd thought the three of them would be 'a family', and that Guy would come to love Christopher as the child they hadn't had. For a moment of unearthly happiness she'd imagined that the torment and pain were over. They weren't over.

"You thought," she heard Guy say, "that I'd have the child, too."

She didn't know what to answer. She couldn't give Guy up. He was her husband, her man, and he'd forgiven her. He wanted her again. If she hesitated, tried to persuade him, he'd imagine that she had loved Andrew and wanted to keep his child. But what of Christopher? It was he who was going to shoulder the burden now. She couldn't pass the buck to a baby of six months. She couldn't. Of them all, he was unoffending.

"You did, didn't you?" she heard Guy repeat.

She said, "Without me, he's—quite alone in the world. He's got no one." And then she said, "Guy, you wouldn't just see him, would you?"

Again his hand gripped her arm.

"Don't ask me that. Please. I know you think that if I saw him, I'd consent to father him; but it wouldn't work. I won't be ungenerous, Gina. I'll do what I can. Fix up anything you like and I'll pay whatever's necessary. Don't stint him of anything he needs. And you know, he won't really miss you. If he were older he might, I'll admit that, but no child of a few months could possibly remember his first surroundings. And it's more than possible that someone will adopt him. . . ."

For a moment the thought came to her to tell him that nothing in earth or heaven would make her give Christopher up. That if he couldn't have her baby then he couldn't have her, but reason said, 'How can you expect him to father a child you had by another man? And he's right, too—what would Christopher's life be if he resented him? You've got to choose Guy or Christopher; Christopher or Guy. You can't have them both. You married Guy and you love him. You ache to go back to Ladysmere. You're sick of this cramped little existence.' It was true, all of it. All true. Quite, quite true. . . .

"Gina," Guy said. "You must understand this thing from my angle. Can't you see that we could never get back to where we were? The boy would always be there, between us. I'm so ready to forget. It's all I want to do. Come back, Gina. Come home to me. . . ."

And suddenly she was too tired, too dreadfully fatigued, to argue any more.

"Yes," she said. "I'll come home. But—you must—let me—see what can be done with him—first."

"It wasn't much good, was it?" said Gina. "All those plans. I might just as well have done what Dardanella's lady did, mightn't I?"

"That impossible name!" Philip answered. "Did they have to call her that?"

"It makes me think of dates," said Gina. "I wonder why. Philip, what am I to do? What *can* I do? I nearly told him to go to hell and that if he couldn't have Christopher he couldn't have me. Yet I can understand it from his angle. And besides, I love him. I do, you know. What do you think?"

What Philip thought was that Guy Taylor had muffed the chance of a lifetime. Had he? No good, if he couldn't face up to the facts. Been merely a question of three lives out of gear, and none of them functioning naturally. Why couldn't the man have taken the chance and saved everybody a great deal of embarrassment? Ten to one he would soon have come to making as big a fool of himself over the child as the next man. Now there was no hope; only a further division in Gina's mind. And the child had to be got rid of, after all. Poor little devil. It always came back on them in the end. What was the best thing to do with him? Take him himself? Repay that old debt? What nonsense! Taylor would merely churn his mind about till he'd persuaded himself that he was the father, after all. No. That was right out of it. An orphanage? Wasn't there something else? Some place which would satisfy Gina and set her free to take up her life again. Mostyn's? It was an idea. Jennifer could never have a child after hysterectomy. That didn't mean that she, or George, would want to adopt one, though. Good home, of course. Public School education and every social advantage. I wonder. Blast that dead Yank, anyway. . . .

"Give me a couple of days," he said to Gina. "There are some people I know. . . ."

Four days later he came over to Melford again.

"I've seen those people," he said, and he watched the blood drain from her face. She sat very still, and suddenly he thought of the American going crazy about her, taking her into his arms and kissing her.

"Yes?" she said.

"He's a chap I knew at Oxford; a barrister. His wife had a hysterectomy done and can't have a baby. She's a nice woman. They live in Kensington. Plenty of money. They made no promises, of course. I don't think the thought of adopting a child had entered their heads as more than a hazy notion. They'd like to see him."

"On appro," she said, and there was a twisted smile on her lips.

"Sort of," he answered shortly. "I suggested they came down. Or would you rather take him up there?"

"Up there. I'd have to see what they were like, wouldn't I? You can tell what people are so much more easily in their own homes, don't you think?"

"Just as you like. Shall I come with you?"

"How can you?"

"Thursday do?"

"Any day."

"I'll ring them and see if that's convenient."

He saw the flowers as he was going. Long-stemmed roses, a couple of dozen of them, incongruous in the little room.

"Guy sent them," she said.

"Nice," he answered, but driving home he supposed the chap had got to do something to compensate himself for failure. Or was it failure? God knew.

The house in Elston Square was thickly carpeted, silent. The furniture was good and the pictures more than good—Renoir, Matisse, a small John and a Devas of Jennifer Mostyn herself. Gina held Christopher in her arms and said to Philip, "Don't let me make a fool of myself. I should so hate to cry before someone I don't know."

"Pride," he said, and lit a cigarette. "Why be ashamed of tears?"

"You are a comfort!" she scorned, and Jennifer Mostyn came in.

She was small, dark, with bright eyes and a gentle mouth. She'd be kind. If only she'd been domineering, it would have been easier to hate her and walk out. She was shy, too. She could barely bring herself to look at Christopher.

"You don't have to have him," Gina said. "Not if he doesn't suit."

"I've never had anything to do with them," Jennifer answered. "I'm rather scared. George will be here in ten minutes," she said to Philip. "I'll ring for tea. May I hold him?" she asked Gina.

She sat uncomfortably on a chair and Gina put the baby into her arms. He looked gravely up into her face, frowned a little and went on staring. She didn't do any of the gruesome things people did to make him laugh. She merely looked back at him as gravely as he looked at her.

"He's quite heavy," she said in her shy voice. "I didn't think they were so."

"He'll be crawling soon," Philip said. "He's strong as a horse."

"I wonder what George will say," she said, and he came in. He wasn't very tall and couldn't, thought Gina, have been anything but a barrister. You could almost see the wig and the bands; hear the 'As your Lordship pleases. My client. . . .'

He didn't fuss. He merely bowed and said, "How do you do." Vaguely he made Gina think of Glynne Thorne.

The tea was brought in and Gina put Christopher back in the carry-cot. He lay there without taking any notice of them. Occasionally he opened his fist and peered at his fingers. Over tea they talked as though he weren't there at all. She wondered as she was eating walnut cake how much Philip had told them.

After tea Jennifer took Christopher again, and George inspected him, while trying to appear merely politely interested.

"He looks all right," he said.

"Don't be a fool," Philip answered. "It's a baby not a brief."

He smiled a little and said, "Have a heart, man. I don't know how to behave towards them."

"So it appears," said Philip. But Gina thought, 'I'd rather have it that way than fulsomeness. Oh God, I believe they like him.' And Christopher, playing to the gallery, chose that moment to smile into Jennifer's face. The smile started in his eyes, a male smile, a devil-may-care, lord-of-creation smile which grew till it ended in his individual, silent guffaw, with wide-open toothless gums.

The deal, thought Gina, is as good as done.

Ten minutes later George took Philip into his study, leaving her alone with Jennifer and the baby.

This is where we have a heart to heart, thought Gina. I hope I shan't be sick.

"I do like him," Jennifer said when the door was closed. "George told me before you came that he left it to me. I can't ever have one," she added.

"I know," said Gina. "Pity."

"I hated it at first," Jennifer told her. "You get used to things, I suppose."

'Even to handing your baby over to strangers,' Gina thought. And she thought, too, 'I can't do it. I can't. But I've got to. Christopher or Guy. Guy or Christopher.'

"I'm—very sorry," she heard Jennifer say. "Philip explained a bit. Will you be able to bear it?"

"I'll have to," said Gina shortly. "I've got to make the choice—baby or husband. A or B. Did Philip tell you who his father was

You'll want to know if you have him, I suppose."

"George did say——" Jennifer began.

He would. The barrister. Get all the facts. Pass the brief.

"I can't, personally, tell you much about him," said Gina in a hard voice. "I hardly knew him. He was Andrew Wharton, the American novelist. I know no more than that."

"I read *Single Track*," Jennifer said. "It was fine, I thought. It seemed tragic that he was killed."

'Supposing he hadn't been,' Gina thought. 'I wonder. . . .' No good going into that.

"There's one thing," she said. "Will you tell your husband, please? I don't know if it can be arranged, but there'd have to be a sort of probationary period, wouldn't there, before you adopted him legally? I'd have to know—*know*—that he was happy and that you cared for him."

"I do understand," Jennifer said, and there were slight tears in her eyes. "It must be so dreadfully difficult. I wish it didn't have to be."

"Well it does," said Gina. And she added, "Sorry. Didn't mean to snap. I know you're nice."

"Women get the knocks, don't they?" said Jennifer.

"I could have said 'No'," Gina replied. "I didn't say 'No'. That's all."

When Philip came back with George, Jennifer said, "Please may we have him, George? I'd like to. I'd like to very much."

Before they left, arrangements were made.

Christopher was to be handed over in a week's time. A nurse would be engaged, and George would get 'something down in writing' to cover the stipulated period of 'probation' before the adoption was legalised. He would, he said, make some very discreet enquiries about Wharton. Fortunately John Holland was a friend of his. . . .

"It's as easy as selling a puppy, isn't it?" Gina said to Philip on the drive back. "No trouble at all."

When Philip answered he said, "It won't always hurt so unbearably. That sounds banal, but it's true."

"'Time heals all things'," she scorned.

He thought her pain was something almost tangible, a fine thin probe of a thing, touching an open wound with exquisite precision.

"Even now," said Gina, "I might retract. Simply bolt with him. Disappear."

"You could," he agreed, "though turning tail is never a solution, is it? Whatever you do you're going to suffer. That's inescapable ——"

"You tell me!" Gina broke in, and he went on, "This way's the best way out of it for everyone, surely. . . ." He broke off as he was in the habit of doing and said, "Why do I have to sound so smug, as though I were necessarily right? I don't mean to. You've seen the Mostyns. You know Christopher will be looked after. They gain all along the line, and you and your husband——"

"Will live happy ever after."

He drew out and passed a lorry piled with wood.

"He needs you pretty badly, too," he said.

"I know."

"Yes."

"It'll be all right, Philip. It's only now—transactions; signing on the dotted line. And Christopher lying there in that silly canvas-bag thing not knowing he's being sold. They exact the price for adultery, don't they?"

He'd forgotten his doubt of himself and was speaking in his normal, definite tones. "You're dealing in terms of flesh and blood, aren't you? In eternal souls, if you believe that way."

"Do you believe that way?"

"I do."

"And yet at the time it was just a dream of a thing, all starlight and champagne and a little song. And that inescapable urge to be made love to. Why does it beat you so, Philip?"

"It's the strongest force there is, isn't it?"

"Then why can't they put barbed-wire round it? Fence it off. They don't give us a chance, do they?"

"Our wills are weakened."

"Were they ever strong?"

"Oh yes. Once they were."

"I think I was left out of that party. Lord, I'm tired."

"Nearly back now. Three miles. Can you take it?"

"Suppose it wasn't you I'd picked out with a pin," she said. "I can't imagine either of the other two becoming a sort of general agent for their erring patients. I suppose," she said, "that if they have Christopher I'd be able to see him sometimes, wouldn't I?"

The lights of Melford were ahead of them, climbing up the hill in the dusk.

"No," Philip answered shortly.

He felt rather than heard her gasp.

"Why?" she said at last. "Philip——"

"You've got to make up your mind to that," he said. "Here and now. It simply wouldn't do. Not for any of your sakes would it do—Christopher's least of all. It's no good, Gina, it just wouldn't be fair to anyone concerned. Besides," he said, "George wouldn't have it. He spoke to me about that very point in the study. It's one of the items he intends to include in the—what do you call it?—agreement, statement, whatever it is."

"Then he can go to hell. He hasn't got Christopher yet and I won't——"

"Yes, you will," Philip said. "You know as well as I do it's the only way. You can't leave the door ajar."

"But—I shan't know. They might beat him, starve him, anything."

"I'll tell you if they do."

"I can't do it. Not if I'm not to be allowed to see him ever. He need never know who I am. I wouldn't say——"

"Use your brains," Philip answered, and she had never heard his tone so sharp. "The situation would be impossible. Jennifer resenting your presence. You gazing wistfully at Christopher—or trying to interfere in their methods. The child conscious of disturbance, possibly still emotionally tied to you, and everyone heading for neurosis. If that's really your intention, you'd better call it off."

'I hate his doctor's damned analytical mind,' Gina thought. 'Everything under the microscope. Probe, probe, probe. Reasons behind the reasons behind the reasons. Is nothing what it seems to be?'

She had a swift, terrifying glimpse of a life that in its expression had no relation to what, fundamentally, it was. Lips smiled and words tripped off the tongue, but all the time a strange, deep, silent thing went on far below the surface. Old, primitive impulses lived in a jungle of a place in the heart, and escaping from it flung aside the surface control, as her desire for Andrew had done. There was no guide through the darkness that was yourself. You were it and it was you, and out of it had come Christopher, fast asleep on the back seat of the car. And he, too, would have his burden of darkness to bear because she and Andrew between them had made him a present of it.

They passed the cinema, turned down Station Road and drew up before the tobacco shop. Set between Mrs. Lightly the dress-maker's and the offices of the Building Society with its discreet frosted-glass windows, it looked sane and normal, and as Philip lifted the carry-cot out, she thought, 'No jungles for Dardanella, I'll bet. Only getting up and taking the kirby-grips out of her hair and saying "Nice day. Ten or twenty?" to the customers and going on doing it till she put the kirby-grips back in her hair again and climbed into bed.'

"I'll get some supper," she said to Philip, as he laid the carry-cot on the couch.

Guy telephoned her that night after Philip had left.

"I know you asked me not to, but I had to. Are you all right?"

"Where are you?" she asked him.

"In London. I'm going down to Ladysmere tomorrow. Gina?"

"Yes?"

"I can't stand this much longer. You are coming home, aren't you?"

Why did he use that word? It opened a door on to their lives, not only at Ladysmere but in the flat, in New York, in France. She thought that she had never needed his comfort more than she did at that moment.

She said, "I'm so deathly tired."

"Why are you so tired?"

"I've been to London. I don't want to talk about it."

She thought he answered just a shade too fast. "Then don't. I don't want to—harass you."

He did want to harass her. He wanted to harass her to dispose of Christopher as fast as she could so that the whole dreadful thing could be put behind them. If only he'd have let her take Christopher home, too! He wouldn't let her. He'd failed her. . . .

"Gina?" he said.

"All right," she answered. "I was thinking."

"I thought you'd gone."

"Are you better?" she asked.

"Oh yes. . . ."

"That means you're not."

"I'm all right. I wish though——"

"Guy, I do know. Arrangements are being made. I'll call you as soon as I can."

He didn't reply for what seemed a long time, then he said, "I can't tell you how much I want you. I've been thinking——"

"Thinking what?"

"We'll go away," he said. "Italy or Egypt or somewhere. Start again."

She shook her head. You couldn't start again. You might try to repudiate your past, but your past wouldn't repudiate you. It was built into you, solid as a concrete slab. It—all of it—had made you what you were, and you couldn't unmake yourself by going to Italy. She wished you could.

"Would you like that?"

"Guy?"

"Yes?"

"I think I'd like it very much. I'm almost sure I would. At the moment I'm a bit muddled."

Egypt, Italy, Timbuktu, Moreton-in-Marsh—did he really think they'd compensate for giving your baby away? The fool. Why had she ever thought she'd go back to him? Insensitive, cruel. . . .

"I thought it would please you. Help . . ." he said. His tone had altered, and she suddenly remembered Korea; the year in prison, his home-coming.

"It does help," she said. "I'd like it, really. I don't think I'm taking things in very well tonight."

She was taking them in perfectly. It was simply that she didn't know what to do with the things when she'd taken them in. There was no arrangement, only a lot of facts that were not related to one another, bobbing up and down in her brain.

"We'll be happy again. It'll be all right," he said.

"Yes," she answered. "Yes. It'll be all right."

Chapter III

THE Mostyns were to come for Christopher on the following Friday at three o'clock—George, Jennifer and the nurse they had engaged.

They arrived dead on time—it wasn't likely George would have permitted unpunctuality, Gina thought—and Christopher was ready for them.

For seven days and seven nights she had swayed from one decision to another. No sooner had she made up her mind, and always irrevocably, to keep Christopher, than pictures of Guy—not the confident man of her first acquaintance, but the man who had returned from Korea, thin and fatigued and pained—came before her, and the 'irrevocable' decision weakened till round swung the wheel again and she knew that it was Christopher who must go. An hour or so later the balance shifted, the sequence of pictures changed once more, and once more she was plunged into indecision until she thought that she would lose her reason. But she washed and ironed Christopher's clothes and packed them into a suitcase, while he, indifferent to it all, slept or woke or sucked his thumb.

Bessie came over from Ladysmere, and she and Dardanella nearly defeated her with their funereal behaviour.

"Isn't it dreadful for you," Dardanella mourned, and the contours of her heavy face drooped. "Poor little Chris. It doesn't seem right, does it? Not now he's just getting to know you."

Bessie gave her a warning stare and said, "Don't be so silly, Dar. He'll be all right. It isn't as if he's going to strangers. I expect he'll be ever so happy. Some children are better with their adopteds than they are with their real parents."

Gina, pouring out sherry for them—for they'd been kind, *kind*—thought, 'This is where that night at Alban Bay's landed me—into having to tolerate Dardanella's condolences as though she were my best friend.' And why not? She and Bessie had been her best friends—and that very fact made the situation more difficult to bear. How strange that those short few hours which at the time had seemed filled to the brim with a primitive beauty had petered out into scenes of a distorted indignity like this one.

"I'll miss hearing you tap overhead," said Dardanella, and she sat on the edge of the chair and crooked her little finger away from the glass of sherry Gina had given her. "I often hear you, and then I think, 'That's Christopher's bottle going on,' or 'Now she's going to bath him.' I always know. It'll be ever so funny when you've gone." She drank the sherry and dabbed at her maroon lipstick with a handkerchief. "Never to hear him cry or anything. I wonder who I'll get next," she added dolefully.

'*Tout passe*,' Gina thought. '*Tout passe*. That was the point, if only you could see it. Everything. Even this. Even this. . . .'

She went to the door and opened it when they left, and while Dardanella plodded with a crab-like motion down the narrow stairs Bessie whispered, "It's all ready for you, Miss Gina. I've cleaned up from top to bottom and"—a strange smile that was part grimace came about her lips—"Mr. Taylor's been ever so kind," she added. "He's just waiting for the day. . . ."

And now 'the day'—or the day before 'the day', for she had decided not to return to Ladysmere till tomorrow—was here.

She heard the car stop and knew that it was the Mostyns. She heard their footsteps on the stairs, but she could not bring herself to so much as glance towards the carry-cot on the sofa where Christopher lay crooning to himself. She heard the irritating tap-tap of Dardanella's 'Mayflower' brass knocker and Jennifer's voice the other side of the match-boarding door saying, "They gave my niece Trufood. It was very successful. . . ."

She thought, 'I can't do it. I can't. God, I can't. It's like death. It really is. Something dying in you. . . .'

But the knocker tapped again, harder this time, and suddenly with one swift gesture of the back of her hand to her mouth, she walked across the room and opened the door.

A quarter of an hour later it was all over. The door was shut again. The nurse's flat-heeled pad and Jennifer Mostyn's high-heeled tap had merged with the sounds of the street and a passing train. She stood by the mantelpiece again in the empty room as the car doors slammed to and the engine started. She still stood there even when she could no longer distinguish the beat of the engine from the other noises of the little town.

She didn't hear the second car draw up or the swift footsteps on the stairs, and even when she heard the rap of knuckles on the door she didn't move from the chair where she had flung herself.

"Gina!"

She didn't want to pull herself from her misery. It wasn't even possible to.

"Gina!"

Philip—she might have known he'd come, but she didn't want to see him.

She scarcely bothered to wipe her eyes as she went across the room and opened the door to him.

He came in and, even as he pushed the door to behind him, he had his arm round her and her head was against his shoulder. He didn't attempt to stop her crying, and he didn't say anything at all till after a time she drew away from him and said, "I've soaked your coat."

She dried her eyes and face, and then wiped her hands on her handkerchief.

"What have I done to him, Philip?" she said. "It's too awful. Unbearable."

"He'll be all right," he answered. "I know that sounds tripe, but he will. Sit down and I'll make you some tea."

He went through to the kitchen and put the kettle on, and hearing the noise of the cups on the saucers she wondered how he knew where they were. It seemed very important.

He came back with the tray and poured out her tea. She drank it, but it tasted of tears.

Suddenly he said, "I've come to take you home."

She looked at him and shook her head.

"I couldn't. . . . Not now. Not today. I must have a few hours. . . ."

"I'm afraid you aren't going to," he said, and his tone was the first thing which had penetrated her misery. It did penetrate it, cleaving a little rift in it, and she saw that there was some new expression on his face.

"You've got to come," he said, "because Guy's ill. He's got influenza, and last evening I took a nurse up there. He's not in very good shape to fight a thing of that kind, you know."

He watched one anxiety change to another on her face, and he thanked heaven for the influenza which had laid Guy out. He couldn't, he told himself, have arranged anything more convenient, not if he'd tried.

Gina's eyes were wide and concentrated and afraid.

"How long's he been ill?"

"Three days."

"You didn't ring me."

"No. I didn't want to complicate matters for you and, anyway, I hoped by this morning he'd be over the worst of it. Normally he should have been, but his constitution isn't all it might be."

"You don't mean he'll die?"

"He's pretty tough," he answered. "But he'll need to go easy."

She lowered her head into her hand. "Philip, I don't think I can bear any more," she said. "I really don't think I can, you know."

"It's a rotten bad patch," he answered, but he knew she would bear it because there was a remedy at hand. It was a stringent one, doubtless, but the point was, it was a remedy.

Half an hour later he was driving her back to Ladysmere.

She sat beside him, her feet high up on the dash-board, her arms tucked inside the loose sleeves of her coat.

There were rows of corn-stooks on the hill-side fields, very neat and tidy, as though a house-proud woman had put them down with pedantic precision, not a blade out of place. And the fields themselves appeared newly swept, aggressively clean. Curved over them was a bland sky, cloudless and frightening in its silent, unbroken blue.

She saw the fields and she saw the sky. She even registered the fear of its immense brooding, but it was a surface seeing and a surface fear. Beyond it was nothing, neither sorrow nor anxiety; only an awareness of a dumb endurance and the movement of the car as

Philip drove it along the smooth surface of the roads towards Ladysmere.

Guy was in bed for three weeks. It was the first time he had been ill in his life, and his attitude was more one of surprise than anything.

When after ten days the immediate distress had left him, he slept a great deal, but the moment he was awake, if Gina was not there he asked for her.

One night when she was sitting in his room while he was still seriously ill, the fever made him slightly delirious. He was, evidently, living over again the day he had returned from Korea, and she heard him say, "Christ, I can't bear it—the stage crowd! So she ran back to them the moment I was out of the way. . . ." Then he called her name and tried to raise himself up in the bed. "Gina! Gina! Where are you?" His head fell back again, and he said, "She won't come back. She was laughing at me all the time." And then, "The one undying thing . . ." he said. "The one undying thing. . . ."

She was deeply affected, for he had seldom, even in the early days of their love, been effusive, but his cry "She was laughing at me . . ." rang in her head long after he was sleeping.

'I must never forget this night,' she told herself as she stood by her bedroom window before she undressed. 'And I must never forget how desperately I've hurt him. It was my fault and mine alone, and I'll have to spend the rest of my life trying to make it up to him. . . .'

One day after he had come down from Guy's room Philip said to her, "He ought to get right away for a time. Not England, over the Channel somewhere. It's the quickest way to clear a thing like this up."

But it was Gina he wanted to get 'right away'. In a short time now Guy would be well enough to take up his work again, and Gina would have time on her hands, and time on her hands was the one thing he didn't want her to have. She wouldn't moon around weeping for her child, he knew that—possibly be simpler for all concerned if she did—but neither would she know how to handle her damaged emotions. She'd analyse and reason and fight, and none of it would get her anywhere. He wasn't optimistic enough to imagine that a 'change of scene' would work a miracle, but it might give them a chance to start their lives again on a somewhat surer foundation than they'd got at the moment. With a strip of water between them and the scenes of the last year, they might come to get a more detached view of themselves.

Gina looked at him. There was a half-smile on her face which meant that she wasn't going to accept anything she thought might be a 'ruse'.

"Do you really believe 'a little change' puts new life into you?" she asked.

"Yes." He rapped the reply out, and he watched her considering the idea. He wished sometimes that she didn't trust his judgment, as she apparently did. It made it easier to—he was going to say 'fool' her, but the word was nauseous. He meant 'persuade' her.

"He's been *physically* ill, hasn't he?" she said slowly.

"He needs sun," he said. "In larger doses than he can get here at this time of year. And food, in larger doses, too—well, more olive-oil with it, then. There's no 'catch' in it," he went on. "I'm not even one of those 'sun-fiends', but I think he ought to go."

"All right. I'll speak to him about it," she answered. "Do you mean for—what? A month?"

"Less wouldn't be much good."

She nodded, and after a time she said, "Have you seen the Mostyns?"

"I was there last Thursday," he answered shortly.

"Christopher . . .?"

"He's settling down very well," he said guardedly.

"I want to know," she said, and her head jerked up. "I'm not a fool."

"They're all very happy," he said. "Very happy."

"Do you think I grudge them their happiness?" she asked in a hard voice. "I want them to love him. Has he grown?" she asked.

"Quite a bit."

"I don't suppose he'd even know me now, would he?" she said.

He looked at the carpet between his feet.

"All right," he heard her say. "You don't have to answer."

"How can I?" he muttered. "I don't know."

She was crying, not noisily but quietly, and he sat there, letting his eye travel up the welt of his shoes, over the toe-caps and down the other side.

"A few tears will do me good, won't they?" she mocked. "Relieve the tension. I swore I wouldn't, too," she added.

"Why be so hard on yourself?"

"Because I have to be. Don't let's bother with it. It's over now." She stood up. "I'll speak to Guy about going away. It'll be quite a second honeymoon, won't it?"

When she went to his room later, Guy was enthusiastic. He was out of bed, sitting in an arm-chair by the window in his dressing-gown. He was very thin, but there was the return of health stamped surely on his face.

"It's what I'd meant to do if I hadn't been ill," he said. "I spoke to you about it. Do you remember?"

She remembered. He'd telephoned her, just after Philip had left, the day they'd taken Christopher to the Mostyns for the first time. Her memory swung back to the little room over Dardanella's shop: to the ship's knocker and the sound of the trains shunting. She remembered being deathly tired and almost hating Guy for suggesting a trip to Egypt, while Christopher lay fast asleep in his cot, quite unaware that he was to be 'given away'.

She wrenched her mind from the memory of that night. It was past. She had made her choice and she had chosen Guy.

"Yes, I remember," she said. "You thought about Egypt then, didn't you?"

"Or would you rather go to Italy?"

His eyes had a new brightness. "I'll get Miss Pangle on the phone in the morning, and she can ring the agents and bring some of their stuff down with her on Thursday."

At the mention of his secretary's name, she smiled, thinking again of Dardanella. 'Miss Pangle', with its hint of circus tights, was just about as ridiculous a misnomer for the pleasant girl who had been down two or three times since Guy's illness as that foisted on Bessie's cousin.

Guy saw the smile and was happy. He had been very ill. In the last few days he'd realised just how ill, and Gina was looking drained, and small wonder. Apart from his own convalescence, it was a good idea for them to get away for a time, shut the door on all this; and when they came home they'd make a new start. Gina wanted to go, that was obvious.

"We'll cut and run directly Blake says I'm strong enough," he said. "We'd better book something for a week or so until I'm back to normal, and then we might wander a bit if we felt inclined. Would you like to go to Paris first?"

'Egypt, Rome, Timbuktu, Moreton-in-Marsh . . .' she'd thought when Guy had telephoned her at Dardanella's flat, 'does he really think any of them would compensate for giving your baby away?'

They *had* to compensate. Christopher was doing *fine*.

"Certainly not Paris first," she said to Guy. "The doctor said you're to have sunshine and olive-oil tipped over everything you eat."

Blake *would* dogmatise about the sun, Guy thought, and a shadow passed over his fragile happiness, but he only said, "Bring up the atlas when next you go down, will you? We'll see if we can get some ideas. . . ."

He leaned back in the chair when she had gone. The autumn nights were drawing in and already dusk was shadowing the hills. What was it the Irishman in the Korean camp had called the twilight? 'Daylagone. . . .' Uttered in his soft voice, it was a beautiful word. Korea. . . . He wouldn't think of Korea. Or of his homecoming. Both had to be put out of mind. He wished—and since he'd been ill and under the fellow's care he'd wished more than ever—that he'd never lost his nerve and said those appalling things about Gina to Blake. He felt that Blake remembered the outburst and put it down to his origins. He never had and he never would like the man, with his know-all attitude. Why that fool Bessie had called *him* of all people the night he'd collapsed, he couldn't think.

Every time he came in he brought the burden of that wretched affair with him, and he had an idea, too, that he was far more intimate with Gina than he pretended to be in his presence. How did he know that the whole thing wasn't a pack of lies, and he and Gina. . . . Steady, he told himself, and he took out his handkerchief and wiped his mouth. He'd sworn he wouldn't go back to that torture of doubt, but when they came home from this trip, Blake could keep out of their lives. And with Blake out of it, Bessie could go, too. He'd get rid of everyone connected with that period. Sack the lot of them and start clear. He'd done it in the factory and he'd do it in his home. There'd been enough of weakness. . . .

The dusk was closing in, but he didn't switch on the light. He made no effort to think, but let his mind drift towards what he knew of Venice, Rome, Egypt. They were hazy pictures, chiefly made up of colour and sun and ease. And strength. Strength in his arms again. Strength in his legs. His body tough, hard, and he able to run upstairs and stride down the street! He thought, too, in the same drifting way of their honeymoon in France, and he felt again the electric excitement of their first love-making, which for him had never staled. And it would be like that again. . . . Thank God he had made Blake give him Gina's address and gone to her that night. And thank God that he'd forgiven her. He so nearly hadn't. And she'd come back to him, and looked after him when he was ill to show her gratitude. And now they would go away. . . .

He heard her step and she opened the door and came in.

"I brought the atlas you asked for," she said. "What a lovely night."

She came across the room and put the book down on the table. After his thoughts of her and in the blue shadows of the dusk, she appeared to have a new mystery about her, some unknown, beckoning quality whose sweetness was as potent as the scent of lilies. He closed his eyes. Then he opened them again, and he held out his hand to her.

"Let's go away very soon," he said. "I want to be with you alone, away from all these people. I want to love you, Gina. . . ."

Chapter IV

THEY left Ladysmere ten days later, flying not, as they had originally intended, to Cairo, but to Cyprus. This change in their plans came about through the visit of J. B. Harris, who stepped from his Daimler one morning at half-past eleven.

He was, so he told Gina, visiting a relation in the district, although she received the impression that this was not strictly true and that he had definite reasons of his own for making the call.

He spent an hour with Guy, and when he came down the stairs, treading delicately on his neat little feet, he, to Gina's embarrassment, for it so happened that Bessie was out for the day, accepted her offer of lunch.

She gave him sherry in the drawing-room, but with an ingenuous smile which masked, she was certain, a will as cool and limpid, and as purposeful, as a river flowing to the sea, he insisted on coming out to the kitchen with her while she prepared the meal. He stood by the window which looked out across the fields, his wine-glass in his hand, scarcely bigger than a child's hand, and she found herself being quietly but firmly persuaded to take Guy to Cyprus rather than to Cairo.

She was fully aware of the 'persuasion', but while part of her mind resented it, another part recognised the common sense of his reasons and, almost willingly, succumbed to his charm.

At lunch he said to her, "And you don't hold it against me that your husband had that regrettable experience in Korea?"

Until that moment she hadn't connected him directly with that year of their lives. Now, catching sight of his child's hands, one holding a peach, the other the fruit-knife, she had a swift sense of their manipulation of the train of events which had begun with Andrew Wharton and ended with Christopher. Those small, delicate, undeflectable hands. . . .

She felt wary, as though stepping from safe hummock to safe hummock over a bog.

"Of course I hold it against you," she answered easily. "Wouldn't any woman?"

Half of the peach in his fingers was still flushed red, half green gold. She had the impression that he had expected another answer.

"It was unfortunate," he said, "that you were away when he came home. He'll be all right now," he added, and he laid the peeled peach on his plate and wiped his fingers on his napkin.

He was, she thought, willing her to tell him what it was that had occurred to prevent her rushing to meet Guy on his release, and for a moment the thought came to her to tell him—to tell him quite coldly, fact by fact, the havoc his hands had wrought in their lives. He would show neither surprise nor contrition, and he would shake the implied blame away with barely a movement of his thin shoulders. . . .

"Yes, it was unfortunate," she heard herself say. "I'm glad I was able to be here while he was so ill."

He speared a piece of the peach on his fork and raised it to his mouth, but there was none of the facile agreement of the polite conversationalist about him. She had the feeling that he knew perfectly well that she had fended him off and that he accepted the fact.

"I have a great regard for your husband," he said quietly.

They spent three weeks in Cyprus. Guy found the journey more fatiguing than he had anticipated, and for the first week he did little but rest. Half-way through the second week a certain amount of strength returned to him, and they hired a car and were able to see something of the island.

Returning from a car-ride one evening, he said to her, "This isn't what I meant it to be. It's dull for you trailing about with me in this state. I hoped I should have been stronger by now."

They were coming down the mountain road. Before them the town appeared as a broken crescent of four-square blocks, white, pink and chrome, laid along the rim of the intensely blue sea. He longed for her to say, "I don't care if I'm in heaven or hell so long as I'm with you." Something extravagant that would sweep his weakness right away, fling him up to the heights which he'd dreamed about while he was crowded into the mud-walled hut in Korea with the Irishman and the little Methodist minister and the others.

"It's not dull," Gina answered. "I think I was tired, too. It's been good to slack. We've only been here ten days, anyway. There's time enough for you to get strong."

'But,' he thought as the coloured blocks began to take on the contours of houses and the unbroken blue of the sea became serrated with the long, even undulation of waves, 'this isn't right at all. It *isn't* what I intended.' And he felt irritated and wondered if Gina were glad that he couldn't make love to her. He remembered the American, too, and a wave of heat and weakness went over him so that he was relieved when they came down into the town and drew up at the hotel.

By the end of the week, though, the change in him was marked, and he began to get things into the sharp focus of health again, instead of viewing them through the confused mist of convalescence.

"I don't want to stay here any longer," he said swiftly one night. "I like it and it's done me good, but I don't think I'll get any stronger here. Let's go to Italy for a week or so. We can fly to Rome and hire a car when we get there. We'll go tomorrow or the day after."

The rest had benefited Gina, too, and she was excited at the prospect of seeing Rome and Florence.

"Yes," she said, "I'd like that. I've never been to Italy."

He had been staying up to dinner for the last few days, and that night they took a short walk parallel with the sea.

He was aware once again of mystery about her, as of some woman he knew but slightly, and the urgent need for her was unbearable; yet he could not bring himself to break through the barrier that was between them. It was gossamer thin but strong as plate-glass. Through it he could see her, talk to her, smile at her, but he couldn't touch her. If he made any move to touch her, he would see only his reflection in the glass. And yet, she was his wife. He had forgiven her infidelity, and now he loved her, wanted her.

"Gina," he said.

She turned her head, almost on a level with his own, and her eyes were faintly surprised, for they had been walking in silence. "Yes?"

He felt as though she had not repulsed him but was quite indifferent to him. And yet even that wasn't true. Her 'Yes?' had held more of casual enquiry than indifference. And yet it had repulsed him. If he so much as put his hand on her arm now, he'd feel as though he were taking a cheap liberty.

"I thought we might go to Venice, if you feel like it," he said, whipping himself to casual enthusiasm. "Be nice to go there before they've swapped all the gondolas for motor-boats, wouldn't it?"

"Be lovely," she answered in her cool tones. They turned and walked back to the hotel. His right hand, inside his jacket pocket, was clenched tight.

But Rome, or rather the hotel in Rome to which they'd been sent by a man they'd met in Nicosia because, so he said, the best cooking in all Italy was to be found there, took the barrier and tossed it into the air above the Eternal City as though it were no more than a bit of muslin blowing in the September wind.

It was such an opulent 'Imperial bedroom', all enormous furniture and faded gold scrolls and cornucopias of fruit, to which the comic-opera little padrone conducted them, and he was so certain, why neither of them could imagine, that they were on their honeymoon that sudden laughter swept the constraint of weeks away. And as suddenly he was able to go to her and to take her into his arms again, and as he felt her relax to him, he thought that only then did he know what relief meant.

Rome, made familiar by photographs, paintings and films, was so like yet so unlike all of them as to give Gina the feeling that she was meeting someone she had known in the past but had not seen for years. It was all so much smaller than she had imagined; so much more casual, and old and new strolled side by side in a curious dis-harmony.

Modern American and Italian cars were parked by Bernini's Fountain. Barefooted children splashed their feet in the water as a party of priests hurried by and an ancient 'victoria' drawn by an old nag plodded up the Via Nationale. A couple of American tourists leaned against the lamp-post pedestals on the Spanish Steps to photograph a Capuchin in his brown habit who passed unconcernedly up, his sandalled feet taking the steps with ease, his athlete's body swinging from the hips. The sunsets from the Pincio Gardens were all the advertisements said they were, and the Colosseum by moonlight was strangely not old, but startlingly modern. The sweep of the arc, cut by the symmetrical sequence of arches, threw triangular shadows sharply defined, and made the whole a gigantic creation of what might have been present-day architecture.

The trams clanged past little shops where strings of onions and bottles of chianti hung round the doors; and snatches of a song drifted down from an upper storey where a red mat hung over a balcony and tourists took on their lips names which were old two thousand years ago as they clicked their cameras at the astonishing 'wedding cake' that was the Victor Emmanuel monument. And over it all hung the blue sky, with the dome of St. Peter's painted on it.

One day there were crowds in St. Peter's Square. The great arms of the Colonnade reached round them as though in an attempted protection, while high on a balcony above their heads there appeared a small white figure, very still. Later the crowds parted, and men carried him shoulder-high through the lane they made for him, Eugène Pacelli, by the grace of God, Vicar of Christ and Bishop of Rome. Like ears of corn before a breeze, the heads bent as he went by, scattering blessings to left and to right, the loneliest man on earth.

All day his loneliness stayed in Gina's mind. He wore it, she fancied, like a cloak about his shoulders, above which his finedrawn, composed face held some quality which teased at her brain demanding a name. But the name escaped her and only the impression of the loneliness remained.

The following day she spent buying clothes. Later, watching her trying on dresses in the hotel bedroom, Guy felt stronger and more confident than he had done for weeks. In Cyprus he had begun to get well; now he was well, and in another ten days he would be ready to go back to England and take up his work again. And Ladysmere, Blake, Bessie . . .? How small and insignificant they appeared now. Not too seriously he considered the idea of selling Ladysmere, starting clear. What with Gina's alterations and the new kitchen and bathrooms, she could make at least two thousand, more possibly, and if he sold it as it stood, furniture and all, he'd net a very pretty sum. It mightn't be a bad idea to buy up property for reconversion as a side-line for Gina. She had a flair for it, and it was quite a profitable game if you knew the way. He'd have a talk with Howard Marley about it some time. As for Bessie and Blake, although from this distance they looked infinitesimally small, mere mosquitoes who were annoying but not dangerous, they would go. He'd write Bessie—no, perhaps not, they'd need someone there to have the place in order for their return. Better hold his hand till they were home, and then they must engage more servants, a cook, a proper parlour-maid, a man possibly. No more of this ramshackle existence. Gina must understand that he had a position to keep up with J. B. Harris and Sir James, and it was fitting and necessary that his home should be in keeping with that position.

"Like it?" he heard Gina say.

She had put on a dress whose predominant colour was red—the red, though he did not know it, that Del Sarto had used and Fra Angelico and Giotto. The dress, he decided, 'did something to her', gave her a new personality. She stood between the two long windows, facing him where he lounged in the Victorian velvet-upholstered chair, and he remembered the hotels and restaurants where he had taken her from time to time, and the swift, interested glances which men and women had given her as she walked across a room. For a while she had lost that quality, now it had returned to her, intensified—or was it with something added?

"It suits you," he said.

"It had better," she answered. "You haven't seen the bill yet. I hid it."

This was how he wanted her to be—light-hearted, gay, enjoying the money he spent on her. If she'd over-spent, he wouldn't have cared. He'd have pretended to be cross, but secretly he'd have been delighted.

"I expect I shall get over the shock," he said.

"Let's hope," she answered, and she went over to the mirror and combed her hair. He saw his wrist lying on the narrow velvet arm of the chair. His hand, fingers relaxed, hung limply down. He saw it resting on a desk, writing a cheque, many cheques. . . . He raised his head and watched Gina, and he remembered the dreary room she had shared with the girl Carrie in Chelsea. He thought how he had taken her out of all that and given her, not riches, though riches would come, but security and a 'frame' for herself and expensive things about her. Without him, she'd still be running round the agents looking for work, and eating sardines out of a tin by the gas-fire with its broken asbestos tubes.

That night at dinner he ordered champagne.

The day before they left Rome, they walked along the Old Appian Road.

"Do we have to walk down the Old Appian Road?" Guy asked Gina.

She was sitting on the chair changing her shoes, and she didn't look up.

"I can't leave Rome without. Even when I was a kid at school, the name fascinated me. Besides, it's so old."

"The rest of Rome being new," Guy answered dryly. "Pity Mussolini can't hear you. . . ."

"Chariots thundering along into the city," said Gina, "and caravans of merchants, and the tramping feet of the soldiers and processions. . . ."

"And funerals," Guy broke in. "It says so in the guide-book, because you had to be buried outside the walls."

"Not a bad idea," Gina answered, and she stood up. "They ought to bury all the Londoners along the Great North Road."

Guy took a clean handkerchief.

"You might keep that idea to yourself," he said. "I happen to have a factory on the Great North Road, and I'd hate the Minister of Interments, when the post is created, to pull it down and plant marble headstones instead."

"I suppose," said Gina, "in another two thousand years tourists *will* walk down the Great North Road and try to picture what it was like with cars and lorries and motor-coaches all making their way into London."

"In a fog," Guy added pleasantly.

"Here you are," he said an hour later. "The Appia Antica. I told you it would look like any other road."

Happiness was as warm and secure as the sun about him. The new strength in his body made him want to shout and laugh. He could, he thought, tackle anything, and he was almost looking forward to getting back to London and work. Almost—but not quite, for the last two weeks had been so much everything he had hoped they would be that he was sad to let them go. Gina was leaning back against a wall looking down the road, her eyes narrowed a little.

"How exciting it must have been," she said. "Days and days of travelling, and then at last to see Rome shining on its seven hills." She pushed herself away from the wall. "But I wish I didn't always think of the Romans as characters in an old film by D. W. Griffiths. It's so childish, and yet I can't stop myself doing it."

They strolled on. There was a church on the left of the road, and a priest with half a dozen people grouped round him was looking up at it. He was evidently acting as guide, and Gina took a few paces forward until she stood within earshot of what he was saying.

"Well, this is the place, Claudia. This is what you've travelled six thousand miles to see," she heard him say. It was, she thought, slightly incongruous to hear his soft southern accent although there were hundreds of American tourists in the city, besides the students at the American College. Why did one always expect anyone wearing a clerical collar to have the enunciation of Balliol?

The youngest of the party, a girl of eight or so, nodded gravely at him.

"Do you really think Saint Peter saw Him right *here*?" the child asked.

The priest nodded. "So legend says." A smile came into his eyes. "He wasn't running away. The Roman persecution of the Church was in full swing, and the idea was to get Saint Peter, who of course was head of the Church, into healthier surroundings."

"Gee, I'm glad he wasn't running away," the child said. "Then what?"

"They got him out of the city, and he was on this very road, which in those days was the great highway out of Rome, and then, just as he reached this place——"

"He met Our Lord," the child broke in.

The priest nodded.

"Yes. He met Our Lord face to face. And Our Lord was walking *towards* Rome, just as Saint Peter was walking away from Rome."

"Did Saint Peter know Him?"

"Ah, yes. Saint Peter knew Him all right. And when he saw Him, he said——"

"*Domine, quo vadis?*" the child broke in quickly.

"And that means?"

"'Lord, where are you going?'"

Again the priest nodded, and his eyes turned to the child were very gentle.

"Yes," he repeated. "'Lord, where are you going?' And what did Our Lord reply?"

"He said, 'I go to Rome to be crucified in your place,'" the child answered, and her face suddenly wore a great sadness.

"That's it, Claudia. He was showing Saint Peter that, even though he was head of the Church, and common sense said it was better for him not to be killed, there was a far greater thing than common sense, and that was—not his life but his death."

"And Saint Peter turned round right here and went back. . . ."

Gina, standing within a few feet of them, had listened fascinated to the conversation. *Domine, quo vadis?* And the reply that rang down the ages, 'I go to Rome to be crucified in your stead. . . .' She had heard the story before, but the child and the priest between them had made it sound living, as though they spoke of people they themselves knew. And into her mind there came the presbytery in London and the Irish priest who had talked to her before she and Guy were married. She turned towards Guy, but he was standing some paces away, looking uncomfortable—as though he were embarrassed because she had listened to the Americans.

She was going to join him when she heard the name which she had first heard spoken by Raines Metcalfe in the garden of the house at Alban Bay.

"Well, now, Mrs. Wharton," one of the women of the party said, "isn't that just wonderful? To think we've stood here on the very place! Claudia's been waiting for this day ever since last fall. Saint Peter's, the Vatican, even the Holy Father himself. . . ."

She had her back to them. She stood very still. Mrs. Wharton. . . .

"Andrew," Raines had called on that afternoon at the bay, "come here and let me introduce you to Gina. Andrew Wharton. . . ." And the house had been white and the sea a deep, deep blue, as blue as his eyes. . . .

There were possibly hundreds, thousands of Whartons scattered over the States. It was childish to imagine. . . .

She heard footsteps. The party was moving, going inside the church. A man's voice said, "You know, Father, I reckon that if they . . ." She heard the footsteps receding and the rest of the sentence was lost. She turned quickly and looked back. The two women were some distance behind the rest, walking slowly. One was tall and slim with dark hair, and she wore a beautifully pleated skirt and the finest of stockings and shoes. The other was an older woman, short and thicker-set, with broad shoulders and white crisp hair.

She tried to recall her features, for she'd only taken a casual glance at her, but she couldn't. And even if she could—what? Go to her and say, "Are you Andrew Wharton the novelist's mother? If you are, you've got to know that your son became my lover three days before he was killed, and nine months later I had his child. My husband wouldn't accept him, so I've given him away to some people called Mostyn, but he's your grandson. . . ."

How impossible! She must be mad even to imagine such rot. And it was probable that, if she did speak to her, the woman would answer, "But I'm Mrs. Wally G. Wharton of Los Angeles or

Chicago or somewhere; and my son's name is Hank or Eleazer or . . ."

Slowly, talking as they went, the two of them were passing on, away from her. She had the impulse to rush after them, to force the woman to admit that she *was* Andrew's mother and then to say to her, "Get Christopher back for me. Get him back. You've got to help me. I must have him back. I must have him back. . . ."

They had passed out of sight. The place where they had been was filled with dancing sunlight and the indifferent song of a bird. Only the Church of Domine Quo Vadis, which marked the spot where the first Vicar of Christ, fleeing from Rome, had met his Lord upon the Appian Way two thousand long years ago, still remained.

"You don't think," Guy said when she joined him, "that they minded you gate-crashing?"

The remark irritated her. "Oh, don't be so provincial, Guy," she said. "What does it matter? This is Rome not Cheltenham."

She felt his humiliation even before he said, "But I am provincial. I thought I'd told you. It's my slum manners, I expect. They taught us in standard three of the council school that it was rude to listen to other people's conversations."

"Do you have to be such a snob?" she answered. "I can't help it that I wasn't educated at a council school. They weren't quite so rigid at the place where I was dragged up."

She'd got the advantage every time; she knew that. And knew the unfairness of it. But . . . Mrs. Wharton. Christopher. *Christopher.*

Guy walked beside her in silence. He was seething under the lash of her words. He had merely half-teased her for hanging on to the Americans, and suddenly she had turned on him with a cut at his upbringing. It was true that he had been to a council school, but at least his father was an honest man. She'd been 'dragged up' at West Deane, the snob-school of the south, at a cost of three or four hundred a year, but it wasn't her father who'd paid the bill, it was the tradesmen.

"Perhaps they didn't tell you," he said coldly, "that it's embarrassing for the man you're with, even if he is only your husband, to be left standing around like a fool while you attach yourself, unasked, to a party of strangers."

Why did we come here just at this particular minute, Gina was thinking. Why did I have to hear that name? I'd tried to forget all that, to forget Christopher, and to a certain extent, I thought I had forgotten. I haven't. I've only pushed him a bit farther down into my mind so that the memory of him doesn't hurt so much. I ache for him. I don't care whose child he is. I want him. *Want* him. . . . But Guy wouldn't have him. He made me give my baby away. Made me? No, he didn't make me. I chose Guy. I've got to remember that. I've got to remember, too, how when he was ill and delirious I told myself that I must never forget that night. I've got to remember. . . .

And now they were walking on the Old Appian Road towards Rome—bickering. She wanted to say that it was her fault; but was it? How did she know that when she listened to the young American priest in the shadow of the church that she was going to meet Christopher face to face?

She stopped, startled out of her argument by the blinding, almost shocking, similarity of the words she had heard only a few moments ago—"Well, he'd got outside the city and was on this very road . . . and then just as he reached this place . . . he saw Him face to face. . . ."

She thought for a moment that it was as though that hidden life that went on deep below the surface—life of laughter and speech and action, of which she'd had a frightening glimpse one night in Philip's car—had suddenly come uppermost and was controlling not only herself, but Guy, the group of Americans, everyone. Quietly, gently and irrevocably it was urging and persuading them towards some end it alone saw and it alone knew.

Somewhere within its knowledge was Andrew Wharton and Christopher and the little church on the Appian Road and the two-thousand-year-old fleeing footsteps of Peter the fisherman. And somewhere, too, the parting of the crowd in Saint Peter's Square, and the white-clad figure with the sad, beautiful face, who passed head-high on his lifted chair bearing loneliness about him like a cloak.

"Guy . . ." she said, but he made no answer. He heard the appeal in her voice, but why, he asked himself, should he give in to her? She had made him look a fool, marching up to the Americans in that brazen 'lord of creation' way, as though, because her relations had all been titled she could make her own standards of behaviour. It was probably the way she looked at that other business, her own rotten unfaithfulness. Gina Randolph, one of the Conway-Coutts lot, could break her marriage vows and have another man's child 'just like that'. No shame. No sorrow even. The same old 'head-in-the-air I'm-a-Randolph' attitude to that, too. And it was he who'd done the suffering—and the forgiving. How many men would have been such fools as to have her back without so much as a word of censure? And she probably thought him weak because of it. She wouldn't understand that it wasn't weakness but strength. It would have been a damned sight easier never to have seen her again; to have let her go clean out of his life and take her illegitimate child with her. . . .

He felt her put her arm through his.

"Sorry, Guy. I'm a bitch. Didn't mean it. I think I've had a bit too much sun or something."

He looked at her quickly.

"You don't feel ill, do you?"

"Not now. I did for a couple of minutes." She pressed his arm. "Forget it."

"I've never known you speak like that before," he said; but there was no conciliation in his tone.

"I've never known myself," she told him. "Can we pick up that taxi?"

He stopped the car, and they sat side by side in it, while alternating light and shade passed over them.

"It was idiotic," Gina said. "Don't let's spoil our last night in Rome."

He stared straight ahead.

"I had no intention of spoiling it," he answered coldly.

Gina laughed a little and laid her hand on his knee.

"So gloomy. Darling, I was only being bloody-minded. Everyone is sometimes. You are yourself. And I have said sorry. Listen. . . . Let's go out somewhere tonight. Let's be terribly expensive, and dress up and drink lots of champagne and forget all about it. . . . Let's pretend it's the first night you've met me and you're besotted with me. Will you? Are you. . . .?"

He struggled for a moment longer, but in that mood of hers he went down like a ninepin. And he knew it.

He turned and saw her large eyes with their black lashes looking up at him. The promise in them caught at his heart.

Chapter V

GUY did not sell Ladysmere. Neither did he fire Bessie. Bessie fired herself because her father's rheumatism got worse and the poor man couldn't even turn over in his bed without help.

But the question of Philip Blake brought discussion.

"You can do what you like," Gina said to Guy. "Nothing would make me go to anyone else." She turned her face away. "Philip Blake kept me out of the river one night."

"That," answered Guy dryly, "is the point."

She looked round at him.

"You don't imagine that by going to Doctor Canon I'd forget what Philip did for me, do you?" she asked. "I shouldn't."

Guy walked across to the mantelpiece and stood there, looking down at the hearth.

"I don't want to talk about it," he said. "I've told you before, I want to forget the whole thing. And I don't want to have anything more to do with Blake."

He couldn't understand Gina's attitude. Surely she wanted to cut clean away from everything that reminded her of that dreadful year. How she could face Blake, he'd often wondered, and again the thought came to him that she had no shame. It was a frightening thought, but it wasn't, by a long shot, the first time he'd had it. Would another woman, he'd wondered, whose husband had taken the attitude he had over the sordid business, behave in her high-handed manner? Wouldn't there be some sign of contrition or of gratitude? God forbid that he wanted her to crawl to him, but, after all, he had taken her back and, so to speak, reinstated her as his wife without so much as a word of his own humiliation. Wasn't that something? Didn't it call for a little appreciation or even a willingness on her part to give in to his wishes over the question of Blake? *Did* she want to go on remembering the fact that she had produced an illegitimate child?

"All right," Gina said suddenly, but there was something in her tone that irritated him more than ever. "Let's hope I'm not ill, because nothing would make me have that man Canon pouring drugs into me. Anyway," she ended with an inconsequence that infuriated him, "he uses hair-oil."

She rang Philip the following day, when Guy was in London.

"May I come and see you?"

"Of course. I heard you were home. How did it go?"

"Oh, all right," she answered. And she added, "Fine, really. I fell in love with Rome."

"Good," Philip answered.

"Will directly after lunch do?" she asked him. "Quarter-past two."

"Half a minute." She pictured him reaching for his appointment book, covered with the incredibly small writing which no one else could possibly decipher.

"Make it two o'clock."

"I'll be there."

"As if," she said to him as she sat back in the chair with the broken spring, "having Canon to take my temperature would make the slightest difference to—that."

She looked, Philip thought, more attractive than he had ever seen her. Her skin was tanned and had a dusky bloom on it. To an outsider she would appear to be the picture of health and contentment. It was only in her eyes. . . .

"He's right, though," he said to her. "Cut out everything connected——"

"Philip, you fool," she broke in. "You can't cut your heart out, can you? Or your memory?"

He smiled slightly.

"I'd be out of a job if you could," he told her.

She frowned. "It's a nuisance," she said, "because it means I shall have to come down like this, surreptitiously. That's bad."

"Why come at all?" he asked.

She looked at him with surprise. "But of course I'll have to." She moved her right hand, and the Italian bracelet she wore shifted lower over her wrist. "How is he?" she asked him.

"Fine," he answered shortly. And he said, "If you didn't come down, you couldn't ask me."

"I'd go mad," she said. "I've got to know. I've got to keep in touch. They haven't adopted him yet. Not legally."

"They will do," he said shortly. "Guy's right," he went on. "Why keep the wound open?"

"Don't go back on me, Philip," she said. "Can't you see that if I don't hear about him occasionally, I shan't be able to bear it? I shan't, you know. Has he grown?"

"Of course."

"Has he—altered?"

"Of course he's altered."

"Is Jennifer still besotted with him?"

"Oh yes." He stood up and walked round his desk and propped himself on the edge of it, looking down at her.

"Couldn't you cut it out?" he asked her. "You ought to, Gina. I should forbid you to come here, refuse to answer your questions. Can't you see that, now the thing's done, you must leave it?"

"And go on being maudlin about it all by myself? What's the point of that?"

"The point is, that with every possible contact obliterated, with the door firmly shut, you'd——"

"But I wouldn't," she said. She sat up. "You think I would because you're a man and your reason and your training tells you I would. But there's something more than reason and training." She put her hands on her abdomen with a gesture which almost shocked him with its hint of the primitive. "It's there a woman carries a child," she said. "Not an idea in her head, but a living creature in her body, whether its conception was legitimately by her husband or not. If your mind forgot, I doubt whether your body would." She lay back in the chair again. "Even you wouldn't understand that," she said. "There isn't a man living who would."

He didn't answer. His hands one each side of him gripped the edge of the desk, and he stared down at his outstretched foot.

Was there, he wondered, any plane at all on which the sexes could meet and share experience—other than in the act of love? Sometimes he doubted it. It was as though, between man and woman there was a great gulf fixed and each viewed life and experience from their own side of the chasm. Only in the unspoken ritual of the body was the gulf truly bridged.

"So you see . . ." said Gina.

"Oh, I see," he answered. "But I don't like it."

"You will," she said, and there was a half-laugh in her tone.

"You ought to make the adoption legal and close the whole episode," he said.

"Christopher isn't an episode," she answered almost dreamily.

"What do you mean?"

She waited a full half-minute before she said, "Philip . . . I can't make the adoption legal yet. Not yet." She prodded the chair-arm with her index finger. "I still sometimes hope that Guy——"

"Good grief!" said Philip, and he jerked away from the desk and stood up. "You're crazy. Guy would never have him, I tell you. Never." He took a pace forward and stood looking down at her. "You must remember," he said, "I know him now. Before, I didn't. And I know what I'm saying."

"And I still think he might," Gina answered, and she went on prodding the shabby leather arm of the chair.

"You're being dishonest," Philip said sternly. "Jennifer and George are only waiting for the moment when you'll agree to a legal adoption. They'd be broken-hearted. And what about Christopher? Have you stopped to think of the effect on him while you bandy him about from pillar to post?"

"Of course I've considered it," said Gina. "It's the only thing I have considered. He's my baby, and George and Jennifer would have to mend each other's broken hearts if I got half a chance of having him back." She looked up at him. "I thought," she said, "when I made the decision to let them have him, that after a time I'd forget." She shook her head slowly, with an old, curiously wise gesture. "You don't forget. There's a sort of gap in your mind that won't knit together again."

"Because you won't give it a chance." There was pleading in

Philip's tone. "See a lawyer and get the adoption legalised, will you, Gina? *Give* yourself a chance. . . ."

She didn't answer, but went on staring at the floor, her head slightly lowered. Suddenly she lifted it and looked directly at him. "No," she answered. "I must wait a little. . . ."

Guy worked hard that winter in order to make up what had amounted to eighteen months' absence. The merger with J. B. Harris had ensured the continuance of his plant and factories—without the merger, he told himself with a grim smile, the absence would not have occurred. There was an accumulation of personal decisions and directions which he alone could deal with, and he was frequently not home till late.

They still knew few people in the district. Influenced as it was by the class distinctions of Victorian England, their coming had caused questions among the residents who, hearing that the new owners of Ladysmere were 'trade', had not called.

It was confusing, when the house was reopened, to hear rumours that Mr. Taylor had been in Korea on some 'top secret' work for the Government and that Mrs. Taylor was one of the Conway-Coutts.

Gina, quite oblivious to all of it, found a jobbing gardener and began work on the garden, but Guy said, "Can't you get the people from Belsted over to lay the place out? Anyone would think I was a miser. Look at your hands!"

"All those little beds and curly paths," Gina scorned. "And precious young men with blue-prints. I like doing it." She looked down at her hands. "They'll wash," she added casually.

Guy frowned. "That's hardly the point. I don't *care* for you to do it."

"Why-ever not?"

"Because I prefer to have it done by a firm," Guy insisted. "Those people know what they're doing."

"I couldn't disagree more," Gina said. "And, anyway, I know what I'm doing." She picked up the fork and bent over the bed she was digging. "Don't fuss," she said. "You'll like it when it's finished."

He turned and walked back to the house, irritated and disappointed. There was no need for her to slave like a navvy in the garden. She had only to ask for money to spend on it and he would have given it to her. It wasn't in keeping either with the house or their position for her and that oaf of a man to be wrestling with it. When he'd first known her—and later in France, in New York, in Italy—she'd always been well-dressed, her hands soft and lovely, now they were hard and work-stained, and half the time she went about in old cord slacks and sweaters. And yet when she changed into one of the dresses he'd bought her in Rome, she managed to make every other woman he'd known appear fussy and overdressed. Then she made him think of the long line of portraits at Harvingdon, but when on one occasion he told her so, she merely made a grimace and said, "Do I really look as dead as that lot?"

"Don't you want to look like them?" he asked her.

She was lighting a cigarette, and she threw the match away before she said indifferently, "Most of them had protruding eyes."

But when at night he took her into his arms, all disappointments and conflicts ceased.

In March, Gina, in London for shopping, met Carrie.

Carrie was superbly overdressed in a fur coat hanging open to show a scarlet frock and three rows of 'pearls'. She also wore a little hat made of red feathers, long ear-rings and lots of jangling bracelets.

"Well!" she said to Gina. "Thought you were dead and buried. What has happened to you?"

"What's happened to *you*?" Gina countered. "You look like a million dollars."

Carrie glanced down at herself. "What, in these old rags? I only wear them for shopping."

"What do you wear to eat your dinner in?" said Gina. "Solid gold?"

"You needn't be a bitch," Carrie answered. "Come and have a drink. I'll buy you a champagne cocktail."

"Not at eleven o'clock in the morning, you won't. You can buy me a coffee."

"Coffee!" scorned Carrie, and she added, "All right. If you want coffee."

She put a handbag of plastic crocodile on the table in the café, and brought out an enormous cigarette-case and a silver lighter.

"Has Meg Metcalfe gone into retirement at last, then?" Gina asked her.

Carrie blew a long banner of smoke from her rounded lips. "Oh, I'm out of show business," she answered airily. "Been out six months now. I'm in food."

"Caviare at that," said Gina. "Where's the food you're in?"

"A friend and I have got a little place in Soho. 'The Black Scampi', it's called. You know what a scampi is, I suppose? Art's an Italian and he's wonderful with sea-food. You'd never know it was fish you were eating." She took a sip of the coffee and grimaced. "They just can't do it, can they?" she said. "If anybody dished up coffee like that to Art, he'd send for the manager."

Gina, remembering the days in Oakley Street when, if funds were low, they'd eaten sardines and drunk coffee essence, kept a smile under control, but Carrie sensed it and she said loftily, "We get West End people, you know. Sir James Morecroft often comes in. And Lord Standon. Glynne Thorne came one night after the show, and two nights later Meg Metcalfe turned up with her new boy. He did look a piece, too. Polished nails. Art had a write-up about 'The Scampi' in the nationals," she went on. "They said it was one of the best places for food in London."

"Lovely," said Gina, and she took a swift look at Carrie's left hand. But nothing escaped Carrie.

"We can't be married," she said, "because Art's got a wife in Italy and they're Catholics. Spoils it rather, but we manage. He'd give me the top brick off the chimney if I asked for it," she added. She looked at Gina. "What happened about that—you know what?" she asked her.

"Oh, that was all right. Fine," Gina replied. "Did you speak to Meg when she came in?"

"I was awfully worried about you," said Carrie. "I wrote to you, but you never answered letters. I am glad it was all right, though. I told you it would be. Are you still at Ladysmere? How's the self-made man?"

"Wonderful," said Gina. "Working very hard."

Carrie let her eyes pass over Gina's coat. "Doing all right still?"

"Well, it's not food, you know."

"No. That's where the 'yeast' is," Carrie answered. Her large eyes softened. "Though I miss show business. Do you?"

"No," Gina answered. And then she said, "Oh, sometimes, I suppose. One misses the excitement, the 'smell of the grease-paint' thing. It was fun while it lasted," she said.

"Meg's got a new play," said Carrie. "The Sheridan. Opening in six weeks."

"Oh; what?"

"It's from a novel that some Yank author she had once wrote. Can't remember the name. He came over here to see Meg and was killed in a car smash. . . . Meg went about in black for weeks afterwards till Anna told her it made her skin yellow. What's the matter?"

"Caught my finger on my cigarette end," said Gina. "Burnt me. Was the book called *Single Track*?"

"That's right," Carrie agreed. "Did you read it?"

"Yes, I read it," Gina answered.

"I saw Toby last week, and he says the play's such a winner that even Meg won't be able to wreck it. Come up some time when it's opened and we'll go to a matinée. Be fun. I can't go at night because it's our busiest time." She fumbled in the immense bag. "Look, here's our card. The phone number's on it, so you can't say you don't know it." She looked at her watch. "I'll have to beat it back. I never come this end much now, but it's Art's birthday on Tuesday and I wanted to get him an electric purée maker, and I thought this dump might know what I'm talking about, but they didn't. . . . You will come and see Meg in her greatest-ever role, won't you, Gina? Promise. . . ." She turned away and then back again. "I've just remembered that chap's name," she said. "Meg's Yank novelist, I mean. It was Andrew Wharton. . . ."

"That's right," Gina answered. "'Bye, Carrie. . . ."

Deliberately she went on shopping, and when she'd finished she had lunch. There was no point in thinking about it, she told herself, and as if that were the password she immediately started to think about it.

It seemed there was no getting away from it ever. Guy could prohibit Philip Blake. Philip could tell her to cut all contacts, and then a chance meeting with Carrie of all people and there was the whole thing coming up fresh as a daisy. And as though the meeting had uttered that password, too, the longing to see Christopher started up again. She saw it coming, knew it was going to take possession of her, and was quite powerless to stop it. "I won't have it," she told herself as she drank the brandy and ginger-ale she'd ordered. "I can't stand the monotony of it. It's like being in love—the thing goes round and round in your brain, and though you don't want it, you can't shake yourself free of it. I've simply *got* to forget him. I've got to forget what it was like to hold him in my arms and feel his head butting into me like some ridiculous little puppy. I've got to forget the way his hair grew and his eyes and that silly guffaw. I've got to forget that his hand clenched round my finger with a grip like a prize-fighter, and that when he slept his lashes were little fans against his cheek. I've got to forget, but I can't. What do you *do* to forget? "Shut the door," says Philip, and the fool doesn't realise you can still hear what's going on the other side of the door. "Fill your mind with something else." Hadn't she tried? Hadn't she lugged tons of earth about the garden at Ladysmere till she was dropping with exhaustion? And Guy? Guy hadn't a clue. Immersed in his money-making, he'd no more idea than Philip Blake, that giving a baby away didn't stop you longing for it. . . . Not that old argument again. She couldn't stand it. Philip would say the thing was an obsession. She knew it, but how did you *stop* it? Or how did you bear it if you didn't stop it? And yet there were other women who had lost their sons. . . . Displaced people, children killed in war or on the roads. . . . But those things were beyond their control, part of the general agony that was life. They hadn't engineered them as she had. If you'd had a son and he'd died, you could mourn decently over him. She wasn't allowed to mourn the loss of her son because his birth was shameful and had to be forgotten. . . . What a fool she'd been to give him away! Now she came to look back, it appeared that she hadn't even tried to influence Guy to have him. She'd just gone down like a spineless idiot. And yet, at the time, she hadn't known where her love or her loyalty lay. Guy ill, shocked, alone. . . . No, not again. That interminable wheel must be stopped because it only churned out arguments without getting any solution. There wasn't any solution. There never would be, unless she left Guy to his money-making, snatched Christopher from the Mostyns and bolted with him.

She was mad, she told herself, as she drove down Knightsbridge. What did she think she was going to do? Knock at the Mostyns' door and demand Christopher? She turned into the square and looked up at the numbers. Hundred and one, three . . . five. . . . That was the house. She drew over to the other side of the road and pulled up by the palings. "Now what?" she said to herself. "Here you are. Over there within a few yards of you is your son. . . . But even if you do knock at the door they won't let you see him because you signed on the dotted line that you wouldn't. What then? Now you've got here, what?"

She hadn't eaten much lunch and she felt slightly dizzy. And foolish. Very foolish. She saw her hands on the steering-wheel. They looked faintly unreal, as though they didn't belong to her.

The door of the house opened, and she looked up and saw the back of a nurse in a blue coat and hat and facing her, a young servant in green, who was laughing and stooping a little as, between them, they edged a perambulator down the three shallow steps. They set it down on the pavement, and the girl ran up the steps again and shut the door, while the nurse turned and made to go up the square.

Then the door opened a second time, and Jennifer Mostyn stood there, small and shy and neat as ever, and she called, "Nanny! Just a moment before you go."

The nurse fixed a safety-catch on the pram wheel and walked back up the steps to the door, and she saw Christopher.

He was sitting up in the pram and the mild sun shone on to his head. He looked enormous. What have they done to him, she thought in a panic. They must have overfed him. . . . He was examining a toy he had with him. He banged it once or twice against the side of the pram, and then, with a swift look towards the back of the nurse, he took it up and dropped it over the side on to the pavement. The nurse, still speaking over her shoulder to Jennifer, came down the steps again. She saw the toy lying on the pavement, and she stooped and picked it up.

"No, Christopher," she said firmly. "That isn't good. Now you mustn't have it."

He stared gravely at her for a moment, then his own audacious grin came over his face. He couldn't, the grin said, have cared less.

Jennifer came down the steps, a smile on her own face. Her eyes beamed love on him.

"'Bye-bye, darling," she said, and she waved her hand.

"'Bye-bye, Mummy. Mummy. Mummy . . ." he called, and the nurse began wheeling the pram away. Jennifer watched them for a moment, and then she went back up the steps and closed the door.

"Well," Gina said to herself, "that's where this obsession's got you. You've seen your son. He looks very strong, very healthy, perfectly cared for. You've heard him call his mother. . . ." She gripped the steering-wheel and braced her feet against the pedal board. "What more do you want? You were within a dozen yards of him and he didn't even know it. He wouldn't have cared if he had. You'd better go home now."

She bent forward and turned the ignition key. Her knee trembled as she put the clutch pedal down. The gear engaged with a snarl, and she drove out of the square again.

Chapter VI

GUY was sitting at his desk, but he wasn't working. Frustration held him in chains. He felt literally weighted, unable to move freely.

The thing, he thought, was intangible, something he couldn't come to grips with. He had never come up against anything like it in his life before. Troubles there'd been in plenty and he'd always gone for them straight. He'd go for this straight, too, if he knew what it was he was aiming at.

He remembered, with a return of the surprise he'd felt then, the first time he and Gina had quarrelled. They were in Rome, and only the night before she'd said to him, "I love you, Guy. I do, you know. You won't let me talk about that—that other thing, but there's something you've got to understand. I never for a moment stopped loving you. Whatever you do, whatever happens to us, believe that."

In the darkness he'd felt her face wet with tears and he'd answered, "I do believe it, if you say so."

Her voice had been urgent. "Yes. You must. Not only because I say so, but because it's true. It was all—all . . . I don't know. I can't explain. It's as though . . ."

He couldn't bear to hear her speak of it and he'd said, "You really mustn't talk about it, Gina. It's behind us. Wiped out. I've told you. It's finished. . . ."

That night he'd have sworn that she spoke the truth. Yet, less than twenty-four hours later, on the Old Appian Road, she'd more or less mocked at his upbringing and scorned his council school education, and all through the winter and right up till yesterday there'd been the same changes of mood in her. Sometimes she'd been gentle and loving, at others withdrawn, condescending and almost hard.

Oh yes, he'd lost his temper, too, and there were times when he'd wished that she were some little slut who'd have thrown something at him, anything to break the tension; but just as he'd told himself that he couldn't stand her mood another hour, change came over her and she'd been sweet to him again. What in creation's name was the cause of it all? He wondered sometimes if everything she'd told him was a pack of lies and the story of the dead American a convenient screen to a love affair that was still going on. Philip Blake.... Was he, not the fictitious American, the father of her child? It was Blake who'd met him on Belsted station. Blake who'd been a constant visitor to the flat in Melford. Blake who'd 'kept her out of the river'....

Had they fooled him between them? Were Blake's damnable doctor's hands touching her flesh with love as they'd touched his own professionally when he was ill?

"I'd hoped, and I think she had, that you'd have found it in your heart to forgive her...." That's what he'd said. "I'd hoped, and I think she had...." Had they made a fool of him? If the story were true, wouldn't she have been overwhelmed with gratitude when he'd forgiven her and had her back? If, as she'd said, she'd loved him all the time, wouldn't her love have been deeper because of what he'd done for her?

But why, if she and Blake were lovers, hadn't they gone off together? His practice? Gina was no fool. To be the wife of a small-town doctor was one thing, but to be the wife of Guy Taylor of Ladysmere and still keep her lover running round taking temperatures—and creeping up to the house when he was away—was another.

The more he thought about it, the more it explained the whole situation. And Blake was an educated man—Winchester and Magdalen. He spoke with her accent; had that indefinable thing which made him 'different'.

He left his desk and walked to the window. He'd kill Blake. And he'd kill her, too, the lying, adulterating little bitch.... Steady.... He'd no proof—yet. But that shouldn't be difficult. There were people who made good incomes by proving just those things. They set men on the tracks of the guilty, men who peered through keyholes and witnessed the shameful act. . . . He couldn't do that to Gina. He'd got to. It was his duty to. Gina was making a mockery of marriage, and marriage was a sacrament, a holy state. And what about Blake? The B.M.A. would be interested in his dealings with his patients. That kind of thing couldn't go on. Someone had to stop it. . . . And when he'd caught them they wouldn't get away with it a second time. You could fool him once, but not twice. No more of those earnest floods of words from Blake. No more tears of shame from Gina. Not again.

He put his hands over his eyes. He'd believed in her, loved her. She'd stood above him, almost out of reach, lovely, cool, faithful. . . . If only she could have an accident, be scarred, blinded, smashed, so that she had to call on him, and he could show her that he loved her more than Blake ever had. He'd look after her. Nurse her with his own hands as he had helped his father nurse his mother. Emptying the slop-pail. . . . Changing the putrid bandages. . . . Carrying them away to be burnt. . . .

His desk telephone rang. It penetrated the back room over the ironmonger's shop where he had been standing. Its buzz hovered over his mother's grey-yellow face on the pillow; over the crucifix which hung above the bed. They faded, backed away into nothing again.

He went across to his desk and picked up the receiver.

"It's nearly three, Mr. Taylor," came Miss Pangle's voice. "Mr. Harris and Sir James will be here in five minutes. The board room is all ready. . . ."

"Thank you," he said. And then, "Would you put a call through to Ladysmere and tell Mrs. Taylor I may be late. Tell her not to wait dinner, will you? . . ."

He didn't leave the office till six. He said good night to Hoskins, the porter, and walked down the three wide steps on to the pavement.

The April evening was floating lightly over the City. Beneath it, outlines were distinct, drawn clearly, with a strong, definite hand. Sounds, too, were clear, with a bell-like ring about them, as though the gentleness of the sky acted as a sounding-board which, instead of amplifying, refined the blurred noises of the streets.

The board meeting had been particularly successful, and he had scored a pretty subtle point off J. B. The little man hadn't liked it much, but there'd been a flick of an expression in Sir James's eye which had been rather pleasant to see. And it had all been done with the very greatest deference, of course. The office-boy daring to suggest to the manager. . . . If they did but know it, they were eating out of his hand. They didn't know it. They thought it was he who was eating out of their hands. It would be convenient if they continued to think so for a little longer.

Gina. . . . She came back into his mind, taking up the whole of it, a dead weight. For a couple of hours he'd put her out of his thinking, but now she was back. He tried to shake himself free of her but he couldn't, and almost before he realised it he had returned to his thoughts of the afternoon, just at the point where he had left them—at his mother's death.

There was something about his mother's death which he had been going to consider when the telephone bell rang. He frowned, and suddenly remembered—the crucifix on the wall. She had asked for it, and his father had taken it down from the nail and she'd held it in her hands. . . . It was in her hands when she died.

He remembered the Requiem Mass, and his father's shuffling footsteps as he followed the coffin across the road to the graveyard. Why did he want to think of that? What had his mother's death to do with Gina?

The crucifix. . . .

He knew, but he didn't want the knowledge. He'd like to believe, as he believed as a child; as his parents had believed. He still did believe in a way, but there seemed a mountain of things in between him and belief. Go to a priest. . . . That was the whisper going on beneath the turmoil of his thinking. Go, not to a private detective, but to a priest. Ask help, not from the little keyhole men but from the old, strong, battling Church. His own religion had been pretty cursory of late, but it was still there; even if it was only childhood habit, it was still there. And the Church would tell him to pray. . . . To pray that Gina would give up Blake and come back to him? And both she and Blake would get off scot free. Why should they? Was he to do all the suffering? He'd given Gina everything: loyalty, money, care, and in the end he'd forgiven her betrayal. Was he to forgive a second betrayal? Steady! He hadn't proved that yet. He must be careful. It might be some other man, not Blake, who was her lover. And how could he find out if he didn't have her watched? The uncertainty was killing him, tearing him to bits. That there *was* another man, he was certain. Someone was 'holding her', he could sense it. Some other man was filling her thought, influencing her, changing her. He'd got to find out who. He'd got to. . . .

"Guy!"

He looked up quickly, unable for a split second to make the jump between the shadowed world he had been living in and the real world of Buckingham Palace Road with its stream of traffic.

"You don't remember me," the woman said again. "You've forgotten."

He hadn't forgotten. He remembered quite, quite clearly. Only now her hair was dark instead of fair.

"Well, Alison," he said. "Nice to see you. How are you?"

She was laughing at him, screwing her eyes up as she always had done.

"As if you cared how I am! You're a fine one! Never a word to your old friends these days."

He'd forgotten how intensely blue and alive her eyes were.

"Oh, come now," he said. "You know perfectly well that I'm married."

"It's written all over you, sweet," she said lightly. "In fact, if I may say so, it looks a little big for you. Outsize."

"You're mistaken," he answered in the same light tone. "That's a board meeting I've just come from. Very large."

She laughed again.

"Guy, it is fun to see you. Where are you going?"

"To have a drink with you, of course."

"That would be wonderful," she answered.

He hailed a passing cab. It pulled up and he opened the door for her, and as he got in and sat beside her he remembered her little flat behind Barker's. The first time he'd been there he'd thought it madly exciting and very elegant. And he'd thought Alison was a society girl, sophisticated and dashing. He didn't know that she served in a 'little' dress shop. She'd been kind to him, though.

"I've missed you," she said.

"You don't expect me to believe that?"

"It's true. But you're very grand now, aren't you?" she asked him, and he saw her glance pass over his suit. "I always knew you'd get on," she added. "You had it stamped all over you."

He laughed, but he was pleased. "Sounds like a tattoo mark."

"You've changed," she said.

"It's quite a while since I saw you, isn't it?"

"It's five years," she answered slowly. "Five years in June."

"How have I changed?"

She didn't reply, and he said, "Come on, tell me the worst."

"You look—rich," she said. "You look as though you didn't have to worry about your bank balance. And your voice has changed, too."

"Is that 'rich' as well?" he fooled.

A smile flicked into her eyes and she nodded her head, a queer little grimace about her mouth. "Yes. It's laced with dollar bills and high society."

"What a ridiculous creature you are!" he said, and he suddenly remembered Gina and that he had been going to see a priest—or a private enquiry agent. He pushed the thought of all three away. He was too tired to think any more. He'd go back to it after he'd bought Alison a drink.

"Don't let's talk about me," he said. "What about you?"

"What about me?"

"Are you still at Marianne's?"

"Oh yes," she answered indifferently. "I'm still there."

"You didn't marry—what was his name? The dark-haired chap?"

"Yes," she answered again, in the same tone. "I married him. He got all my savings out of me and disappeared."

"Oh, my dear," he said quickly. "I'm sorry."

"You don't have to be," she answered. "It was one of those things."

"Did you love him, Alison?"

"Love him!" she scorned. "Of course I didn't love him."

"But you married him?"

"Yes. I did, didn't I? I married him because I *wanted* to be married. I was sick of 'rags' and being on my feet all day. And he was a gentleman. He'd been to Oxford. At least, that's what he told me. I thought I'd—— "She didn't finish the sentence and said, "What's it matter?"

"It does matter. Where is he now?"

She made a little gesture with her hands. "Ask me!"

"I'm terribly sorry," he said.

"You!" she scorned, and the taxi drew in to the kerb.

The bar was full. He found a table and ordered drinks. "This is fun," she said as she lifted her glass. "I've often wondered if I'd ever see you again."

"I live out of London now," he told her. "Then I was in Korea for a year."

"Whatever for? Were you in the army?"

"No. I was in prison."

"In—what?"

He explained briefly, and she said, "Poor Guy! How awful! I can't imagine you shut up."

The thought came to him that he'd wanted someone to say "Poor Guy! How awful!" for a long, long time. No one had.

"It must have been awful for your wife, too," he heard her say, and Gina was there, sitting in his mind again. Gina and Philip Blake and her child and the American and the enquiry agent. He knew he ought to look at them all, but they were too oppressive for him. Too weighty. He was so sick and tired of them.

"Have another drink?" he said to Alison. "Or are you going out somewhere?"

"Not really."

"Same again?"

She nodded. "Please, Guy."

The man brought the drinks, and he lighted her cigarette. She put her hand on his to steady the flame. He remembered now that she had always done that. He remembered other things about her, too—the way she curled up by the fire in a dressing-gown drying her hair after she'd washed it, and that her bedroom smelt heavily of powder and scent.

"She was an actress, wasn't she?" he heard her say. He didn't know what she was talking about and said, "Who?"

"Your wife."

He nodded. "Not a very serious one."

"She isn't acting now, is she?"

"Lord, no," he answered, and then he wondered if that's what she was doing . . . all the time.

"You don't want to talk about her, do you?" she said. "Men never do." He turned to look at her, but her head was bent a little. "A woman always wants to talk about the man she loves. She doesn't care *who* she talks to about him—the char, the sweep, anyone," she said. "But a man's different. The more he loves a girl the less he'll say about her."

"We keep you too deeply in our hearts," he said lightly.

She made a little grimace at him and finished her Martini.

"I'd better go," she said.

The drink had loosened the chains of frustration. He no longer felt as isolated. Even the people in the bar appeared friendly, rather a nice lot; all hoping to have a pleasant evening and forget whatever it was that troubled them.

"You don't have to go, do you?" he asked her. Alison too—such a friendly little soul. He had no sense of strain with her; none of that feeling that he'd got to 'watch his step'.

She was looking at him with her vivid blue eyes.

"Well, do you?" he said.

"Not really."

"Like to have dinner with me?" He looked at his watch. "It'll have to be early, as I've got to get down to Belsted afterwards."

"I'm not dressed for going out," she answered.

He hadn't noticed her clothes; had only had the impression of lightness—neatness—what was it?

"You look fine," he said. "Anyway, I'm straight out of the office. Where shall we go?"

"I don't know, really, that I ought to," she said. And then, as though changing her mind, she added, "Do you remember that little place in Soho we used to go to?"

Vaguely he did remember. Little meals, rather greasy, and cheap wine. And afterwards he'd taken her back to her flat behind Barker's and made love to her.

"There's a very good place now in Greek Street," she said. "Really good. Everyone goes there. It's expensive, though."

"I think I've heard of it," he said. "Like to try that?"

Her eyes were shining. "Love it."

"Come on, then."

Although it was early, The Black Scampi was already nearly full. It didn't appear, Guy thought, any different from a dozen others of its kind in the neighbourhood—the same rather fusty-food smelling room; the poor knives and forks, the Victorian cruets. . . . But it was fun to be back here with Alison, knowing, this time, that if he'd wanted to he could have taken her to the Savoy.

"Now," he said. "What are you going to eat?" He looked at the card.

"I never understand menus," she said. "Why can't they write them in English?"

"Snob value, chiefly."

"You understand them, Guy."

"Oh, more or less," he said vaguely, and he remembered the evenings when he went to a little dried monkey of a man who lived in one room near Kensington Station for French lessons. He went at nine o'clock, and sometimes he hadn't had anything to eat and was giddy with fatigue, but he still went.

"I'd like to be able to speak French," Alison said. "You always feel so silly if you're out with a man who doesn't understand the menu."

That, he remembered, was exactly what he'd thought himself when he first went to the little man. He had had no intention of making himself, or anyone he was with, 'feel silly'.

"It's convenient," he said, and again he thought how sweet Alison was.

"You choose for me," she said. "Please, Guy."

The waiter came and he ordered their meal. Avocado Pear, Fried Scampi and Zabagglione. He ordered two more Martinis, and chose a bottle of Pouilly Fuissé to drink with the Scampi.

"There we are," he said, "and I hope the chap lives up to his reputation. Hungry?"

She nodded. "I am. Are you?"

"I wasn't. Now I am."

She was holding the glass in her hand.

"What's changed you?"

"What d'you think?"

"You mean because you met me. But I don't believe that. What had you been going to do?"

"I hadn't quite made up my mind. There was a man I had to see. . . ." That was true, but whether the man was a priest or a private enquiry agent, he didn't know himself. It didn't matter very much either way at the moment.

"Won't the man mind you not turning up?"

"He didn't know I was coming," he said. "It was only a chance call."

The waiter brought the pears and served them.

"It's certainly good," he told her. "Clever girl."

"I was petrified in case you wouldn't like it," she answered, and he laughed. "It's sort of queer," she said, "to go out with anyone you once knew so well, when you haven't seen them for years. Especially when they've made money. You don't quite know where you are, do you?"

He flicked a glance at her. "Don't you? I don't think it's any different from what it used to be. You soon pick up the threads again."

The waiter took the plates and came back with the Scampi. "Here we are, sir. You will like this, I think. . . . And now the wine. One moment, sir." He whisked away and returned with the bottle folded in a napkin. He drew the cork and poured a little into Guy's glass. "All right, sir?"

It was all very pleasant, Guy thought as they ate, easy and friendly—and a relief. Frustration had gone now, taken out on the tide of the food and wine and little Alison's appreciation. Lord, he thought, how much he'd needed appreciation of late! And how precious little he'd had of it. No one would blame a man for picking it up when he found it lying at his feet. He reached for the bottle to refill her glass, but she put her hand over it.

"I mustn't," she said. "I'll forget——"

"What will you forget?" he asked. "Come on, move your hand. What will you forget?" he repeated. He thought it was frightfully important that he should know. She was looking directly into his eyes.

"I'll forget that it isn't—like it used to be," she said.

"What isn't like it used to be?" he insisted.

"Oh, you know, Guy. Like when you—like it was when we used to go out together before."

"Isn't it?" he said. He put his hand across the table and over hers. "Isn't it?" he asked again. "What's different about it? I'm still your friend, aren't I?"

Carrie, as she came down the three steps from the inner room, saw them and thought, "You'd better watch out, my girl, if you want to remember mother's advice." And then she looked again. "Well, I'll be jiggered!" she said, and went down to the kitchen where Art, having 'got the cooking going', was handing over to his chef and struggling out of a once-white coat into the tailed suit of the *maître d'hôtel*.

"What d'you think, Art?" she said. "You know I told you about Gina who I shared a room with when I was in show business? The one that married what she called a self-made man?"

Art was combing his black hair. She saw a bit of his face reflected in the small mirror.

"Yes. I remember. I remember. The one who was——" He broke off and shouted a broadside of Italian at the chef.

"Yes, that one," said Carrie. "Well, what d'you think? Guy Taylor, that's the self-made man, is in the restaurant having dinner with a dame. Cheap little bit, she looks, too. And he's holding her hand. . . . Can you beat it?"

Art straightened his bow-tie.

"It is his sister, perhaps, yes, my little nosey parker? Eh?"

"Sister, my foot!" said Carrie. "I'd like to see any chap take his sister out to dinner and sit and hold hands with her."

Art turned and dropped a kiss on to the top of her head.

"Then, my garlic-juice, I suggest he is a leetle in love with her. Yes? Eh? And very nice, too," he smiled. He whisked a brown hand over the shoulders of his coat. "Now then, Arturio Marienza," he said to himself. "March!"

Art himself directed the ceremony of their brandy. Tenderly and with infinite care, as though he were the chief priest at some solemn rite, he allowed a tablespoonful of the Remy Martin to descend into the bowels of the glasses.

"There, signor. The end of, I hope, a perfect meal. Everything all right? You have nothing to tell me, signor. No troubles? Signora?"

Good grief, Guy thought. What is this place? A confessional?

"No. Everything has been very good," he said. "I congratulate you."

Art's bow was that of a minister plenipotentiary before his sovereign.

"I thank you, signor. I hope we shall have the pleasure of serving you again. Any time, signor. You must try our Osso Buco Milanaise one day. It is a dream. A poem. . . . Excuse me, signor."

He glided between the tables, on his small, swift feet, his broad shoulders swaying slightly. He settled the little controversy over a customer's wine and swept out and into the passage again. Carrie was just coming upstairs.

"Did you see them?" she asked him. "Were they still holding hands?"

"No man holds a woman's hand when he is drinking brandy," he said. "It is a very important business to drink brandy. It needs all a man's attention." He put one finger under her chin, lifted it a trifle and kissed her lightly. "But he will, my little omelette. Do not be anxious. He will. . . ."

The taxi drew to the kerb and Guy handed Alison in.

"Thirty-four Madison Street," he said to the man, and slammed the door and sat down.

"You remembered that, too," Alison said.

The street lamps, as they passed them, flitted over her face and her stockings, leaving her body in darkness. She sat far back in the seat, one hand on her lap, her legs crossed.

"Yes, I remembered," he said.

He was aware of the inside of the moving cab as it trundled them along the quiet streets. It enclosed the two of them in its own little world, shut off from all contact with the harsh, grating, difficult world outside. All ropes had been cut. All harbours left. Memory was dead and there was no future. There was only the padded upholstery of the seat and the pleasant swaying of the cab, and the lights passing over Alison's face and the slim line of her shin-bone.

'I'm the slightest bit drunk,' he said to himself and he remembered, from somewhere far away, that he'd had no lunch that day. He knew that being the slightest bit drunk meant something very important, but he was too pleasantly comfortable to remember what it was.

"It's been a lovely evening, Guy," Alison said, and her voice was part of the little world of the swaying cab and the flickering light and dark, something not quite real.

"You enjoyed it?"

"Yes. Oh *yes*. It was heaven."

"All this and heaven, too," he said, but the words were just words, without meaning. He'd heard them somewhere, at some time, back in the world of difficulty and things that were hard and rough and sharp-edged.

The car came to a halt at traffic lights. The round red eye beneath the black lid peered out at nothing. It winked shut and a yellow eye peered at nothing. He knew that it would change to green, and when it did he was pleased. 'The green eye of the little yellow god,' he thought, and he wanted to tell Alison, but it was too much trouble. Then the car went forward again, swaying gently through the night.

He felt a movement and Alison's hand lay on his knee. It made a little warm patch on his knee, white against the dark cloth, lightly curled fingers all close together on his knee.

"I don't want it to be over, Guy," he heard her say.

Dear little Alison. He thought how pleasant it would be to go to sleep.

He put his hand over hers. "We won't let it be over," he said, and his eyelids drooped. "We'll just go on like this for ever and ever and ever. . . ."

He was aware of her hand under his own and of his closed eyelids and of his head lolling gently against the upholstery as the cab swayed, but they were no longer separate actions but one action which took place on the very edge of great darkness.

"Darling . . ." he heard Alison say. "Such heaven. . . ."

He pressed his hand over hers and his head nodded forward. He lifted it up and laid it back against the upholstery again, smiling a little. The irresistible darkness reached out for him with great silent rubber hands. He was gathered into a point at which he was aware of his eyelids and his pursed mouth. If only they'd all leave him alone he would sleep.

The cab drew up. He came to the surface of the darkness and looked for the traffic-lights. There were none. There was only a street lamp, rather dimly burning, some distance down the road.

"Here we are," he heard Alison say, and he could have cried with vexation at the disturbance. It was such a shame. Such a *pitiable* shame. . . .

"Don't forget your hat, Guy."

He reached for his hat and put it on. The driver stretched his arm back and opened the door handle. The cool night air came about his head, and he knew they were in the street where Alison lived.

Alison . . .? Alison . . .?

Of course, yes. He'd met Alison and taken her out to dinner at The Black Scampi instead of going to . . .

"Eight and six, sir," the cabby said.

He fished some silver out of his pocket, put it back and took a note from his case.

"Good night," he said to the man and the cab moved off.

Alison stood looking up at him in the gloom. She barely reached his shoulder. What a little thing she was!

"Will you come up and have a drink, Guy?"

He knew there was a reason why he shouldn't go up and have a drink, but he couldn't remember what it was.

"It's only just nine," Alison said.

He was surprised. He'd thought it was midnight or past. Nine was nothing at all, he thought. Lots of people didn't have dinner till nine. Besides, Alison was his friend. He'd known her for years. Years and years.

"Just for ten minutes," he said. "Then I must go and . . ." He couldn't quite remember what it was he had to do, but he knew he ought not to delay it or he'd be too late.

She opened a lower door and he followed her along a hall and up two flights of stairs. She took a key from her bag and opened her flat door and switched on a light.

"It's altered a bit since you were here last," she said. "The chairs are new. And the sofa. And I had that striped wall-paper last year. Do you remember it, Guy?"

"Of course I remember it," he said. "It's a nice house."

She came and stood in front of him, looking up into his face. She was very close to him.

"Will you have whisky and soda?"

He looked down at her. He shook his head. He must, he told himself, wake up. He was so infernally sleepy.

"Oh, Guy. Darling," she said, and she put her hand on his. "It's been so long. . . ."

Once more the thing he'd got to do tugged at his mind, but he couldn't quite remember what it was. Alison's arm lay against the lapel of his coat, her hand touched the back of his head. He bent his head and kissed her.

They were sitting on the sofa and the light, which had been on, was off. She was warm and small and sweet, and he pressed his head down into the curve between her neck and shoulder. Her fingers passed over his lips. But there was something there, a thin probe of a thing, driving into his brain, spoiling the peace and the comfort. He made an effort to fend it off, but it returned, worrying away at him, taking his attention from Alison's lips and the warmth of her arms. For a second or so he eluded it and dropped down into a vibrant darkness, then he was aware of it again, stabbing away at him with a terrible urgency.

"Gina. . . ." It was as though a small, shrill voice had whispered the name from far away, up on a great height above him. "Gina. . . ."

He lay quite still. Gina. His thought cleared. Gina. He remembered that he'd been going to see the priest and then he'd met

Alison. Now he was in Alison's flat, and she'd turned the light off and . . .

He hardly breathed. This—*this* was what had happened to Gina, only Gina had . . . His mind was quite clear now. He knew exactly where he was, what he was doing. Everything, every movement was sharp-edged again; cold.

"Darling," said Alison. "Darling, what's the matter? Kiss me, Guy. . . . Kiss me. . . ."

He put his hands on her shoulders and eased her away from him.

"Why?" she cried. "Why? Guy, what is it?"

He spoke quickly, urgently.

"Alison, my dear. I can't. . . . I. . . . Listen, Alison. I must go. I'm terribly sorry. I've been idiotic. Wretched. You'll have to forgive me. . . ."

Her arms were round his neck. In the gloom he saw her face. It was puckered, distressed.

"What do you mean? You can't go, Guy, now. You can't. I love you. I've always loved you. . . . You can't go. Stay with me, Guy. Please. . . ."

The coldness in him had increased. Her clinging arms were like an octopus round him. The touch of her flesh sickened him faintly. He loosened her arms from round his neck and sat up.

"I must go, Alison. I really am desperately sorry, but I must go. I've got things to do. I'd forgotten, but . . ."

She had turned away from him, and her head was buried in a cushion. A light in a window opposite was switched on and the room glowed palely. She lifted her head and looked at him, her eyes narrowed.

"My God," she said. "You're pretty rotten, aren't you? It's a good moment to remember you're a married man, isn't it? I didn't ask you to take me out to dinner. I didn't ask you to——"

"Alison," he broke in. "I've told you—I'm sorry. I hadn't had any lunch and we had a good bit to drink, and——"

"Oh, get out," she said. "I can't stand any more. You come up here with me, you kiss me. You——"

"For Pete's sake, Alison——" he began.

"Get out," she repeated. "Go on, what are you waiting for?

There's the door. I hate men," she said. "They're all alike, every goddamned one. Selfish, smug as they come. . . ."

"You're being hysterical," he said coldly. "I've apologised."

She laughed. "Oh yes. You've apologised."

"What more do you want?" he said. "Don't let's quarrel, Alison."

"You, a coward," she said. "You." She turned away, her head down. "How they've changed you."

"Because I choose to be loyal to my wife?"

She looked up at him, nodding slightly as though making up her mind about something.

"Well," she said, "there goes the last dream."

He picked up his hat from the table.

"Good-bye, Alison," he said. "Shall I turn the light on?"

"No," she answered. "Go. That's all."

"I wish you understood," he said.

"I do," she answered. "That's the killing part of it. I do. I do."

"I didn't *want* it to be like this."

"Not again," she answered wearily. "I don't want to know. Go, that's all."

He walked to the door and opened it. The light from the hall fell directly on to her. She turned her head away.

"I'm sorry, Alison," he said again. "I can't say any more than that. Good night."

He closed the door again, opened the outer door, shut it and went down the stairs.

Out on the street in the cool night air he stopped and drew in deep breaths of the freshness. "Thank God," he kept saying to himself. "Thank God. Thank God."

He turned and began to walk up towards the High Street. What an escape! And he'd so nearly fallen. So damned nearly. If he had he'd never have forgiven himself. How infernally easy it was to slip into these things! And now, what? He looked at his watch beneath a street lamp. Half-past nine. He'd thought it was much later. It was too late for visiting anyone now, though—enquiry agent or priest. He stopped walking abruptly. If he'd stayed with Alison, he certainly couldn't have gone to an enquiry agent. He could hardly have set a man to spy on Gina when he himself. . . . He walked on, more slowly, and again he said, "Thank God. Thank God."

But what now? Was he going to let everything slip, let Gina go on with her *affaire* with Blake—if it was Blake—without lifting a finger to stop it? The frustration, which for a time he'd completely forgotten, came back. He must, he told himself, he absolutely must take some step that would set his mind at rest. He couldn't go on as he had been going on any longer. For him there was no question of divorce and re-marriage, but he'd rather live apart from Gina for the rest of his life than continue with this torturous suspicion.

He turned into the High Street, and stood on the edge of the kerb looking for a taxi to take him back to the garage behind his offices where his car was.

One thing only, he told himself, was clear at the moment, and that was that it was too late to do anything tonight but drive down to Ladysmere, have a bath and go to bed. And again he thought, "Suppose I'd stayed with her? Suppose I hadn't got out?" And it seemed to him that his escape was the luckiest thing that had ever happened to him.

There was still no taxi, and he turned to walk back to the bus-stop, too impatient to wait any longer. There was only one man waiting beneath the request sign, and he turned as Guy approached.

"Hello," he said. "Haven't seen you for a long time. Taylor, isn't it? What's happened to you?"

This, thought Guy, isn't true. It can't be happening. He put out his hand and said, "Nice to see you, Father. I was only thinking about you earlier in the day. I thought of coming to call on you."

"It's as well you didn't," the priest replied, "for I wasn't there. I'm on my way back now."

What was his name, Guy wondered. He knew it as well as he knew his own; had often talked to him when he lived in the flat. Then he remembered—Dolan. Father Dolan.

"I heard you'd been in the East," he was saying. "And you live down in the country now, they tell me."

"Yes . . ." Guy answered and a taxi came along. He signalled to it and said, "Let me give you a lift. There seems a dearth of buses tonight."

"You may," the priest answered, and he got into the car.

"The presbytery?" Guy asked and gave the address to the driver.

"What was it you wanted with me?" Father Dolan asked him.

"It's—I won't bother you tonight, Father," Guy answered. "It's too late. Perhaps you'd let me come one day when you've time."

"I've never time," came the faintly Irish voice out of the darkness beside him. "What's your trouble?"

Why had he mentioned that he intended calling on him, Guy wondered. Coming on him as he had, ten minutes after he'd left Alison, he'd been taken off his guard. Now the thought of talking about the whole wretched business seemed impossible. And yet he wanted to talk about it. He wanted someone to understand all he'd suffered. The humiliation, the pain. . . .

The taxi turned out of the High Street and thrust through smaller streets. It seemed that tonight he was fated to drive through the back streets of Kensington. The priest sat beside him in silence. He wished he'd give him a little encouragement. But he knew he wouldn't.

The taxi slowed down.

"It's my wife," Guy said. "She had another man's child while I was in Korea, and——"

The cab stopped. The priest sighed lightly.

"You'd best come in," he said.

"And so," Guy said, "she found a home for the child, a very good home, I understand, and I had her back. It wasn't easy to forgive, Father. As it happens, I was taken ill and for the first three weeks after she came back I was in a pretty low state. When I was fit enough we went to Cyprus and then to Rome. She seemed happy. She *was* happy. And I thought the whole thing was put behind us. But now, as I told you, I don't know where I am. Lately I've wondered if the whole story was a lie, that she invented the man's death and that she still sees him. I can't get any peace of mind, any rest. I've done everything I can for her. And I've never once mentioned the other man—never thrown him up at her, I mean. That's not self-praise, but—well, it *hasn't* always been easy."

He stopped, wishing again that he'd never begun; never run into the priest. He was suddenly deathly tired.

"I remember your wife," Father Dolan said. He nodded. "Yes, I remember well. It was a mixed marriage." He sighed lightly, and was silent, staring at the floor.

So it was going to be nothing but a theological scolding, thought Guy. Why had he imagined it would be anything else? It was always the same story. . . .

He looked at the priest's bending face, rugged, tired, a man as he was. What had he hoped for?

"Where did you say the child went?" Father Dolan asked suddenly, but he still kept his head lowered.

"My wife made the arrangements," Guy answered. "She preferred it that way."

"I see."

There was silence again, and Guy thought, 'I must get out of here. He doesn't understand. He can't begin to imagine what these things mean to a man.'

"To defend her and all that was hers," the priest was saying, in a quiet, almost sing-song tone. "That's what you promised, didn't you? All that was hers. . . ."

"It is what——" he began, and then he stopped. He leaned forward in the chair a little, but the priest still stared at the floor. "You don't mean that I—that I should have taken the child?"

There was no answer. No movement whatsoever in the little room.

"It wouldn't have been possible," he said coldly. "I thought of it. Of course I thought of it, but apart from ourselves and our hope of starting our lives together again, I knew from the child's angle alone that it would be impossible. Don't you see that it wouldn't have been *fair* to him?"

"And why not?"

"Because . . ." Guy began. He took his cigarette-case from his pocket. "May I smoke, Father?" He lighted his cigarette and put the match in an ashtray. "I was afraid," he said, "that every time I saw him I'd remember. I wanted to forgive my wife wholly. I wanted to put the entire thing behind us. She saw that. She understood it. She agreed with it. The boy is happy where he is. Don't you see how impossible it would have been?"

"No," Father Dolan answered. And then he drew a breath and looked up and straight at Guy. Guy met his glance and he wouldn't interpret it. There was something behind it that hadn't a name. Something you couldn't label.

"Hard," the priest went on, "but not impossible. Why do you, of all men, shirk the hard way?"

"The child," said Guy again. "Don't you see what the effect would have been on him? How could I have taken him as my own?"

"You couldn't, not in your own strength. Do you think Our Lord wouldn't have rewarded you for such a gesture to one of His children? Ah yes. It's where the trouble lies," he added.

"You mean my wife wants him?"

"I should imagine so."

"But surely she'd want to forget the whole thing, wouldn't she? Wouldn't the baby be a constant reminder? Mightn't she have resented him in the end? She told me she didn't love this man; that the whole thing was a moment of—excitement, delirium almost. Surely the presence of the baby would have been a perpetual—sort of sore."

"Do you think that 'sore' as you call it can heal just because she doesn't see the child? He's still a living soul. Hiding the evidence away doesn't get rid of the fact." Again he sighed lightly. "If the child is legally adopted there's little you can do about it. You'll need to pray hard and you'll need great patience. And great charity."

"I've had great patience——"

"No. You've only had some patience. You'll need to pray for a lot more yet. These things aren't settled in a month or two. Or a year or two. You can't rush them. I'm not, mind you, minimising your own part in the sorry business. Human nature finds those things hard to forgive, I know that. But forgiveness is never a matter of five minutes. It has to be lived out, day by day; hour by hour very often. You'll have to come back to Our Lord in the Blessed Sacrament to give you the help you need for it, won't you? Where else are you to get it? You've tried, so you say, for six months in your own strength, and it hasn't got you very far. I'm not surprised. Nor are you, really, or you wouldn't be sitting in that chair. You know as well as I know myself that there's only one thing to do with a situation of this kind, and that is to put it into God's hands. Doubly so in your case, for your wife, poor soul, hasn't come to it herself yet. Even your forgiveness won't get you far, if you haven't His charity in you. . . ."

And that, thought Guy, driving back to Ladysmere, is that. "Take it to God. . . ." "Go back to the Church. . . ." "Say your prayers. . . ." While Gina and Blake went on having a whale of a time, free as the air. What had he hoped for? It was hardly likely that the priest would have said, "If I were you I'd have her watched. She's evidently playing you up again. . . ." But what had he meant about the child? If giving up the baby was the cause of Gina's behaviour, then all he could say was that she must have loved its father far more than she'd ever loved him. Had she lied about that, too? Yet if that were the answer, why in heaven's name did she come back to him?

It was no good. He'd have to end this torture and find out the truth if it killed him. And the only way to find out the truth was to have her watched.

It wasn't till he was almost home that he remembered Alison and his relief when he found himself outside her flat in the cool night air, and again he muttered, "Thank God. Thank God."

He ought, he supposed, to have mentioned that lapse to Father Dolan, but he'd make a confession of it at a later date. After all, he'd only had a talk with him.

And while he drove and thought, Alison, the rags of humiliation clutched round her, lay in bed watching the memory of the years she had known him become soiled, bitter, something to be remembered, now, only with pain.

He turned into the gates and was surprised to see the drawing-room light still on. He wondered, for a moment of fear, if Blake, thinking that he wasn't coming home, was with Gina. If he was, they'd hear the car and be prepared with their excuses. Gina, he knew it, would be coolly self-possessed, while Blake would put up a screen of his insufferable medical jargon. He wished he'd thought to run down the hill without the engine on, so that he could have surprised them. Why did he hope to find her in Blake's arms? So that he could, at last, find out who this man was who was taking her from him? What else?

He walked up the steps and opened the door. As he shut it again, the drawing-room door opened and Gina stood there. She wore one of her Italian dresses, and in spite of the late hour, looked as though she had just come down from her bedroom.

"Stag party?" she asked lightly, and he knew that she was ready to be kind again. But he couldn't respond. She was turning him into a weakling, a fool, with her deceptions and moods. "You'll need to pray for a lot more patience yet. . . ." The priest's voice rang faintly in his head. He brushed it away, almost disappointed that he hadn't caught her with Blake.

"I was delayed," he answered coldly. "I asked them to telephone you."

She smiled. "You didn't imagine for one moment that Miss Pangle had failed you, did you? How's the dear girl?"

He walked into the drawing-room. A table was drawn up to the fire. There were plates of sandwiches on a lace cloth, glasses, a bottle of champagne.

He frowned.

"Is this in my honour?"

"Not entirely."

"Someone been in?"

He flicked a glance to the windows. Had Blake slipped out as he opened the door?

"Oh no," Gina answered casually. "It's just an occasion." She put her hand on the bottle. "I think it's all right. I've had it on the ice. The sandwiches are good—paté. I got it this afternoon from a little place in Soho."

Soho. The Black Scampi. Alison. . . . But he hadn't stayed. He'd got out.

"You open it," Gina said, and handed him a napkin.

He didn't take the bottle. "What *is* all this?" he asked.

He saw her standing there, vivid, beautiful, her lovely eyes lighted. He tried to shut her out from his mind, from his heart. It was only the same old act over again. He felt himself succumbing to it. He wanted to succumb to it. He wanted to take her into his arms. To crush her to him.

"We're going to have a baby," she said.

He stared at her. She was laughing.

"What do you mean?" he asked.

"I mean what I say. We're going to have a baby." She held out the bottle of champagne. "Do take it, Guy. I feel such an idiot standing here grasping it by the neck and saying 'Baby'."

He took the bottle and put it on the table.

"How do you know?" he asked shortly.

"By the usual natural signs," she answered. "And today I got my guess checked up. No, I didn't go to Philip. I went to London, to a man I used to go to occasionally in Chelsea. I paid him a guinea to tell me what I could have told him. Guy, isn't it extraordinary? After all this time. . . . You're glad. Aren't you?"

He didn't know what he was. Glad, sorry; weak, strong; evil, good—nothing made sense. A baby. But whose? Blake's? Some other man's? The father of her first child? *Her first child.* This wasn't her first child. It was her second child. *Was* it his?

She was looking directly at him. Her eyes were steady as the sky. He'd swear she wasn't lying this time.

"I've been a bit touchy this week," she was saying, "and that's the reason. It makes you. It's rather as though you were going round one way and the world another. Very confusing. Guy, you are glad, aren't you?"

He *was* glad, wasn't he? Suppose that it had been her first child? Their first child? My daughter. . . . He saw a shadowy figure in a rapid sequence of pictures . . . an infant in diminutive filmy dresses; composed and grave at her first Communion; a grinning school-girl; swirling lightly round a dance-floor, laughing over her shoulder. . . . My daughter. But Gina had already had a child. There'd be nothing new in it for her, no first experience they could share. Gina knew the ropes.

"Guy!" she said again.

"I'm sorry," he answered. "I'm a bit stunned, I think. It's rather—unexpected."

"I nearly told you a couple of days ago," she said, "but I thought I'd better make certain first." She took a couple of steps towards him and stood within six inches of him. He thought her skin looked translucent, as though there was a light behind it.

"I want it so much," she said, and he thought he had never heard her speak so quietly.

Suspicion, torture of mind eased. He felt desperately tired again, as though the weight of the confusing day were too unwieldy a burden for him to carry any longer.

He wanted to believe her. He wanted it more than anything in the world. He wanted the ease of her arms, and to lay down all the distrust and torment and bury his head in the curve between her neck and shoulder.

He held out his arms.

Chapter VII

"I DON'T understand women," Philip said.

Gina laughed. "You, talking in clichés!"

Philip frowned. "There's nothing else to talk in on occasion. It's all been said before. I can't see how you could even have come to consider that I should attend you."

"It doesn't appear very complicated to me," Gina answered easily. "You were with me when I had Christopher. But why the argument? I merely said that I wished I could have had you. I can't and that's the end of it."

"The suggestion's indecent," said Philip. "How did Guy take it?"

Gina didn't answer immediately. He watched her expression alter, and after a few moments she leaned her head back against the chair. "If only it had happened when we were first married. Why didn't it, Philip?"

"My dear, I don't know. No one knows. It really is 'one of those things'."

"It seems so damnably unfair," she said. "I wanted a child of his. I did, you know."

He nodded but didn't say anything.

"If I say," she went on, "that I wish with all my heart that this was my first child, then I wish Christopher away. I send him back to being 'nothing', don't I? And I can't do that. I still love him, though I never see him. That's not quite true. I have seen him. . . ."

"What do you mean?" Philip asked sharply. "Gina, you've not——"

"Oh no! I've kept the rules. Don't fuss. But I did see him. I was in London one day and I drove round to Onslow Square. I don't quite know what I intended to do, but I went. I had to go. I parked my car opposite the house, and a few minutes later the nurse brought him out." Her eyes narrowed. "He was sitting up in a pram and he called good-bye to Jennifer."

Philip lowered his head. His hand reached out for the pen on his desk.

"It wasn't a very prudent thing to do, was it?"

"Prudence!" she scorned. "What's prudence to do with love? With hunger, then?" She slumped back in the chair. "No one knew," she said quietly. "Just—another car, pulled up in the square for ten minutes. He'd grown," she added.

"This masochism——" Philip muttered.

He heard her light laugh. "Oh, come, Philip——"

"It is," he insisted. "You never will leave the thing alone. Never will give yourself a chance."

"I've had my chance thrust upon me now," she answered. "I expect it'll be the answer, don't you, Philip?"

"How do I know if it will be the answer?"

"It would be nice if it were," she said. "I might even come to forget Christopher, mightn't I?"

It was what he had been hoping himself, ever since she had walked into the surgery and told him. So often, if a child had died, he'd advised the parents to have another as soon as possible. This was the thing he'd prayed for for her.

"One baby's as good as another," he heard her say. "That's what they tell you, isn't it?"

The remark was a caricature of his own thinking. Didn't he know that none of the clap-trap arguments would do for her, and Christopher, he must remember, was not dead but very much alive.

"I asked you," he said, "how Guy felt about it."

"I think he was reminding himself that this wasn't my first child. I think, for one moment, he wondered if it was merely another adultery on my part."

"Oh no. . . ." The cry broke through his habitual control before he realised it.

"One could hardly blame him," she said slowly. "You never get let off anything, do you? Do you remember when we were driving back from the Mostyns the night after we'd taken Christopher up there I said that to you and you answered, 'It's because we're dealing in flesh and blood, I suppose. In human souls, if you believe that way. . . .' I've thought of that so much during the last few weeks.

I—couldn't face it at the time, but I know now that it's true. That's why I can't bring myself to say I wish Christopher had never been born. And yet, for this child's sake, for Guy's sake, I want to say it. I want to repay Guy with this baby. I want to give myself wholly to it, even now while it's in my womb and I want it to be, what's the word, 'clear-hearted', untouched by any backwash of all that other pain. . . . And yet if only he were here, too," she said, and she covered her eyes. "If only it were the four of us. . . ."

The months passed swiftly through summer to autumn.

This child's coming was like, yet totally unlike, Christopher's coming, thought Gina. There was no hole-and-corner existence in Dardanella's flat; no remorse; no isolation. She had every comfort, every attention and she could walk proudly. And yet the very difference turned her thoughts to Christopher with grief—the one child so longed for, so certain of welcome and home; the other a burden, something to be hurried out of sight. Yet both her children. That she was exaggerating Christopher's position, she knew. He had been 'hurried out of sight', but into care and happiness and love. He didn't know, he possibly never would know, the details of his birth. If, in later years, the Mostyns told him that he was not their own son, they would certainly not tell him any more than that.

Guy, during those months, alternated between delight and suspicion.

Frequently, driving down from London he had imaginary conversations with his daughter—that the child would be a girl he never for a moment doubted. Sometimes she appeared as an infant, sometimes as an adolescent, but always she looked at him with adoring eyes, and between them was a bond strong as steel.

But there were times when suspicion uncoiled in his mind again. Was the child his? He searched Gina's face for the trace of a lie and could find none. But what, he asked himself, did that signify? He remembered when he'd gone over to the flat at Melford expecting to find her soiled-looking and ashamed. But she hadn't been either.

Or was it that she hadn't shown either in her expression? Gina, he must remember, was an actress. She had, too, been through this before. She would be on her guard, quick to pull the wool over his eyes. Even he would be unable to prove that the child was his unless he chose to go through all the sordid paraphernalia of tests. He wouldn't be able to prove it, but he swore by every movement of his blood and beat of his heart that he would know.

During that period one or two of his friends came down, and one night J. B. Harris and Sir James dined with them.

A cook and a parlourmaid had now taken Bessie's place, and the meal was without fault. The garden which Gina had begun had been taken over by a full-time gardener and a boy, and on that evening was looking delightful.

"I congratulate you," J. B. said as he walked beside her towards the rose-garden. "Guy tells me that you designed the entire place yourself."

From ahead of them, where Guy and Sir James paced with slow deliberation, there came a thread of cigar smoke drifting back on the still air. A swift memory of her father slipped into her mind and passed.

"The foundations were there," she said to J. B. "It was more a question of reshuffling than reconstructing. The rose-garden's new, though. There were only one or two pretty poor specimens, and we threw them out. I'm particular about roses."

"You have discrimination," he said, and again she wondered if he were sincere or merely an adept at using the right word.

"I should like to think so," she answered coolly.

He stopped walking and stood still, then turned and surveyed both the house and the land, as though assessing its value. The lights were on in the ground floor of the house, shining out into the approaching dusk, giving the lovely Queen Anne building the appearance of a steady ship ploughing through the waters, not of the sea but of time.

J. B. nodded, as though he had reached a silent conclusion of his own. Then he looked up at her.

"It is the place for children," he said. He turned again and waved his hand—more delicate-looking than ever beneath the black sleeve of his dinner-jacket. "Nurseries, stables, tennis-courts; ponies in the paddock. . . ." He smiled. "Your stage is set. The actors wait in the wings for their cue. . . ."

She thought of the shadowy forms of unborn children who stood on the edge of life waiting to be let in. Then she caught sight of his hand, and she wondered if it was his small hand which had manipulated the events which had led to this child's coming, too.

"Guy," he was saying, "told me that you were to have a child." He gave her a look which pierced her like a probe. She fancied that it thrust through to flick at the secret of Christopher lying at the base of memory. "A first child," he said, "is an exciting occurrence. He'll be all right now," he added, inclining his head towards Guy.

Had she imagined that slight accent on the word 'first'? Was there anything that silent, cunning brain did not know?

"It is good for a man like Guy to found a family," he said. "An heir to inherit the title. . . ."

His words slipped past her notice, then returned. She frowned. Had Guy been hoodwinking him? But the bright red lips between the white beard were parted in the first defined smile she had seen on his face. "It will come," he told her. "Mark my words—it will come."

She lunched one day at The Black Scampi. She was early and there were only a few people in the dining-room. There was no sign of Carrie, and she wondered whether to ask the waiter for her and decided not to. But Carrie came down the steps from the raised part of the room as she was finishing her meal, and she saw her and came to her table.

"Well! Whyever didn't you tell me you were coming?" She flicked a look at her plate. "What have you had? If that darned Achille hasn't served you well, I'll slit his throat. You have to watch them," she added.

"It was delicious," said Gina. "I was this way, and I needed lunch, so I came in."

Carrie nodded, eyeing her. "I've been wondering if you would. How's life?"

"Fine," Gina answered. "And yours?"

"Like an escalator," said Carrie. "You just stand on and you get to the top. Art's thinking about opening up another place; only he's afraid, as there aren't two of him, it mightn't go so good. These food men!" she added. "Talk about rogues! Never known anything like it. Wouldn't stop at murder. And they'd serve their victim's liver up the next day and call it 'Pagliacci' or something. The worst you ever came on in show business were little frolicsome lambs beside them. You never came up to see Meg's play," she said. "I didn't think you would. It's still pulling them in. Always got the Full House notice up if you pass the Sheridan. Even the Press boys couldn't find anything to tear at in it. Did you know Anna's gone into films? I met Nan Theobald the other day in The Avenue, and she said she was playing a bee-utiful spy in a Yank thriller."

"Born for it!" said Gina. "Couldn't have thought up anything better for her myself. Those American casting men have genius, haven't they? Her hair will come in handy, too."

"Oh, she's cut that off," said Carrie. "And dyed it flaming red. Looks queer."

"I can imagine that it might," Gina answered, and Carrie said, "There's Art." She raised her right hand, an outsize emerald ring and two bracelets, and he came over.

Black-haired, black-eyed, taut and with a virility, thought Gina, that knocked you sideways. He flashed gold-stopped teeth at her. He waved his brown, strong hands. He shrugged his square shoulders. He beamed possessively down at the top of Carrie's head, and he, too, inspected her empty plate with a frown.

"All went well? You like your Fetuccini? It was good, eh? But you had no wine! Oh, signora, that was not clever. My Fetuccini is married to chianti. The one cannot live without the other." He turned to Carrie. "Why did you not tell me your friend came? Will you always shame Arturo Marienza? Now she must have—let me see—yes, I think Crêpe Scampi Noire. And afterwards a coffee and cognac." He bowed. "With my compliments, madame." He whisked away and Carrie smiled dreamily.

"Isn't he a piece?" she said. "He's always like that. Hardly ever loses his temper—only with the boys. And then it's all up and over.

I wouldn't go back to show business for all the tea in China." She looked towards Art's back. "He's small," she added, "but he's got what it takes."

And what he'd got had certainly taken Carrie along with it, thought Gina. That emerald hadn't come out of a ten-cent store.

The waiter served her, and she put her fork to the little fat pancake.

"Good?" Carrie prompted.

"Wonderful. But what is it? What's the filling?"

"They all ask that," answered Carrie smugly. "Art invented it. Not even the chef knows. It's a winner, isn't it?"

"Delicious."

Carrie looked at her, her eyes the merest fraction narrowed. "I was surprised to see your husband here that night," she said. "I didn't know you knew Alison Blair."

Gina's 'sixth sense' of danger flipped its red signal. She took a second or two longer to swallow the mouthful of pancake. "I don't know her," she said. "She's an old friend of Guy's. He knew her before he met me."

Who, she wondered, was Alison Blair? And when had Guy brought her here?

"I thought they looked as though they were old friends," Carrie was saying, and Gina knew her far too well to miss the innuendo. It positively shrieked its presence. Guy—and another woman. It was oddly unfamiliar. Incongruous almost. She couldn't quite believe it. "I didn't know who she was at the time," Carrie was saying. "Then about three weeks later she came in with another man. A pretty ropey-looking piece, too. Nan was in while they were here with Toby Wayne. I saw Nan smile at her so I went over and asked her who she was and Nan said, 'Oh, that's Alison Blair. Used to model for Barrenza till she couldn't say no to the cream cakes. Now she sells dresses at Marianne's.' You know," Carrie went on, "that little swank shop near Harrods. She didn't quite look your style, though." She laughed a little. "Thought your self-made man was making a bit on the side," she added.

"Possibly," said Gina lightly. And then, "I believe she's rather a nice creature," she gagged, thinking up the words as she went along. "Guy knew her when they were children, and I hate the thought of his giving up his old friends."

She took a quick glance at Carrie, but Carrie shrugged her shoulders. "Sounds a bit silly to me. If Art wants to take any Lollobrigidas that he knew back in dear old Milano out to dinner, I'll see I go, too. There isn't a man on the face of the earth that I'd trust around the corner of a plate-glass house," she said, and Art, with an attendant waiter bearing the coffee, swept down on them, cognac in hand.

Driving back towards Knightsbridge, Gina was surprised at the jealousy which plagued her. Who was this Alison Blair? What was she to do with Guy? A model, or rather an ex-model who couldn't say 'no' to the cream cakes. There was something in that expression which was nauseatingly suggestive—some hint of a desirous obesity. She'd never given a thought to 'another woman' where Guy was concerned. When she'd first met him she had, because then every woman he'd ever known, besides those he knew then, was a potential danger; but once she realised that it was she whom he loved, the other women had faded into the background. Arrogance? she asked herself. It looked like it. But there was, too, trust and the knowledge that he loved her. Her inward smile was twisted. That's how it had been for him, too. Until Korea and Andrew Wharton. Who was she to blame him for taking Alison Blair out to dinner? But why take her to The Scampi? He knew that Carrie was there. Or didn't he? The day she'd met Carrie in London and Carrie had told her that she was out of 'show business' and in food, was the day she'd driven round to Onslow Square and seen Christopher. Perhaps she hadn't told Guy about Carrie. Was she making a mountain out of a molehill? Why shouldn't he take a woman out to dinner if he wanted to? Was she going to develop into one of those wives who spied on their husband's every moment away from them? God forbid. But if only he had told her! Would men never understand that a woman would accept almost anything from them if they told them the truth about it? They so seldom did. They lied or stalled or kept silent, never realising that when, inevitably, the woman either 'sensed' or found out in some other way, the humiliation was far more difficult to endure than a swift pang of disappointment or jealousy. But the old game of 'hide and seek' went on, and suspicion took the place of trust. And that was the beginning of the end.

She parked the car and walked down past Harrods.

Marianne. The name was written above the window. There was the usual model dress; the usual bowl of flowers; the usual air of slightly strained elegance. She looked at the dress. It didn't attract her. She walked back to the door, opened it and her footsteps fell suddenly silent on the thick carpet.

A girl came from behind a red curtain. She was tall, slim and the mascara was thick on her eyelashes. She looked like every other girl who was learning to sell dresses in 'little' dress shops.

"The dress in the window . . ." said Gina, and she thought, 'I am a fool. What do I hope to get out of this?' "What size is it?" she asked the girl.

"One moment, madam." The words minced through the girl's disastrously red lips. She tippetted back through the curtain on her high heels, hips swaying.

The sound of discreet voices mixed with the smell of silk and the faint scent of the flowers in the window. The curtain parted again and the *vendeuse* came through. She was small and rounded. Dark hair was taken back from her ears and forehead. Her eyes were a peculiarly brilliant blue.

She smiled. It was a wholly professional smile which parted her lips and fluttered her lids, but there was no warmth whatsoever in it. Once, long ago, she had been instructed to smile at the customers. She had, obviously, never forgotten her training.

"You were asking about the little model in the window, madam? It's a Feltin. A lovely dress. Would you like me to have it taken out for you?"

Gina saw the swift glance that passed over her own clothes—a glance which took in make, price, quality in the flick of the bright blue eye.

"I asked what size it is," she answered coolly, and she wondered what in the name of nonsense Guy found in this rather tired-looking little woman with plucked eyebrows.

The blue eyes were regarding her again, running their inch-tape over her. She smiled. "No. It's not for me. I'm not wearing model dresses at the moment."

"No, madam." The words were non-committal but, for a split second, warmth came into the expression. "It is on the small side," the just off-key voice went on. "It was designed for a twenty-four waist and thirty-two bust."

"That is diminutive. How much is it?"

"Forty guineas, madam."

She waited, wondering what else she could say. "Do you have other Feltin models?" she asked. "I want to get one after my child is born. I like his designs."

"Oh yes, madam. They're all the originals of course. We don't stock the copies. The dress in the window is less expensive than usual because it is particularly petite. The cocktail dresses are generally about sixty guineas."

Did she, Gina wondered, entertain Guy with her 'particularly petite' talk? Did she wear her little black silk 'uniform' dress when she sat opposite him at a table in The Black Scampi? It was all so ridiculous that she wanted to laugh. She wondered what the woman would say if she suddenly touched her shoulder and said, "Know who I am? I'm Gina Taylor, and I'm consumed with curiosity to know what happened the night you dined with my husband in Soho."

"Thank you," she said. "I'll come in again later on. I'm afraid the dress you are showing wouldn't suit my purpose."

The little woman walked to the door with her and opened it. The smile was switched on again. The head tilted just slightly to the side in a 'fetching' gesture. "Good afternoon, madam."

So that was Guy's 'young woman'! How odd it would be if, in her gagging to Carrie, she'd hit on the truth and that she had been a friend of his childhood! Nothing on earth would induce her to believe that Guy was in love with the *passé* little soul. And yet—why the dinner at The Black Scampi? Why Carrie's unsubtle innuendo? Why tell her about it?

There was only one way to have those questions answered, and that was to ask Guy. The thing which, she knew it, she would never bring herself to do.

Two days before the baby was due to be born she went to the nursing home. Twenty-four hours later labour began. At the height of pain, when only one small circle of normality remained to her, a voice shouted as though through a megaphone, "I'm paying the debt, Guy. I'm paying the debt. This is for you. For you. . . ." And at the apex of what seemed a dissolution of her entire being, just before they gave her ether, for the birth was difficult, she cried, "Christopher. Christopher. Oh God, don't let them take him. . . ."

Guy received the news at his office. Miss Pangle's tones, controlled as usual, came from the receiver. "The Matron of the Pitt's-Reeves Nursing Home, Mr. Taylor. Will you speak to her?"

"Of course I'll speak to her. . . ."

A click in his ear interrupted his irritation, and a high, precise voice said, "Mr. Taylor? The Matron of the Pitt's-Reeves Nursing Home here. I am happy to tell you that you have a lovely little girl. She was——"

He was trembling and he felt slightly sick. He realised that an inane grin which he couldn't control was stretched across his mouth.

"I didn't hear what you said," he stuttered.

"I said that you have a daughter," the voice repeated as though it were speaking to an imbecile. "I——"

"Yes, yes," he interrupted. "I heard that. I didn't hear the next sentence. . . ."

"I said she was born half an hour ago and is in fine condition. She weighs six and three-quarter pounds, and——"

"My wife?" he broke in.

"A little exhausted," the voice answered. "She is sleeping now. She will be much better when she wakes up. She had rather a difficult labour."

"You don't mean——"

"I mean nothing but that," came back the voice. "Everything is quite in order, but your wife is, as I say, a little exhausted."

"When can I come round?" he asked.

"I should like you to leave it until—say—six-thirty, if you would, Mr. Taylor. This first sleep is so important."

"Yes. Yes. Of course. I understand that. You're sure she *is* all right?"

"Perfectly sure. There is absolutely no cause for concern, let alone anxiety. We shall expect you at six-thirty, then?"

He rang up the florist and ordered flowers. He worked till five, and was still working at a quarter to six when his brain refused to answer his will any longer and he went into his cloakroom, washed, combed his hair and, for the first time, dared to think.

'My daughter.' He'd known it would be a girl. Once Gina had said to him, "Guy, you must stop concentrating on this 'daughter' idea. If the poor little soul turns out to be a boy, he'll be so effeminate you'll loathe him." He hadn't been concerned. He'd known. He stood with the towel in his hands, pressing back the quicks of his nails. The fleeting pictures came back, came between him and his fingers—the small shy child, the laughing girl, the swaying dancing figure in a swirling dress. . . .

The towel was stationary in his hand. He stood very still with constricted throat.

Hoskins beamed as he went through the hall.

"Congratulations, sir. Very glad it's all over, and I'm sure you are."

"Thanks, Hoskins. I am."

"Going round to the nursing home, sir?"

He looked at his watch. "Very soon now."

"Ah, you'll feel better when you've seen them," said Hoskins. "It's an anxious time. Never mind. Over now. I'd like to send Mrs. Taylor my best wishes, sir."

"Thanks, Hoskins. I'll tell her. Good night."

Out into the rain-swept street. He hadn't realised it was raining. Just time for a drink. He needed it. Ten minutes and then he could start off.

He was driving down Park Lane when he thought, 'What if it isn't my child?' It must be his child. Gina couldn't have done that to him. Why not? She'd done it before. But even then she hadn't tried to father the baby on to him. It would have been a tricky matter with himself in Korea. This time he'd been in England. Would he know? He'd felt so sure that he would, but now he wondered.

One baby was very like another. There were cases on record where mistakes had been made and women had been given the wrong child. But the women, rightly or wrongly, usually claimed that they had been aware of the exchange. Suppose he took one look at the child and was certain that it was not his? What was he going to do? He couldn't stand it again. He couldn't. No man could. A picture of Philip Blake's face swung into his memory, each feature delineated and clear. Dear heaven, why did he have to think of him now? He didn't want to think of him. He wanted to throw all doubt from his mind; but the doubt was there. It couldn't be moved, because Gina had had another child before this child.

He turned into Portland Place; came down into Devonshire Street. The dash-board clock showed twenty-eight minutes past six. As the minute hand covered the hour hand he drew up at the nursing home.

There was a shaded table-lamp on a polished table in the bedroom. There were his flowers. And Gina was lying back on half a dozen pillows. She looked almost too beautiful, too frail to approach. The nurse clicked the door to behind her and he stood quite still.

"Hello," she said.

He closed his eyes and opened them again. She held out her hand—it was white and thin as though she had had a long illness. "Nice flowers," she said.

He took a couple of steps forward and held her hand. He stood there, holding it, not saying anything.

"Dumb," she whispered. "Fair struck dumb. Not a word?"

He shook his head. "Are you all right?"

She nodded. "Steam-roller over my middle. All right, though. I wanted you."

He felt the tears in his eyes. To hide them, he knelt by the bed and put his head down against the sheet.

"Darling," said Gina and her hand came down on his hair. "Kid from the ironmonger's shop . . . who's got a daughter?"

Gina reached up and pressed the bulb of the bell. In two minutes

—three—he would see the baby. It must be his daughter. This—this moment, Gina, all of it—couldn't be false, a lie. He was more afraid than he'd ever been in his life. If he could have run away he would have run away—gone steaming out and down the steps and on into the night.

The door opened and the Matron stood there with the bundle in her arms. An unseen presence closed the door and she came into the room.

"Congratulations, Mr. Taylor," came the high, child's voice of the telephone. "She's a darling. . . . I'll put the other light on so that you can see her properly."

A second light came on. The Matron said, "Will you take her, Mrs. Taylor, or would you rather rest?"

"I'm off babies tonight," Gina answered in her tired voice. "You'd better introduce them. He's an awful stickler for convention."

"Now then, Miss Taylor . . ." said the Matron, and she eased the shawl from the baby's head.

Would he know? Would he? He'd been so sure he would. If only he could run away, keep on running. Running and running. . . .

"Your father . . ." came the high, precise voice.

He'd got to move two steps forward. It was not only essential, it was inevitable. He could not escape the movement. It was predestined, as sure as death.

"I believe you're scared . . ." came Gina's voice behind him.

He took the steps.

"There," said the Matron, as though she had just had the baby made to specification in the theatre. "Isn't she beautiful?"

He looked down and, lying against her arm, he saw a red, crumpled, wrinkled caricature, not of himself, not of Gina, not even of his mother or his father, but of his Uncle Ernest who used to keep a second-hand junk-shop in the Lanes at Brighton.

Chapter VIII

GINA was sitting in a chair by the fire, her legs crossed, one hand behind her head.

She smiled and held out her hand.

"You don't have to creep. You can enter to a fanfare of trumpets if you like. You've been reinstated."

Philip frowned suspiciously. "Why?"

"Canon," she said. "Hair-oil. I told Guy that I categorically refused to have anyone but you to come to my daughter, should she —God forbid—need medical attention. Guy agreed."

"Reluctantly," he added.

"Well—without alacrity."

"And if I refuse?"

"You won't. . . . Philip, it is nice to see you."

"You're looking well."

She made a little grimace.

"I didn't enjoy it. It was all much more unpleasant than when I had Christopher. But you were there then."

"Don't be absurd."

"I'm not. I'm being factual. I didn't feel 'at home' at that wretched place and was consequently far more tense."

He smiled. "You'd find a reason for a pig flying."

"It's true."

"Very well. It's true. Where's my patient?"

"Outside in her baby-carriage. They'll be bringing her in in a few moments."

"And Guy?" he asked.

"Besotted. Besotted past all the bounds of reason. He's a man obsessed. He wanted a girl so much that, if she'd been a boy I veritably believe I'd have crawled out of that classy nursing home before he arrived, weak as I was. He adores her."

He waited but didn't say anything. Was it going to be the answer, after all? A moment ago she'd mentioned Christopher's name casually, slipped it into a sentence without apparent thought. It was the first time she had ever done that.

"She is rather a pet," she was saying. "Her features are quite 'formed', not a bit putty-like."

"I've heard that said, by mothers, before," he teased gently.

"Snob!" she answered.

"What are you calling her?"

"Caroline. It's Guy's choice. She is being baptised in a couple of days' time."

"Here?"

"No, in London. Guy wanted the priest who married us to baptise her."

"Nice name," he said.

"You think?" She smiled. "If Guy had wanted her called Dardanella, I don't believe I'd have uttered." She sighed lightly. "She really has 'done something' to him, Philip. If I weren't so thankful, I'd be jealous." She smiled. "When Guy first saw her, he said she was the image of his Uncle Ernest. Can you beat that?"

"I only trust that she won't remain like his Uncle Ernest, unless——"

The door opened and the nurse was there with the baby.

"Leave her, will you, Nanny. I'll ring when I want you to fetch her."

"Nice?" said Gina when the door had closed behind her.

Philip looked down on Caroline. Her eyes were open. She moved her mouth like an old woman.

"She is like Uncle Ernest!" he said. He remembered the first time he had seen Gina with Christopher—her large, still frightened eyes; the marks of anguish on her face. He remembered the little shabby flat over the tobacconist's; the shunting of the trains; the muted sounds of traffic on the main arterial road. And now this odd little scrap of life, he thought. The burden of all that hung on it seemed too heavy for its diminutive person to bear. He wanted to lift it from her; to let her sail free.

"You're feeding her?" he asked Gina.

"Oh yes."

He nodded. "She looks fine."

"She hasn't been vaccinated."

"We'll see to that."

Would she, could she, he wondered, bridge this gap? He pictured her holding out her tiny arms, taking the strain, transmuting by some almost mystical quality in herself, the other tragedy into peace. Stretched on a cross? Weren't we all? He touched her head lightly with his fingers.

The nurse came and took her away again. He looked at his watch. "I must go."

"Philip?" Gina said.

He knew what was coming and he wanted to fend it off.

"Please tell me about Christopher," she said quite calmly. "Is all well?"

There was no need to speak of Jennifer's illness, he decided. It was over now and she was getting about again.

"All's very well," he answered.

She nodded.

"But they're still agitating to get the adoption legalised," he said. "They want to enter him for a school and so on. Think about it when you can, will you?"

He was standing up and couldn't see her face. He heard her say:

"My blood flows in Christopher as it does in Caroline. They ought to be together."

"I'm afraid that's out of the question."

"I wish I could believe you. I can't."

"Perhaps because you won't face it."

"So easy," she murmured. "So easy to say, so hard to do."

"Caroline . . .?" he suggested.

She nodded. "Yes. Caroline. . . ."

"Don't thrash yourself over it now." He put his hand on her shoulder. "I promise you that once you've made the final break you'll feel better about it. I promise you . . ." he repeated.

Chapter IX

GUY said good-bye to J. B. Harris, Sir James and Lord Harben in the vestibule of Claridges just as Waters drove up with his car. The timing was exact.

"The office," he said to Waters, and he leaned back against the upholstery, a slight smile in his eyes, as the car moved off.

Everything was going very nicely. Very nicely indeed. Harben, like himself, had started from scratch, but while he knew that Harben had started from scratch, he didn't know if Harben knew that he had.

He thought of him as the car was caught in a block at Hyde Park Corner. For all his peerage and his success, Harben shouted aloud his origins. He gestured with his short fat hands. His voice had a rasp in it and was too loud. Remove his suit—or even leave it on—and you could have seen his jowled face peering at you over a grubby knotted scarf behind any stall in Petticoat Lane on any Sunday morning.

The luncheon party could so easily have divided itself into two halves—J. B. and Sir James with their Plantagenet pedigrees on the one hand and himself and Harben on the other. But that hadn't been the idea. The idea had been a trio, J. B., Sir James and himself on the one hand and Harben on the other. The idea had been carried out.

It was curious, he thought, how a man like Harben had reached the heights he had—and you'd got to hand it to his brains, will-power and genius for engineering—without making an effort to acquire any of the outward marks of a higher society on his way up. Didn't the man hear that his accent was wrong? Didn't he notice other people's table manners? Or did he simply not care about the impression he was making, secure in the knowledge of his millions and his title? Apparently not, for there he was with his bluff man-in-the-factory manners and shaky aspirates and rough hands—merely an older edition of the boy who had run barefoot round the

Lancashire mills. And according to the Press photographs, his wife was his female counterpart, short and round and over-dressed, beaming a deadly benevolence and good humour on all and sundry as she balanced on high-heeled shoes at charity bazaars or broke champagne bottles over the prows of ships.

Well, that was the way Harben wanted it, obviously, but it wasn't the way he wanted it, and he'd no intention of being 'the second self-made man' of the party. He hadn't been. All the way up from the Brighton slum he'd kept his ears and his eyes open, and each year, he knew it, he'd acquired a greater ease, a more clipped enunciation. Even, when necessary, a touch of coldness. His men obeyed him. And he didn't give an order twice.

And the luncheon? His eyes narrowed. Very successful. He was the youngest of them and he'd still kept that touch of deference in his attitude to the 'great men', and before the brandy came he'd led them round to within a yard of where he wanted them to be. He nodded slightly. It would do. He'd keep quiet now. No over-anxiety. No further approach. The idea had been rammed home at the point of a probe so fine they hadn't felt it going in. Now it would mature in the dark recesses of those fertile brains. And they were fertile brains. Don't let him make any mistake about that. The germination would be exceedingly careful, but the brain behind the hand that had wielded the probe was just as fertile—again a faint smile touched his mouth—perhaps even more so.

The car moved on again. He relaxed against the upholstery, and he noticed the back of Waters's well-cut hair and broad shoulders. He usually preferred to drive himself, but on occasions such as this, it was more convenient and more fitting to employ a man. There was a nice sense of 'finish' in having the car brought to the door by a well-turned-out chauffeur, rather than contending with parking or hanging around for taxis. And not only his time but his energy was money. For a split second a memory of an afternoon of his childhood came into his mind. He was standing in the doorway of the ironmonger's shop, in a patch of thin sunlight, watching his father tipping some nails on to the scales from a little drawer. The shop smelled of iron and paraffin and rubber, a dry mixture of a smell that was dull and heavy in his nostrils, and his father's face as he let the nails slip through his dirty fingers was lined and yellow and tired above his collarless shirt-band.

He shrugged the picture away, wondering what could have brought it out of memory at that moment, and thought of Caroline.

Caroline was six months old tomorrow. Every evening, as he left London in the car, he knew this same lightening of his heart as the miles slipped behind him, bringing him nearer to her and to Ladysmere. He remembered his first sight of that ridiculous crumpled caricature of his Uncle Ernest lying against the Matron's arm, but there was little trace, God be praised, of his Uncle Ernest in her now. She was, people said, a perfect mixture of Gina and himself. She had Gina's brow and eye-setting, but there was a look about the lower half of her face that he knew was a baby replica of his bone structure. And already she had a personality, and a temper, of her own. That was all to the good. Placidity had never appealed to him, a fact which he told himself dryly was fortunate. Soon now she would be crawling, walking, speaking, and after that—a pony, riding lessons, trips in the car with him. And eventually they'd travel, let her see the world—Europe first, then Africa, India and the Far East. She must be taught languages, too; French and Italian and, possibly, German. His eye ran down the programme with satisfaction. She should go on where he left off, and he had the money to make every bit of his plans for her come true. He even allowed himself a brief glimpse of Press notices—'Caroline Taylor, this year's most beautiful débutante'—'Caroline Taylor's dress was designed by Dior'. 'Childish,' he told himself, and added, 'but prophetic.'

Again, he thought, everything is going very well. Very well. Even the fact that Gina herself had taken a long time to pull up her strength after Caroline's birth had not been, in one way, without its advantages, for because of it the nurse had been retained and he, without further argument, had been able to have his way in the matter. And that way was, obviously, the best thing for them all. The nurse was excellent, unofficious and yet firm with Caroline, and Gina was able to shelve all the irksome business of caring for her baby and merely enjoy her presence. He frowned slightly, wishing that Gina could recover her full strength and vitality. There was no doubt about it that she hadn't. She wasn't actively ill, but she wasn't well and there was an apathy about her that he didn't like. He'd forced Blake, against his will, obviously, into getting a second opinion, but even Sir George Ramsden who'd had her in the clinic for a week hadn't found anything wrong, and had given his opinion that she was merely suffering from the after-effects of the difficult birth and would pull up as time went on.

Time had gone on, but although she was better she wasn't right. Not that she complained or even mentioned the fact, but there were perpetual dark circles beneath her eyes and she was far too thin. That she loved Caroline was obvious but . . . The thought broke off in mid-air and he remembered, and tried unsuccessfully to push the memory away, the night he had gone back to the presbytery with Father Dolan and how the priest had suggested that Gina was pining for her illegitimate child. There was a possibility, admit it, that that might have been true at the time, but it could hardly be true now that she had Caroline. Besides, as he'd told himself a hundred times, that incident was over, finished and done with. It was never so much as mentioned between them. There had been only one line to take over the whole affair, and he had taken it. He had forgiven her, and that was the end of it. And Caroline's coming had sealed the door on the whole wretched business. There was no point in even his own consideration of it again. He brushed the thought firmly away, and thought instead of the set of vestments that he had presented to the small and shabby little chapel at Belsted to mark Caroline's birth. The silk had been specially woven on hand-looms and the colours were beautiful. Father Charles Martin, the parish priest, was delighted, and there had been what were suspiciously like tears in his eyes when he had come to the house to thank him.

"The parish," he had said, "is scattered and poor, we are mostly a community of farm hands and small tradesmen, and I can't tell you how heart-warming it is to me to have your very generous support." A sad little smile had touched his mouth and he'd added, "It is good to honour Our Lord with the best that we can give Him, even though it doesn't hide our own shabbiness of heart."

"It doesn't even hide the shabbiness of his boots," Gina had said when he'd gone. "Great holes in the soles and patches on the uppers. It would be out of place, I suppose," she'd said, "to suggest that you'd given him one less cope for the church and a couple of pairs of shoes for himself?"

"*He'd* think it was very out of place," he'd answered. "But I'll see about it."

He had 'seen about it' and, if today's deal went through as he planned, he'd give him a cheque for the new chairs which were so badly needed and he'd have the place redecorated before the winter.

They were driving down Buckingham Palace Road and he suddenly thought of Alison Blair. That chance meeting had so nearly come to grief! If it had done, he might have got himself involved with her again, and that would have been disastrous, for Alison, like so many of her kind, would have been only too glad of a 'gentleman's protection'. Strange that he had run into her on the very night when Gina had told him about Caroline's coming. If he had stayed with Alison. . . . But he hadn't. And now that, too, was past and he had never run into her again. It was unlikely that he would, for they moved in totally different worlds.

Waters drew up at the offices, and he got out of the car and walked up the three shallow steps and passed into the hall and along to his own room. He worked for a couple of hours, and then soon after five, driving himself, he made for home.

There was a battered old estate car outside the house when he reached Ladysmere, and a man and two women drinking sherry with Gina in the drawing-room when he went in.

"Relations!" Gina greeted him. "They've taken a farm at Spine Cross. I hoped I'd finished with my family but they trailed me." She introduced them. "Sir Giles and Lady Conway—Miranda. Ann is Giles's sister, the Hon. Mrs. Easton. I haven't seen Giles and Ann since we were all about eight and loathed one another." She turned to Giles. "Gil, do you remember that Christmas at Aunt Claire's when we caught the curtains alight in the king's bedroom? About ten fire-engines turned up, and old Wilberforce, the Chief Constable, and half the county were milling in front of the house because everyone had panicked and the rumour had gone round that the place was burning down? I have nightmares about it even now."

She inclined her head towards Guy. "I lugged him in to see Aunt Claire when we were near Harvingdon once. She's dottier than ever, isn't she? And dirtier. Does she still have that awful yellow hip-bath taken into her bedroom every morning, or have they made enough out of the public to get a bathroom? I can't imagine why she hangs on to the wretched mausoleum, can you? She'd be far more comfortable in a council house. . . ."

Pouring himself a glass of sherry, Guy felt a sense of well-being enfold him like a warm, comfortable bed, as he listened to their easy talk. Although he had never spoken to Gina about it, he'd often regretted that she had cut herself off so completely from her relations. It was pleasant to think that Giles Conway and his wife had come to live near them. Farmers, and pretty poverty-stricken farmers at that, if the battered car and shabby clothes counted for anything, they might be, but even in a generation which measured everything by the size of a television screen, their name still counted for something. And they were Gina's cousins, his own relations by marriage.

He picked up his glass and joined them.

"How do you think they found us?" Gina asked. "It was all your fault."

"Mine?" he asked.

"They go to your church at Belsted and they know Father Martin. He told them that a rich and respected parishioner named Taylor had presented him with new vestments, and Ann, when she came down to stay, said she believed Taylor was the name of the man I'd married. She'd heard that we'd taken a house down here, and they asked Father Martin and decided that you must be my husband, so they came to see."

He smiled and said casually, "How nice," but the sense of well-being increased.

It really had been a very successful day all round.

The following day was a Saturday and he stayed at home.

The late June morning was perfect, and they had breakfast taken out to the summer-house which he'd had built where the old vegetable garden used to be. The glass doors and windows were wide open, and nothing could be seen from it but the distant hills and the lawn which sloped down to the bend of the river. The coffee, the hot rolls, the honey and the home-made marmalade were all delicious, and as he lighted a cigarette and finished his second cup of coffee, the sense of well-being of the previous evening returned, bringing with it what was almost a sense of triumph.

House, gardens, lawns, flower-beds, Marple, the gardener, passing for a moment across his vision with a basket on his arm; Browne round at the garage washing the cars; the china and the food on the table; Caroline with her nurse up in the nursery; Gina's dress and shoes—they were all, in their way, the external signs of his own brain and will-power. Alone he had fought and worked and sweated. From nothing and by sheer force of holding on with his teeth he had achieved all this. And the end wasn't in sight. He wondered what Gina would say if he told her what was, even now, his exact position, let alone what it would be if his plans of yesterday came home.

He glanced across at her. She was leaning back in her chair looking out at the sunlit hills, quite unaware of him, and as he watched her a shadow came over his satisfaction—a shadow thrown by the expression of sadness which for the first time he recognised, and named, on her thin face.

Irritated and curiously disturbed, he stood up and moved to the step of the summer-house and propped his shoulder against the jamb of the door. What on earth more did she want? Was there no satisfying her? Hadn't she got everything any woman could possibly ask for? Only last night her own relations had openly envied her the house and gardens, her car, the nurseries, even the sherry they were drinking.

"Such opulence!" Giles Conway had said as they were leaving. "Wait till you see the holes in our roof and the so-called bathroom made out of the second kitchen. You're a fortunate little beast, aren't you, Gina?"

And Miranda his wife had said to him as he walked beside her to the battered old estate car in the drive, "It really is a lovely house, isn't it? It's got everything."

But 'everything' wasn't enough apparently. Luxury, ease, a life that millions of other women would give their eyes for wasn't enough. All his years of striving and thrusting, all his achievement, didn't even touch her. He wondered if she had any conception of their value. Of their value *to her*. She took everything he showered on her as her right, with never a thought of the cost in terms of his own work. And with never a thought, either, of the dingy Chelsea room and her own poverty-stricken slap-happy existence in the days when he had first met her.

He wanted to force her to see and acknowledge all that he had done for her. He would have liked to shake her by her thin shoulders and shout at her, "What more do you want? Can't you see what I've done for you? Where I've got you? Can't you show some gratitude? Take that desolation off your face and look cheerful, for God's sake. Wake up to the fact that nine women out of ten would consider you a pampered parasite. . . ."

The thought broke off. He turned and dropped his cigarette end into the ash-tray as the nurse, with Caroline on her arm, came round from the house.

He drove to Belsted to Mass the following morning, and he saw Giles and Miranda Conway in the congregation as he went into the church. The new candlesticks he had given were on the altar, and Father Martin when he came in with his three altar-boys was wearing the red chasuble for the Feast of Saint Peter and Saint Paul.

As he came down the aisle for the Asperges, he felt pleased that the Conways knew it was he who had given the new vestments. He wondered, as a flick of holy water touched his head, if they knew he'd given the candlesticks, too. He thought what a pity it was that Gina wasn't there with him. Perhaps, if she had some religion in her life, she would be more contented, more grateful.

"*In nomine Patris et Filii et Spiritus Sancti*——" Father Martin began, and he knelt with the rest.

The warm June sun filtered on beams of dust motes into the church, lighting cracked plaster and worn carpet. Father Martin's sermon, he was no orator, was an echo of the prevalent drive for finding homes for the army of homeless children. The little man rambled on in his unconvincing way, and Guy's mind wandered to Harben. He saw again the short, gesturing hands, the folds of flesh round the eyes, but the eyes themselves suddenly appeared to stand out from the rest of the padded face and they were small and pin-pointed and hard as granite, and he felt a momentary fear flick like a whip at the base of his thinking. Harben, he knew it, could with one sweep of his fat hand knock down his own smaller edifice, raised now, and Harben would know that, in a bid for opposition. And Harben couldn't be permitted to knock anything down. He'd got to keep a jump ahead of him. He'd got to go over every inch of the ground, and be ready with a counter-move if Harben should put his great feet on a bogged spot. J. B. and Sir James? Little trouble there. No, it was Harben he was up against. Harben who'd started life in a mill-worker's cottage. Harben who'd run around with no shoes on his feet; who'd been poor and hungry and cold. Even as he had. The thought irritated him. He didn't want to remember it. He hated to remember it. There was something shameful and sordid in the memory. For a moment the sheer 'smell' of that life—the unwashed clothes, the reek of garbage in the full dust-bin in the little yard; the odour of his father's body swept over him, sickening him. Then three rows ahead of him he caught sight of Giles Conway's thin profile, and he forced the memory out of his mind. He may have begun like Harben, he told himself, but unlike Harben he'd sloughed off every trace of his beginning. Giles Conway, with his background of Harvingdon, might know of his climb—but he need never know the details of the first step. He himself could laugh quietly back towards it in public when necessary, but he'd take good care that not one of them could label him as men labelled Harben. If he, like Harben, had married an 'Alison Blair' when he'd been too young to discriminate, then he would never have got clean away, because the Alisons of this world wouldn't have had the intelligence, the flair or the courage to rise above their origins. But, luckily for him, he'd steered through those early years, and in the end he'd married Gina.

He came out of his reverie to hear Father Martin saying, "So many of you have pleasant, even luxurious homes. This morning, when you leave this little church where God lives by the road-side, I ask you to spare a thought for that army of children who, through no fault of their own, have none of the joy or comfort or love that your own children have. I have often asked you for money. Sometimes I have asked you for your time. Today I ask you for your love —the love which would be courageous enough to open your own homes to a child who, unlike your own children playing in the garden or the field, already has a forehead marked with lines of anxiety and eyes shadowed with fear. I ask you in the name of Our Lord Himself who said, 'If you receive one of these my little ones, you receive Me,' to ask yourself if you can, if you dare, slam your door on those who call to you to let them in. In the name of the Father and of the Son and of the Holy Ghost. Amen."

He left the reading-desk, took his maniple from the altar-boy, slipped it over his hand and walked with his quiet, strangely dignified tread to the altar and, joining his hands, began the creed.

He came outside the church after the service, and was speaking to Guy when Giles and Miranda Conway joined them.

"Fawning over the brightest jewel in your crown, I see, Father," Giles said lightly. He inclined his head towards Guy. "We were right, you know. He is married to my cousin."

The priest smiled, his mild blue eyes shooting out deep lines from the corners. "So he's just told me." He glanced up at Guy. "Mr. Taylor has been most generous. Most generous. . . ."

"And you'll see he goes on being it, eh, Father?" Giles teased. "Don't bleed him dry. We're hoping to cash in on the relationship ourselves. Have you seen his classy mansion?"

The priest nodded. "Indeed I have."

"How the fellow does it . . ." Giles began, but someone came up and touched the priest on the arm and he turned away.

"Come and have a drink, Guy?" Giles said. "Beer's our mark. Not Tio Pepe."

The congregation—the farm labourers and the small-town tradesmen, with their wives; the shabby little spinsters; the children in their Sunday clothes were drifting down the path, watching them,

Guy noticed, with a diffident interest. Out of the corner of his eye he saw one nudge another and whisper and nod.

"Think I'll get back, thanks," he answered. "Gina's not awfully strong yet."

Giles shot him a look from brilliant blue eyes. He wasn't sure what was behind that look.

"We noticed that. What's wrong?"

They were strolling down the path to the road. Among the little line of cheap cars, the Jaguar, sleek and long and shining, stood out like an orchid in a bunch of daisies.

"She's not really pulled up since Caroline's birth. I got Ramsden to check her over, but he couldn't find anything. I'm hoping to get some time off and take her away later."

"Pity," said Giles, and Miranda said, "It's odd, isn't it? That perfect house, no worries. . . ."

"She had a trying time when Caroline was born," Guy answered, and he put an edge of coldness into his voice.

They had reached the car, and he laid his hand on the door-handle. "It'll do her good to have you people around," he said. "You must come and have dinner with us. I'll get Gina to phone you."

"Thanks," Giles answered. "Good idea."

He raised his hand in a half-salute, Miranda smiled, and they walked across to the shabby old estate car—poised, easy, sure of themselves.

"So damned sure of themselves," he added to himself as he drove back to Ladysmere. "So damned sure. . . ."

At six that same evening the idea came to him, and his first reaction was one of incredulity. The nurse was off duty for the afternoon, and he had just come down from the nursery where Gina had been putting Caroline to bed. Caroline had been in a delightful mood. While Gina bathed and dried her, she flirted and smiled and enticed him, running through all her tricks, till he had been 'on his knees' with near worship.

"You awful little minx," Gina said to her, and to him, "Whenever you're about she turns on the charm. I do hope she's not going to grow into one of those women who get coy every time a man enters the place."

"It's usually the repressed and frustrated who resort to those antics, isn't it?" he'd asked.

"I suppose." Gina was sprinkling powder on Caroline's plump little back, rubbing it in with her own thin hand. "She ought to have half a dozen brothers to beat her up," she said lightly. "Keep your feet on the ground, you uninhibited bit of nonsense."

He left them and came downstairs, pleased and at ease, the undercurrent of his anxiety about Harben shelved for the time being. He poured himself a glass of sherry, lit a cigarette, and stood with the glass in his hand looking out over the gardens and the paddock. And suddenly, without warning, the idea was there.

The glass was half-way to his lips, but he lowered it again, and his narrowed eyes no longer saw the emerald grass or the cool blue bend of the river. They saw Father Martin coming down the aisle of the church, the shining red of the chasuble about his shoulders, and behind him the altar with the six silver candlesticks with the tall candles, their tulip flames sculptured and still in the full June light.

It was impossible, absurd, he told himself. Hadn't he insisted from the beginning that nothing on earth would make him take such a step? Hadn't he told Gina so? But all that was before Caroline had been born. And why now, tonight? The little priest's sermon this morning? He'd hardly listened to it. That wasn't quite true. The last few sentences were clear in his mind—"I ask you in the name of Our Lord Himself . . . if you dare slam your door in the face of those who call to you to let them in. . . ."

But the priest had been referring to children who were orphans, or displaced children from the Middle East countries, not to Gina's illegitimate son. And the child—he realised that he didn't even know the boy's name—was presumably in a good home because Gina wouldn't have let him go to anyone who wasn't able to support him properly. Hadn't he told her in the first place that he would pay any costs there might be? Not that she'd asked him for money. She hadn't—which all pointed to the fact that the arrangements had been satisfactory. Why interfere now? Because of a few words spoken by a priest in a country-town church? And yet wasn't it, in a way, his Christian duty to take the child? He'd got money, plenty of money. He knew, although up to the moment he'd refused to recognise the fact, that Gina wanted the boy with her. He'd thought that Caroline's coming would have altered all that. It hadn't, and in a way he could understand it. Suppose he himself had to lose Caroline. . . . But Caroline was his own daughter, and the boy's father, if the story were true, was dead. Hadn't Gina said to him that night when he went to that dreadful little place in Melford, "Without me, he's quite alone in the world. He's got no one." But was he seriously thinking of going back on his first decision and bringing the child into this house? What did he know of the other man's character? He didn't even know *his* name, either. Blake knew it, though. At least, he supposed he did. Go to Blake and find out? Put himself under an obligation to Blake? God forbid. No, if he went to Blake he'd give his instructions, not ask for help. Surely *that* would bring Gina to her senses? And if there were any local gossip he'd let it be known that Guy Taylor of Ladysmere had, in accordance with the Church's appeal, decided to adopt a child. Gina and Blake, too, must be made to agree with that statement which would by-pass any difficulties. The same reason would serve for Father Martin and the Conways. Luckily his gift of vestments and the candlesticks was all in line. Father Martin would congratulate himself on his successful sermon, and Giles Conway would even perhaps envy his wealth.

But the first thing was to see Blake. . . .

He telephoned him from London the next day and made arrangements to call at his house at six that evening. He would rather have gone about the arrangements some other way, but there was no other way.

Philip himself answered his ring when he reached the house.

"'Evening," he said shortly. "Come through to the surgery, will you?"

Guy followed him down the miserable passage. Why couldn't the fellow have the place done up? Didn't he understand the value of clean paint—especially in his line of business? It was a pity some of these medical people didn't take a refresher course on simple psychology from the industrialists.

Blake indicated a chair and took up his own place behind his desk. He didn't say anything.

"I've come to you," said Guy, "because I've decided to take my wife's child into my home. I want the address of the people he's with and, if you've got it, the name of the boy's father."

Blake raised his head and looked at him, his face expressionless, except for a slight glint in his eye.

"Does your wife know you've come to me?" he asked.

"Obviously not," Guy snapped. "If she did, there wouldn't have been any point in coming to you."

The glint in Blake's eyes flickered.

"I refuse to give it you without your wife's permission," he answered.

"Don't be a fool," said Guy. "I tell you—I've decided to give the child a home. I know that I refused to when I first came back, but I've come to revise my decision. I shall have the boy at Ladysmere."

Gina, thought Philip Blake. Gina's happiness. Gina's health. At last the bill made up, the account squared. And this self-righteous dictator to flourish his signature across the invoice? Once, at the time when the man had come home from Korea, he'd felt sorry for him. Now he didn't feel sorry for him any more. Did he think his damned money could buy everything? Even Christopher? He'd see him in hell first. . . . Steady! That wasn't the issue. He wished it were. The issue this time was between Gina and Christopher—Christopher and the Mostyns. To take Christopher from Jennifer now would kill her, her health was shaky enough as it was. Gina had Caroline and, possibly, the chance of other children. Jennifer hadn't. Why in the name of fortune hadn't he insisted on Gina's legalising the adoption, so that the thing was water-tight? "Guy will never have him," he'd told her half a dozen times. "Once, before I knew him I myself thought he might. Now I know he won't. . . ." So cocksure. So damnably cocksure. But it was Gina's intuition that had come home, not his reason. And the answer was in his hands.

'Why mine?' he asked himself. 'What am I to do with them, any of them? They're not my dependants, my responsibilities. I was dragged into the affair because an unknown woman patient was to have an illegitimate child while her husband was in Korea.' How could he have visualised, when he pressed the bell and the 'next patient' came in, that he was entering on a tangle of personalities and involving himself in that tangle? Gina had leaned back in the chair where her husband now sat bolt upright and said, "I'm going to have a baby," and now there was Christopher and Guy and Jennifer Mostyn and George and Caroline. And himself. And every one of their actions affected all the others. But the man who had set the whole thing in motion, the American, was rotting in his grave. The real cause had possibly had its beginnings a thousand years ago, just as this present situation, where Guy sat waiting for his answer, would bring about another set of circumstances a thousand years hence. And men thought they were free, when even the fall of a leaf was dependent on a process that had started in the dawn of time!

He looked across at Guy and said, "I have nothing further to say. I refuse categorically to give you the address."

Guy leaned forward in the chair and his face was granite.

"Very well. Then I shall ask my wife for it."

"Your wife doesn't know it," Philip said. "So I'm afraid it wouldn't be any help to you to ask her."

Guy stood up. "Of course she knows."

Philip lifted his shoulders slightly and didn't reply.

"Why do you have to be so unco-operative, Blake?" Guy said. "I come here with what surely might be regarded as a generous offer to take that unfortunate child into my home, and you choose to insist on his remaining outcast. Why stand in the child's way?"

'We're like two men shouting at one another from behind sound-proof glass,' Philip thought. 'We're mouthing words that have absolutely no meaning.'

"I'm standing in no one's way," he said. He picked up his pen, took the cap off and put it back again. "You had your chance a couple of years ago, Taylor, but you didn't take it. I'm not saying it wasn't a difficult choice to make, it was, but you turned your thumbs down. You wouldn't give the child house-room. The man who had fathered him was dead, you knew that, and the boy virtually alone, but still you made your conditions. Either your wife must dispose of him or not return to you. As I told you at the time, she'd resisted the impulse either to have an abortion or even to get the baby adopted or put into a Home before you came back. She'd resisted because she held to the faint hope that you would forgive her and——"

"Forgive!" Guy stormed. "Good grief, forgive! I did forgive her, didn't I?"

"I'm merely trying to give you the reasons for my own actions," said Philip. "Yours are no business of mine, one way or the other." Again he removed the pen cap and put it back. "Your wife, after a conflict which exhausted her, agreed to find a home for her son. Fortunately I was acquainted with some people who agreed to adopt him." He looked across at Guy. "Perhaps," he said, "you have never gone into the laws relating to adoption?"

"You know very well I haven't."

Philip nodded. "The husband in this case," he said, "is a barrister and knows the ropes. There isn't likely to be any loophole. And there's another thing"—he laid the pen down—"even if there were I still wouldn't give you their address. These people have done everything for the boy that could be done. They've given him, not only security but love, and not even the rack would make me interfere in that child's life again. He's had one emotional disturbance when his mother was obliged to desert him. He isn't having another."

"All this psychological jargon!" Guy scorned. "If I were suggesting putting the child into a slum with total strangers, I might agree with you. It's hardly likely these people have given him any greater advantages than he'd get in my home, and the fact that I wish the child to return to his mother makes eyewash of all your talk."

"The whole thing's eyewash," Philip answered quietly, "for the simple reason that there isn't the remotest possibility of his adopted parents giving him up."

"Do you mean to tell me that the law can keep a child from its own mother?"

"When its mother has signed him away, yes," Philip said quietly.

"I don't accept that," Guy rapped out. "I shall take advice on it."

"A good idea," Philip answered coolly.

Guy reached for his cigarette-case, took a cigarette and lighted it, his eyes narrowed.

"I don't know what axe you have to grind, Blake, but I don't believe what you say. Obviously, I shall have to get this address from my wife and see these people myself. I didn't want to speak to her about it until the arrangements were completed, but I have no alternative."

Philip didn't answer for a moment, and when he did he said, "When the child first went to his foster-parents your wife certainly knew where they lived. Since that time they've left London, and Mrs. Taylor has no knowledge of their present address." He looked up at Guy. "You can speak to your wife and you can question her, Taylor, but I should go very carefully if I were you. Nothing you say or do, no amount of legal advice nor private detection, will make one iota of difference. But, as Mrs. Taylor's doctor, I say again, go carefully. The conflict your wife went through was more severe than you know. It is operative in the long time it has taken her to pull up after your daughter's birth. She is pulling up. Slowly, I admit. But I see nothing but further strain for her, plus a bad effect on Caroline, if you stir up this business to no purpose. And it will be to no purpose."

"I," said Guy, "am the best judge of that."

"You are no judge of it," Philip answered. "And if you fox yourself that you are, then God help you."

"All these dire forebodings," rapped Guy. "If my wife's present state of health is, as you say, due to the loss of her son, surely my decision to give him a home is going to be beneficial, not cause her further strain?"

Philip drew a long breath. The man was blind, immersed in his own circumscribed little world made up of cheque-books and factories and the power and the glory that went with being able to outwit the next man in cunning and set yourself up as a little tin dictator. They were all alike, the whole boiling of them. They'd bricked themselves up behind a wall of pound notes, and they'd forgotten, if they ever knew, that outside was a world of pain and heartbreak.

"I've already told you," he said, "that the boy is happy where he is and there is no possibility of your having him. You'd better get it into your head, Taylor, that what I said in the beginning is true—you had your chance and you didn't take it. You're two years too late. . . ."

Along the passage the bell rang and a door opened and closed. There were footsteps on the worn linoleum, the sound of voices. Philip looked at his watch. "You'll have to excuse me. My surgery patients are arriving."

He stood up and Guy looked across at him.

"I'd like to know why you've chosen to stand in my way," he said. "Why you've chosen to stand in the child's way. There's something about all this that doesn't ring true."

"It is the child's way I'm not standing in," Philip answered. "You're accustomed to dealing in guns, Taylor, and guns don't have emotions and they don't have nervous systems. Neither do they suffer for other people's sins and selfishness. That child's had a poor enough inheritance as it is, and I'd stick at nothing to keep him in the peace and security he's got now. I'd stick at nothing," he added.

He walked to the door and opened it. "Good night to you," he said.

He closed the door again and went to a cupboard, took out his white coat and put it on. Then he walked to the window, and stood looking out on to the little patch of untidy garden and the tower of the church looming over the near-by roofs.

Why, he asked himself, had he bluffed Taylor, lied to him? For Christopher's sake? Was the poor little brute to be shuttlecocked about whenever Taylor chose to lay down the law? Was Jennifer to suffer a shock of that kind so that Taylor's conscience might be eased? No. The thing was done now. Nothing but harm would come from interference with the present arrangement. In any muddle of this kind, you could only go on the lines of the greatest good for the greatest number, and to leave Christopher where he was added up to just that. But Taylor had sensed his own lie, even if he couldn't prove it. Would he go to Gina, or had he scared him with his threat of what further strain might do to her? It was a fact that the Mostyns had left Onslow Square and that Gina didn't know it, but if Taylor did go to her he'd soon find out that there was no legal adoption. And the answer to that one? Gina's realisation that he had stabbed her in the back. Refused the one thing her heart ached for. Never again would she trust him, believe in him. She wouldn't even recognise the danger to Christopher nor the damage to Jennifer. She would only see what she'd designate as his own Judas action.

He bent forward a little and rested his head against the cool glass. "I had to do it, my dear," he said. "There was no other way. The whole thing isn't simple any more. It's passed beyond the 'yes' or 'no' stage long since. There are too many people involved now. It's no longer you alone. . . ."

He straightened up and glanced at his watch as the door-bell rang again and more footsteps came down the passage.

He walked over to his desk and sat down, but before he pressed the bell for the first patient, he thought, What does she see in that self-righteous pontifical fool of a man? Is it really love that keeps her tied to him or only the fear of being without boundaries, without security? And now there was Caroline and a further strand woven into the chain. But this time, Taylor hadn't had it all his own way, and if his luck held Taylor wouldn't have it all his own way. He'd half-killed Gina when he'd forced her to desert Christopher two years ago, and now he was oblivious to any effect this bouncing about from one to another might have on the boy.

And if Christopher had gone to Ladysmere, there'd have been a nice neat four-square solution at last. The little happy family gathered under one roof—and Gina on her knees with gratitude to Taylor, fawning over him because the great 'I am' had given her son back into her arms. . . . Was that why he'd held out against Taylor? Not Christopher's welfare but his own hatred of Gina's husband?

He pushed his chair back and rang the bell.

Was there no end, he asked himself, to this schizophrenic watching of himself?

Guy swung the gate of the house to, got into his car and drove back to Ladysmere.

How much of what Blake had said was true, that was the point. On the question of the totality of legal adoption, his lawyer would supply advice soon enough. And if Gina had 'signed her son away' for good. . . .?

His hands were easy on the wheel of the car, but his mouth was a thin hard line. Could the law be so imbecile that it could refuse a child to its own mother? Possibly. He'd got to admit that, but the law wasn't the only means available. These people, whoever they were, must be brought to see that the child's place was with Gina. If what Blake said was true, then it wasn't likely that money would influence them. There must be some other way. If he knew who they were and could get into touch with them, he could explain the position to them. No one with any feeling whatsoever could insist on keeping a child when its mother was prepared to give it both natural parental love and every possible social and material advantage. There was, too, the question of Gina's health. That was another factor which they'd have to be made to understand. But Blake had refused, point blank, to give him any information about them. Even Gina, according to him, didn't know where they were. But Gina knew who they were. And Blake, a mistake there, had dropped the information that the man was a barrister. Find out their name and the rest shouldn't be difficult. But how right was Blake when he hinted that any approach to Gina would be bad for her? Was that true or merely an exaggeration? He couldn't be sure, one way or the other. One thing only was certain—if Blake were merely opposing his decision for his own reasons, he would find some means of undercutting him somehow or other. When he made a decision, he made a decision, and he would ensure that his plans were not scotched by any know-all small-town doctor. Whether Blake liked it or whether he didn't, whether he chose to oppose or be co-operative, the fact remained—Gina's son should come to Ladysmere.

He turned off the main road and ran down the lane which led up to the house, and as he passed the vivid green fronds of the larches in the little wood, he heard Blake saying, "You're two years too late, Taylor. . . ."

He came out from the shadow of the larches into the broad sweep of field and meadow and downland, and his eyes were hard.

One day Blake would be sorry he'd said that.

Gina, the parlour-maid told him, was lying down with a headache, and he went to his downstairs cloakroom and washed his hands and sluiced tepid water over his face before going upstairs. This business was becoming absurd. There was absolutely nothing wrong with her. If there had been, then Ramsden would have discovered it. The man hadn't got a knighthood for nothing.

He went upstairs, and heard Caroline's voice chattering away in her own language in the nursery and went into the bedroom. Gina was lying on the bed. She looked pale and the circles beneath her eyes were darker than ever. She pursed her lips at him in a little grimace and said, "I'm not enjoying bad health! I hate it."

"What's the matter?" he asked her.

"I think I sat too long in the sun without a hat. Stupid."

That, from Gina, was nearly humorous. Even in the Mediterranean heat she sat for hours in the sun without a hat, and now after an hour in an English garden in June, she was complaining of a headache. The thing was ridiculous.

"Have you taken anything for it?" he asked her.

"Oh yes. It'll be all right in half an hour."

The whole set-up was nothing but self-pity, he told himself. Even if the basic cause were this question of the child, she ought to come to grips with it. She'd gone to bed with this man in full possession of her senses, and she ought to be able to acknowledge the fact and face the consequences. If she saw it squarely, she'd realise that the loss of the boy was, in a way, the price of disloyalty. No one could commit that sin and expect to get away with it. Life wasn't like that. The law of retribution was pretty exact. Perhaps it wouldn't hurt her to realise it before he made arrangements to have the boy here.

"It's been hot, hasn't it?" Gina said. "Did you have a good day?"

His thought flicked to Blake. "Much as usual," he answered. "It was stifling in London."

What had happened to him, Gina wondered. Where had he, Guy, 'the kid from the ironmonger's shop', gone? Was he still there, hidden under layers of this stranger he had become, or was it only that she herself had created that image of him in her own mind? The thought was frightening, and she closed her eyes on a stab of pain through her temples. No. It was no image of her own, she swore it, that she'd loved. France, America, that moment in the Stratocruiser when she had touched his shoulder for comfort in a sudden excess of fear; laughter in New York; the fun and excitement of his first 'visit' to Ladysmere; his love-making that stirred and satisfied her so deeply—those weren't imaginary. They were real, solid as concrete. What then? As if she didn't know! It was she who'd torn all that down. Wipe out that night at Alban Bay and Guy would still be Guy. If only it could be wiped out! 'Nor all thy Piety nor Wit shall lure it back to cancel half a line, nor all thy Tears wash out a Word of it.' Would that debt never be settled or must it go on for ever? She'd told herself, that night when he was ill, that whatever happened she'd got to go on making it up to him. She'd tried to. She'd given Christopher up, had Caroline, but not even Caroline had broken through the shell with which he'd covered himself. Would nothing break through it? She thought that the longing for his old tenderness and love was sweeping through her on a wave which broke in her own tears, deep in her heart. If only she could hate him, but she didn't. She still loved him. Or did she still love the man he had been? She didn't know. She was too tired almost to care.

"Will you have a drink?" Guy asked her. He was standing by the window, his figure silhouetted against the light, and she thought that the words they spoke to one another got lost in the chasm that was between them.

"It mightn't agree with the aspirin. You go and have yours," she answered.

He turned from the window, and as he moved and the evening light played over his face, it appeared to change, become younger, untensed, the face of the man she had first met at Toby's party. She wanted to hold that change, but as he stepped to the end of the bed and said, "Will you be coming down to dinner?" she saw that, already, the momentary illusion had gone.

"Oh yes. I'll be down in half an hour."

"Right," he said shortly and left her.

He was irritated because she wasn't well, she knew that. A sudden illness or a broken leg he could understand, but this kind of thing was something slightly disgraceful, near neurotic. 'What is the matter with me,' she wondered. That suave Savile Row suit of a Ramsden said there was nothing, and even Philip agrees that there's nothing wrong physically. But Philip had also said that she'd never be well until she'd got the question of Christopher settled. Was that the cause of this eternal fatigue? And would all illness fly away in some miraculous manner once she had 'given him away' with no hope of return? Suppose she went to Philip and said, "I've decided. . . . Tell the Mostyns they can go ahead. I'll sign the papers if you'll let me have them. . . ." Close the door. Tear every last memory of him out of her mind and live only for Guy and Caroline. But even if she did, it wouldn't make any difference to Guy—to what she had done to Guy. That night at Alban Bay would still be there, even if Christopher were in a Tibetan monastery. Nothing could alter it now.

She put her arm over her eyes and wished that, like Guy and Giles and Miranda, she could go to Father Martin and pour out the whole story to him and receive some certitude of understanding, some hope of peace of heart again. She thought of him sitting in the drawing-room, a small hunched black figure with a washable rubber collar, his patched shoes planted on the carpet, saying, "It is good to give Our Lord the best we have, even if it doesn't hide the shabbiness of our own hearts." Was it the "shabbiness of her own heart" that had been the beginning of the whole thing? Looking back, that night with Andrew was as hazy as a dream. She even thought of it as something that had happened to someone else, because it was so remote from herself. And yet, she and Andrew Wharton had "dealt in flesh and blood, in human souls. . . ."

She heard the nursery door close and Guy's footsteps on the stairs.

"Oh God, make it right," she cried silently. "Somehow make it right. . . ."

Guy poured out his Martini, and as he drank it his mind returned to Philip Blake. It was as though Gina herself was siding with the man. How bring the subject of these people up when she was lying on the bed grey with fatigue? A fine scene there'd have been if he had approached her and she'd become hysterical and he'd had to call Blake. The whole situation was absurd. He should have stuck to his first decision and never had the man in the house again—or else moved from the district. All very well to be hounded out of his own home by Blake!

He was sitting down facing Gina's bureau without actually seeing it. Suddenly he did see it. It took on significance. It was almost certain that in it were papers, letters, some trace of the name of these people who had the child. He drew back from the thought, startled. Did he propose to rifle her desk, read her letters? Extreme circumstances demanded extreme measures, and wasn't his whole motive to give her back her child? Surely he, if anyone, had the right to take any steps he thought necessary for her good. Blake had warned him against further strain if he spoke openly to her—very well, then. He was fully justified in taking any action which would give him the information he wanted in the most peaceful way.

The key was in the bureau. He turned it and the bow front slid down. He frowned at the disorder of letters and papers tossed inside. He took up one of the letters and saw a scrawled, "Art's calling. I must go. Carrie," and he put it down again, a picture of Gina's old room in Oakley Street slipping into his mind and out again. He thought he heard a movement overhead and he stood still, his right hand on the lid ready to pull it up, but when there was silence again he went on with his search.

He saw Gina's address book and took it up. An address book had small claim to privacy—hardly more than a telephone directory. He opened it and glanced at each address, mentally checking the names written there. "Alton, James. . . ." Some people they'd met in Rome. "Conway-Coutts, Ardeley, Hertford. . . . Green, Bessie, 2 Council Cottages. . . ." H, I, J, K—he could account for all of them; acquaintances in London, odd people they'd made friends with in various places. "L . . . Lancaster, Lorrimer, Lynas. . . ." No one strange there. "M . . ." He stared at the only name written on the page, oddly certain that it was the name he was looking for. "Mostyn, George, 105 Elston Square, S.W.7." Mostyn. *Mostyn.* He tried to remember the names of the theatre people she'd spoken about when he'd first known her. Toby Vane, Anna Delahenty, the Metcalfes, Ann Forrester. . . . His mind ran down the list of her relations—Conways, Randolphs, Lancasters, Moultons. . . . Even childhood friends she'd told him about flicked across his thought—Peggy Van Zeller; Jane Moorehouse; Lizzie Somerset; Mark Wainwright; John Easton. . . . They were all there, remembered, clear. But the name Mostyn was not there.

He took out his pocket diary and pen and copied the name and address, then he put the book back, quietly pulled up the front of the bureau and turned the key in the lock.

When Gina came down he was reading the paper.

Chapter X

THE following day Gina telephoned Philip. "Any chance of your being out this way today?"

She'd been in his mind ever since Guy had left last evening, and her voice was hardly more real than the voice which had been ringing in his head for most of the twenty-four hours. He wondered if Guy, in spite of his trying to put the fear of God into him, had spoken to her, after all.

"What's the matter?" he asked her, as casually as he could.

"Nothing, really. Headache. Tired—same old thing. But it isn't that—I want to talk to you."

He tried to reach out across the few miles to what was troubling her. He couldn't bring himself to ask the direct question.

"Of course," he answered lightly. "Four o'clock do?"

"Oh, nice. I'll give you some tea."

"I shan't have much time . . ." he began, and he heard her slight laugh.

"As if I didn't know! You can drink the tea while I talk."

"You don't feel worse, do you?" he asked, because he had to know if Guy had spoken to her.

"No. Not really. It would be nice to feel well," she added.

"I'll be up at four," he said.

He walked back to the dispensary and went on making up prescriptions. If Guy had torn down all the strength he'd been trying to give her; if he'd told her that he'd opposed this idea of Christopher's going back to her. . . . His eye moved slowly along the bottles on the open cabinet shelf.

Appalled at the unspoken thought, he took his key-ring from his pocket, selected the key and locked the door.

"You fool," he told himself, but for the first time since he'd become a medical student, he was afraid of the poisons which, normally, were no more to him than cold tea.

Gina was sitting under the trees on a rug, playing with Caroline, when he got to Ladysmere. She looked, he thought, little more than a child herself, till she heard his step and turned to smile up at him, and then he saw that the hurt was still smudged round her eyes—that hurt which, only last night, he himself had rewritten there.

"No little bag?" she said. "You look like an ordinary man. Very odd. Caroline's got a tooth—well, nearly. Isn't she clever?"

"Inherited," he answered. "Mother's side, of course."

Had Taylor told her? He tried to find the answer in her tired eyes, and couldn't. He realised, sharply, at rapier point, that less than twenty-four hours ago, he'd wrenched from her hands the one thing she longed for in all the world. Why had he? Did Jennifer count with him more than she did? He saw himself looking at the poison cabinet. What *was* truth?

Gina had taken Caroline on to her knee. She sat there like a little ridiculous queen, a doll of a thing, considering him with large, grave eyes. Suddenly the gravity departed, and she smiled and held out her arms and turned her hands on her wrists, enticing him with her head on one side.

"Charmer!" he said, and took her on to his knee. "Let's look at this tooth."

He held her in the crook of his arm, and she put up her hand and stroked his face, crooning to herself.

"Would you say another Du Barry?" Gina asked. "Rather alarming, isn't it? She goes on like that with every man who crosses her path—even Marple. Do you think it's all right?"

"Couldn't be all-righter. I only wish I could think she'll remain like it. She won't, of course. You'll send her to some darned school where they'll teach her to giggle and play hockey. What crimes we commit!"

"You couldn't let her loose on an unsuspecting society like that, though," said Gina.

"Why not? Do society good. Wake it up, possibly. It's comatose, anyway."

"You are in a sweet mood," said Gina, and the nurse came across the grass.

"Margaret's taken the tea into the summer-house," she said to Gina. "Come along, Caroline. Orange juice."

Caroline clung to Philip and had to be forcibly removed. She went off kicking like a little fury till Marple appeared, trudging along with his barrow, when her crying stopped like magic.

"What did I tell you?" said Gina. "Even Marple, and he's sixty he's a day!"

In the summer-house, she poured the tea and passed it to him and indicated the cake. "Cut yourself some if you want it."

He took up the knife. "You?"

She shook her head. "Too hot."

He cut himself a slice and she said, "It's about Christopher."

He felt absolutely quiet, as though for a moment all life in him had ceased, and yet he was aware of every single object within his vision—the gold band on the china, the exact shade of the nuts on the cake; the striped border of the table-cloth; a bee which went buzzing past the open doors, cutting across the picture of lawn and flower-beds and river and the scalloped line of the distant hills. And he was aware of the moment itself, as though it hung in a vacuum, suspended in a warm solitariness between time that had passed and time that was still to come. And the only living things in that moment were himself and Gina. They were shut into it as though its walls were of concrete.

"Yes," he said and his voice readjusted time. It flowed on again, merging into the day, into the channel of its passing. He thought of Guy and hated him.

"I've decided," said Gina, "to do what you've always been at me to do—to legalise the adoption."

He didn't understand. He simply didn't know what she was talking about. It didn't make sense.

"To what?" he said.

"What do you mean—'to what?'?" she asked, and there was reproach in her tone. "*Haven't* you always been on at me to do it?"

He tried to force himself to be normal. To think, to reason, to gauge the trend of what had happened: if Guy had told her of his visit to him; if he'd told her that he'd lied about the adoption, refused to give the Mostyns' address; if she knew there had even been a chance of her having Christopher. . . . No, none of that made sense. What was this, then? Coincidence? It didn't seem possible, the reversal of everything was too fine.

"Sorry," he said. "I'm a bit dim." He drank some tea. "What's decided you?" he shot out.

"Aspirins," she answered, and lay back in the chair, her legs at full stretch. "I took some because I had a headache and while I was lying down Guy came home." She sighed. "Something's got to be done," she said. "I can't go on like this, just dragging through life. He hates it. You told me, you've kept on telling me, haven't you, that if I 'shut that door', put Christopher right out of my life, that I'd get strong again? I've never quite believed you, you know that, because, back of my mind somewhere, I'd always thought, hoped then, that the miracle would happen and Guy would let me have him here with us. You've told me a dozen times that I was mad to go on hoping." She stopped talking, and the bee came back, buzzing across the tea-table and sailing out again into the warm, still air. "You've won," she said at last. "I know now that you're right. He'll never have him, so the Mostyns might just as well finish the deal off."

He couldn't answer, couldn't find a thing to say. Why be surprised, he asked himself. Wasn't this just the kind of queer trick life played you? But why yesterday of all days, when Guy had come to the surgery demanding the Mostyns' address and he'd refused it? It was almost as though the thought in their two minds had been implanted into Gina's mind, but twisted, turned upside-down.

"You're very strangely dumb," Gina said. "Why?"

"I wasn't expecting it," he temporised. "You've always been so adamant."

She smiled slightly. "I've never been adamant in my life. Only weak and stubborn and . . . You know what I am." She turned her head towards him. "Well, aren't you going to say, 'Now you'll be the fine, healthy, strapping girl you were'? That's what you ought to say."

He was looking at the boards beneath his feet. He felt humiliated, almost as though she'd taken the decision with the purpose of shaming him. And yet his action of the night before had been morally right. What other could he have taken?

He said, "A divided state of mind is hell, one thing warring against another. You're beaten before you start."

"I suppose so," she said, but she didn't sound convinced. "I still can't see how it can affect Guy, though."

"In what way?"

She didn't answer at once and then, still looking out through the doors to all the splendour of the view beyond the summer-house, she said, "You didn't know him before. I did. He's a different person. Even Caroline. . . ." She stopped and said, "I thought, you thought—you did, didn't you?—that Caroline would"—she lifted her hand and let it drop back on to her lap—"adjust the balance, make it all right again. He adores her, of course he adores her, but even Caroline hasn't touched—that thing. I don't mean he's ever spoken about it, not even reproached me with it, but it's there, in his mind. How can my giving Christopher away for good alter that? Even his death couldn't. How can I blame him?"

Because he was a self-righteous prig who hadn't the capacity either to understand or to love, thought Philip. What did Gina's suffering and remorse matter to him? He couldn't even see it, though it was under his nose twenty-four hours a day. He remembered that first time when he'd said to him, "Have you never made love to another man's wife, Taylor?" It was a pity he didn't make love to another man's wife; give her a baby even. Then he might understand. But there was little likelihood of that. Strange how humility, and love, were so often born, not in the respectable but in the 'fallen'. Small wonder that many of the saints had been sinners. It was possible that it was down in the gutter of life that they learned to be ashamed—and to love.

"And yet," he said, and wondered why he bothered to defend Guy, "it's possible it will make a difference. If you were at peace in your own mind, you'd give out peace, wouldn't you? You can't live with anyone and not be aware of their conflict, even if you politely ignore it."

"And you think my name on a bit of paper will blow all the troubles away like a dandelion clock?"

He made a little grimace and was silent.

"Will you let them know, then?" Gina said. "You'd better do it soon before I weaken."

"I'll phone George tonight."

She moved and stretched out her arm.

"Hold my hand, Philip. I'm afraid. . . ."

Guy sat in Meredith Galway's office, surrounded by the smell of old books, yellowing parchments and cigar smoke.

The lawyer tucked his handkerchief into his breast pocket, pulled the edge out till it showed the correct half an inch above the dark cloth, and said, "If an adoption is legalised, I'm afraid there is no hope of the child's being freed. No hope at all. I could, of course, go through the agreement to make certain of the precise nature of the terms."

"I'll have to consult the people concerned about that," Guy said. "I am merely making this enquiry for them."

"I understand," the lawyer answered. "I'm afraid I can't suggest anything else."

Guy stood up and looked down on the tonsure, symmetrical as though measured by a compass, on the silver head.

"If I can get hold of the papers I'll let you have them," he said. He made to move and then turned back. "Oh, by the way, do you happen to know a counsel named Mostyn? Used to live in Elston Square, though I believe he's moved now."

The little man had his blue-veined hands one on each arm of the chair ready to help himself to his feet, but he lifted them and clasped them together above the blotter, and he raised his head and looked up at Guy, a frosty smile in his unsmiling eyes. "I know him exceedingly well. A very fine man and an excellent counsel. He has chambers in Lincoln's Inn. I didn't know he was a friend of yours."

"He isn't," Guy answered. "Some people I know speak very highly of him. I merely wondered if you knew him personally."

"He was at Balliol with my son," said old Galway. "Charming fellow." The frosty smile flicked into his eyes again. "I trust you will never need to meet him *on the other side*," he said dryly.

"Good as that, is he?" answered Guy lightly. "We'd have to make sure, in that case, that he was on our side." He looked at his watch. "I must get back." He straightened the chair he had been sitting on. "He must have been just round the corner from me when I lived in Kensington. They're out of London now, I believe."

"Yes. They moved after his wife's illness. She isn't strong, you know. He was very fortunate, picked up a lovely little place just outside Bridge Hill in East Sussex at a most convenient price. It belonged to a client of mine who died."

"I don't know much about that part," said Guy.

"Delightful in the spring," old Galway answered, "though I don't know that I'd care for it in the winter. A little isolated. . . ." He walked beside Guy to the door and opened it. "At my age one is less enthusiastic about apple-blossom and more enthusiastic about a window on Pall Mall, I find, Taylor. Unfortunate, but true. . . . Good day to you. Let me know if we can give you any further advice on the adoption question. . . ."

So his intuition had been right, Guy thought as he walked down Welbeck Street and hailed a taxi. He had no idea where Bridge Hill was, but finding out would be a simple matter. Unless he got into touch with Mostyn at his chambers. He frowned slightly, not altogether happy about the notion of meeting Mostyn on, so to speak, his professional ground. The private house would be more fitting. Better, too, to approach the two of them together, a woman would be more responsive to the situation than a man, especially a barrister. In fact, he wasn't at all sure, now he came to think of it, that the best plan wouldn't be to side-slip Mostyn altogether and approach the wife alone. It would be no great matter to run down to the place one day and chance finding her at home. He'd got a pretty full week ahead, but next week. . . . He took his diary out of his pocket and steadied it as the taxi jerked to a sudden stop. . . . Monday, Tuesday. . . . If Cartwright could manage to deal with Saunders on the Wednesday, he might manage it then.

At the same moment Philip Blake was telephoning George Mostyn.

"That you, George? Philip here. I saw Mrs. Taylor yesterday. She's agreed for you to go ahead with the adoption. Thought I'd let you know"

George's distinct enunciation came, controlled as ever, over the wire. "Thanks, Philip. Very good news. Jennifer will be delighted. I'll get on to it immediately."

"Jennifer all right?"

"I'm not very happy about her. Ramsden came over last week—he's only a couple of miles from us now—and he's suggested Jones-Griffiths has another look at her heart."

"He's a good man. You'll let him?"

"Oh yes. She's to see him at the end of the week, but I hope this news will give her a lift. It should do. She's never felt too certain of the position. Understandable. She's devoted to the boy."

"Yes, I know," Philip said. And he added, "I thought she'd be pleased."

Thank God he'd lied to Taylor! Last night, after he'd seen Gina, he'd been torn with near remorse. Now he could see clearly, and he knew that he'd been right. If Jennifer had had to lose Christopher now. . . .

"Tell Mrs. Taylor that I'll get on to it at once, will you?" he heard George say. And then, "One can hardly thank her, can one? Too ironical. Does she feel better about it now they have the other child?"

"The baby's a certain panacea, I suppose. I think she'll probably find it easier once this thing's settled."

"Wretched position all round."

"Yes. I shan't be sorry myself when it's over."

"Nor I."

"You haven't thought any more about the South African thing, I suppose?"

"Not at the moment. Ramsden didn't think much of such an upheaval for Jennifer, and of course there's the question of climate. I'll give it another year or two."

Pity, Philip thought. With the Mostyns—and Christopher—settled in Africa, there'd have been a good few thousands of miles of geographical as well as legal separation between Gina and the boy. Not even the remotest chance of their meeting. Not even the chance of seeing George's name in the Press report of a court case.

"Right, then. I'll tell Mrs. Taylor you'll let her have the stuff to sign. Sooner the better. I'll come across and see you one Sunday if I can."

"Good idea. We've made quite a few changes since you were over."

"Love to Jennifer. . . ."

Philip put the receiver down. The last lap, he thought.

Guy drove fast down the arterial road, but after that the going was cross-country and the roads winding and narrow. The heat wave had passed and the sky belonged more to winter than summer, with fast-moving clouds driven before a south-west wind beating up from the Channel. The wind thrummed about the Jaguar's windows and thrashed the leaf-heavy trees and sent grey-green waves whipping over the barley fields. Every now and then there was a break in the clouds, and high above them a circle of brilliant blue sky and a sudden blaze of light which silvered the tossing leaves and turned the grass to a shining deep emerald, while the clouds banking up in the south-west became as blue-black as the smoke from old dank wood.

He had little difficulty in finding the village, but he was not sure on which side of it the house itself lay, and seeing a man getting into a car, he stopped and enquired. The man was about his own age, a 'gentleman farmer' type, and he noticed that his hair was bleached almost white by the sun, which emphasised his very dark brown eyes.

He told him where the house was, and then, with an inclination of his head towards the Jaguar and a slight smile, he said, "That's a nice-looking beast." He gave a comical glance at his own mud-spattered old Ford. "Wouldn't care to swop?"

"I'd have to consider it," Guy answered lightly. "Needs a bit of thinking about."

"Ah, pity. Never mind. . . ." He raised his hand in salute and opened the Ford door, and Guy drove on.

He found the house a mile and a half farther on, and turned in at the drive gates. The place was obviously a converted farmhouse, old and weathered, with a beautiful spreading roof and Elizabethan chimney-stacks. He glanced up at it, and then went into the rose-covered porch and rang the bell.

A young girl—a village girl obviously—opened the door and he asked for Mrs. Mostyn. She did not ask for his name, but took him into a room off the square hall to the right and said, "I'll tell her."

He glanced round the room, noticing the foot-wide beams, the pleasant easy chairs and the good solid furniture, and he wondered what kind of a woman he was going to see. He had a feeling that she would be tall and toothy and managing—the kind who sat on women's committees and adopted 'unfortunate children'. She would know all about the law and . . .

The door opened. He saw a small, fragile child of a woman standing there looking up at him from wistful deep blue eyes. Her face was very grave but singularly untroubled. She said, "I am Mrs. Mostyn. You wanted to see me?"

Chapter XI

PHILIP sat with his head lowered into his hands. He ought, he told himself, to have been prepared for it. He was a doctor, and he'd known all along that she'd never really pulled up after that last bout of pneumonia. And only ten days ago George had told him that Jones-Griffiths was going to have a look at her heart. . . . Yes, all that, and still George's voice over the phone telling him of her death had pained him as nothing had for years. Behind the palms of his hands, she was there, more living than she'd ever been, small and grave and shy. Fighting a battle too large for her.

She'd died last night, just snuffed out like a candle, and George hadn't even been there, because he'd had to go to a Law Society dinner or something of the kind. They'd phoned him, but she'd died before he got home. He couldn't question George, obviously, but he asked him if Jones-Griffiths had told him that she might collapse, but George merely said that he'd advised her to rest as much as possible until the cardiographs which he wanted were taken.

"She hadn't done anything out of the ordinary, had she?" he asked.

"No. Everything was as usual," George said. "The nurse had taken Christopher to tea with the Lawson children and Jennifer only had to make her own. The daily left it ready on a tray for her. She told the nurse she didn't feel very well when she came back with Christopher, and the girl was anxious and phoned the doctor. She died at half-past eight."

Philip had a totally irrational feeling of guilt, as though, had he been there himself he might have saved her. He shook that off, knowing the idiocy of it, but he found it difficult to take in the fact that she was dead.

And if he found it difficult, what about George? He suddenly remembered a May-day morning at Oxford when he and George and Mathew Galway had got up at five and rowed up the river to hear the choir singing from Magdalen Tower. There were new willows trailing their chenille strands in the grey early-morning water, and the devil of a noise coming from dozens of other people in punts who'd all had the same idea. And then as six struck there was a sudden deep silence, and drifting down over the river, literally borne on the wings of the rising sun, came the chant of the Te Deum. He'd shifted his position slightly and caught sight of George's head, sculptured like a young Roman against the morning, and he'd thought, 'I shall remember this when I'm old.' Now Jennifer was dead and George was a widower.

He pushed that old memory away and he raised his head from his hands, and his eyebrows drew together as he wondered if George had dealt with the adoption papers. He didn't believe Gina had had them or she would have let him know, but it would be damnable for George to have to see to them now that Jennifer was dead. He thought he'd call in and see Gina, and find out if she'd heard anything.

He went up to Ladysmere after lunch, but even before he'd had time to ask her Gina told him that she'd heard nothing from George.

"I thought they were so mad keen on signing for my son that they couldn't wait," she reproached him. "It's over ten days since I spoke to you about it, and I haven't had so much as a postcard from him."

He didn't want to mention Jennifer's death, the situation was too confused, so he merely muttered something about the snail's pace of the law and left it at that.

"You can tell George Mostyn from me," said Gina, "that I might change my mind while he's strutting around Lincoln's Inn dotting the i's and crossing the t's." Her eyes saddened. "Philip, do say that it isn't easy to hover on the very brink like this. . . ."

But driving back to Belsted he wondered how long it would be before he'd be able to give that message to George, because George hadn't even a 'brink' any more, the ground had given way and he'd fallen headlong on to rocks so sharp they must have near killed him.

Guy, too, was wondering when he was likely to hear from the Mostyns.

Contrary to his expectations, there'd been no wrangling, no difficult argument. He'd told Mrs. Mostyn who he was and that he'd decided to have the child at Ladysmere, and how he hoped that she and her husband would agree with him that his right place was with his natural mother, and not stick to the letter of any legal agreement that had been made. Mrs. Mostyn had said very little at all, merely, in effect, that she would tell her husband that he had called and what he had said, and get him to deal with the matter. Her attitude had surprised him, but then she herself had surprised him—he'd been so certain of a masterful, domineering type who would have created a scene or been argumentative. In fact, her child-like gentleness and her acceptance of the whole thing had confused him, making him feel as though he'd gone to lift a heavy weight and found, as he grasped it, that it was feather-light. Only as he'd said good-bye to her, there'd been some expression in her eyes that he couldn't interpret. Driving home he'd wondered about it, but it wasn't till he was approaching London that he suddenly remembered a stray dog he'd found cowering under the pier at Brighton when he was a boy. The comparison irritated him. There was little of the 'stray dog' element about the Mostyns, with their old, charming house and obvious signs of well-being. They were, he would say at a guess, sensible, reasonable people—certainly she had appeared to be so—who would understand the position and, he hoped anyway, would defer to his wishes in this matter of Gina's child. For all that, he was rather surprised that he'd neither heard from them nor from Blake. Especially from Blake! Did that mean that the Mostyns were going to come to terms with him without further fuss? It certainly looked like it, otherwise surely they'd have told Blake of his visit. Or was Blake's story of their being friends of his poppycock? It well might be, just as it might be possible that they weren't sorry at the thought of parting with the child. Certainly Mrs. Mostyn hadn't shown any particularly sign of dismay or even disturbance.

He decided he'd give them another week and then write to them, but owing to a strike in the Birmingham works and his having to go up there with J. B. Harris, he didn't write to them. In the end he and J. B. were in the Midlands for the best part of a fortnight, and when they got back they found Harben with a fistful of tricky questions and a smile on his bull-dog face that Guy didn't like.

Philip drove across to Bridge Hill for Jennifer's funeral. It was all desperately painful, and he thought he'd never seen anyone look so solitary as George did when he walked behind her coffin down the aisle of the church and across to the gaping hole in the green turf that was her grave. Mathew Galway was in the church with Ann, his wife, and he went back to their farm with them afterwards and had tea there. They'd taken over Christopher and the nurse to relieve George of any added burden, and after tea Ann fetched him down from the old nurseries, no longer used now that their two sons were at school.

He wasn't, thought Philip, in the least like Gina. His eyes in a tanned face were Nordic blue, and his hair, which fell in a cock's-comb over one eye, was bleached almost as white as Mathew Galway's. He'd got a boxer's shoulders and looked as strong as a young ox. He was quite unself-conscious, and chattered to Ann who apparently understood his language. And he laughed. The laugh was his old guffaw with wide-open mouth and wicked, dancing eyes, but now it was no longer silent but a ridiculous, bass chuckle. The only likeness to Gina was a faint similarity of an expression which crossed his face in repose as he stood at Mathew's knee and watched him light his pipe. When Mathew blew a cloud of smoke from his mouth he raised his hand and brushed it away; and his hands, oddly, were beautifully shaped with long sensitive fingers. A queer mixture of the ox and the artist, Philip thought, and added, "Poor little devil!"

Ann, reading his thought, said, "I suppose George will keep him."

Her doubt surprised him and he said, "Thank God, he's got him!" and he thought of the adoption papers.

"What's happened to the girl—the mother?" Ann asked. "Jennifer told me she'd had another baby."

"She's all right," he answered. "Well, more or less. They did have a baby. Little girl."

"I felt sorry for her," Ann said. "Jennifer said she was nice."

He nodded. "She is."

"Would she have gone off with his father if he'd not been killed, Philip?"

"No," he answered shortly and left it at that.

"I suppose," said Ann, "it's the kind of thing that might happen to any of us."

"Only sometimes," he replied; "the bill is rather heavy."

Ann nodded. "Very," she answered, and she put her arm round Christopher in a kind of protection. "But I'm glad Jennifer had him, you know, even though it's ended like this. I think for the last eighteen months she's been utterly happy. You could almost see her happiness growing. She adored him, and now—well, nothing can ever spoil it, can it? She had that time with him."

They were all three silent, and even Christopher, leaning against Ann as she knelt on the floor, didn't make a sound.

Philip stood up. "I must get back. The twins all right?"

"Barring a little matter of a five pound bill for broken windows, fine," said Mathew. "We couldn't get down for the half, so Dad went and gave them such a blow-out that they're praying we'll never be able to go again. I'm expecting castor-oil as an extra on this term's bill—a gallon of it."

"God forbid," said Philip fervently.

"We may be up your way before the summer's over," said Mathew. "There's a body, name of Giles Conway, come to live near you somewhere. . . ."

Philip looked at him. "Giles Conway! How do you know Giles Conway?"

"Why shouldn't I know Giles Conway? What's he done to you, in heaven's name?" Mathew asked with quizzically raised eyebrows. "He was at Charterhouse with me," he added.

"But do you know who he is?" Philip asked.

Mathew took his pipe out of his mouth.

"What do you mean—who he is? He's Giles Conway, grandson of the Earl of ——"

"Don't be a fool," Philip broke in. "I know all that." He pointed down at Christopher. "His mother is Giles Conway's cousin."

"Well I'll be damned!" exclaimed Mathew. "Jennifer never said."

"No, and I shouldn't have said either. Oh, blast! Keep that to yourselves, you two, will you? I must be slipping. What with Jennifer's death and one thing and another."

"Don't worry," Mathew answered easily. "You never said it." He jerked his pipe stem towards Ann. "The old girl's safe as houses, thank God."

They walked to the car with him, and as he drove away he saw them standing there, Mathew and Ann and Gina's child, Christopher. But he was angry with himself. He should never have told them who Christopher's mother was.

Ten days later he had dinner with George in London and George asked him if by any chance he knew anyone who would be likely to adopt Christopher because, if he did, he was hoping to sell up everything he possessed in England and take the job he'd been offered in North Africa.

Philip was astonished. He put his coffee-cup down and stared across the table at George, but George, his head bent, was turning his cigarette thoughtfully from side to side in the ash-tray and didn't even look up.

"I couldn't take him out there with me," George was saying. "The nurse won't entertain the idea of living in Africa and, anyway, it's hardly a very healthy spot for a two-year-old European to grow up in. I did consider leaving him in her charge for a year or two, and maybe having him out later, but she told me two or three days ago that she hopes to be married soon and her fiancé wasn't enthralled with the idea of starting life with a two-year-old baby in tow." A slight smile touched his mouth. "A complication that could be embarrassing. So I decided to ask you what your views were and if you knew of anyone who would be interested. It isn't," he ended, "as though the adoption had been legalised. As you know, I was dealing with that when Jennifer died, so that there wouldn't be any difficult complications."

"But surely Christopher will——" Philip began, and he stopped, for he was trespassing on fenced ground.

George was still intent on edging minute specks of ash from his cigarette, and he didn't look up. "I want to get away from everything here," he said. "I've got to, Philip. As far as I'm concerned, there's"—he lifted his hand an inch and lowered it—"nothing, no one. As for the boy—oh yes, I was fond of him, but it was she who wanted him. I agreed to have him because she wanted him. I only wanted her——"

He stopped speaking, and Philip thought of Guy Taylor's demands and his own refusal—and now here was George looking for someone to take Christopher. It looked as though once more it was Taylor who was going to 'cash in', get his own way again—unless he didn't tell Taylor but found someone else altogether. The thought, quite involuntary as it was, troubled him. What on earth was the state of his mind and heart that he could contemplate further injury to Gina in order to spite Taylor? A nice friend. . . .

He told George of Guy's visit to him, and the strained expression eased from his mouth a little and his eyes brightened.

"That's fortuitous, isn't it?"

"Very."

"I'd been feeling a bit of a monster, I don't mind telling you. But with his own mother able to have him. . . ." He squashed the cigarette out finally and added, "It's what Jennifer would have wanted more than anything in the world. I'm certain of that." He brushed his fingers together over the ash-tray. "You'll let them know, will you?"

But which of them was he to 'let know', Philip wondered. His impulse was to go straight to Gina, but that was out of the question because Gina didn't know that Guy had already been to him, and she wouldn't imagine for a moment that he'd consider having Christopher. There was only one answer—to get into touch with Guy again, and Guy, the great 'I am', the sinless, forgiving husband, would make the final gesture and return the child to Gina. And Gina's debt to him would pile up.

And Christopher? Once again the little shuttlecock would bounce back. Strange new faces to get accustomed to. A new environment. New ways. Guy to father him instead of George.

Gina to mother him instead of Jennifer—that at least was the best and the most natural part of it all. And there was Caroline. He remembered how, the first time he'd seen her, he'd pictured her with her small arms stretched out across the chasm of their two lives. Now she'd have Christopher—but whether she'd take to him or not had yet to be proved. Only one thing was certain as the day—that the light would come back into Gina's eyes again.

He telephoned Guy at his office, and asked him to call and see him as soon as he could. He came the following evening, and he told him of Jennifer's death and that George had decided it would be better for Christopher to be in the care of a woman rather than of a man alone, so that if he were of the same mind about Christopher's going to Ladysmere. . . .

Guy, who had come prepared for a battle with Blake and the disclosure of the fact that he had been to Bridge Hill to see Mrs. Mostyn, was astonished, but his brain worked fast and he decided, under the circumstances, to say nothing about that visit, for Blake obviously didn't know of it. But when, he wondered, had Mrs. Mostyn died? She'd appeared perfectly well when he'd seen her just over three weeks ago. He'd have liked to ask Blake more about her death, but thought it better to leave things undisturbed—especially as everything seemed to be working out very well on its own. He was sorry that Mrs. Mostyn was dead, but her death had certainly cleared the ground and saved further argument, and it was useless to pretend to a grief he didn't feel. As for Blake—Blake had done everything he could to stand in his way, but all his efforts had come to nothing, and now here he was more or less offering him the child he had done his best to prevent him from having.

How often the circle came full cycle if one left it alone, kept the hands off it! Too often people interfered with the course of events and became anxious and flustered. Even the letter he'd intended to write Mostyn this week wouldn't now be necessary. Without his doing anything, it had all come into his hands. He could almost feel sorry for Blake. . . .

In a few concise sentences he made the necessary arrangements for Christopher's transference from Bridge Hill to Ladysmere and a tentative date was fixed for the journey.

"You say this man's a barrister," he said. "He will, I presume, attend to the legal side. I don't want any complications, and I shall get my own lawyer to make sure everything is in order."

A smile hovered in Philip's mind. So much pomposity and all over something non-existent, built up round his own lying inference. He drove the smile away and said, "I am sure everything will be carried out in an exemplary manner."

"So am I," Guy answered, but there was no smile on his face. He looked directly at Philip. "The ways of Providence are very strange, Blake," he said, and an expression crept into his eyes which made Philip tighten his grip on his pen.

"Providence?" he asked coldly, and he thought of the gaping hole in the new green turf that was Jennifer's grave and of George setting off, quite alone, to Africa.

"As I told you," said Guy, "the child's place is at Ladysmere."

Not a muscle of Philip's face moved, and he forced his tone to remain quite even, quite controlled.

"And you're pleased to think that Providence has killed Mrs. Mostyn so that your will may be served, Taylor? That it? Aren't you making the action of the Deity more incomprehensible than even the theologians would permit?" He stood up. "You will remember, perhaps, that the devil also has his angels."

Guy, too, stood up and his eyes were steel. "I remember it only too well," he answered, "though I was under the impression that Providence is able to foil the plans of both the devil and his angels when and as he pleases." He flicked a look at Philip. "I don't know what you have against my wife or me, Blake, that you tried to prevent my plans for the child going through, but not much has come of your interference, has it?"

How in God's name could Gina love this blind, insensitive fool, thought Philip, and in the same moment he remembered her saying, "You didn't know him before. . . . How can I blame him?" *Was* it possible that that one incident had changed him so much? Could it change a man past all recognition? His impulse was to lift his fist and crash it into that cold self-righteous face—and in doing so to bring wrath down on Gina's head and finally cut off every hope of seeing her again himself. And yet words, argument, were useless. The man could see nothing beyond the range of himself.

"I've nothing against either you or Mrs. Taylor," he answered coolly. "Why should I have? While Mrs. Mostyn was alive and the child happy, there seemed more harm than good in your trying to disrupt the arrangements." He walked to the door and opened it. "You'll forgive me if I get on. I've some prescriptions to make up before surgery."

Guy was seething under the man's quiet tone, but he, too, kept a grip on himself.

"Well, it's all ended most satisfactorily," he said, "as indeed one had foreseen. I'll confirm the date I gave you by telephone, Blake." And as he reached the door which Philip was holding open, "Tell Mostyn that I'll sign any necessary papers myself, will you? There's no need for my wife to be bothered with the legal side. . . ."

Philip went to the outer door with him, opened that, and said a cold "Good evening" as he passed in front of him and out on to the street; but instead of going back to the surgery he went into his dining-room and poured himself a whisky and soda. It was seldom he drank while he was working, but as he put the glass down he said to himself, 'I deserved that.'

'And I think,' thought Guy as he drove home, 'that the trick goes to me.' For all Blake's high-falutin' talk, he'd had to ask him to have the boy, and after a lot of time wasted they had reached the precise spot which he had intended they should reach, whether Mrs. Mostyn had lived or died.

His thought flicked to the slight, grave figure standing just inside the doorway saying, "I am Mrs. Mostyn. You wanted to see me?" and he wondered if there'd been an accident, for she'd appeared to be in perfectly good health then. Poor little woman. But, after all, death was an unpredictable inevitability. We all had to meet it somewhere, somehow, and he couldn't stand an attitude of false sentimentality about the newly-dead. It was that implied attitude of Blake's which had so irritated him. That and the mantle of theology he'd tried, quite ridiculously, to wear. Why bother with the man? All his inept fumblings hadn't made the slightest difference to the outcome, and now he was on his way home to tell Gina. A thrill of excitement such as he'd long forgotten came over him as he drove the last half-mile, and he was aware of the lifting of the darkness which had been about him, and with the lifting the promise of a return to a brighter day.

But the thrill dissolved in irritation when he reached Ladysmere and found that Gina wasn't home. She hadn't said that she'd be out, and he felt resentful that she should have chosen this evening of all evenings not to be there. It was, he felt, her fault, that the hoped-for lightness drained away in frustration long before he heard her car scattering the pebbles on the drive. And when she did come walking swiftly up the steps, more swiftly than he'd seen her walk since Caroline's birth, a queer paralysis came over him so that instead of, as he'd intended, telling her at once, he couldn't bring himself to utter a word of it, and it wasn't until after dinner that he did tell her.

It was a cool, grey evening and the girl had lighted the fire. Gina, who had just taken some sugar, was stirring her coffee.

He saw the lids come down over her eyes, and she sat there with her eyes closed and the spoon stationary in her hand for what seemed a long time. At last she opened her eyes, put the spoon back in the saucer and stood the coffee on a table before she looked at him and he saw the tears rolling down her cheeks. She opened her lips as though to speak, but no words came. She moved her head from one side to the other, then raised her hand and lowered her forehead on to her fingers. And he found himself sitting back in the chair watching every movement, every expression, with a mesmerised fascination.

Her hand came away from her forehead, and again she looked across at him and said, "Did you see Philip, then?"

"Yes."

"I can't take it in," she whispered, and he could only just hear what she said. "What made you change your mind, Guy?"

"Need we go into that?"

She brushed the tears from her face.

"I feel confused. I didn't think the Mostyns would give him up. Did Jennifer mind?"

"Jennifer Mostyn died not long after I first went to Blake," he told her.

"Oh no! Oh, Guy, no! I can't believe it. She was so. . . ." She stopped and said, "George! What will he do? He adored her. Philip told me once that he lived for Jennifer. I can't bear it for him." She remembered taking Christopher to their flat, and that Jennifer had sat very upright and afraid on the chair, with Christopher on her knee, and later she'd said, "May we have him, George? I'd like to. I'd like to very much."

A troubled frown came on her forehead. Wouldn't George have wanted to keep Christopher because Jennifer had loved him? It would be cruel to force him to give him up now that she had died and he was alone. Much as she wanted him, longed and ached for him, she doubted whether she could wrench that one small comfort from George. When there had been the two of them, yes, for they would still have had one another, but not George alone. . . .

"Blake said he wanted to leave England and settle in Africa," Guy answered when she told him of her thought. "I gather that it was his idea not to take the child, anyway."

She nodded, fighting down a momentary irritation at Guy's veiled implication that Christopher was 'for sale' again, unwanted, someone who was a burden and in the way. But irritation now was idiotic. Christopher was coming back to her. He was coming home. He'd never be lonely or unwanted again in all his life. And it was Guy who had, in the end, made this wonderful thing possible.

She was out of the chair and kneeling on the rug beside him, her arms on his crossed knee, her face lifted to his.

"What can I say to you?" she asked, and again the tears were in her eyes. "I can't tell you. . . . I've wanted him so much. So much. I thought when I had Caroline, our baby, I wouldn't mind any more, wouldn't miss him. Guy, it's been awful, like something cut out of you. An ache that never goes. I have tried to fight it off, you know, but . . ." She shook her head. "It doesn't matter now, does it? He's coming back. Coming home. And it's you who've given him to me again. Oh, darling, it's so perfect, I can't help crying. . . ."

He looked down at her and saw her face torn, almost ugly, with her tears, and he remembered Blake saying, "You had your chance, Taylor. You're two years too late. . . ." And again he looked down at Gina on her knees at his feet.

Chapter XII

A FORTNIGHT later Christopher came to Ladysmere.

To avoid any village 'talk', either in Bridge Hill or in Belsted, it had been arranged that the Mostyns' nurse should take him to London, meet Gina there, and the three of them return to Ladysmere. The nurse had agreed to spend a week with the Taylors in order to "settle Christopher in".

As far as the Conways, Father Martin, and their own staff were concerned, the inference was that Mr. and Mrs. Taylor were adopting a child whose mother had died. They had, obviously, the means to do so, a lovely home and a child of their own, so that there was nothing particularly startling in the idea.

The only people who were aware of the facts were George, Philip and, though Gina did not know this, the Galways. For the rest, Giles and Miranda Conway thought they were slightly mad and the majority of their friends agreed with that opinion. Father Martin, on the other hand, went into the church and said a prayer before the Blessed Sacrament in thankfulness to God that his words had gone straight into the heart of one of his congregation.

The nurseries were in perfect order, and Kathleen Harrison, Caroline's nurse, had dressed her in a nonsense of a dress, all white silk and blue smocking. She had combed her hair into ringlets, and given her, by some miracle, the appearance of an Early Victorian dowager. She herself, in a clean white overall, was sitting on the rug under the tree beside her, a neat little heap of mending at her left hand. She hoped that the adopted child's nurse would be pleasant, and she was glad that she would be staying only a week. She didn't like the thought of interference with her ways. As for the little boy. . . . It was rather wonderful of the Taylors, she thought, to take on a friend's child, but it was the kind of thing Mr. Taylor would do. She was sure that the idea had originated with him, because he was the most generous, most wonderful man that she had ever known. She hugged the secret of her aching love for him to her, pressing it to the pain-filled void that was her heart.

She heard the car come in through the gates and stop at the house door, and she saw Stevens go round to get the luggage out. She lifted Caroline up and sat her on a pillow and, as she heard their voices, she put up her hand and smoothed her straight, tidy hair. As she lifted her head she saw Mrs. Taylor leading a fair-haired boy by the hand across the grass. Beside her walked a girl in a navy-blue suit with a white blouse.

Gina, as she came towards them, was aware of nothing but the sense of dream which had hung over the whole day. There had been none of the thrill, none of the fierce joy she had pictured, only this strange dream-like atmosphere of a muted reality.

Even when she'd walked into the Grosvenor Hotel and seen Christopher, his feet stuck straight out before him, sitting by the nurse's side, the sense of unreality hadn't lifted. She went across the room to them, held out her hand to the nurse and said, "I am Mrs. Taylor. You're Miss Carrington, aren't you?" And then she'd looked down on that white-fair head and said, "And this is Christopher."

Perhaps, she told herself, it was the necessary restraint, the half-hypocritical manner she'd had to adopt, that had dimmed the bright edge of wonder. Or was it that the longing for him had become so much a part of her life that she wasn't able to realise that now it was over?

He had sat next to her in the train and she'd felt his small sturdy little body against her own thigh, but he had been quiet and grave and, she thought, bewildered, and after a time his head had dropped sideways and he'd slept.

He woke just before they drew into Belsted, and sat there yawning and still sleepy till, as they stood up to leave the train, he said, "Shall we see Mummy, Nanny? I like to see Mummy. Please, Nanny."

She thought then that there were tears not in her eyes but in her heart, and she knew that never before had she fully realised that, to him, she was a total stranger. The nurse, a younger girl than the 'nanny' who had come with Jennifer to fetch him from Melford, looked at her with a sad, helpless expression on her face and said, "It's so hard to make them understand, isn't it? He keeps thinking she'll come back."

"We'll have to give him time," she answered. "It must be very bewildering for him." And she had the ridiculous feeling that he'd been travelling about the world quite alone, but that now he'd reached a harbour.

At last they were at Ladysmere and he was walking beside her over the grass towards Caroline, his hand tightly clasped—he'd always had a grip like a bruiser—round her first finger.

"Well, Nanny," she said. "Here we are. This is Christopher. . . ." She introduced the two women and half-smiled to herself at their guarded 'keep off my grass' approach to one another. "I thought perhaps you'd like to take Miss Carrington to her room, Nanny. I'll stay with these people till you come down. Don't hurry," she called after them. "There's still twenty minutes before tea."

She watched the two sedate figures walking back over the grass. Then she took her hat off and threw it on the rug, and knelt down, one arm round Christopher.

Caroline, still keeping up her Early Victorian dowager role, hadn't moved. She sat quite still, with her absurd hands clasped across her little round stomach, staring at Christopher with fascinated eyes.

"I've brought you a man of your very own," said Gina. "Now perhaps you'll leave Marple alone."

Caroline swung her eyes up to her with an expression which, for all the world, looked as though she had understood the introduction and was amused at the inference that a 'man of her own' would stop her passion for Marple, then her lashes fluttered and she gazed at Christopher again, drawing in her breath on a long satisfying sigh.

"Look, Christopher," said Gina, "that's Caroline. She lives here, and you're going to stay with us, too. Do you think you'll like her?"

She felt his broad, sturdy little shoulders under her arm, and suddenly, swiftly, Andrew Wharton was there, splashing through the shallow water to the strand, his broad shoulders looking as though they'd been oiled in the strong sunlight, and she thought that, for the first time, the fact came home to her that he had been a living man with his own personal desires and satisfactions, his own dreams and failures. Now he was dead. She felt as though she wanted to mourn for him, to be sad and grieved, because he had died on a strange road in a strange country. Poor Andrew. . . .

Christopher looked up at her from his Nordic eyes, startlingly blue in his tanned face, and a shy half-smile came over his face. He too sighed and he lowered his head again, and then raised his hand and pointed his finger at Caroline.

"She's a minx," said Gina. "A hussy. I hope you'll be able to keep her in order."

This, she told herself, was the moment that she had longed for, hoped for and relinquished hope for—the afternoon sun flooding the garden; the house silent, the morning's work over, and she and Christopher and Caroline sitting under the cedar tree together, never to be parted again.

Caroline saw Christopher's pointing finger and suddenly she discarded her Victorianism. She unclasped her hands, lifted them from her lap and held out her arms, then with her head on one side and a bewitching smile on her face, she moved her hands on her wrists, her fingers spread, enticing Christopher as she enticed Guy, Marple, Stevens and, when possible, the tradesmen who called at the back door.

For a moment Christopher, bewildered with the abrupt change, stared at her fascinated, then he raised an amused but cautious face to Gina.

"She wants you to go to her," Gina explained.

He lowered his head and stared at Caroline again, then quite deliberately he left the circle of Gina's arm, marched the few steps forward, and with a gentle push sent Caroline tumbling backwards.

"That's learned her," said Gina softly, and the next moment they were both tumbling together on the rug, laughing.

How strange, she thought later, was happiness. It passed so quietly, so gently. There was little of the spectacular in it more often than not, and sometimes, unless you said to yourself, 'This is happiness. Now, at this moment, I am happy', you were not even aware of your happiness.

She was sitting in the drawing-room waiting for Guy to come home. They were dining with friends of Giles and Miranda, who lived at the other side of Arundel, and she had changed early.

She lay back in the chair and closed her eyes as waves of peace washed over her. This was joy, fulfilment—Guy and Christopher, her 'men', under the same roof with Caroline and herself. The sheltering arms of their lovely home round them. The evening coming down across the hills. But even at the heart of joy was the faint echo of pain. Only by Jennifer's death had her own happiness been born. Once she had said to Philip that if Guy would let her have Christopher, she'd take him without scruple, and that George and Jennifer would have to mend their own broken hearts. She hadn't realised then the cruelty of that. Perhaps it had taken Jennifer's death to make her realise it. She turned away from a horrible picture of Jennifer, so shy, so grave, mouldering away in a cemetery, and she thought, 'I wouldn't have taken him from you. Not at that price. I wanted him, of course I did; I ached for him, but I'd rather you'd lived and—yes, I mean it—kept him. I would, you know. I didn't want you to die. . . .'

But it seemed that there was always death in the heart of joy. Someone's death. Was that the condition of happiness?

She heard the car draw up, and a few seconds later Guy came in. For the last couple of weeks, since he had told her that he'd been to Philip about having Christopher, she thought that he was beginning to return to the Guy she'd first known; the 'kid from the ironmonger's shop' who'd fought and tussled his way out of a slum, because he'd hated the poverty and ugliness. What a fight he'd made of it—the little ragged boy to the owner of Ladysmere; a pair of rusty roller-skates to a Jaguar and an Alvis. And now he had given her Christopher. Could love do more?

He came in, and she felt suddenly constrained, sharply aware that Christopher was upstairs with Caroline being put to bed.

He was looking at his watch. "I got held up," he said. "I'd better go and change straight away." He sent her a swift glance. "Everything go all right?"

The constraint increased. She felt it was almost impossible to speak of her meeting with Christopher.

"Yes," she managed. "It was all very easy. We were back here again by a quarter to four."

He nodded. "Good," he said, and added, "I'll change, then."

He didn't move for a moment, but stood there, as though undecided, his head bent.

She said, "Would you—will you be going in to see Caroline?"

Again he looked at his watch.

"Just about. Shan't have to be long. What time did you say we'd pick Giles and Miranda up?"

"At a quarter-past seven."

"I thought you said seven. Quarter-past. . . ."

She stood up, feeling she had to do something, take some step, make some move, anything to ease the constraint which had suddenly become impossible.

"Will you come and see Christopher, then?" she said.

He was dressed for bed in a blue pyjama suit and he looked very clean.

As they opened the door he was standing at the nurse's knee watching her feed Caroline from a mug. He turned when he heard them and, as he saw Guy, a startled, almost fearful look came over his face and he trotted over to Nurse Carrington who was folding up his clothes, and stood beside her, very straight, his eyes bluer than ever above the blue sleeping-suit.

Caroline, a rime of milk round her mouth, danced her lashes at Guy, and then looked at Christopher and waved her one free arm.

"Careful, Caroline," said the nurse, and Gina walked towards Christopher, her hand out.

"Won't you come and say how d'you do, Christopher?"

Nurse Carrington gave him a little touch on the shoulder. "Say how d'you do," she urged.

You could almost, thought Gina, watch the conflict going on in his baby mind—the fear and the courage; the desire to please, the urge to turn away and hide from things and people too large for him, too bewildering. If she could she would have spared him all that, for tonight at least, but Guy had given him back to her, and she wanted above all things that he should love him.

Suddenly, his battle won, he marched forward, his hand outstretched, and Guy stooped and took it in his own.

Happiness woke and lived with her, something tangible, to be seen and felt.

Philip, who came up a few days later, was struck by the change in her. In less than a week vitality had returned to her movements, her walk, her speech even, and he thought he saw, for the first time, the person she had been before Guy had gone to Korea and she had met Andrew Wharton one night at Alban Bay.

Watching her playing with the two babies, her skin tanned by the hot summer, her eyes deep and bright again, he told himself that the American could hardly be blamed, though heaven knew the man had left her with a heavy enough burden to carry. But that time was over. For good? God knew. He brushed the doubt aside. He might dislike Taylor, but she loved him. The love and the vitality had resurrected together.

He still wondered if Taylor had told her that he had refused to give him the Mostyns' name and address when he had first approached him. He had an idea that he hadn't, for Gina, apparently, bore no resentment towards him—unless any that she had borne was dissolved in her present happiness. And yet, there was something odd in the fact that Taylor hadn't taken the chance to degrade him in her eyes. Why hadn't he? Certainly not from love of him! He was slightly puzzled, aware of some quirk in the way things had worked out.

Christopher, bored with Caroline, got up from the rug and began to push his wheelbarrow over the grass. But Caroline, writhing in the frustration that chained her small limbs to immobility, opened her mouth and let out a roar of anger and flayed about with her arms as though they at least might enable her to get up and join him.

"Hell holds no fury . . ." said Philip, and he smiled down at the tiny threshing figure on the rug.

Christopher, who had only taken a few steps away from them, turned and stared at Caroline, surprise stamped not only on his face but in every line of his sturdy frame. He stood there for a moment, the handles of the barrow in his fists, then he lowered the legs on to the grass, went back to the rug, bent over Caroline and gave her a firm slap on one fat thigh.

Caroline had never been so astonished in her life. The roar stopped in mid-utterance, and she lay with her mouth open, her eyes wide, while Christopher stood over her, not saying a word. Then, while the tears still clung to her lashes and rolled down her cheeks, she smiled up at him; a smile of total bliss and satisfaction.

"Masochism . . ." muttered Philip. "You women wield it like a sabre. Poor Christopher."

But Christopher had his own methods. He stood over Caroline for a few seconds longer, then he squatted down on his knees, gave her a swift and casual kiss, got to his feet again and walked determinedly back to his barrow. And Caroline watched him—in silence.

Philip laughed.

"Nice work," he said. "That chap's got something."

The smile faded on Gina's face and quite seriously she said, "He's got a personality, even now. What d'you think of him?"

Still lightly, he answered, "I'm lost in envy. He should go far. He's the first man I've met who isn't afraid of a woman."

"I meant seriously," Gina urged. "He has got quite a character, hasn't he?"

His own face became grave. "He's nice."

"I wanted you to think so." She picked some shorn blades of grass and ran them through her fingers on to the lawn again. "They—Jennifer, I suppose, really—have looked after him wonderfully. I so often think of her," she went on. "It's almost as though a bit of her is here, with him, still." She sighed. "I hated it because it had to be that way, Philip. It seems so unfair, as though she lost everything and I gained it all."

"It's done now," he said gently. "She had her moment. Don't grieve over it."

"There's no use," she answered. "How's George?"

He lifted his shoulders slightly. "Not finding it easy, poor devil. He may be better when he gets across to Africa."

She sat there silent with her head bent and he said, "And Guy?"

"I think it'll be all right," she answered, but she didn't look up. "It's a bit strange all round at first. He's been—wonderful," she added.

"Has he?" he asked, and cursed himself for a fool.

She looked at him quickly. "But, Philip, of course he has. How many men would have let me have Christopher?"

And how many men would have been so infernally smug about letting you have him, he asked himself. It was no good, he couldn't stand Taylor. Reason told him that the man had taken a hammering —to be presented with your wife's illegitimate child after a year in a Korean jail took some bearing, God knew—and yet his attitude of 'I, the sinless' galled and irritated him. And now 'the sinless' had become 'the charitable', the 'wonderful' and 'forgiving' husband. And Gina, as he knew she would, adored him more than ever.

"You don't like Guy, do you?" she said.

"We're different types," he answered easily. "And I don't know him very well, you know. Who am I to like or not like your husband, anyway?"

She was pulling at the grass again, watching the short green blades fall into a little heap. "You're my friend," she said.

"Yes."

"I wish I could make you understand what I did to him. I *know*." She sighed. "Perhaps it will be all right now," she added.

"You've suffered, too," he said quietly.

"If only we alone suffered for our own mistakes, our own sins," she said. "That's the agonising part of it—we don't. It's the damage to the people we love that's so terrible, isn't it?"

"Remember that they share our goodness and joy as well," he told her.

"Yes," she answered. "Yes. I mustn't forget that."

While they were having dinner she told Guy of Christopher's handling of Caroline. "Philip Blake was here," she ended, "and he said Caroline was showing signs of female masochism already."

She saw his expression change.

"Is someone ill?" he asked.

"Ill? No, why?"

"Then why was Blake here?"

"He'd just come in to see us," she answered.

He put his knife and fork down.

"We've had this out before," he said. "I don't like Blake, and I don't want him coming to the place unless and until he's sent for. I gave in to you when you wanted to keep him on as your doctor, and I think you might consider me now."

"But, Guy, good heavens, he was only here a quarter of an hour. He happened to be passing the gate and——"

"Listen, Gina," he broke in, "I'm not interested in where he was going to or coming from, all I say is, I don't want him dropping in here whenever the fancy takes him."

"You forget," she said, "that he's a friend of mine. Surely you don't want to cut me off from friendship."

He drank his wine and put the glass down.

"You have plenty of other friends," he said. "And now you have your relations within a stone's throw of you as well. I can't force you not to have Blake here, but I ask you not to." He picked up his knife and fork again. "It doesn't seem to me to be a very great demand to make of you."

But it was, Gina thought. It was a dreadful interference with her liberty of choice. Why shouldn't she see Philip? No human being had ever done as much for her as he had done. Never before had she realised the depth, the 'drawing together' that was friendship. She could even say that she loved him, not as she loved Guy or Caroline and Christopher, but love all the same. She wouldn't give up seeing him. Guy had no right to make such a demand. Hadn't he? She sighed. Yes, he had. By the very virtue of his giving Christopher back to her he had.

Realising it, she was suddenly afraid.

Nurse Carrington left the following day.

Kathleen Harrison was not sorry to see her go, although there had been no trouble; in fact, everything had gone smoothly. But, last night, when 'he' came into the nursery to see the children and to say good-bye to Nurse Carrington—he never forgot things like that—she saw the smile the girl gave him and it sent a sick pain through her heart—not only a sick pain, but a sudden, terrifying desire to smash into the girl's face, to maim and disfigure it and to feel the flesh and bones giving beneath hammer-blows. The swift force of that primitive urge left her appalled and shaking—she who found it difficult to kill a mosquito.

There had been a scene with Christopher, who cried and clung to the girl when he realised that he was not going with her and she'd had to wake Caroline up from her afternoon nap to distract his attention. When Mrs. Taylor came into the nursery, he went to her and held her skirt in his hands and cried, "I want to go to Mummy. Please may I see Mummy? I want her."

Mrs. Taylor had looked very sad, and she'd picked him up—not, she thought, a very good idea—and had taken him off with her.

"I'll give him a run in the car, Nanny. It'll take his mind off it, perhaps."

"I think it would be better to leave him with Caroline, Mrs. Taylor," she'd advised. "After all, he's got to get used to it here without his nurse, hasn't he?"

"Yes, I know," she'd answered. "But we mustn't be too hard on him. These things hurt so terribly, don't they?"

It was, she thought, rather a foolish remark, treating Christopher as though he were adult. And what, she wondered, did Gina Taylor know about being 'hurt'? She'd 'got everything'—money, clothes, a lovely home, a car, and—Guy. Unless . . . She'd wondered sometimes. Doctor Blake . . . She'd often heard them laughing together, and yesterday, under the trees, she'd seen him put his hand on her shoulder. Did that mean . . .? Suppose it did? One day they might go off together and leave Guy, and he would turn to her and at last, at last, she'd be able to shower all the wealth and glory of her love on him. Such tenderness, such understanding, such, oh God, such care for him. Not almost cold, as 'she' so often was cold, but warm and loving and gentle. And he would lie with his head on her breast and say, "Oh, Kate, Kate . . . I've wanted you so much. It's been so long . . . so very long. . . ."

Christopher sat beside Gina as she drove, his legs in bright red denim trousers stuck straight before him, his feet vertical, a small and shabby little tip-cart clutched in his hand.

She looked sideways at him and saw that his head was down and the tears still hung on his lashes, and as she turned away she heard him draw in his breath on a sob. His solitariness was terrible. She felt it in her own heart, as though she, too, bore it with and for him. In a way she did, for the fact that he could not turn to her for comfort was a sharp grief which was the measure of her own isolation from him.

She said, "We'll go into a shop and see what we can find. Would you like that?"

"Mummy," he whispered, his head still down. "I like to go to Mummy. . . ."

She thought she knew, for the first time, what it meant to be unable to comfort your own child's pain. There was nothing she could do for him. Nothing. She knew very well that, in a week or so, sooner possibly, the memory of Jennifer would go from him and the pain of his loss would go with it, but now, at this moment, he must bear it quite alone. And it was she herself who had, in the first instance, inflicted it on him.

She wanted to fold him close to her and say, "I'm your mother, son, and I'll never desert you again as long as I live. . . ." But that was as impossible as it was idiotic. All she could do was to drive him into Belsted and buy him a toy at the little shop.

He chose a tip-cart, almost identical with the one he held, politely refusing every other suggestion, and he was very grave; but when he came out of the shop, clutching one tip-cart in each hand, the tears had dried on his lashes.

Gina did other shopping and, as it was by then half-past four, she went into the tea-shop in the square for tea. He drank some milk and ate a little cake, and she sat beside him and brushed the crumbs from his mouth and felt conspiratorial and blessedly happy.

"I like going out with you," she said. "Do you like going out with me?"

He looked up at her, his eyes shy, but more confident.

"We'll escape sometimes," she said. "When you're a bit bigger, we'll go off for a whole day. We'll take our breakfast and have it on the hills. How about that? And we'll go out in the night and see the stars. . . ."

She was talking nonsense to him and she knew it, but it gave her a certain comfort. There was so much to show him, so much to share with him. Her mind slipped along the track into the future. . . . Sailing, climbing, cooking supper out in the open as the night came down. . . . Poetry, paintings, Rome. . . . So much to share with him.

Clutching the tip-carts, he trotted beside her to the car.

She was surprised to see Guy's car on the drive when they got home. He came down the steps as she drew up.

"You're early!"

"I had to see a man in Croydon as I came down. It didn't take as long as I thought."

"Nice. Have you had tea?"

"They're getting me some."

Christopher stood very still, looking up at him, his eyes anxious.

"He was so miserable after the nurse went that I took him out for a run," Gina said. "I offered him every toy in Collins's shop, but he chose a replica of the little cart he had. I'm afraid he's got a one-track mind."

She saw Guy looking down at him, and although his expression hadn't changed, there came a faint warning into her mind, as though a distant alarm had sounded.

"You didn't take Caroline," he said.

"Not this time," she answered briskly. "We slipped away quickly to take his mind off his tears. Caroline would have meant Nanny and a very great palaver. We bolted, didn't we, Christopher?"

She spoke quickly, fending off the irritation she sensed rising in him. Was he really jealous because she had taken Christopher and left Caroline? The idea was ridiculous.

"I see," he answered, and she took Christopher's hand to take him back to the nursery. He clutched her very tightly, and kept close to her until they had got into the house and he was climbing the stairs, his little round, red-covered seat bobbing as he took each step.

As she followed him up, she thought, 'I've got to be very careful. Very careful,' and she sighed lightly.

Two nights later she forgot both care and carefulness in a wave of joy which she hadn't experienced since the days before Guy had gone to Korea.

The Marsdens, people they'd come to know who lived six miles away, gave a party for their daughter's birthday in the Tudor manor-house where they lived. There was nothing spectacular about the party, and yet, as sometimes happens, it was warm-hearted, natural and very successful from the first half-hour. And Gina, for the first time for nearly three years, threw off the veil of fatigue and anxiety which had dimmed both vitality and hope. Life flowed through her again, and as she walked up the two stone steps, worn into a dip by the passing of many feet over the centuries and on into the oak-panelled hall with the hammer-beam ceiling and the minstrels' gallery and the sombre faces of long-dead Marsdens looking, as she thought, longer dead than ever in their heavy gold frames, she felt a final lifting of a weight and laughter woke in her heart again.

Guy, too, seemed influenced by some indefinable charm about the old house and, watching him across the dinner-table, she saw that the strained appearance had gone from his face and his mouth was relaxed, smiling. She felt excited, on the crest of a new wave, as though some other life were just about to be revealed to her.

After dinner they went into the Long Gallery and danced, and when Guy came to her and took her into his arms, she knew an uprush of love for him, an opening of her heart which had been constricted for so long. Wave after wave of gratitude to him went over her, and she thought, now at this moment I have everything—Guy, Caroline and Christopher. And love. I love Guy. Some time ago I wondered if I did still love him. I know now that nothing will ever kill my love because I love *him*, not my own mental image of him. The little Catholic priest was right—marriage is permanent. In spite of that night with Andrew, it's still permanent—the one undying thing, as we said that night on our honeymoon.

She looked up at Guy, and he, caught up in the same magic, looked down at her, and she knew that, in that moment, the barriers had gone and they saw one another, not 'through a glass darkly', but 'face to face'—two people of the thousands of millions who had passed across the track of the world; two people who, by some miracle of chance, had been born into the same time, to meet, to know and to love.

And yet, less than a month later she looked back on that night and wondered if she had imagined the delight of it.

Chapter XIII

WHAT more, she asked herself, did Guy want? What awful inner un-peace was eating him up now?

Why ask yourself questions to which you know the answers, she flayed herself. Guy, it was obvious, disliked Christopher. To use the word 'dislike' to describe an antagonism between a man of nearly forty-five and a baby of two was ludicrous, and yet he did appear actively to dislike him.

Could anyone dislike Christopher? He was a boy, certainly, full of mischief and enterprise, but he was obedient and to her, anyway, he seemed to be striving so hard to please in this new bewildering life. And Caroline adored him. When he went off round the garden on some important male affair of his own, she watched him with fascinated wonder, an almost maternal smile of satisfaction on her face. And when he condescended to her and came to dally a few moments away on her play-rug, she patted his face, or held out her ridiculous, enticing hands to him, or merely sat still, breathing deep sighs of an overflowing bounty, her eyes fixed on his every movement.

And apart from Caroline, everyone who came to the house—besides their own staff—appeared to care for him.

Miranda Conway was nearly as besotted as Caroline.

"He's so fascinating, Gina," she said to her one day when she was up at Ladysmere. "Wouldn't you give anything to know about his parents?"

"We do know a certain amount," Gina answered, with a faint inward smile. "I believe his father was an artist or writer."

"I shouldn't be surprised. He's got a sort of distinction about him even now, hasn't he?" Her eyes followed Christopher as he walked beside Marple—two men, engaged with some momentous and grave consideration, and she said, "I wonder what he'll be. In a way, it's even more exciting when you haven't any clues to guide you, isn't it?" She laughed. "All I'm willing to wager is that whatever he becomes will include bevies of young women, fluttering their eyes at him. And Caroline," she added, "will smile her way over the lot of them and have him for her own in the finish. 'As it was in the beginning. . . .'"

"But she couldn't . . ." Gina began quickly, and she stopped, realising that the sentence mustn't be continued.

"They aren't *related*," said Miranda. "I think it would be charming if they fell in love eventually." She lay back in the chair. "No one could say, 'Marry in haste, repent at leisure' to them. I'm not so sure that it wouldn't be rather nice to marry someone you'd grown up with. It would be very—peaceful, wouldn't it?"

Miranda's suggestion with all its confusion of implication frightened her, but she had to put the thought away. The future must take care of itself. The present was bewildering enough.

Her thought returned to the Marsdens again. At their house that night it had seemed to her that they had touched a depth of happiness unknown before. Its sweetness had spilled over on to the following days, and once or twice she'd thought that it was as though the pain and heartache of the last three years had not only intensified her present happiness but actually made it possible. Gratitude to Guy filled her, and she thought she could never love him enough for ending the torture of her longing and giving Christopher back to her. There had been no doubt in her mind that from now on the four of them would be a unit, a family. She hadn't been foolish or irrational about it. There'd been no false romanticism, no extravagant hopes of some Utopian existence far removed from reality. Guy and she were a man and a woman with wills and minds and temperaments of their own, and the children were children, unformed, mischievous, tiresome; but the fact that Guy had let her have Christopher had united what had been divided, and it had also been a tangible expression of his total forgiveness.

It had, hadn't it? What else? If it wasn't that, why had he given him back to her? He'd gone to see Philip about it some time before Jennifer Mostyn had died. It wasn't even as though George had asked them to have him—it was Guy and Guy alone who had made the first move. Then why this perpetual, carping dislike of Christopher? And why, dear God, why the apparent total repudiation of that lovely night at the Marsdens' and the week of sheer happiness that followed it? Could he have forgotten so soon? Or had that night when he had loved her with all the passion of the first days of their marriage been nothing but 'an act', or, what was somehow worse, more degrading, his own physical need for her? Was that, she wondered, the basis of it all—of his 'love' for her? Was it nothing but that? No care for her as a person, another soul, only the fact that, by chance, she could satisfy his sexual needs? She turned away from that, sick at heart, and she thought of the time when she had first met him. Was that all it had been then? Surely not. They'd been friends, companions, eager to know one another, to reveal and share the thoughts of their minds and their hearts. The physical union, wonderful and passionate as it had been, was the expression of that love, the fierce need to get ever nearer, more and more united. It was so, wasn't it? Or had she only imagined the 'devotion', the 'caring'? If she had, then the night of the Marsdens' party and the following week of their reawakened love were not what she had thought them at all. They were merely moments which, now, made her feel ashamed, almost degraded.

'I've got to stop this introspection,' she told herself. The moment you started delving for the motives of your own—or other people's—actions you were lost in a fog of suspicion and speculation, and there was no safe ground under your feet anywhere. Black became white and white black, and before you knew where you were you could make false every truth and suspect every kindness. There was only one thing you could do, and that was to take the present as it was and work from that. And the 'present' was that Guy, having decided on his own initiative to let her have Christopher at Ladysmere, now seemed to regret that move and hate Christopher.

Once again she told herself, 'I must be careful. Very careful.' But she added, 'Nothing will separate me from Christopher a second time. Nothing.'

But no amount of 'carefulness', no determination to keep everything 'on an even keel', made much difference, and two days later, at the week-end, it was only by sheer luck that a 'scene' was stopped in mid-act. And it was all so puerile, so over 'nothing at all'.

The children had been playing together. Caroline, now able, to her gratification, to crawl had, somehow or other, managed to get her hand under the wheel of Christopher's barrow. The hurt was superficial, but Caroline made a dramatic business of it, and her screams might have been the screams of someone in mortal agony. The nurse, had she been there, would have made short shrift of her histrionics; but she wasn't there, she was in Belsted having a tooth removed, and it was Guy who was first on the scene with Gina a second or two behind him.

Gina took a quick look at Caroline's hand—Guy had picked her up and was holding her in his arms—and saw there was no grave damage, and she turned to Christopher who was standing staring up at her, white-faced and obviously shocked. She knelt on the grass and put her arm round him and said, "It's all right, Christopher. You haven't hurt her badly. We'll all go in and get some milk. . . ."

But Christopher was almost rigid, his terrified eyes staring, she realised, not at Caroline but at Guy.

And turning, swiftly, she saw an expression on Guy's face which stunned her.

"Guy!" She had cried his name before she realised it.

He shifted his glance from Christopher to herself, but the cold, hard expression was still in his eyes. "Guy," she said again, "what are you looking like that for?"

Caroline had stopped screaming, and was staring down at Christopher, the tears still on her lashes.

"I'm tired of this revolting favouritism," Guy answered her in a clipped, low voice. "I didn't know when I decided to have your child here that he was to be preferred before my own daughter."

"What are you saying?" she asked him. "There's no favouritism, no preference——"

"There's both," he said. "And on every possible occasion and at all times. The boy wilfully injures Caroline—and it's he who has to be coddled and made much of. And it's always the same. He's only to cry a few crocodile tears and you rush to protect him. Two days ago——"

"But, Guy, you don't understand. Two days ago he'd suddenly asked for Jennifer. He hasn't forgotten yet, and every now and then he misses her so dreadfully. What could I do but comfort him? You happened to come in and——"

"That wasn't an isolated instance, and you know it. It's perfectly obvious to anyone that you've a far greater love for him than for Caroline."

"That's not true. You know it's not true. I love them both. How could I not, Guy? They're both my children . . .?"

The words were uttered before she realised their import and almost at once Guy's bitter retort came, "Exactly. But they are *not* both my children and, as I say, your preference is obvious. And sickening. If I'd known that this boy was to be elevated and smarmed over on every occasion, while Caroline is more or less ignored, I shouldn't have considered having him here. I didn't know. I imagined that you'd be so grateful to have him at all that you'd at least treat our own daughter with the same affection. The boy's becoming a little upstart. . . ."

The malice was pouring out of him, seething up from behind the barrier of repression in his heart. It was the old set-up. . . . Once again he had made her this last and final gift—her illegitimate son, and was she grateful? Grateful! After the first day or two of a pretended gratitude, she'd swung back to her usual high-handed 'Gina-Randolph-Conway-Coutts' attitude. For half an hour she'd been on her knees to him, but once the child was safely installed, there'd been an end to gratitude. And, in spite of her justification, her favouritism was obvious. And, as he'd just said, sickening. There was no doubt now, in his mind, that her original story of a 'sudden temptation' was merely another scheme to 'pull the wool over his eyes'. Sudden temptation! It was ludicrous. But the whole thing was clear now, and if he hadn't been a fool he'd have seen it all before. He had seen it all before, but he'd shut his eyes to it, because he'd made up his mind to forgive her and to have her back as his wife. Of course she'd loved the boy's father. Would she have sighed and yearned for the child if she hadn't loved him? Wouldn't she have been delighted to obliterate all traces of her 'sudden temptation'? Of course she would! But she hadn't. She'd made herself ill by her insane longing for her lover's child, and now that he, in his innocence, had given the boy back to her, she was unable to hide her adoration of him. She didn't even try to hide it. She flaunted it, making a fool of the boy, while his daughter was treated with what amounted to indifference. And he wasn't alone in that opinion. Although she hadn't said so in so many words, the nurse had noticed it. Only last night there'd been a meaning look in the woman's eyes when she'd said to him, "Mrs. Taylor seems to have taken to him very much, doesn't she?" Was he to have the scorn and pity of the servants thrust on him? If only they knew! He felt he wanted to go to them and tell them. To say, 'I gave Christopher back to her. He's her child by another man, but I forgave her and now I've even had her son brought here to my home. . . . All this I've done for her, and what does she care?' Care! She takes it all for granted just as she's taken my forgiveness for granted. Why shouldn't Gina Randolph be forgiven? The Conway-Coutts aren't bound by the laws that affect the common herd. They're above them. They can do as they please. Gratitude! God, no. Merely their accepted right and privilege. *In their own eyes*. In the eyes of God they're adulterers, just like any ordinary people. They're sinners. Gina's a sinner. She wouldn't admit it, but she is. She's soiled and dirty, and the boy, the outcome of her disloyalty, is soiled, too. And all this, all this, I forgave. . . .

He realised that he was standing under the tree with Caroline in his arms and that Gina was still kneeling on the grass, one arm round Christopher's shoulder, her face lifted to his own. He felt shaken and physically sick, and he fought down an urge to knock the snivelling boy down, to remove that white, frightened face from the circle of his vision. It was he who'd come between them. He Gina loved, just as she'd loved his father. Just as once she'd loved him. . . .

Caroline drew a long, shuddering breath, the finale to her outburst. He felt her small body tremble in his arms, then she held out her hand to Christopher. Even Caroline. . . .

"Guy," said Gina, "you're so wrong, so . . ." And then, over the grass, came Miranda, on her greyhound legs; thin as a lath, her narrow feet passing lightly over the shorn blades, a smile on her lips.

"Hyah!" she called. "What's going on around here?"

Another of them, thought Guy. As loose as the rest, possibly. How often had she let Giles Conway down? Or didn't he care if she had?

"Hello!" said Gina, and he noticed that in a split second she'd 'right about faced', all shame and even distress wiped from her face. "A major crisis," she said lightly to Miranda. "We thought Christopher had murdered Caroline, but it's more noise than anything. Nurse is in Belsted at the dentist's," she added. "She would be! Shall I have Caroline, Guy? I'll take them in and give them some milk. They're all right now."

"I'll have her," said Miranda. "You manage Christopher. Coming, Caroline?"

She swung the strap of her handbag up her arm and held out her hands. Caroline smiled delightfully, one white tooth showing.

Guy watched them as they walked back to the house. Just for a second a door opened in his mind and he saw everything in a totally different light—clear-cut, gentle, true; then the door slammed to again and he watched Gina bend down and take Christopher's hand.

She couldn't even walk over the grass back to the house without the urge to touch him.

Christopher lay on his back under the tree. Through the leaves he could see the sky, and every now and then when the wind blew and turned the leaves inside out, the piece of sky grew larger. He was hot and his trousers were sticking to him. He wriggled his hips but the trousers still stuck to him. He might have used his hands to pull them away from his flesh, but he was holding the tip-carts and he didn't want to let go of them. The edges of them cut into each of his palms, but he had to go on holding them. He tried moving his legs up and down to make a draught to cool himself. As each leg came up he saw his foot and his red sandal appear within his vision. Then a bird flew on to a branch of the tree and sat there. It had a long beak and shining green feathers. Suddenly it bent its head and sent its beak diving in behind its wing. He stopped moving his legs and watched to see if the bird would do it again, but it didn't. It only sat on the branch swaying slightly and opening its beak every now and then as though it were trying to sing.

He sighed and he remembered another garden. It was different from this one, but he didn't know why. It was filled with light, and there was a presence in it which touched his heart with comfort. Dimly he remembered someone's face. It bent over him, smiling gently, and he knew that he loved it. He would have liked very much to be in that place again and to put out his hand and touch the hand that was there. He thought he was going to cry, and then he turned his head and saw Caroline. She had woken up from her sleep, and had rolled over on to her side and was looking at him. She smiled and took her thumb from her mouth and held out her hand towards him, moving her fingers. He edged over till he was close to her, and he laid his arm across her and felt the warmth of her body through the thin dress she wore, and he smelt the known smell of her flesh, and was comforted.

They lay there quietly under the trees together.

Chapter XIV

"YOU'VE got to give it time," Gina told herself. "You can't throw your hand in now. You can't. . . . If only you can keep your temper, remain calm. . . . If only you can understand. . . ."

That was all very well but almost impossible. Nothing Christopher could do was right for Guy. If there was a quarrel between the children, then it was Christopher's fault. If there was an accident, Christopher caused it. And the constant tension was already telling on Christopher. When he'd first come to them, he'd been like a little sapling, growing straight and true, and his eyes had been unafraid. Now he was no longer unafraid, and the fear made him more difficult, edgy. The realisation appalled her, for it was, stupidly, the one thing she hadn't foreseen. In all his small life he had only known love—her own or Jennifer's. Now he was experiencing, if not actual hatred, irritation and dislike—and fear. And for how long could she subject him to it? It was all very well to say, "Give it time," but he'd already been at Ladysmere two months, and the situation, if anything, was worse than it had been. And that damned nurse didn't do much to help it, either. She had never liked the woman, and now she had the feeling that she, too, disliked Christopher and was very careful to 'show him up' when Guy was around. That, of course, was because she was drooling after Guy herself. As if she didn't know! At one time she'd felt humorously sorry for the poor prim little woman, but there'd been a sort of secret malice in her behaviour lately that had sent all pity for her out of her mind. She hated her obvious discrimination between Caroline, the daughter of the house, and 'the little orphan' who had come to them. The sheer snobbery of it was sickening, and there were times when she'd had to hold herself in with iron bands to stop herself telling the fool woman who and what Christopher was. And if ever her iron will broke and she did tell her—then the whole situation would disintegrate.

That, she knew it, would be the day she'd leave Ladysmere—and this time there'd be no return. She and Christopher would get out for good. . . . She stopped, horrified, for her thoughts had been running on involuntarily. Had she really contemplated such a thing? She must be mad. How could she think—even think—of leaving Caroline? She adored Caroline. So did Christopher. Caroline was his one security, his one sure anchor. It wouldn't be possible to separate them. And, oh God, hadn't he had enough of this being bashed about? And Guy? Leave Guy? And for good? For this time there would be no return, that was obvious. Easier to leave Guy than Caroline? This Guy, this man he'd become, yes. Take both children and get out? No money. Nothing to keep them on. To take them from plenty—good food, care, financial security—to nothing? To a mother who'd have to go out to work to keep them? To take Caroline from Guy who loved her. He did love her. If there was one thing in all this tangled skein that was true, it was that—Guy loved Caroline. And if she couldn't take Caroline from Guy and she couldn't take Christopher from Caroline—what was there to do but stick it out? Wait and hope and pray that somehow life would adjust itself.

"Time heals all things," she mocked to herself. But nobody said what happened to the nerves of those who waited for time to do its healing.

'I've made a mess of it from the beginning,' she thought. 'And now the thing's so tangled there's no way out. I ought to have stayed with Christopher and never gone back to Guy when he came home from Korea. And Caroline? Caroline would never have been.' And that was just about as impossible a thing to think as all her other thoughts. She half smiled. Caroline was far too much of a personality to be waved back into oblivion quite so easily. Having come on the scene, she stole the show. And back went her mind to the beginning again. Alban Bay. . . . Andrew. . . . Yes, there it was with its awful monotony, the core and reason of all the rest. 'There was a night when my burden was love . . .' Glynne had sung while the stars sailed in the sky and the little waves lapped at the hidden sand far beyond the groynes where the emerald sea-weed clung to the weathered wood. That irresistible urge; that primitive drive that nothing and no one could stop. And not even a memory of delight remained. However hard she forced herself to remember delight, she couldn't do it. There wasn't so much as a glimmer of it left. There wasn't even shame. There was just—nothing. And she'd bartered a few hours of 'nothing' for all that had happened since. It didn't seem possible. It simply didn't seem possible. Again she forced herself to remember how, after Meg's birthday dinner, Andrew, his hand over hers, his body in line with her own, had whispered, "What's happening to us, Gina?" She made a tremendous effort of will to recapture a flick of the thrill that had swept over her and caught at her very being, but again there was nothing but two queerly wooden people muttering wooden phrases in a wooden setting. Glynne's 'burden of love' had become a burden indeed—but a burden that was crushing the last of life out of her.

And yet, strangely, there was no resentment towards Andrew in her mind. There ought to be, but there wasn't. If anything, she felt an odd sort of compassion towards him, as though they were two people who had stumbled into a bog. Was that because she knew, at heart, that the assent had been hers? She'd said that to Jennifer Mostyn on that afternoon she and Philip had first taken Christopher to Elston Square. "I could have said 'No'," she'd told her. "I didn't say no—that's all." That at least was true. The assent had been hers. It had been hers, just as it always was a woman's, in spite of all the nonsense talked. All through nature that strand remained and would remain, but while the birds and the beasts knew and lived it by instinct, in humans that pride of selection had become dissipated. What modern mother would explain that to her child? Her thought went to Caroline. One day Caroline, too, would come up to that fence. One day Caroline would, perhaps, have her 'Alban Bay' to live through. How could she tell her, how explain, how defend her from that tinsel attraction which flamed up into the dark sky like a rocket and fell to the ground again in a spatter of little false stars? For Caroline, too, was a woman. . . . She smiled slightly, thinking of her absurd little figure sitting watching Christopher with maternal satisfaction, and for the first time she felt a bond between them that she hadn't realised before. Caroline, too, was a woman. And ten minutes ago she'd contemplated leaving her. . . .

She walked to the window of her bedroom, and looked out on to the garden, russet now, with autumn. Was there to be no answer, ever, but only these agonising choices? She longed for peace of heart; for the wholeness and simplicity of their family life, and for the security and companionship of Guy's love. But between them was nothing but a veiled antagonism; a dreadful watching of one another. There was no freedom, no laughter. And less love. How could she love him when he treated Christopher as he did?

She leaned her head against the glass, worn out with the sheer monotony of her own questioning. She was so incredibly tired of it. She longed for escape. To put it right away from her. To laugh again and walk on the hills and not be weighed down with care and her tortured thoughts.

Philip. . . . He came into her mind—his quiet voice, his gentle eyes—and she knew how desperately she missed his casual dropping in at the house. Guy had even resented and forbidden her friendship with him. Was she to give in to his absurd, medieval restrictions as well as to his treatment of Christopher? She wanted to see Philip more than she'd ever wanted to see anyone. Philip cared for her, understood. His understanding had never failed. His help had never failed. . . .

She looked at her watch. It was ten to four. She wondered if he would be there if she went down to Belsted. He might or he might be out on his rounds. Should she chance it, drive down there, and if he were in, have a talk with him? If he were out, come home. . . .

She heard the wheels of the pram on the drive and looking down she saw Caroline, her cheeks apple-red in the cold air, riding regally while Christopher, a small outrider in his scarlet coat, padded in her wake. In his hand he held the original and paintless tip-cart. They passed under the gable out of her sight, and she went to the wardrobe and took her coat from it.

Philip would understand. . . .

She was actually sitting in her car with her finger on the starter when the housemaid came running into the garage.

"Father Martin's just come," she told her. "I said I didn't know if you'd gone. . . ."

She felt irritated, and her first impulse was to say, "Tell him I can't see him, Margaret. I have to go out. . . ."

What did the little man want? More money for his church? Possibly. And what was his church to do with her? It was Guy who was the Christian; Guy, the believer. Guy who hated Christopher, who was virtually cruel to him. . . . And she wanted to see Philip. She needed to see Philip. She longed for his understanding and his care as she'd never longed for it before. He'd take all this pain and turmoil into his steady hands and ease it, lift the burden from her.

Choice—it was there again. She was aware of it as she'd never been aware of it in her life, as though here, now, was significance. But why? She frowned, dimly conscious of the working of something she didn't understand; of that 'other life' that she'd glimpsed once outside the church on the Old Appian Road and, before that, in Philip's car the night they drove back from the Mostyns', a life that went on its way regardless of what she or any of them had planned—a dovetailing of events, a welding-together of loose strands, a uniting of disunity. It moved them about as it willed. It guided the pin in her hand on to Doctor Blake's name. It produced Dardanella and the little flat at Melford. It sent Father Martin riding up the hill on his bicycle from Belsted. To prevent her going to Philip? What nonsense! Philip was her friend. . . .

"Shall I tell him you've gone?" the girl asked.

"Yes," she answered swiftly. "Tell him. . . ." She took her finger from the self-starter and dropped her hand into her lap. "Oh, I'd better come, Margaret. He was probably hoping for some tea."

She took up her handbag and got out of the car.

'Choice?' she thought as she walked back to the house. She'd made her choice, and in the same breath she'd rescinded it. Or had it been rescinded for her? Had she prevented herself or had she been prevented from going to Philip? And if she had, why? She brushed the speculation away. Strain was making her neurotically imaginative. She'd have to get away for a day. Tomorrow she'd go to London and do some shopping. . . .

The priest stood up as she went into the drawing-room, and as he smiled she remembered his clear eyes and the network of lines round them.

"You were going out," he said apologetically. "I mustn't detain you."

She put her handbag and gloves on a table. "It wasn't important. . . ."

Wasn't it? Suddenly it was—very. What a fool she'd been to come back to talk to this shabby little cleric.

"I was up this way," he said, "so I thought I'd call. I haven't been to see you for a long time. And you know," he said, taking her into his confidence with a look, "I've never seen the boy yet. I wondered if I might? Lady Conway tells me he's a charmer."

She smiled at his use of the word, and she said, "Of course you shall see him. I'll get them to bring him down. And you'll have some tea, won't you?"

"I'd love some tea," he answered, and he added, "Last time you gave me tea it was chocolate walnut cake."

"Oh dear!" she laughed. "I hope cook's got some today. I can't guarantee it."

He shook his head gently. "Gluttony! One of the deadly sins. I find chocolate walnut cake a dreadful temptation. But I hope there is some, just the same." The twinkle left his eyes. "Is the boy settling down? Not causing you trouble, I hope?"

Polite conversation or intuition, she wondered, and answered, "I think he's happy. Caroline adores him."

"Ah, good." He settled his shoes on the rug, and she saw the thick, hand-knitted grey socks above them, wrinkling round his ankles. "It was wonderful of your husband—of you both—to have him. This lovely home. . . ." He glanced round the room and back to her. "I must see Mr. Taylor about his baptism. He wasn't sure if he'd been baptised or not when we spoke of it. He was going to find out."

'Was he!' Gina exclaimed to herself. He'd not mentioned a word of it to her.

Another skein in the tangle, she thought wearily. To the priest Guy was Christopher's legal guardian and adopted father, and he'd take it for granted that he would be baptised into the Church as Caroline had been. But Christopher was hers, nothing to do with Guy.

She pressed the bell and when Margaret came in she said, "Will you ask Nanny to send Christopher down? You can bring him, Margaret. And Father Martin will have tea with us."

She turned to the priest again, and she saw that he was looking directly at her. There was something in his expression that disturbed her, and she talked of Miranda and Giles until Margaret came back with Christopher.

She knew a sharp sense of shock when he came in. The change in him, particularly in his eyes, appeared suddenly marked. Or was she imagining it? She held out her hand to him.

"Come and say how d'you do to Father Martin, Christopher."

He turned his eyes to the priest quickly—too quickly. Too fearfully. Then he looked back to her. She smiled at him, trying to send him confidence.

"You've got a tip-cart," she heard Father Martin say in a matter-of-fact tone.

Christopher brought his hand up an inch or so and peered down at the cart, then he looked at Father Martin and a half-smile came over his face. It was a conspiratorial, man to man smile, recognising the rational assessment of the importance of tip-carts.

"I'd like to see it," said the priest gravely. "Please," he added.

For a moment longer Christopher hesitated, then he marched forward and, standing at the priest's knee, handed over the cart. Father Martin examined it in silence. He turned it over, twiddled the wheels, let the back flap down and clicked it to again. And at last he said, "Does it hold sand?"

Christopher nodded.

"And little stones?"

"And leaves," said Christopher. "And biscuits. Once," he said, "I putted sugar in it. But Nanny was cross."

"Women don't understand these things," said Father Martin, and with a quizzical glance at Gina he said, "But you mustn't put sugar in it if they tell you not to. Want to use your sense. Keep the peace."

They went on conversing about the tip-cart and Gina thought, 'They're about the same age'; but she saw that the fear had gone from Christopher's eyes and that he stood close to the priest, one hand on his knee.

She had never seen him stand close to Guy, one hand on his knee.

She sat back in her chair watching the two of them analyse the tip-cart and discuss, with gravity and proper decorum, the various merits of buses, wheelbarrows and pen-knives, and she thought, 'This is what he needs—another man's companionship,' and she smiled to herself. But it was true. Tension had gone from him. He chatted and explained as he used to do, and once he opened his mouth in his old manner and chortled out his deep laugh. 'His life can't be twisted out of shape, made a thing of fear,' she thought. 'I've got to stop it. Got to protect him.' But how? And back came the answer—'Take him away. He'll never be happy here. He'll always be fettered, afraid.'

She fancied she saw Jennifer there, standing with pain in her eyes, and she said to her, 'I'd rather you'd have kept him for ever than this. I'd rather never have seen him again. . . . Because with you and George he had love.'

Father Martin was demonstrating some abstruse mystery with his own pen-knife when Margaret came for Christopher.

"I must see you again," the priest said. "I've got some goldfish in a tank. I call them Eb and Flo—it's short for Ebenezer and Florence. Get them to bring you down some time. . . ."

He laid his hand on Christopher's head in a brief gesture, and Margaret took him off.

The door closed behind them and he turned his gentle eyes to Gina.

"He's a beautiful child. Most lovable. How his own mother, God rest her, would bless you if she knew what you were doing for him. I'm sure——"

She sat up very straight in the chair, her arms tightly folded pressing against her breasts and suddenly she drew a breath and said, "Please don't go on. I am his mother."

She didn't even ask herself why she'd told him. It was done. That was all.

The merest flick of the tail end of an expression showed for a second in his eyes, then they were quiet again, untroubled.

"You poor child," he said.

She still sat up very straight, and she spoke in short, rapping little sentences.

"No. I'm neither poor nor a child. I'm a woman, adult. I knew what I was doing, knew quite well. . . ." And still rigid, her arms pressing on to her breasts, in the same tone, cold as the fall of little pebbles on to concrete, she told him all of it, right from the beginning. "It hadn't even the dignity of love. . . . He was killed. . . . Guy in a Communist prison. . . . Philip Blake. . . . The Mostyns. . . . She died of heart failure. . . . Caroline. . . . He hates him," she ended. "I pretend I don't know why, but I do know why. It's as he said it would be in the beginning when he first refused to have him, his very presence shrieks the fact that another man made love to me. That I betrayed him while he was in captivity. He can't forget it, and Christopher is a living reminder. I'm an adulteress, aren't I? That's what you'd call me. It's what he calls me in his heart. I'm outcast, aren't I? I committed the unforgivable sin. . . ."

He sat there very still, his eyes cast down as though he were embarrassed. Possibly he was. Then, without looking up or moving, he said, "There is no such thing as an unforgivable sin. Our Lord Himself said so, didn't He? He told us that our sins whatever they were would be forgiven in the measure in which we forgave." He raised his head and looked at her. "You have forgiven much," he said to her.

Something in his tone started the tears in her eyes, and she saw him through them, queerly caricatured, a little black beetle hunched in the chair.

"It isn't I who have anything to forgive," she said coldly, and she thought, 'Poor little man. Poor little celibate. He doesn't understand. How could he?'

"It is a greater grace than you know to be able to say that," he said, and he glanced at her sharply. "A far greater grace." He looked down again. "So many of us see only what we want to see," he said. "So many of us."

"I don't know what you're talking about," she answered shortly. "Nobody forced me. None of it would have happened if I hadn't fallen for a handful of stars and a little song."

"You didn't mean to," he said. "There was nothing coldly deliberate, premeditated. You fell for the strongest force there is. It might happen to any of us."

"Your Church condemns it," she said scornfully.

He smiled very slightly.

"'*My*' Church forgives it," he answered, "because Our Lord forgave. It not only forgives, it forgets," he said, and he shot her another little look. "It wipes it right out. Our Lord wipes the slate clean."

"But Christopher, Guy," she said. "All of them. All that's happened since. Guy's dislike of Christopher. Christopher's fear. It can't wipe all that out. Nothing can."

"It can all be mended, made lovely again," he said. "It can be made even more lovely than in the beginning, because now there's Christopher, too. *O felix culpa* . . ." he muttered to himself.

"You don't understand," she said. "You don't know Guy."

"No," he answered softly.

"I loved him," she said. "I did, you know. He'd battled through so much. And he loved me. I killed his faith in me. Don't you see that? I know he's been wretched since, but how can I blame him? To him it *is* the unforgivable sin."

"You mustn't say that. Really you mustn't," he said. "There just isn't such a thing. And he knows it. You see," he said, "it isn't we, you, I, or anybody, who forgive. We couldn't. Haven't got it in us. We just haven't got it in us," he repeated. "We have to pray for it to be given us," he said. "A free, gratis and for nothing gift. I expect you feel that you can't forgive Guy for disliking Christopher. You say to yourself, 'How can I forgive him that?' You're right, you can't. It's beyond you. But Our Lord can give you forgiveness. Don't smile and say, 'That funny little man sitting there talking nonsense'. It's true. A fact. You ask Him to give it you. He will."

The door opened and Margaret came in with her tray. She pulled the table forward, spread the cloth, put cups and saucers down, and a new chocolate cake with the walnuts making indentations in the smooth icing.

"It is chocolate-layer," he said, when she'd shut the door again. "Now isn't God good?"

She filled the cups and watched him eat a large slice of the cake, and she wondered what on earth had made her pour all that out to this childlike man with the cake crumbs round his mouth. Just what did she think he could do? And yet she hadn't been able to lie to him.

He talked of other things till he'd finished his tea and then he said, "You know, I've got to go now. Isn't that impolite? But I have to be at the Poor Clares by six." He sat forward, his hands on his knees. "You've been very courageous," he said, "and very generous-hearted. You'll go on being it, won't you? Don't give up. God leads us in very roundabout ways sometimes. I shall pray for you," he said.

Again his tone brought tears to her throat, but she said sharply, "I'm past praying for."

"None of us are that, thank God," he answered.

She walked to the front door with him, strangely loth to let him go.

"I'll come and see you again very soon," he said. "And in the meantime—God bless you."

He had left his bicycle outside the gates and she stood on the steps watching him walk down the drive, and as she saw his black retreating figure, she suddenly remembered the day in Rome when the crowds in Saint Peter's Square parted and they'd carried the Pope through the lane they'd made. And she thought that there was the same quality of loneliness about his diminishing back, as though they both shared some deep and secret purpose which no amount of talking would get into words.

She was up with the children when Guy came home, and she heard him go straight along to his study. His presence in the house brought constraint, but changing her dress a quarter of an hour later, she remembered Father Martin saying, "It can all be made lovely again. . . ." Could it? Even now she wanted to believe it could, though reason and sense told her that her hope was futile, nothing but wishful thinking.

An hour later she was convinced, if she needed further convincing, of the futility.

She'd gone down to dinner with a faint spark of new hope, as though the priest's sheer kindliness had spilled over and left a residue of warmth in her. She'd even imagined that Guy might be pleased to think that he had called, and when she first told him, there'd been a softening of the lines of his face, an interest in his eyes.

And then—would she never learn?—she'd said, "He asked to see Christopher, so I got Nanny to send him down and he was sweet to him. . . ."

Just that one sentence, that was all. One unthought-out natural remark. But it was enough. Guy didn't say anything, didn't make a scene, but she watched the momentary softness leave his face, saw the cold lines settle again.

Christopher had been brought down to the drawing-room to see the priest, but Caroline hadn't. Caroline had been left upstairs.

She didn't need telling. She knew it all as clearly as though he'd shouted it at her. Andrew Wharton's child had been 'preferred' to his own child. Once more he'd been 'flaunted', 'made much of'.

She felt sick with the sheer hopelessness of it. 'Made lovely again?' No. It couldn't be made *anything* again. She thought it was as though she and Guy had set out on a journey, and at the cross-roads, that was the night at Alban Bay, they'd separated, each going on a different road. For a little while, at the time of Caroline's birth, they'd caught sight of one another again, but only for a few brief steps. Now, every day, the distance was widening. 'Made lovely again!' The priest's pathetic hope was the hope of an idealist, so far removed from reality that he couldn't even see the facts as they were. And in the end it was Guy he'd have to support, because Guy was one of his parishioners. And even as she ate the pineapple-shortcake on her plate the old deadly wheel of monotonous query started again. Why did he have Christopher only to hate him? Was it nothing but a cold, premeditated plan to 'punish' her through her son? The sadism of that tormented her, snapping the last strands of normality.

She looked at Guy's cold face and was afraid. She'd been afraid before, but not with this kind of fear. This kind of fear was insidious, you couldn't come to grips with it because it hit, not at you, but at your children, at one of your children. The other? Caroline danced into her mind on a smile, holding out her hands, her parted lips showing two brand-new teeth.

She felt trapped, caught in a cage.

Chapter XV

SHE kept to her plan to spend the next day in London, and decided to go up by train from Belsted instead of by car. Guy had a dinner to attend and was staying in London for the night. The very fact gave her a sense of freedom.

'Perhaps,' she thought, driving down to the town, 'a day right away from it all will give me a new slant. I'm too near it. . . .'

She recalled, as she parked the car, the expression on the nurse's face as she'd told her that she would be away all day and didn't know what time she'd be back. She hadn't taken it in at the moment, but now it returned to her, troubling her slightly. There was something in that expression which she couldn't quite place; some hidden secret, not malice exactly, but . . . Her thought broke off as she saw Philip walking towards her.

"I thought that was your car," he said. "Nice."

Yesterday she'd been on her way to see him when the priest had come. Today, escaping from all of it, she'd run into him. It didn't matter what you planned or didn't plan, she thought. It simply didn't matter.

He was, he told her, going to lunch with George because George was flying to Africa next week. He was meeting a surgeon he wanted to see in the afternoon, and then driving down in George's car, which he'd bought from him, in the early evening. And what, he asked her, was she doing?

"Running away," she answered lightly. "I shall probably buy a hat. That's what women are supposed to do when things are irksome, isn't it?"

"Are things irksome?"

"Not really," she answered. "It's nice to make a fuss."

She didn't miss the look he shot at her, but she didn't want to discuss it on a crowded platform with the train coming in.

He talked casually on the way up until a quarter of an hour from Victoria he said, "You wouldn't like to come down with me in

George's car, I suppose? We might have dinner first. Or on the way home, if you'd rather."

She thought, how very odd. In all the time I've known him, I've never really had anything to do with him other than, in a way, professionally. He took me in his car to the Mostyns', and he drove me back from Melford to Ladysmere after Jennifer had taken Christopher. And both those drives were 'part of it', as all his visits to the house and to the flat at Melford were 'part of it' as well. He was my friend, but he was 'the doctor' too. Now, suddenly, he's someone different, neither the doctor nor 'Philip', someone I'm not sure if I even know.

"I'd like to very much," she said suddenly. "I hadn't made any plans."

They made arrangements to meet at The Ritz Bar at half-past six.

Didn't she know herself well enough yet to realise that London's civilised impersonality wasn't likely to distract her thoughts from either Guy or Christopher, she asked herself. Shop windows full of clothes that she didn't need were more of an irritation than a panacea, and the problem of Guy and Christopher, of what to do, of what not to do, marched just as monotonously beside her as they did in the lanes round Ladysmere.

She left Regent Street, and on an impulse took a bus to the corner of Shaftesbury Avenue. 'The Roadway of Romance', she thought on a half-bitter note, and yet at one time the thought of her name above a theatre had spelled all the happiness there was likely to be. Could she, if she left Guy, go back? She tried to picture that life again, but it remained wooden, unvital and without reality or meaning. Even the memory of Carrie and the rooms in Oakley Street didn't come to life. Nothing of it did, not even the weariness and distaste which were weighing her down when she first met Guy.

Meg's photograph and one of Toby Wayne and Glynne were outside the Sheridan. She hadn't seen either of them since that night at Alban Bay, and their life-sized faces gave her a shock. Did Meg really look like that? Did Glynne? Of course they were stage photographs and, as such, unreal, but she thought that their faces were masks, behind which was—what? Anything? Or had years of acting, years of being 'on show', so swallowed up their real personalities that only the mask, the 'thing' they had made themselves, remained?

It was a frightening thought, and for a moment the solid crowded pavement of twentieth-century London rocked, making a fissure into which if you peered you caught sight of queer inhuman shapes staring up at you with blank, lost eyes.

'I need lunch,' she thought, and in the same instant decided to go to The Black Scampi. Carrie, at least, she told herself, was real, solid and set-square as the Albert Memorial.

It was much later than she'd realised, and there were only two or three people finishing their meal when she walked into the restaurant. The room wore the sordid, soiled air of a place where food had lately been eaten. There were dirty plates and glasses on some of the tables. Chairs were askew and the smell of stale cooking was strong. She wished she had gone somewhere else, but now she was here she'd have something to eat, if the mercurial Art could provide it.

She walked towards the cleanest looking of the tables, and at the same moment saw a woman dressed in a bright emerald suit, who was slumped in a chair, one elbow leaning on a stained cloth, looking at a newspaper. *Was* it Carrie?

The woman raised her head, and surprise wiped the glum expression from her face. She lumbered to her feet and came across the room, bracelets jangling.

"Land sakes!" she exclaimed in mock-American. "Fancy you coming in just then. . . ."

Carrie, too, thought Gina. Carrie, too. . . . She must weigh twelve stone. There were little pads of fat round her eyes. Her jaw-line was hidden as though it had never been. The rings cut into her tiny podgy white hands. But it wasn't only that. Carrie herself—she was 'curling at the edges', not much but a little. The last of youth had left her. The last of something else—was it of *expectation*?—had left her, too. A process had begun which would continue now to an inevitable end.

"Am I too late for some lunch, Carrie? Anything will do."

A waiter came in and Carrie beckoned him over and spoke to him in a quiet voice, and when he'd gone out again she sat down opposite Gina and said, "God, aren't you thin still!" She held up her own hand and looked at it. "I'll have to slim," she said, not zealously. "How's tricks?" she asked.

"Fine," Gina answered. "I've had a daughter since I saw you."

"I wouldn't mind kids," said Carrie, "but Art isn't interested. Says you can't mix kids and food. Suppose you can't really."

An edge to her voice? A flick of a hint that the gilt had faded? Carrie, too. . . . Did nothing last, ever? Was everything transient, reaching a point of joy and dying again? She could have wept for the transience, clutched at the passing with her hands, begging it to remain. To remain lovely, fresh, new.

Art came in, and in a split second those sloe eyes had recognised her and he was coming across to their table.

"You remember Gina," said Carrie, and he bowed with a flash of teeth in which, now, there were more gold fillings.

"How could I forget?" he said in his flat Italian tones.

"I've told Beppo to bring her Osso Buco Milanaise," said Carrie. "Get us a drink, Art."

Art, too. The zest, the sparkle—not gone, but 'curled at the edges'. No longer light, spontaneous. His smile now was forced, professional. A smile for business sake, amen.

"And what will you drink, signora?" he asked, and Carrie said, "Bring a bottle of that special chianti, Art. Then she can drink it with the Osso Buco."

The frown didn't even register on his brow, but it was there just the same in his mind. The one-time demands of love had become the irritating dictation of the commonplace.

But Art had the quality of the Cæsars somewhere in his comic-opera being, and he kept up the farce which had, once, been amusing. "But certainly, my little dumpling. Always I obey your commands," he said with another bow, but Gina had the impression he could have hit her fat arm.

He came back with the bottle, called a waiter, who polished glasses, and then he poured the wine. "There, signora. You will like that." He winked one eye. "They drink it in Paradiso," he told her. "All the blessed saints. It is the nectar of gods. Excuse, please. . . ."

He swept off, shoulders swaying, and Carrie lifted her glass and said, "Cheers."

She had laid the newspaper she had been looking at on the table, and with an oblique glance at Gina she picked it up.

"See they've brought in suicide on Alison Blair?" she asked.

The name struck a chord in Gina's mind. Alison Blair. The stage? Then she remembered Carrie saying, "I didn't know you knew Alison Blair." She'd been aware of danger and had 'put on an act', and Carrie, her voice loaded with insinuation, had told her that Guy and Alison Blair had dined at The Scampi—and from what Carrie didn't say it was obvious that there was 'something in it'. And when she'd left Carrie, she'd called in at the dress shop near Harrods, and the little *vendeuse* with the bright blue eyes and the camel-like grin fixed to her face had come pattering out on high heels from behind a red curtain, and chattered of 'particularly petite' fittings in her pseudo-refined voice.

Guy's young woman, she'd thought to herself, incredulously. And she wondered what on earth he could have to do with the funny faded little thing—and then she'd forgotten all about it because she'd driven round to Elston Square and seen Christopher.

"I didn't know she was dead," she said to Carrie.

Again Carrie shot her that oblique look.

"The escalator she was on was only going one way—down," said Carrie. "She'd been on the booze for over a year. Got the sack from Marianne's a couple of months back. Once a girl takes to booze, the end's in sight," she said.

"Poor woman," said Gina, and she remembered the sudden genuine smile that had lighted the blue eyes when she'd told her that she was to have a baby. And she remembered, too, wondering what she'd have done if she'd suddenly said, "I'm Gina Taylor, Guy Taylor's wife," to her.

Again she was aware of something behind Carrie's expression.

"Nan Theobald says that it all started because she was keen on a man who threw her over," she said. "He used to live with her at one time, then he got married. Some while after he went back to her and she thought it was going to be O.K. again, but he was only fooling and flung her back on the heap. Nan said she never got over it." She drank some wine. "Catch me eating sleeping-pills for any man on earth," she said. "Silly lot of clods. God, they stink! The whole boiling of them."

What was Carrie saying, Gina wondered. Who was the man who had 'thrown Alison Blair back on the heap'? Was it Guy? Was that what Carrie was insinuating? She felt desperately troubled, but it wasn't possible to ask Carrie what her veiled hint had meant. It wasn't possible.

"Picture of her here," said Carrie, and she passed the paper across.

Gina picked it up and read the caption under the blurred photograph—'Alison Blair, the ex-model who died from an overdose of sodium amytal. Report page 2.'

The photograph was, obviously, an old one, and Gina stared down at the laughing eyes and gay smile. She had the irrational feeling that if she stared deeply enough into the face, it would reveal the secret of its death.

"Here's the food," said Carrie, and the waiter was there, whipping the cover off the dish.

She ploughed through the meal, no longer hungry, and she drank the wine and smoked a cigarette.

The last people left the restaurant, and a tangible dreariness settled over it, leaving Carrie like a plump fish washed up on a littered tide-mark.

She was glad to get out into the street again.

She took a taxi straight to a cinema, and sat there till it was time to meet Philip.

She was at The Ritz Bar a few moments before him, and when she saw him come hurrying in, she thought he brought an almost clinical normality with him. He came across to her with his nice smile, and she, relieved, smiled back at him.

He ordered the sherry, and she leaned back in the chair feeling relaxed and comforted, and he told her of his meeting with George. She asked how George was and he frowned slightly. "On the surface, he's exactly the same," he answered, "but it's cut him pretty deep. She was his whole life," he added, and then he said, "Perhaps

Africa will do something. I don't know." He looked across at her. "He asked after Christopher."

She nodded but didn't say anything, and he went on talking about George and Jennifer.

"Was her heart very bad?" she asked him.

A troubled expression came into his eyes. "None of us thought it was all that bad—not even Jones-Griffiths. Of course they hadn't got the cardiographs to go by—she was to have had them taken the following week—but . . ." He lifted his shoulders. "It's all rather baffling. If she'd sustained a shock or had had any strain one could account for such a sudden collapse, but she hadn't. She may have felt worse than any of us realised, I suppose. She wouldn't have talked about that, not even to George. She was one of the most totally selfless people I've ever met, and I think possibly her spirit had driven her body for longer than we knew."

"Poor Jennifer," said Gina. "She was nice."

"She liked you," he told her.

"I'm glad."

"You were the means of giving her a great deal of happiness," he said. "I know that."

"Perhaps that's something."

"It was more than either of us knew at the time," he answered. He was silent for a moment or so, and then, as though laying the subject down, he said, "I've looked forward to this all day. Where would you like to have dinner? Here? Or would you rather stop at The Angel at Wainhurst? It's only a few miles out of our way."

"The Angel," she answered. "The sooner I'm out of London today the better."

"Couldn't you find the hat?" he asked lightly.

"There wasn't one without a rose," she answered in the same tone. "And I only like roses in gardens."

The night was cold and crisp, with the first hint of winter in it. Philip drove, not fast and with a flair, as Guy drove, but steadily, deliberately and, in the traffic, with caution. He didn't talk much till they were clear of Kingston, then once again he said, "This is nice. Do you know, I've never been out with you before? Not unprofessionally," he added.

"I was thinking that earlier," she answered, and she thought, for the first time, how angry Guy would be if he knew she was with Philip. Why did Guy dislike him so much, she wondered. Because it was he who had met him at Belsted and told him of Christopher's birth? It seemed rather unfair to Philip. But there was so much that was unfair in the whole tangled skein of it. And all stemming from that one thing. . . .

They reached The Angel at half-past seven. In the panelled dining-room the candle-light was not a deliberate forcing of antiquity, but fitting, quietly soothing. And being with Philip, she thought, was the easiest thing in the world; for there was no need to explain either herself or anything they talked about, because they spoke, as it were, from the same view-point. She realised, with sudden clarity, that she had never experienced that closeness of understanding with anyone else in her life. With Philip she could be herself, without reservations.

They didn't hurry over their meal, and it was half-past nine before they came out of the hotel to a sky full of stars, and their very remoteness and cold beauty brought to the surface of her mind all the anxiety she had deliberately laid aside. Guy, Christopher, Caroline, fear, frustration, indecision, it was all there again, each strand of it leading back to the one question—what to do? And as the headlights of George's car, that was now Philip's, picked up the gunmetal ribbon of the Belsted road she said, "I nearly came to see you yesterday and then, just as I was leaving, Father Martin came in and I had to give him tea." She stopped and drew a breath, and then, "It's not going to work, you know, Philip," she said. "I think Guy hates Christopher. I don't know how long I shall be able to bear it."

He'd known on the station that morning that she was troubled, and he'd wondered, during the evening, if she were going to say anything about it.

Had he ever, he asked himself, thought it would work? And yet, the answer to that was—yes, he had. One part of his mind had even pictured her doting on Guy more than ever because he'd given her back her son. One part of his mind. The other had doubted the arrangement from the first.

"Hatred's a strong word," he said to her.

"I know that," she answered. "And yet it is a kind of hatred. It's affecting Christopher, Philip. I believe he's always afraid."

Hatred brought on by jealousy, a perpetual resentment of his presence. Then why had the man ever considered having him at Ladysmere? No one had been more surprised than he himself when Guy had first 'demanded' the Mostyns' address. If Jennifer hadn't died, he'd never have had it—or Christopher. And on the night he'd dined with George in London and George had asked him if he knew anyone who'd take the boy, he'd hesitated for a while and considered the idea of finding new foster-parents. He'd even, he remembered, been ashamed of that notion, because he'd recognised in it the desire to puncture Guy's infernal pride. Had there, perhaps, been a deeper, truer intuition at the base of his thinking—the intuition that in spite of Guy's apparent and exterior change, the thing wouldn't work? Now what?

"I've been a fool from the start," he heard Gina say. "Such a fool. I should never have told Guy Christopher wasn't his. I see that now. Andrew Wharton was dead, and there was no one on earth who could have contradicted me. And I don't suppose a doubt would have entered Guy's head after that year in Korea. Even if he'd gone into the mathematics of it, it wouldn't have proved anything—a couple of months one way or the other isn't evidence of non-paternity. I could have saved all this—every bit of it."

"And lived the lie?"

"Why not? Plenty of other women have. Wouldn't living a lie have been better than all this havoc? Where has the truth got me—any of us, Philip? I and I alone would have lived the lie. The truth has affected half a dozen lives, not just one. And it's going on affecting them. It hasn't ended yet. Sometimes I wonder if it will ever end. . . ."

Was she right, Philip thought. Ought he to have persuaded her to 'swing' the boy on to Guy? At the time he'd questioned himself—and her—as to whether she'd have been able to live the lie out for the rest of her life, and they'd both decided that she wouldn't. To him it had been, not so much a question of expedience as the effect the living of the lie might have had on her mind. The human personality was still a mystery, and to live out, day after day, year after year, a fundamental untruth might twist a soul out of shape, cause an almost schizophrenic rift in it. But who was he to weigh the balance between the value of one soul and the effect the truth had had, was having and would continue to have, on at least four lives? Was it because he'd loved her, even then, that his one thought had been for her? In the state she was in at the time he could, he knew it only too well, have swayed her towards the lie with ease. He hadn't. And because of it he'd had his part—Part? The entire responsibility more like—of the havoc the truth had caused. He'd counted on Guy's forgiveness and on his acceptance of the child because they themselves had had no children. And he'd counted wrong. And brought her such a load of conflict and strain as to make any rift of soul appear child's play. Or wasn't that true? Wouldn't the lived-out lie have affected all those lives, too? It might have made the external conditions more comfortable, but wouldn't it have reached out and touched—and twisted—all their lives just the same, only in a hidden, more insidious way? Who could tell? God alone, in the last analysis, for God alone saw the working out as it was, not as it appeared to be.

But it was the existent facts that had to be considered now.

"How long can I let Christopher bear the brunt of my stupidity?" Gina said. "It's beginning to twist him already, Philip. There's a shadow in his eyes now—a baby of two. Oh no, the N.S.P.C.C. won't have us up, because he's well-fed and well-clothed, but the cruelty's there just the same. Guy says I 'flaunt' him and ignore Caroline. I don't, of course. It's simply that he's piling on to Christopher the fact that I committed adultery with his father. Every time he sees Christopher cross his path, he sees that. . . ." She stopped speaking, and he drew the car to the side of the road on to the grass verge and switched the engine off. "That was why, in the first place, he refused to have Christopher," she went on. "He said then that it wouldn't be fair to him, that he himself wouldn't be able to live it out. But why change his mind and *have* him, only to hate him? It's me he ought to hate, not Christopher."

His hatred of her superimposed on the boy? The thought made Guy a monster, a sadist. Was it that? Such refinement of torture was the action of a maniac. But Guy wasn't a maniac. He might be hard as nails and self-righteous and proud, but he wasn't a maniac. Unless jealousy and resentment had made him so. That, of course, was the core of it. He'd never forgiven Gina. Deep in his heart the injury remained, festering, turning sour on him. He'd got to make her suffer; go on making her suffer to compensate himself for his own hurt pride. Oh God, he thought, the twists and turns of man's mind! The defences we put up. The lies we tell ourselves. We can justify hatred and murder as easily as we can justify a flash of temper. We were lost in the labyrinth of our own hearts. But no man who wasn't sinless had the right to make anyone suffer as Guy had made Gina suffer. He might pat himself on the back because he hadn't made love to another man's wife, but the long-drawn-out torture he was inflicting on her was a far worse crime. Thinking of it, anger swept over him, blinding the last of reason. A cold fury shook him as it had on the day he'd locked the poison cabinet. In that moment, if he could have seen Guy writhing in pain, he wouldn't have put out a hand to help him. He could have stood by and watched him racked and tortured and crying and he'd have been glad. Why did they ever let him out of his Communist jail? Or why in the first place did he have to go to Korea, anyway? Money. That was the answer to that one. Money gathered into the till because he'd invented a more torturous way of killing more people than the next man. Oh God, the insanity of it all. One set of men growing rich on death, another set, himself among them, wearing themselves out in the fight against death. And the rest of humanity running blindly between the two, shouting, 'Save us from the atom' to the arms men, and 'Save us from cancer' to the doctors. And outside, beyond the car where he and Gina were huddled, the great procession of the stars in space went on its silent, indifferent way.

He turned and looked at her beside him and anger was swallowed up in the protection he longed to give her. But the time was not yet. He knew that. The whole situation was breaking up, disintegrating, but one false step now might wreck the entire thing. And he was a doctor. He'd got to remember that before everything else. If Guy could accuse him before the B.M.A., he would; and not only would his income but the very purpose of his life be stripped from him. And a life without that one driving necessity of healing which had never lost its grip on him since he was a child of ten was unthinkable. Three generations of the blood of doctors in his veins was too strong a stream to be diverted now. And yet he loved her, longed and ached to take her into his arms and comfort her. He put his hand over her own and she turned and smiled slightly at him.

"I seem fated to sit in cars with you making moan," she said. "Poor Philip."

"I'm racking my brains to think how to help you."

"You're there. That helps more than you know."

He was silent, still with his hand over hers, till he said, "Would you leave him, Gina?"

A car swept down the hill in front of them, swung up the rise and ripped past before she answered. "My life is a roundabout, isn't it? Never a straight line. If I leave him, I leave Caroline."

That shocked him.

"You wouldn't! Gina, you couldn't. You'd start the whole process again."

She nodded.

"That's what I mean. A roundabout. It is, isn't it? But how could I take Caroline from him, Philip? If there's one thing in all this that's true, it is his love for Caroline. He adores her. He does, you know. Even I couldn't do that to him. . . ."

A faint cold breath blew over him.

He put his finger on the starter and the engine came to life.

Chapter XVI

It was ten-past one in the morning and Guy was pouring himself out a cup of tea in his hotel bedroom. The strong tea was, he told himself, the one link with his 'slum days' which he had deliberately, though secretly, fostered. But what up till tonight had been a questionable social habit would, from now on, become merely an amusing eccentricity permitted to men of note. In future if he chose to order strong tea with his *hors-d'œuvre*, then strong tea he'd order. Not, he smiled slightly, that such an original idea would be likely to appeal to him.

He sat back in the chair, sipping the tea. The line was reeled in at last, and he knew now how great the strain of the past few months had been and how desperately tired he was. But it was over, and Harben, that wily trout, had been landed. Not that Harben knew he'd been landed. On the contrary, Harben thought that he'd landed Taylor—Taylor and J. B. and Sir James, together with all that concern with its five companies known to the world as The British Home and Imperial Industries. And that little misconception of Harben's had been the trickiest move and the triumph of the whole deal. For Harben was seventy-one. Five years more for him? Six? And then even that great ocean-going monstrous slab of a man would begin to go the way of all flesh. But Taylor would still only be in his forties, with twenty-five years ahead of him. And J. B. and Sir James? Sixty-five apiece, and—he smiled again—eating out of his hand after tonight's 'celebration' dinner with all it portended. It had been touch and go once or twice, and they'd both been scared stiff, tried even to restrain him, make him rein in, but he'd known as surely as though the result were already headlining the *Financial Times* that his playing of old trout Harben couldn't fail. It hadn't failed. And all he'd ever determined to achieve was not only a possibility but a certainty. The last of the ropes that had tethered him to the ironmonger's shop in Bell Street had been cut, the future he had visualised all those years ago up in his little back bedroom stretched before him. Soon now he'd draw level with Gina and her people. March side by side with them; 'one of them', not by courtesy, toleration or condescension, but in his own right, earned by his own brain, Sir Guy Taylor. Lord Aberlane of Ladysmere. The scarlet and ermine. The coronet. His seat in the Upper House. The well-known London residence famous for the brilliance of the entertaining. Caroline at a presentation party. . . .

And Gina? His eyes narrowed. Harvingdon? Giles Conway? Maltravers Berry with its five-hundred-year-old gardens? None of it would be of great moment to Lord Aberlane, chiefly because he would have the advantage, the considerable advantage, of possessing riches as well as honours while the 'Conway-Coutts' were scrabbling along on a fast tottering glory and the few hundreds they could scrape together from letting the public into their homes at half a crown a time.

But Gina herself? Gina and her son?

He finished his tea, put the cup down and suddenly covered his eyes with his hands. Why had she ever driven that knife into his back when he was sweating it out in that reeking mud hut in Korea? Those first years of their marriage had been heaven. When he'd made love to her it had been with the whole of himself, mind and heart as well as his body; and he thought it had been the same for her, God help him.

But she'd gone off with the first man she'd come across, and she'd even denied that she'd loved him and the very fact of her denial had branded her promiscuous. He'd been mad to have her back. He'd gone to Melford that night intending to shame her, but when he saw her he'd been overcome with pity. And his pity was his weakness, both then and three months ago, when he'd decided to have her child into his home. Always his pity was his weakness.

Why go on? She'd taken his forgiveness as her right, just as she'd taken his having the child as her right. The gratitude she'd assumed for a day or so had soon died. Gina Randolph didn't need to exhibit gratitude. He should count himself privileged to have been betrayed by her. He should count himself privileged to have her lover's son flaunted in front of him; given all her love and affection while his child was kept in the background. She had no religion, yet even when the priest called it was her son who was sent for. Her son who had to be admired.

He was aware that he had been drinking, and the champagne, exhilarating a couple of hours ago, was now a dead weight in his veins. He knew it, yet couldn't stop the heavy trend of his thoughts. What more did she want of him? God knew. He hadn't intended to dislike her child. He'd thought that she'd be on her knees with gratitude, that she'd love him again. But she only loved the boy, and every time he saw him anger and irritation gnawed at him. Who could blame him? Surely he was more sinned against than sinning? God Himself could hardly have demanded more from him —not only forgiveness, but the child brought into his home to take his place with his own daughter. Surely that was love, if anything was. . . .

But what a night this would have been for him if Gina had remained faithful to him! If the boy, Christopher, had never been. With what delight now, late as it was, he'd have picked up the telephone and told her of his success. He thought of a night, shortly before he'd gone to Korea, when he'd said to her, "I want to give you everything in the world," and she, weeping a little because he was leaving her, answered, "Do *you* know what to feed a hippopotamus on?" She'd been gay and light-hearted then, interested in everything he did and had done, and he'd imagined, besotted as he was with her, that that's how it would be always.

He'd taken her to the opera when they were in Paris on their honeymoon, and on the way back to the hotel, as they were walking by the Seine, she'd said, "We must always hold this night in our hearts, Guy. We must always hold the singing in our hearts." Extravagant? Sentimental? Possibly. And in the light of what she had done since—humorous. But then he'd believed her. That and her other phrase, 'The one undying thing', were linked together in his mind, hall-marked with her own individuality. He'd forgotten that she was Gina Randolph, the actress.

But he had remained faithful to her. And as he'd said to the man Blake, God's Providence worked in the most minute and exact manner. Blake had tried to stop his having the boy, but in the end he'd been obliged to ask him to have him. And now, tonight, all that he'd ever prayed for had come into his hands.

He looked at his watch. It was twenty minutes to two. Should he telephone Gina? He'd only to reach out his hand, pick up the receiver and ask for the number. And when she answered he'd say, 'I had to call you. This is the biggest night of my life and I wanted to share it with you. I told you I'd get you back where you belonged. . . .'

Fool! Was he such a puerile weakling as that? God forbid! She wouldn't even understand what he was talking about. What did she know of the days of strain, the plans, the risks, the fears, which were the measure of every cheque she wrote with unconsidered indifference? What did she know of the silent tussle with Harben, the horror of failure that gripped you by the throat in the night? The bankruptcy and disgrace that lurked in waiting behind every mistake you might make? She would neither know, nor, if she knew, care, while there was money in her account, a cheque-book in her desk.

And if he did call her she'd think that he was crawling to her again; condoning her flaunted preference for her lover's child. Condoning that leprous adultery of hers which had soiled their lives. In these days people thought that the sins of the flesh didn't matter. They did matter. The very word 'adultery' meant 'to make impure', to soil. That's what Gina had done. She'd made herself impure. Soiled not only herself but their marriage. And the boy was the child of that impurity. . . .

The champagne, he knew, was making him maudlin, but he was too tired now to fight it. He wanted to be maudlin, to feel pity for himself. Why not? No one else felt pity for him.

He would, he decided, go to bed.

He picked up the evening paper from the table and opened it, yawning.

And then he saw the photograph, and he stared down at it, all thought of sleep gone.

Alison. . . . The snapshot he himself had taken of her at Rottingdean years ago. But, good God. . . .

Rapidly he read the report. 'Suicide while the balance of her mind. . . . Sodium amytal. . . . One-time model. . . . Actors, authors and industrialists among her friends. . . . Felicity Lamare, saleswoman, 38, told the coroner that Miss Blair had been depressed for the last eighteen months. Asked if she could give any reason for the depression, she said that she believed it was connected with an unhappy love affair. Answering further questions she said that since April 1955 Miss Blair had changed very much and had seemed to lose interest in herself. It was true that since that time she had known her drink too much on occasion. Lamare said that she did not know the name of the man concerned. . . .'

He lowered the paper, shocked. Alison—a suicide. He couldn't take it in. What on earth had driven her to kill herself? There certainly hadn't been anything either depressed or suicidal about her that night he'd run into her in Buckingham Palace Road. Her eyes had been as clear and laughing as they'd been all those years ago when he'd first known her, and she'd been decently dressed, too, no obvious signs of poverty about her. Besides, she hadn't given him the impression of a woman on the edge of neurosis. Or of death. Of course you could never tell with the Alisons of this world. . . . She might even have picked up trouble. They were always open to that risk. Poor little Alison. Poor little thing.

He took up the paper and looked at the report again. 'Actors, authors and industrialists among her friends. . . .' Industrialists. Where had the reporters got that from? They'd ferret out every needle in every haystack once they knew there was a needle to be found. Industrialists. It couldn't be a veiled reference to himself, because in the days when he'd known Alison well he couldn't have been referred to as 'an industrialist', and it was hardly likely anyone would know of that chance meeting eighteen months ago. Eighteen months ago. The words became rapier sharp in his mind, and again he looked at the report. 'Felicity Lamare, saleswoman, 38, told the coroner that Miss Blair had been depressed for the last eighteen months. Asked if she could give any reason for the depression, she said she believed it was connected with an unhappy love affair. Answering further questions . . . since April 1955 Blair had changed . . . lost interest in herself . . . drank too much . . . did not know the name of the man. . . .'

April 1955. Eighteen months. It was eighteen months ago, at the end of April 1955, that he had run into her in Buckingham Palace Road. He hadn't even recognised her at first. . . . Then the drinks at the Troc Bar; dinner at that place in Soho. . . . No lunch, and he slightly and pleasantly drunk in the taxi that took them back to Kensington. . . . Her flat . . . the light out. . . . And his sudden 'coming to' to realise what he was doing. Her pleading with him. "Stay with me, Guy. I love you. I've always loved you. Guy, please. . . ." And then her anger. "You're pretty rotten, aren't you? . . ." "You, a coward! How they've changed you. . . ." And finally that expression of scorn which he'd never quite forgotten on her face and her, "There goes the last dream. . . ."

But, good grief, what was all this? As if that chance meeting eighteen months ago had anything to do with her suicide! Was every man who ran into a one-time woman friend and spent an hour or so in her company to accuse himself of her death? There would be some extraordinary situations created if they did. And the Alisons of this world were quite capable of taking care of themselves. They knew the ropes. And he didn't kid himself that he was the only man she'd had up to her flat. Once he might have been, admit that, but not of late years. And hadn't she told him herself that she'd been married and that the man had left her?

He was being most alarmingly and ridiculously scrupulous. Just because the poor girl had begun to go downhill about the time he'd last seen her, was he to connect himself with her descent? And what had he done to her? Nothing. Just that, God be thanked. He'd come to himself in time. Got out. Escaped. If he'd stayed, he might have been mixed up in the scandal of her death.

And once more he thought, 'Thank God. Thank God.'

Before he got into bed he said an Our Father for her. God knew she'd need prayers.

Chapter XVII

THE following day was a Saturday. He went to his office, where a skeleton staff was working, for a couple of hours and then drove home.

He couldn't forget the report he'd read of Alison's death. It nagged at the back of his mind, casting a blight on his earlier sense of triumph over the Harben amalgamation, and its very presence in his thought irritated him. The irritation made him feel slightly ashamed, and he asked himself why he couldn't merely feel grief for her death and leave it at that. Perhaps if it had been a natural death it would have been easier to forget it. But it was idiotic and ultra-sensitive of him to thrash himself into a ferment because, by sheer coincidence, she had begun to go downhill about the time he had last seen her. As he'd told himself last night, her death couldn't possibly have any connection with his own brief meeting with her, and he must remember that, even in the early days, he hadn't been either her first or only lover. But she'd been sweet to him and she'd taught him a lot, and he'd always felt a certain kindly gratitude towards her. As he forged ahead, they'd drifted apart, and naturally he hadn't seen her after he and Gina were married, except on that one occasion.

After all, he told himself, it was hardly likely that a man would read of the death by suicide of someone he had known intimately in the past without being affected by it. He would have been more concerned if he hadn't been affected by it, for in that case he might have thought that success had hardened his heart and made him a snob. God forbid that it should have done either.

He reached Belsted soon after half-past twelve and parked his car in the square while he went into the tobacconist's. As he walked the few steps from the car to the shop he caught sight of Philip Blake standing talking to another man outside his house. He looked straight ahead, as though he hadn't realised that he was there.

Philip himself opened the door when the bell rang soon after twelve, but he didn't expect to see Mathew Galway standing there.

"I told you we might be up before the winter," Mathew said. "We're staying the night with the Conways on our way to Charterhouse to see the twins. Ann and Miranda are shopping, so I said I'd slip round and see if you were in."

"Nice," said Philip. "We'd better go and have a quick one at The Bell. I had lunch with George yesterday."

"How was the old boy?"

Philip shut the door and they walked across the square to The Bell.

"He's trying hard; that's about all you can say," he answered. "Seems keen enough to be on his way."

"Best thing for him, I suppose," said Mathew. "Wouldn't be my idea, I must say. Takes more courage than I've got to cut myself off from everything and everyone I'm familiar with and start in on a new line quite alone."

"Shock tactics, I think," Philip said. "Maybe he's right."

They went into The Bell and ordered their drinks.

"Christopher?" Mathew asked.

Philip nodded. "Takes a bit of time to get his roots down, naturally. He'll be all right."

No point, he told himself, in discussing all that with Mathew. Too chancy, anyway. Mathew might mention it to Ann, Ann to Miranda, and back it would get to Gina. He'd made a bad enough mistake when, after Jennifer's funeral, he'd virtually told them who Christopher's mother was without adding to it. In this life to keep the mouth firmly shut was the only way to avoid complications.

"Giles mentioned to us that his cousin lived in these parts," Mathew said dryly. He looked at Philip over his glass. "He also mentioned that she and her husband had recently adopted a child."

Philip made a slight grimace and took a long drink from his tankard.

"Poor old Ann," said Mathew, "nearly burst with the desire to ask how the kid was, but by a superhuman effort controlled herself."

"Good for Ann," murmured Philip.

"We thought they were going to lug us up there, wherever it is, for a drink this evening, but the idea's been shelved. Just as well."

"*Just* as well," Philip echoed. And after what Gina had said to him last night—more than just as well.

They talked about other things, finished their drinks and Mathew looked at his watch.

"They said they'd only be quarter of an hour," he told Philip. "I've given them half. Should think that would do."

"Where did you leave the car?"

"Round some little back street Miranda favours. Up by a baker's shop if I remember rightly."

"I'll show you," said Philip, and they left The Bell and strolled back towards his house. "There you are." Philip pointed across the square. "There's your baker's shop, and I should say you parked your car up that street alongside it."

"That's it," said Mathew. "Thanks." He looked at the Queen Anne houses lining the square. "Nice old town."

He saw a Jaguar car swing in from the main road and draw up a few yards beyond them. A man got out of it, came towards them a few paces, then went into a shop.

"I know that chap," said Mathew.

Philip had recognised the Jaguar as it pulled in, and when he saw Guy get out of it, the cold, almost calculating anger of the night before came over him.

"Which chap?" he asked Mathew, but he was thinking of Gina sitting beside him in George's car saying, "He hates him, Philip."

"Fellow in the Jaguar," Mathew answered, and Philip was jerked flat into the present.

"I don't think you do," he said.

"Tell you I do," Mathew insisted. He frowned. "Can't think where I met him. . . . I can tell you what his voice is like though. . . . Oh, blast. . . ." His face relaxed suddenly. "Got it! He's the chap who asked me the way to the Mostyns' once. I knew I'd seen him somewhere. I remembered the classy car. Is he a local?"

"You must be mistaken," Philip said shortly.

"I'm not mistaken, blow you," Mathew answered. "I tell you he's the chap who asked me the way to the Mostyns'. I recall the whole thing now. There'd been the father and mother of a gale, and a tree on my land had blown down and was blocking the right of way to the manor. I'd just been across to see what was to be done, and before I got into the old farm Ford, this chap in the Jag. pulls up and says, 'I'm looking for a house called Prendergast, people name of Mostyn. Can you direct me?' I told him how to get there, and then, in my jocular way, I pointed to the sanctified tin can he was driving and said, 'Pretty little run-about. You wouldn't care to swap, I suppose . . .' or words to that effect. The chap was nearly as classy as his car—Savile Row and a proud look and a high stomach and I quite expected him to say, 'Be quiet, boy, and next time you refer to my automobile take your boots off,' but as a point of fact he astonished me by the human quality of his reply. With the most awful gravity, he said, 'I'd have to consider it. Needs a bit of thinking about,' which," said Mathew, "you must admit was quite tidy." He glanced at Philip. "I don't see why you should look so ferocious about it. The brief little episode was both moral and sanitary, and the chap and I had every right to be on the Queen's Highway. At least, I had. . . ."

Philip was hardly listening. He had heard enough. So Guy had found out the Mostyns' address and gone down there. That's why he'd not mentioned his own refusal to put him in touch with George to Gina. And then Jennifer had died. . . . Good God!

"Mathew," he said quickly. "Stop drooling, for Pete's sake. This matters. Listen. That man will be coming out of the tobacconist's any minute. I want you to keep your eyes skinned and take another look at him before he gets into his car. I want you to make quite certain that he is the man who asked you the way to the Mostyns'."

"What is all this?" said Mathew. "You're behaving like a sleuth."

"Never you mind how I'm behaving. Keep your eyes on the tobacconist's."

"You make me feel a perishing fool," said Mathew. "Have you taken to reading strip cartoons instead of *The Lancet*? . . ." The sentence broke off as Guy came out of the tobacconist's, walked a few paces up the road, turned left and opened the car door. As he bent slightly to reach the handle, his profile was clearly visible.

"No question," said Mathew. "Besides, the car registration's the same, though I couldn't swear to the numbers. I know it was PPO though, because, in my infantile and mentally retarded manner I remember noticing it and thinking, Plutocratic Persons Only. I'm often madly witty when I'm by myself."

"Shut up," said Philip.

"Certainly . . ." Mathew muttered. "But I'd just like to know——"

"You don't, I suppose, remember when it was you saw this man?" Philip asked him.

"I told you," Mathew answered. "There'd been a frightful gale and——" He stopped and his dark eyes became troubled. "It was the day Jennifer died," he ended quietly.

"Time?" Philip asked.

Mathew frowned. And then, "Quarter-past three, I should say. Might have been half-past. You're not suggesting——"

"I'm not suggesting anything," Philip answered. "I'm asking a few questions, that's all."

"Yes, but you might——"

"I know I might," Philip broke in. "And I will later. At the moment there's something else I want to know. Do you remember, or can you tell me, just who was in the house the afternoon of the day Jennifer died? Or, rather, who might have been in the house at about, say, three-thirty to four in the afternoon?"

Mathew looked down at his foot, and moved it sideways, as though brushing away sand.

"Wasn't the nurse out?" Philip prompted. "If I remember rightly, George told me that she'd taken Christopher somewhere. . . ."

"The Lawsons'," Mathew said. "It was Sally's birthday. The weather had cleared up a bit by then, so I suppose if she'd walked she'd have left about half-past three."

"And Jennifer would have been there alone?"

"If Violet had left by then."

"The daily?"

"Yes. Violet Stubbings. She's the daughter of my cowman. Her mother used to go there occasionally, too, but only for an hour or so in the morning. Violet stayed to wash up the lunch-things."

"That's right," said Philip. "And she laid Jennifer's tea on a tray.

I remember now. Do you know what time she usually left?"

"Not really. I suppose it would depend on what time she was finished. Ann would know."

"I'd rather keep this to ourselves at the moment," Philip told him. "I'm not quite certain of my bearings. It's just that I've got a hunch. . . ." He stopped and said, "It would be quite feasible, then, to say that Violet Stubbings might conceivably have been at the house at half-past three and that it's possible she might have answered the door to a visitor, shown him into the drawing-room and then left?"

"I suppose so. Don't see why not."

"Nor do I," Philip said. "What's happened to Violet since George gave up the house?"

Mathew shot him a look.

"Changed her job," he said shortly. "She milks my cows alongside her dad now."

"Convenient," exclaimed Philip.

"If you say so," Mathew muttered, and he saw Ann and Miranda come down past the baker's shop and into the square. "Here come the women," he added. And he said, "You can't leave me holding this bit of knitting without the pattern. What are you suggesting? Murder?"

"There are various kinds of murder," Philip answered. "You don't necessarily have to use physical violence. Listen, Mathew," he said, and he spoke quickly as Ann and Miranda crossed the square towards them. "I know it's irritating to be left without the clue to all this, but it's how it has to be for the moment. Just one thing more—when will you be home again?"

"Monday lunch-time. Near as makes no odds."

"I suppose I could have a word with your Violet Stubbings if I came over one evening?"

"Don't see what's to stop you."

"Then I might do that." He lifted his hand in salute to Ann and Miranda as they reached the pavement. "Not a word even to the angels of God, Galway," he added as Ann, turning to Miranda, said, "And I'll lay you a sherry to a ginger-pop that they've just crept out of the local."

Guy shut the car door and took the Aberlane Road out of Belsted, and as he passed the one-time rifle-range, which was the church, he thought of the promise he'd made to himself back in the summer—that if his plans came to anything he'd have the place redecorated. He would have to see Father Martin about that as soon as he could fit it in, although it might be too late to have much done this year. But if things matured as they surely must—the characteristic narrowing of his far-seeing eyes was drawn on his face—a new church altogether? Not a converted rifle-range, but architect-designed of Purbeck Stone, with a wide sanctuary and carved wooden Stations of the Cross; a red carpet. . . . The church that Sir Guy Francis Taylor had given to Belsted. . . . He saw it rising, stone by stone, on the windscreen as he drove. Clear-cut, modern, yet with none of your meaningless slabs-of-concrete look about it. Small but perfect. A church that would stand long after he was dead; that would, in its way, be his memorial. . . .

Thinking of it, picturing the laying of the foundation-stone, the consecration, he quite forgot Alison's death. As he turned in at the drive gates, he recalled seeing Blake standing outside his house talking to another man. Vaguely he wondered who he was, but though he thought he'd run into him before somewhere, he couldn't place him.

He and Gina were alone for lunch, but he found it quite impossible to speak to her of the Harben amalgamation. Or, for that matter, of anything else. The constraint between them was almost solid, a wall that bricked each of them round in isolation.

"I thought Miranda was coming to lunch," he said, more to break the silence than anything.

"They had some people ask themselves for the week-end," Gina answered. "She rang and left a message about it yesterday while I was out."

"Were you out yesterday?" he asked.

She raised her eyebrows slightly.

"I do go out sometimes," she replied lightly, and she thought, 'For the first time since I've known him, I can't tell him where I was, or rather whom I was with, because if he knew I'd dined with Philip there'd be further trouble. He'd never believe that my meeting him was accidental. It doesn't even sound accidental. Whatever happens, I must keep controlled and calm until I can see clearly what I've got to do.' And she remembered that Philip had said, "Would you leave him, Gina?"

Now, sitting opposite him eating lunch, the thought of leaving him—of leaving Ladysmere, her home, their home—seemed fantastic, impossible. Yet how go on like this? What more could she do? What more was there to do? She'd said once that she'd spend the rest of her life making up to him for that one night. She'd tried to do that, and she would still go on trying to do it; but where was the good—or even the sense—if he refused to accept what she tried to give him? You couldn't 'make anything up' to anyone if they didn't reach out their hand to take your gift. If they remained for ever cold and condemning and suspicious. If they hated your child. . . . She forced down the emotion which she knew was all too insecurely battened under the thin crust of her tired will.

That thin layer of will must hold. If it gave, she felt that all the restraint and constraint and pain and anger and frustration and humiliation might come surging and crashing out of her in great gushes and gobbets of violence which neither she nor anyone else could stop.

They finished lunch in silence. She heard Guy go out, and thought he had gone on his 'tour of inspection' of the gardens, as he often did at the week-end. The first awareness of anything wrong was a sharp thrust of intuition which tensed her every nerve, even before she heard Christopher's scream and Guy's raised voice.

The late autumn sun had been pouring in through the french windows of the drawing-room and she had opened them so that the sound carried clearly. With the sharp certainty of crisis, she got up from her chair and ran over the grass in the direction of the sound. Before she actually reached them she saw that Guy had hold of Christopher by the shoulders and was shaking him. She called his name, "Guy . . . Guy . . ."; but if he heard he took no notice. Just before she reached them he stopped shaking Christopher and threw him from him. Christopher landed full-length on the grass and lay still.

As she picked him up she thought, 'If he is dead, I shall kill Guy'; but the thought was without temper, very cold, a statement of fact. It wasn't till she realised that, though white and odd-looking, with his eyes closed, he was breathing that she began to try to take in the rest of the scene; discover what had happened.

It wasn't difficult; the evidence was too strong—the ruined bed of stylosa and helleborus which Guy had bought at the Chelsea Flower Show in the spring and which should have been blooming at Christmas. The wheel marks of Christopher's barrow criss-crossing the earth, and his footmarks, enlarged to giant size, imprinted in the dark, damp mould. The barrow itself with half a dozen plants falling from it, lying on its side in the middle of the bed. His dirty hands. The mould thick on his red Wellington boots. . . .

Why on earth had he done it? She'd explained to him a dozen times that he mustn't touch the beds. Was it that he was pretending to be that almighty and glorious deity of his child life—Marple? Did he think that the plants were weeds which had to be removed? Or had he trampled the bed down with evil intent for purely destructive reasons, or even with, somewhere in his confused and unhappy little mind, the urge to hurt Guy for all the hurt he had given him?

She was aware of Guy's face. His lids had dropped over his eyes, and there was a dreadful look about his nostrils as he took two or three deep breaths. His cheeks had sudden, strange depressions in them and his flesh had become grey-tinged.

He opened his eyes, and they stared at one another in a silence that was gashed into time with a sword. She thought it was as though in that moment she saw time slipping over him—all the time that had passed since she had first met him that night at Toby's party; all the delight, all the pain. Time washing over him, over them both, changing them, leaving them the people, the strangers, they now were.

"I lost my temper," he said, and he shot a quick look to where she knelt on the ground holding Christopher.

"If you've injured him, I shall kill you," she answered in an echo of his own lifeless tones.

"He isn't hurt. I only shook him. . . ."

"I saw you. You flung him on the ground like an animal. You hate him. You've always hated him. . . ."

He lifted his hands, and let them drop again as though he were helpless against the hatred.

"He's not hurt," he said again.

She didn't answer. She got to her feet, holding Christopher in her arms. He opened his eyes and stared up at her, then closed them again. She pressed him closer to her, and she sagged a little under his weight.

"I'll take him. . . ."

She shook her head but didn't speak. She took a few steps forward and came level with him. "Gina!" he called sharply. "Gina! What are you doing? Where are you going?"

"I don't know," she answered. "I don't know."

"I can't stand this," he began. "I can't *stand* it."

"*You* can't stand it! *You* can't. . . ."

"What more do you want?" he asked her. "Tell me that—what more do you want?"

"I don't want any more. Ever. Nothing at all. Nothing. . . ."

"Haven't I given you everything?" he said. "Right from the beginning. What more could I do? I forgave you your adultery, didn't I? I had you back here as my wife. I've even had your child here. . . . What more can I do?"

"Your forgiveness!" she said, and he thought that her eyes were like live coals in her white face. "Your bloody forgiveness. . . . Dear Christ, the burden of it." She lowered her eyes for a second only, and raised them to him again. "I'd rather have had your anger," she said. "I'd rather have had you use physical violence to me, beat me, knock me about, anything, *anything* but the intolerable burden of your forgiveness. It's crushed me, killed me, mangled me, and now it's crushed and mangled my son. Every time you've spoken the word, every time you've thought it, you've thanked your God that you're without sin. Are you without sin? Are you? What about Alison Blair, Guy? What about her?"

She'd had no intention of mentioning Alison Blair's name. She heard herself use it, heard it come hurtling out of her lips, and she saw the merest flick of a change come over Guy's set face.

Christopher stirred in her arms. She looked down and saw his frightened eyes. "It's all right," she said. "All right. I've got you. I won't leave you." She stared up at Guy. "P'raps you killed her, too, with your forgiveness," she said. "Your damned Christian forgiveness. . . . Your damned Christian righteousness. . . . Your damned Christian charity. . . ."

"Gina!" Guy shouted. "You're hysterical. You're——"

"All right, then, I'm hysterical," she said. "And I'd rather be hysterical than cold-hearted and self-righteous and cruel. And I'd rather hate than forgive. There's something cold and clean and terrible in hatred, but forgiveness. . . . Oh, forgiveness. . . ."

She swayed a little and he made a move as though to take Christopher from her, but she shook her head. "No," she said. "No. Don't touch him. Don't touch me. Either of us. Not any more. Not any more. . . ."

She moved on away from him, her body bent under Christopher's weight, over the grass, across the brick path and into the house.

The nurse had taken Caroline to get some forgotten shopping at Tarn, two miles away. Fortunately? Possibly, Gina thought, though she would have been glad of reassurance about Christopher.

She laid him on the nursery bed, and he opened his eyes and looked up at her. She thought he seemed to be more shocked and dazed than injured. Pity and love for him rose in her throat on a fierce wave. She did love him, loved him with a depth which now was a great burden in her heart. But all her love had only brought him pain. . . . She ran her hands gently over his body. There seemed to be no bones broken. She went into the little nursery kitchen, and made some milk warm on the stove and brought it to him to drink. She propped him up so that he was leaning against her arm, and he took a long drink of the milk and then looked up at her again, and there was more colour in his face, more life in his eyes. He raised his hand and rubbed at his right shoulder, and when she pulled his jersey from it she saw the mark where he had fallen, the scarlet branding of Guy's hatred, growing on his white child's flesh.

"We'll put some stuff on it," she said. "And then we'll go and see Doctor Philip. He'll make it better."

Philip. The name steadied her, gave her confidence. Philip would do something. Philip would take it all into his hands.

Christopher breathed a deep sigh, and she pressed his head against her arm. He raised his hand and put his thumb in his mouth and sucked it—a thing she had never seen him do since he had come to them. For a time he stayed as he was, making a queer little animal noise as he pulled on his thumb; then quite suddenly, as though a mild electric charge had gone through him, he fidgeted a little, moved his legs and began to edge himself from the bed. In another moment he was running his tip-cart over the window-seat.

He was still playing with it as she fetched the suit-cases from the box-room and packed his and her own immediate necessities. She did it quite methodically, quite coldly, thinking out in detail what was needed, what could be left till later.

She heard the sound of the car, and saw the Jaguar swing out from the garage and pass rapidly down the drive.

Guy had gone out.

The phrase was quite meaningless, it barely penetrated her reason. She might just as well have said 'Apple-pie' to herself. Guy had gone out.

The packing was finished. She dressed Christopher, went down to her bureau for money, cheque-book and keys; and when everything was ready she went to the garage and got her car out, and carried the cases down to it herself.

How much the people in the kitchen had seen or heard of Guy's outburst she didn't know. All she did know was the impossibility of attempting explanations or, even, of speaking to anyone. There was only one instinct, one driving necessity—to get Christopher away, out of the house, now, at once, before anyone or anything could stop her.

She took his hand to help him down the stairs. "We're going out in the car," she said.

He changed his tip-cart over into his left hand and looked up at her. "Car-line?" he asked.

"No," she answered. "Not Caroline. Not this time."

The words echoed and re-echoed in her brain as they went down the stairs and across the hall and over the paved terrace to the car. They went on echoing and re-echoing as she lifted him on to the seat, got in herself, started the engine and drove out of the gates. "Not Caroline. Not this time. Not Caroline. Not this time. Not Caroline. . . ."

Philip, said Mrs. Firth, the housekeeper, wasn't at home.

She found it difficult to believe, and she stood on the step of the house looking round the square, trying to take it in.

It hadn't struck her for a moment that he wouldn't be there. The thought of him had been, not actively, except for that one moment when she ran her hands over Christopher's body, but passively in her mind all the time.

"You don't know when he might be back?" she asked the woman, and even then, while all the present with its confusion and pain and bewilderment was piling up around her, she found herself remembering the fan of white paper in the grate during the summer months, and she pictured the woman kneeling on the rug, her broad buttocks pressing on to the heels of her shoes, folding the paper, 'ironing' her fist along the creases to produce a knife-like edge, and finally tucking it behind the black bars, and opening out the fan till it covered the decent fire-blackened back with the obscene prettiness of its false modesty.

"He said not till tonight," she answered. "Doctor Canon's dealing with anything urgent," she added.

Gina looked back at the woman, and found her mind running off into ridiculous speculation again. Had this slab of formless flesh ever been torn and swayed and fainting with love? Had she lain in 'Mr. Firth's' arms, her hair streaming out on the pillow, her mouth bruised with his kisses . . .?

"I think," she said, "I'll leave a note, if I may. Perhaps you could let me have paper and an envelope?"

The housekeeper didn't like that. The measure of her dislike radiated from her back like an aura as she thumped down the corridor, but she brought the paper, and Gina, leaning against the wall and balancing it on her handbag propped on her raised knee, wrote, 'I've left Ladysmere and am going to Ardene for the night. Shall stay at The George there. Give me time to think. Perhaps you'd telephone—Ardene 2. Christopher is with me.'

She hesitated for a moment and then merely scrawled 'Gina' across the paper. She wrote 'Dr. Blake' on the envelope and wondered how long it would be before Mrs. Firth was steaming open the flap. She felt the woman's antagonism leaving her body with every breath. She wondered why. Perhaps she was in love with Philip. She must be sixty. What had that got to do with it? Love didn't die with age. It was the one thing that didn't. As if all that mattered—now. But whatever happened in your personal life, however deep the grief or tragedy, the processes of your mind went on just as usual. The mechanisms of observation, thought, analysis and wonder, continued their work with awful precision at a point just below the base of your own pain or grief. You were even aware of some strange woman's grudging dislike. . . .

Suddenly, she turned the envelope face downward and wrote, 'The George Hotel, Ardene. Phone Ardene 2,' across the flap. As she handed it to the housekeeper she said, "Should he telephone, perhaps you'd say I called. I've put the address and phone number on the envelope."

She felt faintly sorry for the woman's defeat, and the next moment despised herself for her suspicion that she'd intended to read the note. What did it matter one way or the other? But if Philip telephoned his home, he would know that she'd called and where she was.

"Thank you," she said to Mrs. Firth, but there was hardly so much as a crack on the respectable façade of 'natural' skin, colourless lips and hard, pale eyes.

As she crossed the pavement to the car she wouldn't have been surprised to hear the woman shout, 'Adulteress . . . Wanton . . . Deserter . . . Shame . . .' after her.

"Home?" asked Christopher when she started the car again.

Was it 'home' to him, she wondered. Could it be 'home' to him? As if he'd understand the meaning of the word! But it was the first time he'd used it. To her, anyway.

"No," she said to him. "We're going for a ride in the car and then we're going to sleep in another house. Just you and I."

"Not Car-line?" he said.

"No," she answered. "Just you and I."

Ardene was a hamlet on the river estuary, fifteen miles from Belsted. At low tide there were mud-flats where the gulls congregated round the skeleton hulls of old boats, and emerald sea-weed wreathed the bleached wood of the groynes along the concrete wall. But at full tide on a calm day the water was deep blue, reflecting the little gay shops along the quayside and the Queen Anne façade of the George Inn.

She had known the inn from childhood days, when Giles's parents had had a boat moored there, and she had driven down not long ago with Miranda.

The holiday people had been gone for some weeks, and there were only two or three boats tied up to the quay and few people about when they reached the hotel.

By the time she had engaged a room and garaged the car, it was still only half-past four.

She couldn't believe that it was so early. It seemed an age ago since she and Guy had been sitting opposite one another having lunch. But that thought she quickly thrust aside. She would not think. Not yet. Later perhaps, but not yet. . . .

The rain started soon after tea, and by six, when she was bathing Christopher, there was half a gale blowing. It thundered across the mud-flats and flung salty rain at the inn windows, and sent white-capped waves scudding up the narrow channel of low-tide water.

Christopher was tired and fretful, and when she saw his bruised shoulder again, she wondered if she ought to have taken him to another doctor. But he drank his milk and ate some biscuits, and was asleep as soon as he was in bed.

She took a long time folding up his clothes and unpacking her own, and all the while she knew that thought was there, a jinx on her shoulder, waiting for the moment when there would be a rift in the mechanical ritual she set herself.

It came when the last things were done and she stood at the bedroom window watching the wild, darkening sky and the night coming turbulently up over the marshes on the other side of the water.

She had left Guy.

She had not only left Guy, but she had left Ladysmere, her home. She had left all her personal possessions, all security. And she had left Caroline. She tried to whip herself into feeling of some kind, but there was no feeling in her.

She told herself that she must feel something, that it was unnatural, even indecent, not to feel loss or grief or even despair, but she felt only rather a chilly desire to come to terms with the fact that she had left.

It was the only step she could have taken. Today's scene was merely the final breaking-point of the tension which had been deepening ever since Christopher came. There was no sense in getting either emotional or hysterical about it.

Guy had been physically cruel, and it simply couldn't go on. If it was in him to lose control of himself like that, one day he might do Christopher some irreparable damage.

And back came the never-answered question—why had he had him, then? If only she could find an answer to that! She never had. She never would.

She walked over to the bed where Christopher slept. Accustomed to seeing him in his cot, he looked very small. He must have been tired, for he had scarcely moved. The clothes were still tucked round him, one hand was under his cheek and his fair hair was still smooth from its last brushing. Looking down at him, she thought that he had about him all the incomprehensible mystery of a person asleep.

The mystery caught at her throat. Her child, but who was he? Who were any of us? Where were we bound for? What was our destination? Nowhere? Nothing? Were we precipitated into being by that violent moment of sexual love, to live like the may-fly for a few hours and rot back into the earth again? Though he—any of us—might know love and friendship, joy and health, that loneliness would remain, for however close you might get to another person, no one could ever cross that final barrier of yourself. Alone you lived. Alone you died.

And Guy, whom she had loved as she had never thought to love anyone, had shaken that lonely, sleeping child, and flung him from him as though he were something soiled, evil. She thought of Guy, then, as she had seen him in the garden when she ran over the grass. She remembered the drawn, dreadful look round his mouth and nostrils, and Christopher lying on the ground. She could understand all the rest, right from the beginning—his hatred of her when he came back from Korea, his refusal to have Christopher, his suspicion, the awful, frightening change in him—all that she could understand, but not that he could vent his hatred on a baby of three. Not that.

She knelt by the bed, her head pressed down on to the blankets. That was the unforgivable thing. . . .

The words struck a chord in her mind, and she thought of Father Martin sitting in the drawing-room with his grey, hand-knitted socks wrinkling round his ankles, saying, "There is no such thing as an unforgivable sin. . . . Our Lord Himself told us so, didn't He?" "Your Church condemns it," she'd said to him, and he, a slight smile in his eyes, answered. "'*My*' Church forgives. . . ." Then, like a child himself he had eaten chocolate cake for his tea and before he left he said, "We can't forgive. We haven't got it in us. . . . You can't forgive Guy for being cruel to Christopher. You haven't got it in you. But if you pray to Our Lord He'll give you His forgiveness—a free, gratis and for nothing gift. . . ."

She saw herself, a strangely wild creature in retrospect, holding Christopher in her arms, saying to Guy, 'Forgiveness! Your bloody forgiveness. . . . The burden of it. . . . I'd rather hate than forgive. There's something cold and clean in hatred. . . .'

That was true, wasn't it? What did it matter if it was true or not? She could never forgive Guy for what he'd done to Christopher. She didn't even want to try to forgive him.

She raised her head and looked at Christopher again, and there swept over her, like a faint far-off scent, a picture of the white house shining phosphorescently beneath the stars on that June night at Alban Bay.

"Andrew, come and meet Gina. . . ."

He walked across her mind—the broad shoulders, the fine hands, the low, charming voice. But what had he been like, that man she'd known less than twenty-four hours? Had he been kind? Understanding? Would he have been sorry that he had left her to bear all the consequences of that fierce, primitive attraction by herself? She remembered the book, *Single Track*, the depth in it, the sympathy for the defeated. If only she could go to him now and say, 'Help me, Andrew. I'm alone with our son. . . .'

The room had darkened. The rain slashed at the windows. The blanket was rough against her forehead. She felt as though she were reaching out to him across the darkness, straining to find him; to find some comfort that only he could give—because he was Christopher's father.

"It's been too heavy for me," she cried to him. "Don't you see that? You broke free. You died, Andrew, but I lived. And your son lived. And I've loved him. *Loved* him. But now I'm tired and broken and alone. I can't go on any longer. I can't go on. . . ."

She was kneeling there when the bedside telephone rang, and the reception clerk told her that Doctor Blake would like to speak to her. He was in the lounge.

Chapter XVIII

WHEN Mathew Galway, with Ann and Miranda, had gone, Philip went back into the house, thinking of the coincidence which had sent Guy Taylor driving into the square at Belsted just as Mathew was standing talking to him. A few seconds either way and Mathew would never have seen Guy—or remembered where it was that he'd seen him before.

He thought over what Mathew had said in a queer sort of excitement. He'd known all along that there was some missing word in the little paragraph that was Jennifer's death, and now, in this odd manner, he'd caught up with that missing word—and it spelled a name, Guy Taylor. If ever a man had killed, then that man was Taylor. With his industrialist's cunning and with all his money behind him, he'd found out the Mostyns' address, gone down there and . . .

Steady on! That's what it looked as though he'd done, but there was no certainty. He'd asked Mathew the way to the house on the afternoon of the day Jennifer died, but though the rest was glaringly obvious, there was no proof that he'd seen Jennifer. Only one person could clarify that point and that was the girl Violet Stubbings, and as he'd said to Mathew, he'd go across to Bridge Hill next week to see the girl.

Why next week, he asked himself. Why not today, this afternoon? It was, to all intents and purposes, his day off, but as he'd been to London only yesterday. . . . He went to his desk and picked up his diary. There was no surgery on a Saturday night. He'd already made the urgent calls of the morning, and possibly Joe Canon would deal with any emergencies for him.

He picked up the telephone and called his number.

Ten minutes later he went into the kitchen and asked Mrs. Firth to bring him something to eat right away because he had to go out as soon as he'd had a meal. Before he left he told her to switch any urgent calls over to Doctor Canon, and to leave all other messages on his desk as usual.

By half-past one he was in his car heading for the other side of the county and the little village of Bridge Hill. He reached it soon after three, and driving through the main street in the direction of Mathew's farm, he remembered the last time he had come down that road, on the day of Jennifer's funeral, and as he thought of it and of George's lonely figure following her little coffin across to the graveyard, his face hardened and again that whipped-up feeling of excitement was there.

If ever a man should pay for that afternoon's work, Taylor should.

The house itself was closed for the week-end, but it didn't take him long to find Stubbings, a short, thick-set little man with the dried-up leathery neck of the farm-worker. He explained that he was a friend of both the Galways and the Mostyns, that Mathew had told him that his daughter now worked at the farm and that, if she was home on this Saturday afternoon, he'd like to see her for just a few moments.

Everything was very simple, clicking into place like clockwork. He found the cottage down a lane near the farm, spoke to a cheerful little woman who took him into the inevitable 'front room' crowded with large furniture and photographs of long-past weddings, and five minutes later Violet herself came in.

She was the type of village girl of nineteen who, with curious and not very prudent ambition, had modelled herself on the lush exhibitionism of the more extrovert film stars. The result was astonishing, for her young breasts beneath the soiled jumper were strung up to exaggerated points, and the dull matted mane of her hair hung to her shoulders, giving her a deformed and vaguely aboriginal appearance.

He thought at first that she was going to be difficult, but after he'd given her a cigarette and explained that all he wanted was to find out if a friend of his had called on Mrs. Mostyn on the afternoon of the day she died, she became more co-operative.

Not, she said, that there was much to tell him. They'd had lunch and she'd washed up and laid Mrs. Mostyn's tea-tray as usual. It wasn't a very nice day, so she'd decided to stay and clean the silver instead of doing it the following day, Thursday, because Thursday she wanted to get off early and catch the afternoon bus into Millhurst. She'd just got done by the time Nurse was ready to take Christopher over to the Lawsons to the party. That must have been about twenty to four. She helped Nurse out with the pram, and went back and washed her hands and was just going when the gentleman came. No, she didn't ask his name. Yes, he was in a big black car, because she both saw it when she opened the door and had another look at it as she went out.

"And you, I suppose, took him into the drawing-room and then told Mrs. Mostyn," Philip said. "Was she resting?"

"Yes, sir," Violet answered. "We wasn't supposed to disturb her till four as she hadn't been well, but as Nurse was out and it was nearly quarter to by then, I went up and knocked on her door and told her he was there."

"Didn't Mrs. Mostyn ask you his name?" he enquired.

The girl lowered her eyes. "Yes, she did," she answered. "She told me I ought to have asked him. Then she said, 'All right, Violet. I'll come down.'"

He thought the girl was near to tears, and he said, "You've been very helpful and there's only one thing more I want to ask you. Mrs. Mostyn didn't appear to you to be any worse than she had been when you went to her bedroom, did she?"

The girl was crying openly, fishing into the pocket of her jeans for a handkerchief which, obviously, wasn't there. He passed his own across to her and said, "Does it grieve you very much to talk about it? It's all finished now. I won't ask you any more."

She lifted her face, and he saw that there was a terrible fear behind her eyes. "It wasn't me getting her up early that made her die," she cried. "She didn't look no iller than what she had done. I know I didn't ought to have gone up and got her, but——" The sentence tailed away on a sobbing breath.

For a moment he couldn't see what she was driving at, then it became clear and he put his hand on her arm. "Listen to me," he said, "and you must believe what I say. I'm a doctor, you know, and I understand these things. Of course your disturbing Mrs.

Mostyn earlier than you should have done didn't have anything to do with her death. It wouldn't have made the slightest difference. It wasn't that that killed her."

"I kept thinking of it," she said, and she drew a long, shuddering breath. "That's why I didn't tell anybody, not even Mum, that the gentleman came and I fetched her down. I didn't know she'd be dead next day."

Poor child, he thought. The awful burden she must have been carrying beneath that cheap turtle-necked sweater—the dead-weight of self-blame. And if Mathew Galway hadn't stopped at Belsted on his way to the twins at Charterhouse and hadn't seen Guy Taylor get out of his Jaguar in the square, she'd possibly have carried it for the rest of her life. Another mark on the slate against Taylor.

"There! That's all right now, isn't it? And you'll promise me that you'll never think Mrs. Mostyn's death was anything to do with you again?"

She nodded, wiping her eyes.

"I was ever so fond of Mrs. Mostyn," she said.

He nodded. "We all were." He stood up, but she remained where she was, her red hands clasping his handkerchief, her large feet in the peep-toe sandals planted on the shabby carpet. "Now I'm going back, Violet." He smiled slightly. "I'd like to go into town and buy you a box of chocolates, but I haven't got time." He drew a note from his case and laid it on the table. "You won't be offended if I ask you to buy it for me next time you're in Millhurst?"

"I don't want no money," she said. "I haven't done anything."

"You've done more than you know," he told her. "Much more."

He thought of her as he left the village and turned on to the main arterial road, and he remembered Taylor's blasphemous reference to 'the ways of Providence' that he'd trotted out that day in the surgery. But he hadn't got away with it, even at the time. "And you are pleased to think that Providence has killed Mrs. Mostyn so that your will may be served?" he'd asked him. Providence! It wasn't the will of God that had killed Jennifer Mostyn, it was Guy Taylor's will. He'd not only killed her, but he'd sent George off to bear his lonely grief in Africa, and not content with that, having got Christopher into his hands, he'd turned his malice on to the child. But for all this careful planning, he'd tripped up. Or was it the Providence whose guidance he claimed with such self-righteous enthusiasm who had tripped him up? You could call it coincidence or you could call it Providence. And you could also, he thought, with a hardening of his expression, say that your sins would find you out. And having found you out, they were going to be brought home to you. He hadn't forgotten that it was Gina's own unfaithfulness that was the cause of all the rest. He remembered all right, just as he realised the shock and humiliation the whole miserable business had been to Guy. But what the man had never comprehended for a split second was the anguish of Gina's own suffering and remorse, and of how she had even been willing to give the baby up to compensate him for that one tragic lapse. To all that he'd been as blind as a bat.

But Taylor the Sinless was sinless no longer. As sure as the sun was in the sky, he'd caused Jennifer's death. Gina, God help her, had 'sinned' and brought forth life. But Taylor was a murderer.

He stopped for tea in Lewes, and after he'd finished he telephoned through to the house to find out if anything might have come in. There was nothing of any moment, Mrs. Firth told him, but Mrs. Taylor had called soon after he had gone and had left a note and an address and telephone number, which she wanted him to have if he rang up.

He scribbled the name of the hotel and the phone number on an envelope, and decided to go straight down to Ardene before going home.

It looked as though Gina had reached an end.

The rather coy little 'ship's galley' lounge of The George was fortunately empty. He sent a message up to Gina that he was there and he ordered a drink. A quarter of an hour later she came down. The expression on her face and her tear-marked eyes told him the facts as loudly as though he'd heard them spoken.

"Sorry I was out," he said. "I came as soon as I could."

"I've thrown my hand in, Philip," she said, and he saw that her fingers trembled slightly. "I've got Christopher with me."

He nodded and pressed the bell for the waiter.

"Have a drink," he said. "Look as though you need it. You didn't bring Caroline?"

"No. Only Christopher."

The waiter came in, a metal tray tucked under his arm.

"Better have a brandy, hadn't you?" he asked her.

"Perhaps."

"Bring a double brandy and ginger-ale," he said to the man, and when he'd gone out he pulled a chair to the fire and said, "Want to tell me, or not?"

"When you weren't there this afternoon I was frightened," she said with a faint smile. "I kept thinking about the fan of paper in your grate. . . ."

He turned and shot a penetrating look at her.

"No, I'm not insane," she said. "Things like your fan of paper come into your mind when you daren't look at what's really there, don't they?"

"I didn't know there was a fan of paper in my grate. I must have a look at it."

"I've often wondered if you did," she said, and the waiter came in with her drink. Philip poured the ginger-ale into the glass.

"Have a good go at that," he said. "It's better than sipping at it."

"Thanks, Philip." She drank some of the brandy and said, "It was all so unexpected—and yet not, really. We'd just had lunch and Guy had gone out into the garden. . . ."

She told him how she had heard Christopher's cry and Guy's raised voice, and that she ran over the grass to where they were.

"I've never known Christopher go on to the flower-beds before," she said. "I can't think what made him do it." She lifted her hand. "But it wasn't that. I think it might have happened if he'd only spilt his milk or done something quite insignificant. At a certain point the thing—broke."

"Where was Caroline?" he asked her.

"Nurse had forgotten something she needed, and she'd left soon after nursery lunch to walk to Tarn."

"You'll have to have Caroline with you, of course," he said quickly.

He thought she 'crumpled' as she sat in the chair, not exteriorly but interiorly—an emotional caving in.

"How can I? Now?"

"How can't you? You couldn't go through all that again. You're not the type of woman who can walk out on your children. Don't you know that yet?"

"I wish I were," she said.

"Thank God you're not," he answered shortly. He frowned. "I wish George were here."

"Why George, Philip?"

He turned and looked at her. "My dear, I'd like to know where you stand—legally. You don't want to lose Caroline."

"Legally," she repeated. "Legally." She closed her eyes. "I hadn't thought of—legally."

"It's got to be thought of," he said. "You've the rest of your life to face—and the children's lives."

"Legally," she said again. "The law makes everything so—sordid."

"It protects you, too."

"I suppose——"

She thought of reports in the papers; all the dreadful intimate little details that had once meant delight, joy, dragged before the sniggering readers. Mental cruelty. The child walked on the flower-beds. Defendant lost his temper and shook him. The bruise on the shoulder. Not his own son. His wife's illegitimate child by Andrew Wharton, the deceased American novelist. Yes, he had taken both his wife and the child into his home. The daughter to remain in the custody of the father. . . .

"For God's sake, don't thrash yourself into a ferment about it tonight," she heard Philip say. "I oughtn't to have mentioned it. It's my analytical mind trying to gather in all the facts, and naturally I thought of George."

"If George had been here," she said, "and Jennifer alive, it wouldn't have happened, would it?"

He thought of his drive down to Bridge Hill, and of Violet Stubbings in her jeans and soiled jumper. "I showed the gentleman into the drawing-room and went up and told her he was there. . . ." And Jennifer, all unsuspecting, had gone downstairs, and Guy. . . . Had he threatened her? Had he found out that the adoption wasn't legalised, that the Mostyns had no absolute right to keep the boy? What did the exact kind of weapon he'd used matter? Jennifer, standing quite alone in the drawing-room, had taken the thrust right in her heart—and George wasn't in England to be consulted any more. He was half a world away.

He finished his drink and said, "Have you made any plans? Where to go?"

She shook her head. "I haven't done anything but—come here. There seemed only one thought in my mind—to get away. I didn't even know where to go till I stood on your doorstep, and then I suddenly remembered this place."

"I wish I could have you at the house and look after you."

A faint smile touched her lips again.

"Mrs. Firth," she said, "and all Belsted, and the B.M.A. and your practice rocking? Ah no, Philip."

He was staring down at the rug between his feet.

"How much does it matter?" he said.

"It matters very much." She put her glass on the table. "I've made enough mistakes. God forbid that I drag anyone else into the mess."

He looked up and saw the light from a shaded lamp playing on her face. The sadness drawn on it stabbed down into his heart.

"I shall stay here for a few days," she said, "and try to think things out a bit. Nothing seems very clear at the moment. I wonder where Guy went," she added.

"Did he go anywhere?"

"I'd almost forgotten. . . . I saw the car go down the drive, and my one thought was to get away before he or anyone else could stop me. It was as though something just—snapped. I know everyone says that, but it's what happens. I packed the cases—and left." She stopped and drew a breath. "Christopher keeps asking for Caroline," she said.

He put his hand on her arm.

"Try not to let that flay you tonight, Gina. I don't know but—

I have an idea that you'll get Caroline all right."

"Guy would never let her go," she said. "Besides . . . how could I take her from him? I told you once before, if there's one thing that's true in all this it's that . . . he loves her. He does, you know."

"Until she opposes his will. Then what? Caroline beaten up as Christopher was!"

"Don't say that. It isn't true. It simply isn't, you know. I'm certain he'd never touch her. She's—his life." She stopped and then said, "You see, he never loved Christopher."

He thought he'd remember that phrase always.

"Would you like me to have a look at him?" he asked her. "Ease your mind?"

"Have you time?"

"Yes," he answered. "I've only one more call tonight. That's all. Another drink?"

"No. No more."

She stood up. "Will you see Christopher now?"

"I'll just go and get my case out of the car. Wouldn't be a bad idea for you to take a sedative."

A faint trace of her old self returned.

"A nice little sleep will make you fresh as a daisy," she said.

Christopher barely stirred while Gina slipped the jacket from his shoulder. The bruise had darkened in colour and had spread over the top of his shoulder.

Philip didn't say anything, but he felt his jaws strain together. He ran his hands over Christopher's arms, shoulders and neck, and felt the bump on his head. He held his wrist in his hand and took the beat of his pulse.

"They fall relaxed, luckily," he said. "I don't think there's any damage. I'll give you something to put on that bruise. It doesn't look as though he'll wake, but I'll leave you a tablet to give him if he does. And I'll have another look at him tomorrow."

He laid his hand lightly on Christopher's head. Always, all the time, the children carried the can. But it wasn't till you saw a baby of three literally shouldering the burden that you wanted to cry out to men to resist with everything they'd got. And this child, by and large, was lucky. At least his mother had stood by him. It was all the others, the neglected and the starved and the beaten; children who were conceived in drunken squalor and flung on the muck-heap of life that were the cross-bearers.

Five minutes later he was driving along the Belsted road, but just before he reached the town he took the right-hand turning which led to Adversane.

Jo Canon could hang on for another half-hour. There was something he had to say to Guy Taylor.

Chapter XIX

GUY saw Gina walk over the grass with Christopher in her arms. His first instinctive reaction was to go after her and explain what had happened, but a total impotence kept him standing there watching her retreating figure.

For the first time in his life he felt incapable to stop what seemed like a gigantic breaker rushing towards him. He put his hand to his head, trying to steady himself, to see reason; but reason eluded him, lost in the maelstrom of weight bearing down on him.

He turned from the ruined bed, walked over the grass to the garage and got into the car. There was only one need—to get away; to be quite alone. To fight his way to the cold truth that was still there behind the confusion all about him. For a moment he thought of Christopher lying on the ground, but the boy, he told himself, wasn't hurt.

He started the engine, and without thought of where he was going turned right at the gates and went up the lane. A mile farther on he took the little cart-track that skirted the disused chalk-pit and brought him to the top of the hill. He left the track, bumped over the grass and switched off the engine. The abrupt silence came at him with a stab of surprise, and he saw himself trembling with rage, taking hold of Christopher and shaking him. He felt the touch of his shoulders, saw the wide-opened eyes, felt the little body rocking in his arms, the head wobbling loosely like the head of a rag doll.

He put his hands on to the top of the steering-wheel and lowered his head on to them.

The child had screamed once, a queer animal cry of fear, but he'd gone on shaking him, and then he'd flung him from him and the small body had hit the grass with a little thud. If anyone had told him that he could bring himself to do such a thing he'd have laughed. What cog had slipped in his mind throwing up that terrifying impulse to hurt; to kill? He thought for a moment that he stood on the brink of himself, peering down into the blackness of his own heart, which, beneath the veneer of decency and good clothes, held those sadistic and obscene desires. He turned away from that gaping pit and tried to think out what had actually occurred.

He'd driven down from London, stopped at Belsted, and as he passed the church on his way out of the town he'd thought about the redecoration, even visualised a new church rising on the ruins of the old converted rifle-range. In the forefront of his mind was gratification over the amalgamation and a longing to tell Gina about it. He saw himself hurrying into the house, calling her name, and he looked up as she came running downstairs. "Gina, I've done it! It wasn't J. B. and Sir James, it was me. Harben's part of our combine now. No, it's not we who are part of Harben. Harben is part of us. Knighthood. . . . The peerage. . . . Nothing can stop me." He saw her standing on the bottom stair, her eyes bright, saying in her own 'tossed-off' way, "Why all the commotion? All I don't understand is why you've been so *long* about it. . . ." And then she flung herself into his arms and said, "I always knew you were the most wonderful man in the world. That's why I picked you," and they laughed and opened the champagne.

That had been the bright image in his mind, but when he reached Ladysmere and walked into the house the image dissolved before the barrier that was between them. He didn't call her name. She didn't run down the stairs. Coolly, in her damned 'Gina Randolph' way, she said, "Hello. Thought I heard the car," and passed on across the hall, a bowl of flowers in her hand. What did she care if he'd just pulled off one of the biggest deals of a lifetime? Why had he ever imagined she'd care? Once, before he'd been to Korea, he'd thought she cared, but then he'd come home from Korea. . . .

They'd had lunch, and although he wanted, casually, not as though it mattered to him, to tell her about Harben, he hadn't been able to. He hadn't been able to break through that damned barrier. . . . And then she'd spoken of Miranda's not coming to lunch. No mention of where she'd been, just that 'I was out'—the phrase she'd have used to a servant. Where had she been? Was she having another '*affaire*' with someone? Showering her love on some other man as she'd showered it on Christopher's father? Gratitude to him for having the boy into his home? God, no. He was merely her 'stooge', the machine that provided the money on which she could entertain her lovers. So he hadn't mentioned Harben and the amalgamation, and they'd finished lunch in silence and then he'd gone out into the garden and come on Christopher pulling out the plants. Then what? It was as though something had 'gone' in his brain, as though all his pain had been concentrated in the figure of the child pushing his barrow over the bed. If Christopher had never been, none of it would have happened. Gina would still have loved him; looked up to him. She would have run down the stairs and flung herself into his arms. She would have spoken those words of praise. . . . It was the child who was the barrier. And wilfully, evilly he had trampled down the green shoots. This other man's son. . . . This interloper. . . .

He'd put out his hand to hit him, but he'd ducked away. He'd reached after him, and his hand had come down on him. He'd shaken him like a little rat, and then he'd thrown him from him and he'd heard the thud of his body . . . and Gina was there. She bent over the boy, took him into her arms—and the expression on her face was burnt into his brain. She'd said, "If he is injured I shall kill you."

"What more could I have done?" he'd shouted at her. "Haven't I forgiven you?" And she, standing with the boy heavy in her arms, had said, "The intolerable burden of your forgiveness! Every time you've mentioned the word, every time you've thought of it, you've thanked God you were sinless."

It wasn't true. *Hadn't* he forgiven her? Had her back? Yes, after he'd forced her to give the child away. . . .

'Whosoever receiveth one of these children in my name, receiveth me. . . .'

He tried to thrust the words from him, but they were there, now, living in his mind. Received Our Lord Himself. Received the Christ living in man. Not Christopher but Christ. It was Christ he had grabbed by the shoulders and had shaken till his head wobbled. Christ he had flung on the ground. Christ whose body had fallen with a thud.

He lifted his head and lowered it again, twisting it on to his folded hands against the wheel.

'Is my reason going,' he wondered. 'Am I insane? What's happening to me?'

And Gina, her face marked with that dreadful grief, had sat on the ground and taken Christopher into her arms and looked down on the little, still figure.... 'They took Him down from the cross and His mother was there....' Not Christopher but Christ.... Christ crucified again in a child. Christ crucified by him, Guy Taylor, the man who went to church every Sunday, who gave the vestments and the altar candlesticks; who dreamed of building a church....

And if Christopher were really injured? If in the fall he had struck his head, damaged his brain? Christopher in his bright red trousers trotting over the grass clutching his tip-cart, an idiot? God, no. To know always and for ever that it was he who had made him so? It wouldn't be bearable. It just wouldn't be bearable.

He tried to get a grip on himself, but the wave was breaking all about him, tossing him around like a bit of driftwood. There was no sure ground beneath his feet, nothing to stand on. Only the words going round and round in his head—Not Christopher but Christ. Not Christopher but Christ. . . .

And what to do now? He hadn't even stayed to find out if Christopher was all right. The nurse was out and Gina was there alone. He'd made a move to go to her, but she'd walked on, bent a little with the boy's weight. "No, don't touch him. Don't touch either of us."

He'd got to go back, get down to the house again. He'd got to find out what he'd done to Christopher.

He lifted his head from his hands on the wheel. After the darkness of his closed eyes, the grass and sky were unreal. For a moment he saw himself as a child running ragged and bare-foot on the hills above Brighton. The laces of his broken shoes were tied together round his neck, his hands were stained purple with blackberry juice. He felt the wind with the faint smell of the sea in it about his face, looked down and saw his own feet, his toes grimed with dirt. He called to the other boys, and ran on, holding the paper bag with the blackberries in it. . . .

He pressed the self-starter and the engine of the Jaguar purred into action. He turned, bumped over the grass and down the track.

The house was very quiet, the drawing-room and dining-room were empty. He went upstairs and heard the nurse's voice from behind the closed nursery door. He opened it. Caroline was sitting in her little chair, and the nurse was bending over her, feeding her from a cup. There was a ring of milky food round Caroline's mouth, but when she saw him, she smiled, twinkling up her eyes and holding out her hands to him. Looking down at her, he thought that something in his heart broke and dissolved in weakness.

He looked at the nurse. There was an expression he couldn't interpret on her face—a queer kind of masked satisfaction. He wondered if she knew about Christopher.

"Do you know where my wife is?" he asked her.

Her eyes darkened, and she lowered her lids over them.

"I believe Mrs. Taylor is—out," she answered, and he wondered if he had imagined the slight hesitation before the word.

"You don't know where?"

"I'm afraid I don't. . . ."

"Is Christopher with her?"

Again that strange satisfaction was there on the woman's face.

"I think he must be."

"I see." He wanted to ask her if she knew what had happened, but he couldn't bring himself to do it. "Had they left before you came back?" he said.

"Yes, they had."

"I'll go and see if anyone downstairs knows," he said, and once more he was aware of the woman's dark eyes above her prim, vaguely smiling mouth.

He went downstairs again and pressed the drawing-room bell. Margaret came in, her eyebrows lifted in surprise.

"I didn't know you were back, sir. I'll get your tea. . . ."

Margaret, too—an odd expression on her round face.

"Can you tell me when Mrs. Taylor went out?" he asked her.

Her blue eyes were turned away from him. "Well, I can't be quite sure. It was about half an hour after you went. I shouldn't have known she was going, but I happened to see the car. . . ."

Had Margaret seen the whole thing from the kitchen window? He had the feeling that she had seen it all, knew where Gina had gone, but had no intention of telling him.

"Will you have some tea, sir?"

He nodded. "Yes. Nothing to eat."

She went out, and he was alone—as alone as he'd ever been in his life. He felt isolated from everything; everyone.

He lowered his head into his hands, and he thought that if only he could see Christopher come running in, he'd go on his knees to him, take him into his arms, love him. . . .

But there was no sound in the house. Not even a door opening. . . . Where had they gone? He thought if he couldn't find out, his reason would snap. Blake. . . . If the boy were injured she'd have rushed him down to Blake. She would have told Blake what had happened. Blake, too, would know. . . . Even that, it didn't matter. He'd got to find out where they were.

He went across to the telephone and called Blake's number. A woman's voice answered him. No, Doctor wasn't in. Doctor Canon was taking any urgent calls. If he'd like to ring Belsted 47. . . . No, she didn't know what time he'd be back. He hadn't said. He'd gone out after lunch. Would he care to leave a message . . .?

Not Blake, then, unless Christopher was seriously hurt and Blake had gone to the hospital with her. Ring the hospital? Enquire if they were there? To hell with what they thought. . . .

Again he picked up the telephone and called the hospital. A brisk, bright, impersonal voice said it would put him through to the children's ward. He waited a full five minutes before, at last, a high-pitched voice with a slight lisp told him that no child of that name had been admitted that afternoon.

He was putting the receiver back when Margaret came in with his tea. She left it without a word and went out again, and he poured himself a cup and drank it standing up. When he'd finished it he stood with his head lowered, remembering the night of Caroline's birth; remembering that frail look about Gina as she lay on the nursing-home bed, propped up by pillows, and of how he had gone to her and knelt on the floor and pressed his head into the blankets.

But even on the way to the nursing home he'd wondered if it were his child. He looked down the years, saw himself watching her, disbelieving her, for ever suspicious that she was having another '*affaire*'. How could he help it? She'd been everything to him—all the truth and purity and sweetness he'd ever known. He'd believed in her love for him, believed in her loyalty. 'The one undying thing. . . .' And then he'd come home from Korea to—that. Could any man have believed in her after it? Wasn't the whole thing soiled, sordid, slashed across with mud that would never go?

Two hours ago she'd said, "Your forgiveness has crushed me, mangled me, and now it's crushed and mangled my son. . . . Every time you've spoken the word, every time you've thought it, you've thanked God you were without sin. . . ."

His mind swung back to the night he'd run into Father Dolan at the bus stop, the night he'd had dinner with Alison. He saw himself sitting in the presbytery, saw the rugged lines of the priest's lowered head. "'To defend her and all that was hers'—that's what you promised, didn't you?"

"You don't mean that I should have taken the child? Don't you see how impossible it would have been?"

"Why do you, of all men, shirk the hard way?"

"The child. . . . The effect on him. . . . How could I have taken him as my own?"

"You'll need to pray hard and you'll need great patience."

"I've had great patience."

"You've only had some patience. You'll need to pray for a lot more yet. Forgiveness is never a matter of five minutes. It has to be lived out day by day, hour by hour. Your forgiveness won't get you far if you haven't His charity in you. . . ."

He'd driven away half-irritated. "Take it to God. . . ." "Say your prayers. . . ." What did this little Irish celibate know about the agony he'd suffered in Korea; his homecoming to that?

Your forgiveness won't get you far if you haven't His charity in you. . . .

Again he thought he stood on the brink of himself, peering down into the darkness of his own heart, into that strange, shadowed self which lived its caged existence beneath the façade of Guy Taylor, industrialist, and again what he saw there sickened him. . . . He saw Gina, the tears in her eyes, saying "I never stopped loving you, Guy. I was caught in a wave, lost. . . ." He saw himself forgiving her, standing there cloaked in his own sinlessness, damnably condescending. He saw himself in church, gloating over his expensive gifts. . . . Guy Taylor, the generous parishioner. . . . He saw himself standing outside Alison's flat in the darkness muttering, "Thank God. . . . Thank God. . . ." He saw himself watching Gina's every movement, waiting for her to be unfaithful to him again; saw himself in his office deciding to have her watched. He saw himself on his knees praying, receiving Communion, rattling off the familiar "Forgive us our trespasses as we forgive them that trespass against us. . . ." He saw Gina standing in the garden with Christopher in her arms. "The intolerable burden of your forgiveness. . . ." He saw Christopher's wobbling head as he shook the small body, shook it and shook it. . . . Not Christopher but Christ. . . .

Like a blind man he groped with his hands for a moment, and then was kneeling on the floor, his head buried in the chair.

This—this was himself.

Shadow had filled the room when at last he lifted his head.

He got to his feet, switched on the light and the room came to life. He saw it with surprise—all the familiar things; the furniture, the curtains, the bowl of flowers that Gina had been carrying through the hall as he came in.

He looked back at the morning as though it were a sunlit country he could never reach again.

Where were they? If only he knew. If only he knew if Christopher was all right.

Giles and Miranda! He'd forgotten them. Perhaps she'd taken Christopher there. He went across to the telephone and gave their number. A man's voice answered: "Belsted 3458."

"That you, Giles?"

"Sorry, he's out. Did you want him?"

"Is Miranda there?"

"She's out, too, I'm afraid. I'm the only living soul in the place at the moment. Giles won't be long. He's only taken Miranda and my wife over to Tarn. I should think they'd be back in quarter of an hour. Like to leave a message?"

He remembered, then, that Gina had said that they had friends staying for the week-end. This must be one of them. He thought the voice was faintly familiar, but Gina obviously wasn't there.

"No, it was nothing important," he said. "I'll ring again some time. . . ."

It was quite dark now and the polished window acted as a mirror. In it he saw himself sitting at the table and behind him the room, strangely cut by the lights of Belsted which were alight down in the valley.

Then he saw the headlights of a car come in through the gates, sweep up the drive and stop.

Gina. . . .

He went to move, but weakness caught at him. For the first time in his life he thought he was going to faint. Through the wavering dark and the noise in his ears, he heard the bell ring and voices in the hall.

Not Gina. . . . Gina wouldn't have rung the bell. Someone else. . . . They'd come to tell him that Christopher was in hospital, that Gina. . . . He made one final effort that sent the beads of sweat on to his upper lip, and the waves of darkness rolled back a little. As the door opened, he got to his feet.

"Doctor Blake would like to see you, sir," said Margaret, and he saw Philip standing behind her. A second later he was in the room and Margaret had shut the door.

He didn't need to ask Philip if he knew what had happened. It was written on every line of his set face. But some last ribbon of pride was left to him, and he met his unsmiling eyes.

"You've come from my wife . . .?" he said.

Philip nodded. "Yes," he answered shortly.

"Where is she?"

Even as he looked at him, the doctor in Philip noticed the colour of his skin, his dilated pupils, the signs of acute strain, but he brushed away the stirring of compassion and the almost mechanical need to relieve suffering.

"You asked me that question once before, Taylor—and I told you. I told you because your wife, then, wanted to see you. Now she doesn't want to see you."

He watched the muscles tighten in Guy's cheeks, saw his eyes harden.

"She sent you to tell me that?"

"No, she didn't send me to tell you that. She didn't 'send me' at all. I've seen her and I've seen her son. I've seen what you've done to her son, and I've seen what you've done to her. I've not only seen it tonight, but I've watched it happening over the last two years. I've watched your damned unforgiving self-righteousness breaking her spirit and her health. And for the last three months I've watched your spite being vented on Christopher. You'd have done better if you'd beaten your wife, not a baby of less than three years. She wouldn't have bruised so easily. . . ."

He moved his hand slightly as though brushing away something unimportant. "That's done." His eyes narrowed. "When I met you on Belsted station three years ago, I was sorry for you. It was a pretty terrible knock to come home from Korea to face what you had to face. I tried to explain to you that your wife had fallen to a temptation that any one of us, God knows, might fall to, but you didn't believe that. You chose to believe that she was promiscuous and that she'd been deceiving you for years. You had your share of suffering to face, but you didn't realise then, and you've never realised since, that she suffered, too. I was with her when she gave in to your demand to get rid of the child—in case his presence might remind you of her unfaithfulness and of your injured pride. She loved him, not because of his father for she never knew him, but because he was *her child*—the baby she'd longed for. But you were so busy nursing your own hurt that you never noticed hers. You were too damned satisfied with yourself and your forgiveness." He stopped speaking for a moment, but Guy didn't move. He stood as he had been standing when he had first come into the room, one hand on the back of the chair, and his face showed no expression whatsoever. "But you've been unlucky, Taylor," he went on. "You've been found out. And I, with luck or with the help of the Providence you so glibly assume is concerned solely with your particular schemes, have found you out. It isn't your wife who needs forgiveness, it's you. She was unfaithful to you, but you've got the mark of murder on your soul just as surely as Christopher's got the mark of your spite on his shoulder—for it was you who killed Jennifer Mostyn. You came to me for their address. Remember? I refused to give it to you because I knew that if Jennifer had to give Christopher up it would kill her, because she had suspected angina and had been warned to avoid strain. But nothing mattered to you but your 'Christian duty'. It was all of a piece with the vestments and the candlesticks you gave to the church; all part of the picture of 'Guy Taylor' the generous parishioner, the forgiving husband. I don't know how you found out who the Mostyns were and where they lived. You did find out, and you went down to Bridge Hill and you saw Jennifer. I don't know what you said to her—only you know that—but within three hours of your leaving Bridge Hill she was dead. . . . Your threat to take Christopher from her had killed her as surely as though you'd driven a knife in her heart." He drew a breath. "That's what I've come here to say to you tonight. You're a Catholic, aren't you? Go and confess that to your priest, Father Martin. Go and tell him that you're not only a child-beater but that you're a murderer." He shook his head. "You won't! You'll find some excuse, some justification for all of it in yourself. If Gina hadn't been unfaithful to you, you'd never have beaten Christopher up. That's the line, isn't it? It wasn't your fault that Jennifer Mostyn had a bad heart; you did your duty. So easy! Just see what you want to see. Shut your eyes to anything else. And Father Martin, that dear gullible little man, will give you absolution. Yes, you can fox yourself and you can fox other people; you can even fox your priests in the confessional, but there's one thing you can't do and that's fox the Providence who arranges all your affairs with such zeal. You can't fox God. . . ."

He stopped speaking abruptly, as though, at last, the accumulated hatred of months had been satisfied; as though at last Gina and Christopher and Jennifer Mostyn had been avenged. He felt tired, empty, as he used to feel as a young doctor when he had helped someone to die. And still Guy hadn't moved. He still stood with one hand on the back of the chair, his face grey. Philip had expected a dose of the self-righteous sarcasm he'd had before in the surgery. He'd half expected—half hoped—that Guy might raise his fist to him. Had he, at last, punctured that damned hypocritical self-righteousness? Or was the man a coward? Even as the thought came to him he was aware of surprise. He'd never have credited Guy with cowardice.

"Nothing to say?" he asked. "Isn't Providence going to come across with another of those pleasant little miracles to smooth your path this time?"

Guy was staring straight back at him, but the expression drawn on his face shook him. And then Guy rapped out, "No. Nothing to say. P'raps you'd like to go now."

There was something going on, thought Philip, that he didn't quite understand. None of Guy's reactions were as he'd imagined they'd be. He remembered the day he'd seen him come towards him down the platform at Belsted station, a scarecrow of a man who'd been in a Korean prison for a year, and he'd got that same tattered dignity he'd had then about him now.

"Yes," he said, "I'll go now. I've said all I want to say—except this. Your wife didn't take Caroline with her because her one thought was to get Christopher out of the place with his skin whole. Half an hour ago she said to me, 'I couldn't take Caroline from him. . . .' She couldn't, but I could. And if the law wants a medical report on your behaviour I shall see that it gets it. Gina can't go through all that again." He turned to go, but swung back on his heel to half face Guy. "Jennifer Mostyn," he said, "was my step-sister. If she hadn't been, I should have married her. I shall use your part in her death, too, if it would help to release Caroline."

Without another word he turned, opened the door, walked across the hall and let himself out into the driving rain.

Guy heard the door shut and the engine start. The headlights came on and the gear engaged. The stones scattered as they always did as the car turned, and he heard it go off down the drive.

Now he had reached an end. He knew that. The last defence had been stripped down. There was nothing left.

"You've got the stain of murder on your soul as surely as Christopher's got the stain of your spite on his shoulder. . . ."

It almost didn't matter any more.

Coolly, without emotion, he saw himself driving down to Bridge Hill; saw the drawing-room door open and the grave child-like eyes looking up at him. "I am Jennifer Mostyn. . . ."

His will. His determination to have his own way. . . . But he hadn't known that her heart was bad. He *hadn't* known. He'd rifled Gina's desk to get their name. He'd tricked old Galway into giving him their address. He'd decided to see Mrs. Mostyn alone; to work on her softer emotions. . . . He had worked on her emotions and, in doing it, he'd killed her. She'd loved Christopher as he loved Caroline, and the thought of losing him had been, for her, the final strain that had snapped the thin bands of her life. He saw the house at Bridge Hill as he'd seen it on that stormy afternoon. He saw the door open, the men carrying her coffin out under the rose-grown porch. He saw the windows closed, and a 'For Sale' notice at the gate and the weeds growing on the brick path. He saw a vague figure with a suitcase in his hand walking alone across the tarmac to the plane. . . .

He saw it all quite clearly, knife sharp, and again he raised his hands and lowered his head into them.

This man, too, was himself.

Father Martin sat very still and he kept his eyes lowered as Guy's toneless voice went on piecing together the story, so much of which he already knew perfectly well.

So many similar stories. . . . So many men and women sitting in the arm-chair, as Taylor sat now, sick with the revelation of the unguessed-at twists of their own personalities. Dozens and dozens of them, vomiting up their gobbets of pain and malice, released at last by the emetic of God's grace working its painful, cleansing way on their hearts and minds. And when the sickness had passed, Christ Himself, through the Church, through him, would wipe the last rancid stain from the lips and, like any hospital nurse, carry the mess away and come back with a drink of the cold water of absolution.

And while with half of his mind, so long trained to listening, he heard Guy's voice, he remembered Gina sitting with her arms clasped round her, saying, "I am his mother. . . ." "I committed the unforgivable sin, didn't I?" "Your Church condemns it. . . ."

How little they knew. How little they understood of the silent, healing process of grace, going on beneath the surface. How little he himself knew. . . . But she had been generous-hearted, not foisting the blame on anyone but herself; seeing her own weakness as the cause of all the rest. He remembered leaving the house and cycling down the hill to Belsted and up to the Sisters at the Convent, and how he had asked the Mother Abbess, her eyes still the laughing clear eyes of Susie Carmichael, the little torment of a cousin he'd gone sailing with on the Fal forty-odd years ago, to pray for them. And—he half smiled to himself—Susie had marshalled her Sisters, and gone into action with all the faith and fervour she'd used when the two of them had been lost on Dartmoor in a fog. But neither the girl nor Taylor would ever know that, for like Christ's own healing process of integration, it was silent, hidden, as the engines that drove a liner across the Atlantic were hidden from the passengers on the promenade deck, and all they knew, without even surprise, was that they'd reached harbour. Susie the stoker . . . he thought irreverently, and lowered his lids over the smile in his eyes.

But it was God's hand that was on the helm.

Chapter XX

THE lounge of the George Hotel at Ardene looked, in the morning light, exactly what it was—the lounge of the George Hotel at Ardene. The wicker tables with the glass tops were clean. The wicker arm-chairs with the showy blue-and-white cushions were set about them with precision. The over-coloured prints of barques and schooners, all in full sail on cobalt seas, each hung dead centre of its allotted square of dark oak panelling. Papers and magazines were set neatly on a side-table and a small fire burned in the 'mock Tudor' grate.

The gale had returned and the rain lashed against the windows, but now the mud-flats were hidden and the broad river was grey and angry, swirling up-stream on scurrying white-capped waves.

Gina stood at one of the windows, her back turned to the terrifying impersonality of the room. Why, she wondered, had she come here of all places? Because she had connected it with childhood and summer holidays? But in those days The George had been old and fusty and comfortable, with oilskins and Burberrys hung anyhow on the hooks in the passage, and a dear old relic of a waiter known as 'Mary', who served the meals from an enormous sideboard in the dining-room. And this room—there hadn't been a trace of a neat little wicker table. There'd been a bamboo one, though, with a ledge underneath and copies of the *Sketch* and *Tatler* and *The Queen* were piled on it anyhow, and the chairs were large and old and shabby, and there was—she'd forgotten that—a complicated and fearsome oil-lamp hanging from the ceiling, all strange funnels and curling brass, with a shade like a coolie's hat over the whole contraption to keep the ceiling from getting black—only it didn't! And at night the talk was of ships and ropes and tides; of sheets and boom and galley, and her father and Uncle Rod and the others got up and helped themselves to drinks from bottles which 'Mary' set ready for them after dinner, while she and Giles and Ann and anyone else who was there sat on the sheepskin rug by the wood fire, alight wet or fine, cold or hot, and talked or read or listened to the 'grown-up' stories while they sucked, with holy relish, 'curiously extra-strong peppermints', bought at the little shop down the road that sold fishing-nets and plimsolls and post-cards and shells. Why drool over all that now? Because the deadly uniformity of the Sunday-morning appearance of the room behind her made her weep over change? Would it have made much difference if it had still been as she remembered it? What did it matter? The point was that she was here. Yesterday she'd left Guy. A flick of a picture of the drawing-room at Ladysmere came into her mind, but she saw it in time and flung it out. That, too, was as forbidden as memories of The George. Sentimental reminiscence got you nowhere.

But where—literally—did she go from here? This was bearable for the week-end; but where next? She couldn't picture herself hanging around in 'little' hotels or boarding-houses. She loathed the places. Besides, how could she coop Christopher up in one of them all the winter? She looked round and saw him. He was sitting on the floor between two of the arty little tables playing for a moment with some bricks. He'd woken up soon after six—it seemed an interminable age ago—and he'd been fretful and 'on edge' ever since, and every little while he'd asked for Caroline. She thought, 'It's Caroline, not me, who means home to him, if anything does.' It was possible that even the nurse meant more to him, in a way, than she did. Children, like puppies, turned to the hand that fed them. But he'd soon forget Caroline. . . . Her thought broke on the precipice of that, but she steadied herself, and watching him move the bricks his solitariness tore at her and she fancied that he was 'out on the road' again—on the march like the Wandering Jew. . . . She thrust that fancy down, too, and tried reason again.

She'd have to get a home for him, of course. Another 'Melford' flat. Another 'Dardanella' creeping heavily downstairs with her hair in kirby-grips? God forbid. . . . That depended on what money she would be likely to have. Guy would have to give her money, wouldn't he? She didn't even know that. As Philip had said last night, it depended on the 'legal' position. She'd have to see a solicitor, explain the whole thing. . . . "I had a child by another man while my husband was imprisoned in Korea. . . ." That thought sickened her, too, so she dropped it. She'd have to get her clothes, though. Yesterday, in the stress of that awful moment, she'd taken only the barest necessities, hardly enough to tide her over the week-end. How on earth was she to get the rest of her things? And Christopher's? Go up there during the week, while Guy was in London? Face that wretched, sanctimonious nurse again? And Margaret and Cook and Marple? Let Christopher see Caroline for an hour—and then drag him away? Herself see Caroline . . .? She felt the tears gathering into an ache in her throat, but she forced them down. She must think clearly, without emotion. She couldn't go back there, not even for her clothes and personal possessions. There were all Christopher's toys, too . . . and her fur coat and the two Sheraton chairs which her father had let her have in the Oakley Street rooms; and a couple of pictures Aunt Claire had given her once. . . . She closed her eyes. It was all too complicated, too involved. Yesterday, when her one thought had been that an end had been reached, and that she must get Christopher away, she had acted on the 'crest of a wave' which was rushing her along too fast for detailed thought. Now the 'detailed thought' had caught up with her.

What did people do when they left their husbands? Not in the big broad things, but in the little things like 'whose were the fish-knives?' As if it mattered! Yet these things were all part of it. No one could tear up their roots in one jerk. Like ground-elder, you might snap the main root, but there were a thousand other small 'leaders' still left in the earth. She glanced out of the window again, but the gale was still lashing across the flat land beyond the wide river. She turned from that desolation to the almost equal desolation of the room, and she wondered if they'd lighted the fire in the drawing-room at Ladysmere. Oh lord, not again. . . . She'd had to get Christopher away from Guy. *Had* to. It wasn't a question of just that one incident, it was a question of the whole relationship and its dreadful effect on Christopher. Guy hated him—and that was the end of it. She knew why he hated him, and as far as she could see he'd never do anything else but hate him. Whatever she did, however hard she tried, nothing could alter the fact that he wasn't

Guy's child, and nothing could alter the fact that Guy would never forgive her for having him. Even if she wanted to go back for her own sake, she couldn't go back for Christopher's sake. Christopher had had enough.

She had gone over to the miserable little fire and was hovering over it, her feet in the hearth. Was this how it would be always? Cheerless little rooms belonging to someone else, nothing of your own. . . . She beat the self-pity down. Of course it wouldn't. She'd find a home for them, make him happy again.

He got to his feet and came over to her and stood at her knee, one of the bricks in his hand.

"I like to see Car-line. Shall we go and see Car-line? In the car?" He stopped speaking, and put his thumb in his mouth and sucked it, looking up at her. There were dark smudges under his eyes, and he seemed tired, listless.

"No, we can't go and see Caroline, darling. Not——" She was going to say 'Not yet'. Why lie to him? Why pretend, even to a child?

He took his thumb out of his mouth and sighed, then he lifted the brick and rubbed it up and down her arm. "I like to see Car-line," he said.

She reached for her handbag, and took out a bar of chocolate and broke him off a piece. She went to put it into his mouth, but he turned his head away.

"Don't want it?"

He looked at the chocolate in her fingers, and rubbed the brick up and down her arm again, twisting his body sideways as he leaned against her.

"I like to see Car-line," he said.

She thought, 'I can't bear it. I simply can't bear another thing. I'm too tired. . . .'

"It's nice chocolate," she told him mechanically. "Come on. Eat it."

He took it into his mouth, and a little brown-tinged dribble slipped between his lips.

She took out her handkerchief and wiped it away, then she looked at her watch. It was still only half-past eleven.

Christopher went back to his bricks and she picked up one of the papers from the table and tried to concentrate on it, but she hadn't the slightest idea what she read. And then, as she held the paper open looking at the inside page, a small photograph caught her eye. She stared down at the man and woman pictured there, read the caption underneath. 'Mrs. Joseph Wharton with Father Ronald Wharton at London Airport. See "Gift for poor parish".' Swiftly she found the heading, read the paragraph.

> 'Mrs. Joseph Wharton, mother of Andrew Wharton, the American novelist who was killed in a car smash at Washington, Sussex, three years ago while on the way to an appointment with John Hammond, his English publishers, has given the proceeds of the première of *Single Track*, the film made from her son's best-selling novel, to Father Ronald Wharton, another son, towards the building of a permanent church in his first parish. Father Wharton studied at the American College in Rome and was ordained in 1943.'

His brother. . . . And the short woman with the crisp grey hair his mother. She'd stood within a couple of feet of them both, and not even here in England but in Rome. She stared into the blurred photograph, trying to trace some likeness to Andrew in either of them, till she realised, with a shock, that she couldn't recall his face with any clarity, all that remained was an impression of broad shoulders and deep-set blue eyes and of a quiet strength.

She looked down at Christopher and back at the priest. There was the likeness; quite unmistakable. The same-shaped head; same bone formation; even some hovering similarity of expression. . . . Christopher—and his unknown, unknowing uncle.

She lowered the paper on to her knee, nearer to the held-back tears than she had been all the morning. Neither of them would ever know that their son and brother had had a child. Neither know that she had watched them, heard them talking quietly together outside the little church on the old Appian Way.

Sunlight and shadow on the road. The priest's broad shoulders, the child's long plaits and little bumpy figure; Guy, standing some distance away. . . . The essence and the 'feel' of Rome that was in the very air.

Always and always, the strange interweaving of events. The meetings that never took place. The loves or friendships missed by a second of time. . . . All that we didn't know. . . .

She picked up the paper again and looked at the photograph. Would they understand? The mother might despise her, but the brother, the priest?

Her mind flung away from them to the dreary little room in the presbytery of the Church of the Assumption, and to Father Dolan speaking to her of the sacrament of marriage and of how she had smiled to herself and thought, 'Whatever he does to it, he can't make it too permanent for my liking. . . .' She'd meant it; how she'd meant it! 'The one undying thing. . . .' Not the glitter and the fun of going about with Guy. Not the sheer relief of the material comfort he could give her, but—Guy himself. The person he was, with all his twists and odd, funny quirks; with his sensitiveness and his determination, and his half-pride, half-shame, that he'd come from the 'ironmonger's shop'. She'd thought then that if they'd cut him up and brought him to her in little pieces in a sack, she'd still love him.

'The Church guards the whole personality of man, that's why there can be only one permanent sacramental marriage . . .' Father Dolan had said, and she, who'd have staked her life on her own love, had smashed it up. And now it was all over, done with. She'd let Christopher go once, but she couldn't let him go again. She wondered what 'Father Ronald Wharton' would say if she could go to him and tell him the whole story. Would he tell her to leave Christopher and go back to Guy and Caroline? Throw Christopher back on the junk-heap? Whatever he said, there was no solution. She'd either got to leave Caroline or Christopher. One or the other. But possibly, like Father Martin, he'd say, "I will pray for you."

Probably Father Martin had prayed for her, but God hadn't heard his prayers.

She thought of the little man, sitting like a spry black beetle in the chair saying, "'*My*' Church forgives. . . . Our Lord wipes the slate clean. . . ." If only it were true.

The door swung open and Philip came in.

She thought she had never been so glad to see anyone in her life. She held out her hand to him, and he strode across the room and took it, looking down at her.

"You all right? I couldn't get here any earlier."

"Oh, damn, Philip. I'm crying. It's the weather."

He smiled slightly. "Yes. It's vile outside. Did you sleep?"

"Christopher woke at six."

Christopher left his bricks and came across to them. He looked up at Philip, tilting his head far back to see his facc.

"Car-line?" he asked him. "In the car?"

Philip gave a quick glance at Gina.

"He's been asking for her all the morning. If only one could explain to him."

Philip drew out a chair, and sat down and took Christopher on to his knee.

"You'll see Caroline again soon, old boy. Just wait a little while."

Gina closed her eyes and opened them again. "Oh, Philip, no! It's no good saying that to him. I know he's only a baby and doesn't understand, but he might think it's true. I'm not being silly . . ." she ended vaguely.

He looked across at her over Christopher's head. "Neither am I," he answered. "I meant it."

"How can you mean it? I've told you. . . ." She stopped and shook her head. "I can't go through it again. I can't. I've had enough, Philip. I have, you know."

"D'you think I don't know that? Here, wait a minute. . . ." He held Christopher with one arm and fished in his pocket with his left hand. "Look, Christopher. What d'you think of this?" He held up the miniature red engine and ran it over his right palm. "Like it? Let's see if it'll run on the floor."

He took Christopher from his knee, and bent down and sent the engine shooting off between the tables. It moved round to the right between the chair-legs and followed the slope of the old floor to the far wall, where it hit the skirting and stopped. "She goes well, doesn't she?"

Christopher stood looking at the little engine for a moment, then he sighed once and trotted off after it. He reached it and picked it up, and then he sat down on the floor, his red-trousered legs apart, and ran it up and down in the little triangle of space between them.

"I'll look at that shoulder in a minute," said Philip, and he went back to the chair and sat down, bending forward to Gina, his hands clasped between his knees.

"My dear, I told you last night, you must have Caroline with you."

Again she shook her head. "You don't understand. . . . He'd never let Caroline go. I know he wouldn't. . . ."

"He will let Caroline go. . . ."

She looked up at his tone, a slight frown on her face. "What do you mean?"

"I've got something to tell you. I wasn't going to say anything about it yet, but I've changed my mind. Last night, after I left here, I went to Ladysmere and I saw Guy."

"You didn't tell him I was here?"

"Of course not."

"Did he ask you where I was?"

"Yes. At least he said, 'I suppose you have come from my wife.'"

"What was he doing?"

"Doing? He was in the drawing-room when I went in."

"Was he all right?"

"As far as I could tell. He looked a bit strained."

"*Why* did you go there? What was the point? Don't you see nothing can be done with any of it?"

"Let me tell you," he answered. "I didn't, in one way at least, go there on your account. There was something I had to say to him." He stopped speaking for a second or so and then he said, "I've been in this thing with you from the beginning. I hoped, as you hoped, that when Guy came back from Korea he'd forgive you and accept Christopher. He didn't accept Christopher and he's never forgiven you. You know that as well as I know it. Why he changed his mind and had Christopher after Caroline's birth remains a mystery. He did. And every time he saw him it brought the whole thing back to him—because he'd never forgiven you. His treatment of Christopher yesterday was only another instance of his non-forgiveness. You know that's true. He took it on himself to visit the sins of the parent on the child—but unfortunately he wasn't the Deity. Like the rest of us, he wasn't blameless."

Gina was staring at him with a puzzled frown. "What do you mean? What are you trying to say to me?"

"Gina—don't let this shock you—it was Guy who was directly responsible for Jennifer Mostyn's death. He——"

"Guy!" she exclaimed. "Responsible for *Jennifer's* death? How could he be? He didn't even know her. What are you talking about?"

"You're wrong," he said. "He did know her. Or rather, he met her—once."

Quietly, in short sentences, he told her all of it; how Guy had come to him for the Mostyns' address; how when he refused it he had discovered who they were and had gone down to Bridge Hill. How, by chance, through Mathew Galway's coming to stay with the Conways, he had found out about it.

"I'd known all along," he said, "that there was some missing link in the circumstances of Jennifer's death. I told you so at the time. She ought not to have died, unless she'd had some shock or strain. She did have the shock. Guy administered it. And it killed her. He wouldn't accept my refusal to let him have Christopher. He wouldn't accept what I told him—that the boy was happy, that the foster-parents loved him, that it wasn't fair to either them or him. He had to have his own way. He got it, and he killed Jennifer. It was *that* that I went to tell him last night."

Gina sat very still, her head bent, her hand across her eyes.

"It will finish him," she whispered.

"No," he answered. "It won't 'finish' him. But, if he thought it would become public and smirch the picture of the respectable, generous Christ-like Taylor who lavishes gifts on the Church, it might make him give up Caroline without a fuss. Just as if what he'd done to Christopher became public he'd give Caroline up. I told him that, too."

"It will kill him," she repeated. "That—and to lose Caroline."

"Gina!" he said sharply.

She didn't move her hand from her forehead.

"What did he say?" she asked him.

"Say? What could he say?" Suddenly he remembered the expression on Guy's face, the queer tattered dignity about him. "There wasn't anything for him to say. Don't you see—you'll get Caroline. You'll be able to start again—you and both the children...."

"You don't understand," she said, in the same toneless voice. "It's just—one more thing, isn't it? One more effect in the chain of effects that have come from that night at Alban Bay. It's—never ending, is it?"

"You're hysterical," he said.

"No," she answered. "No, I'm not hysterical. It's just that I can see."

"Do you have to attribute everything that's happened since that night to yourself? It's sheer masochism."

"No. It's not that, either. It's just—true. Can't you see it's true?" She nodded her head slowly. "All of it, Philip. The change in Guy, Christopher's being bandied about like a little shuttlecock, Jennifer's death, George going off to Africa. . . . Even this last thing, Guy's hurting Christopher, and me here in this dreadful little hotel and your accusing Guy of killing Jennifer. . . . It's as though I touched a switch and one after another the lights have gone out."

He got to his feet and looked down at her. "If you're going to start on chain-reaction, you're never going to stop. If you'd never met Guy at all——" He lifted his hand and lowered it again.

"That was a good thing. The other wasn't. You said to me once yourself—'You were dealing in flesh and blood. In human souls, if you believe that way.'"

"I must have been feeling sanctimonious," he answered shortly.

"I shall have to go to him," she said.

He pushed himself away from the mantelpiece.

"You'll have to what?"

She didn't move; still sat there with her head bent. "The agony of mind," she said, almost as though she were speaking to herself. "To know, for always, that you had—killed someone. . . . The remorse. . . ." She looked up at him, her eyes dark. "I know what that is," she said.

He bent over her and laid his hands on her shoulders.

"Gina! For pity's sake! What are you saying? Go to him! This is nothing but reaction from the strain of yesterday. You can't go back. Good grief! You said yourself just now—you'd had enough. It's true. You can't, no one can, keep on living under the perpetual strain you've been living under lately. And what about Christopher? Are you going to take him back for another dose?" He dropped his hands from her shoulders and straightened. "You can't," he said. "It's against all reason. All common sense. Do you imagine that, because he knows he caused Jennifer's death he'll have changed? He won't. You'll merely start the whole sequence over again. You can't do it."

He looked down at the top of her head and his heart ached for her. And yet—he knew it—he couldn't force her; couldn't even advise her. He'd done that once. . . . But now he understood her—the way her mind worked, her reactions. Once this was over he'd care for her, build her up again, let her out into the sunlight. He'd show her what companionship meant. "The marriage of true minds. . . ."

"Gina . . ." he said. "Gina. . . ."

She still sat as she had been sitting, her head bent, and when she spoke it was, again, as though she were thinking aloud.

"All this argument . . ." she said. "I suppose it is that I love him and always shall. In spite of what he's done to me or Christopher or Jennifer. . . . And when you love, you've got to be with the person you love if they're suffering, in trouble."

He drew back into himself, lowered his hand stretched out to touch her. He couldn't believe it. She couldn't *love* a man who'd treated her as Taylor had. She couldn't love a man who was a self-righteous hypocrite; who'd beaten her child; who'd killed Jennifer. . . . Surely she couldn't contemplate *living* with him again.

He had the terrifying feeling that he didn't know her, after all. . . . Didn't know the first thing about her.

"I don't understand you," he said.

She had lifted her head and was leaning it against the chair back and her eyes were closed. "I don't understand myself."

And suddenly, involuntarily, looking down at her strained face, the doctor in him took over.

"You must realise that this is merely reaction," he said sharply. "You had a wretched day yesterday; you haven't slept and you're worn out. All your judgments are fogged by the physical and emotional conditions. Give yourself a couple of days, a week, to come to grips with this change, and you'll see that it's right." His voice softened, lost its professional note. "I know how desperately difficult it's been. You've had such courage. Don't let it fail you now. Don't you see, my dear, that if you go back to all that strain it'll kill you. . . ."

She heard his voice, was aware of the room with the wicker chairs and tables and the over-coloured prints and the life-belts on the walls, and superimposed on them the dusty road, the hot sun beating down, the little group in front of the church.

"*Domine, quo vadis?*"

"Lord, where are you going?"

"I go to Rome to be crucified in your place. . . ."

"That's it, Claudia. He was showing Saint Peter that, even though he was the head of the Church and common sense said it was better for him not to be killed, there was a far greater thing than common sense, and that was, not his life, but his death. . . ."

"And Saint Peter turned around right here and went back. . . ."

Why that, now? Because it was Andrew's brother who had spoken those words? And afterwards, when they'd gone into the church, she'd thought that it was as though some hidden life was going on beneath the surface-life of speech and action, and was controlling not only herself and Guy but the Americans, everyone, everything. Quietly, gently and irrevocably, it was urging and persuading them towards some end it alone saw, it alone knew. Somewhere within its knowledge was Andrew Wharton and Christopher and the two-thousand-year-old fleeing footsteps of Peter the Fisherman. And somewhere, too, the parting of the crowd in Saint Peter's Square and the white-clad figure who passed head-high bearing his loneliness about him like a cloak. . . . Somewhere, too, now, Caroline, and Father Martin eating chocolate cake in the drawing-room at Ladysmere, and Jennifer Mostyn lying in her grave, and George alone in Africa, and Philip. . . .

The great silent wave of it surged about her, pressing her forward, taking her on its tide.

"I've got to go back, Philip," she said.

Chapter XXI

THE car drew up with a scatter of little stones.

The rain had stopped for a time, and a stormy sunset turned the grass and trees to deep emerald. The side of the house facing the flaming west might have been washed with ochre. There were lights upstairs in the nursery.

She lifted Christopher down. He dropped his tip-cart, stooped to pick it up and started to run off over the gravel drive towards the house.

She left the suitcase in the car and followed him. The door must have been ajar, for by the time she reached it and went into the hall, she saw his red-clad legs taking the last stairs at the top of the flight. A second later she heard the light thumping of his feet as he ran along the corridor to the nursery.

She stood quite still for a moment in the hall. She felt that it should have changed, that there should have been some vast alteration, but it was just as she had left it yesterday.

A door closed upstairs and she remembered, with a stirring of fear and embarrassment, that she would have to face Margaret, the cook, the kitchenmaid, Marple—and the nurse. They would all know; all have talked the whole thing over between themselves; all have their own views of what had occurred. They would look at her with suspicion. Or pity.

For a second or two the realisation made her falter, then she walked on across the hall to the study door and opened it.

Guy had heard the car draw up. There was no need to look out of the window to see who had come. He knew the sound of Gina's particular turn-in to the gates and swing round on to the gravel too well. He got to his feet and stood dead still, taking short, silent breaths, as though afraid to be discovered. Through the thick closed door he heard faint movements and then silence. Had she come back to fetch Caroline? Was Blake with her? Christopher? "I've got to go and see," he told himself. "Am I a coward, too?"

But he didn't move. He stood exactly as he was, breathing with short silent inhalations. He was aware of his teeth clamped together and of his ears strained to catch the slightest sound, while a jumble of pictures went flicking across his closed eyes—Blake stood with his hands in his overcoat pockets saying, "I shall use Jennifer Mostyn's death, too, to release Caroline. . . ." Father Martin sat in an upright arm-chair, head bent, his eyes looking down as though in embarrassment, his voice weighted and quiet. "The mortal sin of anger. . . . Reparation. . . . The child. . . . You did not go out with the intention to kill the foster-mother. Only God knows whether you were the cause of her death. . . . Your wife's generous heart. . . ." The dimly lighted church, the faint outline of the priest's bending figure the other side of the grille; his own voice marshalling the suspicion and the malice and the self-will, telling it out in short halting words, laying it before the barely seen crucifix level with his forehead.

"*Passio Domine Nostri Jesu Christi*. . . ." The priest's hand moving upwards and sideways. The merits of Christ's death applied to the anger, the pain, the remorse. . . .

The silent house. The rain lashing on the windows. And then the nurse, hardly recognisable out of her uniform, with a strange expression in her eyes. . . . That fantastic moment that followed and her voice still ringing round the study. "She's been fooling you all along. Do you think I don't know that Christopher is her child . . .? I've seen them together in the garden. I've seen the doctor put his hand on her. Two nights ago when you were away he brought her back here in his car after midnight. I want to look after you, care for you. . . . She never loved you. . . ." And out of the embarrassment and the nausea his own voice again. "I shall have to ask you to go now, tonight. I will ring for a car to take you to London in an hour's time. Please don't get hysterical. . . ." Voices upstairs. Doors opening and closing. His fingers round the pen writing a cheque while he tried to fight off the sound of her voice. "I've seen them together in the garden. He put his hand on her. . . ." Then the car drawing up, waiting; going off again; and Margaret, round-eyed and frightened, saying that she would see to Caroline. Midnight and the lights of Belsted no longer streaming weakly through the lashing rain. The wind dying down. The silence deepening. . . .

The door opened and he looked up and saw Gina standing on the threshold with her coat round her shoulders.

"I've come back," she said.

He stared at her, shocked and surprised, though he knew she was in the house; knew he would have to see her. He unclenched his teeth, felt the muscles slacken in his jaws. Her hair was blown about by the wind. He'd got to say something.

"Christopher?" he said.

"He rushed up the stairs to Caroline. He didn't wait for me."

"Is he all right?"

She didn't answer for a moment, then she said, "He's bruised, Guy."

He raised his hand to his forehead. "Oh God. . . ."

He wanted to tell her all of it—how he'd gone up on to the hill-top and looked down into that awful pit of himself. Wanted to tell her that if he could have seen Christopher come running in, he'd have gone on his knees and put his arms round him. He wanted to tell her of Father Martin sitting in the upright arm-chair in the presbytery, his eyes lowered; of following his bobbing black back into the silent church; of his own voice telling out the suspicion and malice and pain. . . .

He couldn't tell her. It was all there, the whole experience that had taken him and shaken him as he had shaken Christopher; but he couldn't tell her. He would never be able to tell her.

He raised his head again and looked at her.

"What are you going to do?" he said. "Is Blake with you?"

"Philip? No. Why should he be?"

"I thought you'd come to fetch Caroline."

"Would you let me take Caroline?" She saw a shadow of the old arrogance come over his face and go again, leaving his dark eyes looking back at her.

"Yes," he answered shortly.

She shook her head. "It wouldn't be any solution," she said, and she thought that the pain on his face seemed as though drawn there with thin steel. "Christopher and Caroline can't be separated. Christopher and I can't be separated. You and Caroline can't be separated. You and I"—her voice faltered for a moment—"can we be separated, Guy?"

She thought he flinched a little as though someone had struck him.

"Blake." He rapped the single word out.

"You've always thought there was something between Philip and me, haven't you? How can I tell you that there isn't, there never has been? I do love him in a way. I think he has shown me what friendship means. But you are my husband."

Again he was conscious of all there was to tell her, to explain, but now it had receded, was behind him somewhere, and he couldn't get at it. He could only say, "I was cruel to Christopher."

She was looking back at him, her eyes dark and tired.

"You've thought, sometimes, that Christopher was Philip's son, haven't you? That all I said to you wasn't true. But it was true. If only you'd let me talk about it, but you wouldn't. And I was afraid of hurting you more than I had already hurt you." She stopped speaking, and he saw her hand go to her coat pocket and bring out a small piece of paper. "I want to show you this," she said.

She walked across the room from the shadow where she stood to where the red glow from the sunset streamed obliquely through the tall window. She was taking a chance, and she knew it and knew that it had to be taken now, tonight, before the ordinary, external things of life crowded in again.

"Look, Guy."

He took the couple of steps to her side, and glanced down to where her forefinger was laid below a Press photograph.

"Mrs. Joseph Wharton and Father Ronald Wharton at London Airport."

Her finger moved to a marked paragraph. 'Gift for poor parish.' She was silent while he read it, frowning slightly, his bending head on a level with her hair.

"Andrew Wharton was Christopher's father," he heard her say

at last. "That"—her finger passed back to the priest's black coat—"is his brother." Her voice faltered on the last word, and then she said, "Christopher is very like him. I wanted you to see it. So that you would never doubt that, at least, again. . . ."

"Gina," he said, "I——"

There came a light thumping of feet on the wood floor and Christopher raced into the room. They both turned as he came flying out of the shadow into the rectangle of the light. He ran full tilt up to Guy, grabbed the crease in his trousers in his fist, tipped his head far back to look up at him, as he poured out some unintelligible story in which the only understandable word was "Car-line".

But his action spoke more clearly than his words as he pulled at Guy's trousers, trying to make him move.

"Christopher!" Gina said. "What are you trying to say? Go slower, darling."

He flung her a swift glance only and looked back up to Guy again, the tangled words coming out faster than ever. And sudden comprehension dawned on Guy's face.

"Oh lord," he said. "It may be Margaret in a fix. I sacked that damned nurse last night and Margaret's putting Caroline to bed."

"You sacked the nurse!" Gina echoed. "Why didn't you tell me?"

"I forgot."

"But what did you sack her for?" She bent down and picked Christopher up in her arms. "All right, Christopher, I'm coming."

"We had a difference of opinion," he said. "She——"

But Christopher was struggling to get down and Gina stooped and put him back on the floor. "Run and tell Margaret I'm coming," she said to him. "I'll follow you up."

He turned and scooted across the room and out of the door, and she heard the thump-thump of his feet crossing the hall and silence again as he reached the stairs.

"She, what?" she asked Guy.

"I'll tell you later," he said, "when the children are settled."

The light was fading quickly. The red had gone, swallowed swiftly by the black clouds banking up in the west again.

"I'd better go and see what's happening," she said.

He watched her turn from him, take a step, and then she faced him again.

She held out her hand.

Philip stood at the surgery window looking out at the church tower drawn against the red sky.

Would it work out? God knew. The actions and reactions of the human mind were past tabulation or prophecy. Was it possible that anyone of her character and temperament could live in any degree of harmony with a man like Taylor? Even if they made some sort of working compromise, would she ever be able to forgive him for his attack on the boy? Or for his damned smug self-righteousness?

A faint not wholly bitter smile came over his mouth. If he'd not told her that he'd gone up to Ladysmere and accused Taylor of Jennifer's death. . . . Even that, who could tell? Possibly she'd have gone back to him, anyway. "All this argument," she'd said, "and I suppose it is that I love him and always shall." But that even Gina possessed that feminine streak of masochism was baffling. Or wasn't it? The old inheritance of the cave-woman? The fundamental need for male domination? Could be. But wasn't there something else, some truer unity based on mutual respect and understanding? Something untouched by that female desire for *capitulation.*

He shrugged his shoulders. Perhaps not. But he hated to think of Gina crawling back to Taylor again. There was something nauseating about it, for Taylor wouldn't have the remotest idea of the strength of her love or the courage she'd shown all along, to say nothing of the courage she'd had in going back to him today. He'd either take the view that she couldn't live without him or that she 'knew her place'. And as for his murder of Jennifer and the break-up of *that* home—he wouldn't even consider that he had any responsibility for it whatsoever. And even so Gina had tried to defend him, to take the blame on herself. True enough that it was she who'd set the whole sequence in action in the first place, but as he'd said to her, you could go on along the road of chain-reaction till all was blue without getting to a definite starting-point.

And if he'd persuaded her to lie, to foist the child on to Taylor, none of it would have occurred and—he drew in his breath, suddenly shocked—Jennifer would be alive today. His hand, too, holding the knife that struck her? God, no. . . . And yet you could say that. . . . He'd had his part in it. . . . No, the thing was too big a tangle to analyse because while the lie might have saved Jennifer's life, she would never have known those two years of joy. . . .

The telephone rang, cutting into his thought. He let it ring for a moment as he watched the last light go from the church tower, leaving it grey, then he walked across and picked up the receiver.

"Doctor Blake speaking. Yes. Yes. What time? All right. I'll be along within half an hour. No. Good-bye. . . ."

He walked over to his desk and picked up his note-book and stood turning the pages. . . .

Father Martin was kneeling before the altar in the chapel of the Poor Clares up on the hill.

The daylight had nearly gone and the nave was shadowed and grey, but the six tall candles and the smaller five-branch Benediction candles made a lovely glow about the Host in the gold Monstrance on the altar.

He always felt happy when he gave Benediction up at the Poor Clares. He liked the gentle voices of the nuns coming from behind the enclosure, and he could never quite stop himself thinking of Susie kneeling there within a few yards of him, joining with him in praising God in the Church's lovely old liturgy. And tonight he felt especially near to her because of Guy Taylor's visit to him. How penetrating was the light that God sent streaming down into a man's intelligence to pierce the darkness and show him a glimpse of himself, not as he thought he was, but as he *really* was. And once a man had felt that touch of God's finger he was a different person, and whatever happened to him in the future he would never quite forget it. '*Emitte lucem tuam, et veritatem tuam* . . .' he thought to himself. 'Send forth Thy light and Thy truth, for they have brought me into Thy tabernacle and to Thy holy hill. . . .'

So many and various the ways that God used to bring men to Himself. All the devious and strange highways and by-ways of the world; all the trains and the buses and the machine shops and the factories and the pubs; all the meetings and the conversations and the comings and the goings; all the words spoken or not spoken; all the men and women, good, bad and indifferent; all the children and the cats and the dogs . . . everyone of them a part of the plan to bring men to the feet of His Love. . . .

The last notes of the Sisters' voices singing the *O Salutaris* died away. He gave the little nervous cough he always gave before he started the prayers. . . .

PRINTED AND BOUND IN ENGLAND BY
HAZELL WATSON AND VINEY LTD
AYLESBURY AND SLOUGH